CW00543070

THE WALL

Also by Adrian Goldsworthy

The Vindolanda Series

Vindolanda
The Encircling Sea
Brigantia

The City of Victory Series

The Fort
The City

Non-Fiction

Hadrian's Wall
Philip and Alexander
The Eagle and the Lion

THE WALL

CITY OF VICTORY, BOOK 3

ADRIAN GOLDSWORTHY

An Aries Book

First published in the UK in 2023 by Head of Zeus,
part of Bloomsbury Publishing Plc

9 7 5 3 1 2 4 6 8

A catalogue record for this book is available from the British Library.

ISBN (HB): 9781789545821
ISBN (XTPB): 9781789545838
ISBN (E): 9781789545814

Cover design: Matt Bray
Map design: Jeff Edwards

Printed and bound in Great Britain by
CPI Group (UK) Ltd, Croydon CR0 4YY

Head of Zeus
First Floor East
5–8 Hardwick Street
London EC1R 4RG
WWW.HEADOFZEUS.COM

For all the Hadrian's Wall scholars past, present and future. May they continue to fascinate, enlighten and confuse us as they seek to understand that unique monument.

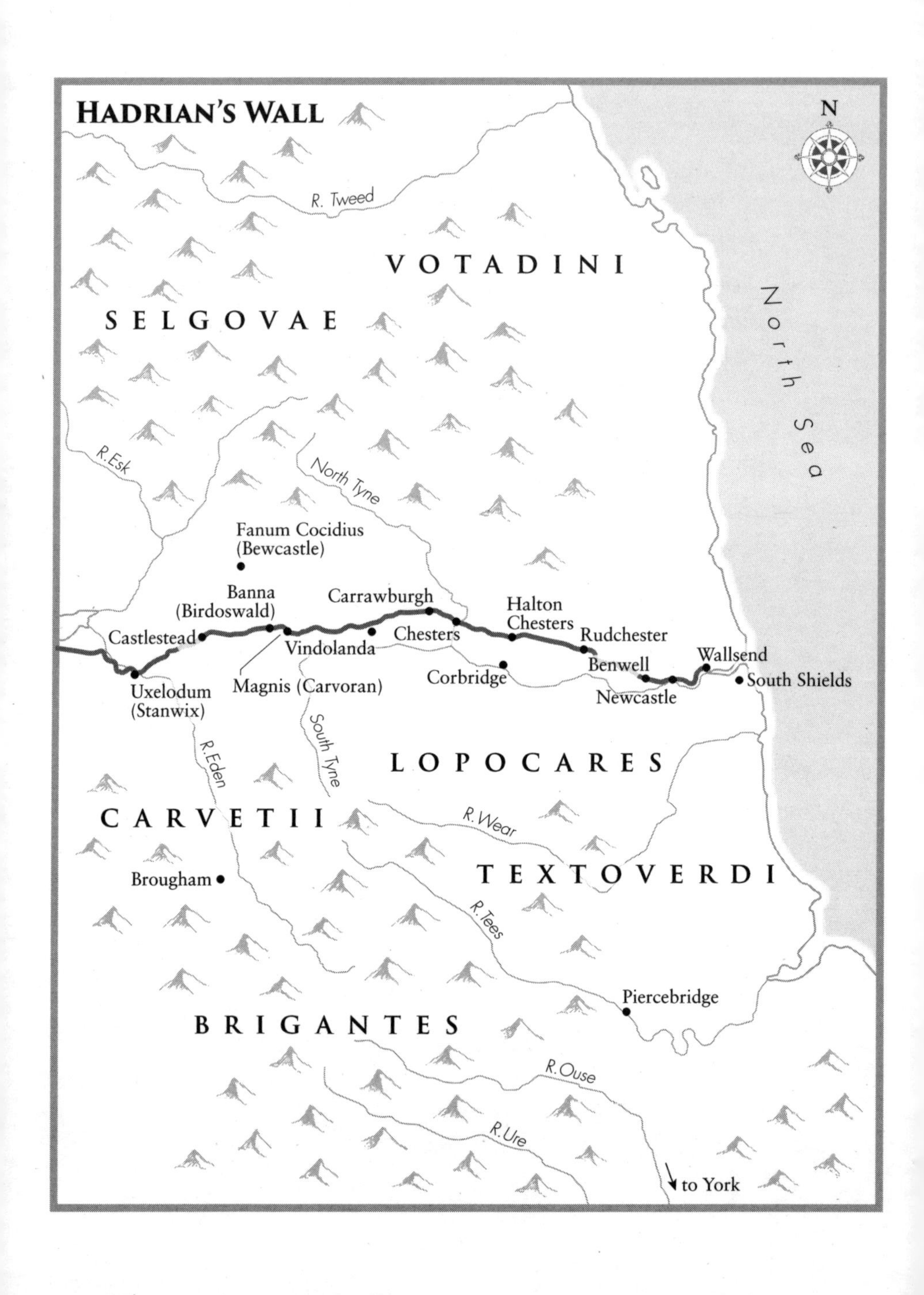
HADRIAN'S WALL
N
R. Tweed
VOTADINI
SELGOVAE
North Sea
R. Esk
North Tyne
Fanum Cocidius
(Bewcastle)
Banna
(Birdoswald)
Carrawburgh
Halton
Chesters
Castlestead
Chesters
Rudchester
Vindolanda
Wallsend
Benwell
Corbridge
South Shields
Uxelodum
(Stanwix)
Magnis (Carvoran)
Newcastle
South Tyne
R. Eden
LOPOCARES
CARVETII
R. Wear
TEXTOVERDI
Brougham
R. Tees
Piercebridge
BRIGANTES
R. Ouse
R. Ure
to York

ACT I

PROLOGUE

The house of the legatus Augusti of Syria, Antioch on the Orontes, seventeenth day before the Kalends of September, in the consulship of Q. Aquilius Niger and M. Rebilius Apronianus[*]

HADRIAN SIGHED AS he turned back to the intercepted letter. The writer was a decent enough fellow and good at his job, but so naïve. A lot of former slaves were shrewd, but Phaedimus the imperial chamberlain wrote with an indiscretion out of character for a man so punctilious in his duties. It was as if he believed no one could ever eavesdrop to words on a page as they might to a spoken conversation.

> I worry for the health of the princeps, our Lord Trajan, the best of masters, who has treated me so fairly and who gave me my freedom all those years ago. His rules are strict and precise, his standards high, as we who serve in his familia know all too well. Yet if you are diligent and follow those same rules, he has always been kind. Few households have been as happy, whether we were in Rome, in the country, or off to the wars.
>
> The princeps is no longer young, it is true, but those of

* 16 August AD 117.

us who have seen him in these last years in the mountains of Armenia and the deserts of Assyria could not but marvel at the vigour of a man in his sixty-second year, who marched as hard and rode as far as any soldier in the army.

That was true. The older Trajan had become, the more he had felt the need to prove his vigour to everyone – most of all himself.

The Lord Trajan is always happiest when he is with his army in the field, heavy with sweat, his grey hair and face plastered with dust or drenched with rain. The body slaves shake their heads when they tell of how much work has to be done to make him decent again, but by dinner he is immaculate once more in tunic and cloak, or sometimes even toga, and spotless shoes, and the next morning he will be ready before dawn, armour gleaming, boots and leathers polished.

Trajan would have enjoyed all that, always wanting to be the gruff military man. The lure of fighting and victory drew him even more than wine, and he had always been a heavy drinker.

Only lately has his appetite declined, as I should know, for it is my task to supervise every meal. He and his officers and comites used to eat heartily, always plenty of meat, and everything served and chosen with some style and discernment, though I say it myself. It was all in the finest of taste, for I cannot resist the pun—

No, you couldn't, could you, Hadrian thought.

—without ever descending into the vulgarity of too many rich men, senators included, who believe that something has merit simply because it is rare, expensive or indulgent. These were good, decent meals for the best and most decent of emperors, and that is exactly what the Lord Trajan demanded and received. He ate well, although often the dishes were cold because he loved to talk and laugh. I am forbidden to prepare copies of each one, starting at different times, so that as the conversation began to fade, I could have the slaves smoothly substitute the cold platters with ones that were just ready.

Hadrian could hear his cousin's voice, as if Trajan was actually in the room. 'Leave that sort of thing to the likes of Mark Antony and his tart.'

He skimmed through the next lines, as Phaedimus extended himself to discuss meals and their preparation, and what was proper for a *princeps* and his guests. Slaves and freedmen often had very fixed views on such things, for most men naturally came to believe that the concerns of their day were genuinely of the gravest importance to the wider world. After more than a page of this, the chamberlain expressed mild disapproval at the drunkenness of many meals at the emperor's table.

That is the emperor's influence, for he drinks as hard or harder than all, without ever quite losing control. His attendants say that getting him to bed was always easy, and that he woke without needing to be roused. He is one of the best behaved and tidiest drunks anyone knows.

Hadrian sniffed in amusement. Trajan would be pleased

enough with the comment privately, but would not want it spread abroad. It was so easy to forget that slaves and freedmen got to know their master or mistress better than anyone else. They judged them too, usually shrewdly if from a particular point of view. A wise man took this as a warning, and remembered not to be too free with actions or words.

> He drinks less now, and only after I have sampled the cup, and some of that is suspicion and some is his health. The change in his eating habits is greater still. The princeps used to eat well, whether the food was hot or stone cold, but now he picks at his food, and all too often is plagued with stomach pains or loose bowels. Hard travel and fighting in harsh lands will not put meat on anyone's bones. You may not believe it, but even I am positively thin! The Lord Trajan became gaunt in the last years, making him look older for all his vigour. Since his illness last month he is wasting away, his limbs thin as sticks where once they were muscled. He struggles to move his left arm at all, while the leg is stiff, so that he limps.
>
> The Lord Trajan believes that he is being poisoned, and I count it the greatest compliment of my life that he still trusts me – and only me – to test his wine and his food.

Well, that was enough to make sure that this letter would never be read by anyone else. There were rumours – there were always rumours, but Phaedimus, who would not matter in any other circumstance, could not be permitted to voice such concerns.

> I do not know whether or not this is true, but I know my master, my patron, and he is a brave man who has faced death many times without flinching.

No one could ever doubt Trajan's courage. Two years ago, in this very city he was trapped when his house collapsed as the earth shook and the buildings were torn apart. He spent hours in a cavern formed by the debris, encouraging the slaves entombed with him, until rescuers managed to get them out.

A year ago he had almost drowned when his ship capsized on the Tigris. Others perished and he simply swam to the bank. Much the same thing had happened to Alexander all those centuries before. They say that Trajan showed more emotion when they reached Charax at the mouth of the great river, and he saw a ship setting sail for the long voyage to India. Some said he wept because he was too old to do what Alexander had done, and lead his armies there. Hadrian doubted it, for the princeps was always master of his emotions in public and would not be so weak as to shed tears. The longing would have been real enough, but like many urges, something his cousin would control.

All of that was before the war turned sour. Trajan had created new provinces on land taken from the Parthians and their allies, and suddenly rebellions broke out at the same time in many different places. Perhaps it was chance, perhaps not, for there were many influential Jews living in Babylonia, but the Jewish population in Egypt, Cyrenaica and beyond also erupted in a savage war, slaughtering their neighbours and routing the depleted Roman garrisons.

After months of victory, Trajan faced one threat after another. His armies were tired and spread thinly across the new conquests. Taken by surprise, they could not be strong everywhere at once, and there were defeats and more than one outright disaster. Phaedimus noticed the change.

... as the war turned sour and rebellions broke out over so

much of the newly conquered provinces, my Lord Trajan's mood became grim and he carried his years more heavily than before.

I should not have doubted him. One morning the princeps woke and it was if decades had fallen from his shoulders. He had found his path and sent out orders while leading one column of the army himself. From then on, all the news was of victories. He proclaimed a new king of kings in the royal city of Ctesiphon, making his own man ruler of the great Parthian empire. Lusius Quietus, that African who seems to age almost as well as the Lord Trajan, was let loose and took city after city. When the rebels were cowed, he was sent to Judaea where he stopped the locals from joining their kin in rebellion.

Lusius Quietus was a remarkably able man and one of the finest commanders alive today, who had risen from prince of Mauretania to the Senate and now the consulship on sheer talent. His career was a long succession of getting tough jobs and always succeeding. Plenty of senators envied him, but those who met him tended to like him. He had charm.

Those were hard days, worst of all when the emperor led us to Hatra, that strong walled city in the middle of a barren, fly-infested wasteland. For months we baked in the day, froze at night, and vainly tried to brush the flies off our food. The Lord Trajan nearly died, riding forward to inspect the breach we had made in the city walls. He was wearing the plain uniform of a trooper, but no helmet, and his grey-white hair must have stood out even at that distance. A bolt from an engine passed inches from his shoulder to kill the man riding behind him.

Trajan was lucky, as the stars had always made clear to anyone with the wit and learning to understand them. Yet he had failed at Hatra and had to abandon the siege. Elsewhere in his new provinces control was tenuous at best. There were simply not enough soldiers to dominate everywhere, and not enough time to convince local leaders that accepting Roman rule was the sensible thing to do. That might change in time, but Trajan would never know.

> I do fear for the Lord Trajan. He is fading before our eyes. Not that I need worry for myself, for his generosity means that I have a house and more than enough set aside to pass the rest of my life in considerable comfort. I fear for him because he is a good man and the best of emperors, and who knows what will follow if he is no longer there to lead the res publica.

Well, they would find out, for Trajan was dead. Hadrian knew it to be true, but even so after all these years of waiting and wondering, part of him struggled to accept that Trajan was no more.

For all his many virtues, Trajan had never been a man to plan too far ahead. That was one reason why his wars in the east had gone so badly wrong. Even in these last years, as his health began to fail, he pretended that all was well and went off to play at being a great commander who would never or could never die. Because of this he made no preparations for the future, and in that sense failed his duty to Rome and the empire. For a man with no children, indeed who had never shown the slightest interest in having children, it was irresponsible.

Rome needed a princeps. The Senate had toyed with the idea of doing without one and guiding the state themselves for no more than a few hours after the murder of Caligula before realising that they were living in the distant past. Instead, they discussed which of them should be proclaimed as the new princeps, only to discover that the Praetorian Guard had already named the dead emperor's uncle. Six hundred old men could not hope to oppose thousands of well-equipped soldiers, even assuming the six hundred could agree on anything for more than a few moments. So the Senate accepted the choice made by the guardsmen and Claudius became the ruler of the world.

More than once Trajan had hinted that the Senate should pick his successor when the time came, perhaps from a list he would give them when he got around to drawing it up. He had mentioned a few names, which was unfortunate, but never done more than that. There were well-established ways to mark a man down as heir, just as Nerva had done so quickly when he picked Trajan to succeed him.

Everyone expected a princeps without a son of his own to look among his nearest relatives for a candidate. That was just the natural way for everyone to think, Romans as well as Greeks and all the other races who did not feel the need to pretend that they did not have an imperial family.

Hadrian was Trajan's cousin, a generation removed so a suitable age, and there was no closer relation. As tribune, just eighteen years old, it was Hadrian who had travelled hard to congratulate Trajan with the news of his adoption by Nerva. Since then, Trajan had given him a succession of posts in the city and with the army. Most recently, after a brief spell as acting legate of Syria a couple of years ago, the emperor had put him in charge of the province again, as properly appointed governor this time. Trajan had also awarded him the rare honour of a second consulship. Hadrian read the words of the letter again.

… and who knows what will follow if he is no longer there to lead the res publica.

Who indeed?

Trajan had never really liked him. Perhaps that, as well as the old man's refusal to accept the inevitable end of life, had made him stop short of recognising him as successor. Now it meant that everything would be more difficult than it needed to be, and that was bad for the empire.

Trajan was dead. He had fallen ill in Cilicia on his way back to Rome. Whether it was poison or simply natural frailty that had taken him in the end did not matter, as long as no evidence was made public.

Before he had died the emperor had announced that he was adopting Hadrian as his son. That was all that it took, the recognition that his closest male relative would be his heir. Trajan's wife – widow now – Plotina had convinced her husband in his last hours to take this final step. She had always liked Hadrian, and he had cultivated her, not least during those long months at Antioch where she had waited for the emperor to return home from the wars.

Hadrian trusted her to have been discreet. If poison was necessary to hasten the inevitable then it would have been done with care, even kindness, and would not be discovered. The same was true whether Trajan had actually bitten back his distaste and spoken – or written – his choice of heir, or whether Plotina had arranged for his voice and hand to be mimicked. Men might talk, but nothing could be proven.

Much needed to be done and done quickly. Much was already in place, or would be acted upon now that he had sent word. The two prefects, joint commanders of the Praetorian Guard, were aware of what had happened and were pledged to him. So were almost all of the nearest provincial governors and a good few farther afield. As news went out of Trajan's death, of his ascension to heaven like all good emperors, and of his choice of Hadrian as successor, praetorians and other soldiers alike would also hear of the generous bounty they were to receive from their new princeps.

Some precautions were necessary. His order would not reach Jerusalem for another day or two, but reliable officers would then arrest Lusius Quietus and remove him from his post as provincial legate. His term in the post would simply finish earlier than was usual. Hopefully the man would have the sense to accept comfortable retirement. A few other men, unpredictable by character and as dangerously capable, would also be removed. Again, he preferred to hope that this would be sufficient. Other senators did not have to like him as long as they had the sense to accept him.

Yet there were bound to be some deaths. That was regrettable, but inevitable, for there were always men who were too ambitious or too foolish or both.

One death had already occurred. Phaedimus fell violently ill and died only a few days after his master. That was a shame, for he had been a good and loyal chamberlain and before that a faithful slave, but it was better if the man did not talk. This letter was proof of his lack of discretion.

Hadrian sighed and held the papyrus above the flame of the lamp until it caught fire. He waved it to spread the flames, feeling the heat on his fingers, then dropped it into the bronze bucket filled with ashes of other documents too sensitive to be allowed to survive.

Trajan's failure to prepare for the succession meant that everything would be messier, and the mood far less certain than ought to have been the case. Hadrian knew that it was his destiny to rule, but had no illusions about the task ahead. It meant endless work, much of it drudgery, and taking responsibility to do what was best for the *res publica*. He smiled at the thought of the former slave writing the old, very Roman, phrase in his letter. Yet that was one of the greatest secrets of Rome, to take most of the world and convince everyone that they were Roman.

The empire brought order, peace and prosperity. All that required stability and firm, consistent leadership. Hadrian sighed again, not for the dead freedman, but because he relished the task as much as he feared it. There was so much to do.

A cough interrupted his thoughts. One of his own slaves was in the doorway.

'Sosius, my lord,' the man announced. He knew his master well enough not to add that he had been told to bring him as soon as he arrived. Nor did Hadrian show any surprise and simply nodded to him.

'It is done?' Hadrian said once the slave had gone and the thickset, bald Sosius come into the room. The man had once been a cook in his wife's household, one of the few practical benefits the union had brought, until an incident let the freedman reveal his full potential. Over time, he became the most effective, cleverest and wholly ruthless agent at his command.

'Yes, my lord.'

'Any complications?'

'None, my lord.'

'Fine.' An emperor needed to be strong and sometimes ruthless. That meant making use of men even more ruthless. 'Now,' Hadrian said, 'I have work for you in the far north.'

Five days later. Near the road between Magnis and Vindolanda in the north of Britannia

THIS WAS THE *last chance and he knew it.*

That was not reason enough to be careless. They moved slowly through the night, stopping often, and in the last few miles they waited, lying flat in complete silence, listening and watching. They were still more than they moved.

People rarely understood how far sounds travelled on a quiet night like this. At least there was no wind, for while a strong gale could hide many things, a fitful, gusting wind made it hard to tell whether a noise would be muffled or carry a long way. They might give themselves away without realising it, or stumble straight into someone else abroad for reasons of their own. There could be other hunters about, or more likely simple wanderers. He had no desire to kill either without good reason, but if it came to the point all must die, and die quickly and silently, and it was hard to be sure of that in a sudden encounter.

The route was easy to find. He had travelled it himself, several times, even during the short nights of early summer, for he had wanted to leave as little to chance as possible.

'We do not go out to fight,' the Lord of the Hills had often said. 'We go out to kill.' That was the way of war of his people, the Silures, and the way he and all the others had been raised as boys. It was the way he had done his best to teach his warriors, only one of whom came from his own tribe, and he had left

that man behind with the horses to be sure that his instructions were followed.

After a long wait, so still that a hunting owl swept past within arm's reach and did not pay them any heed, he raised himself to a crouch, waited again, and then tapped the shaft of his javelin just enough to make a little sound. The others rose on the signal, and he led them on. They were almost there.

On the first night everything had gone well, so that they reached the spot in plenty of time and prepared for what must be done. He was pleased with his lads, pleased with the way they hid themselves as he had taught them, and even more pleased at how patiently they had waited, not one of them breathing a word.

That night, like the preceding day, had been cloudy, until as they waited the clouds parted to show a bright field of stars. There were also a couple of fiery stars, blazing across the Heavens. That was not a good omen, especially among the Selgovae and he had two of that tribe with him. He had tapped his spear shaft and stood up. No one had said anything, but all had understood. They left and went back to their camp without anyone saying a word. When they were there, she told them that they had done the right thing and no one doubted her power.

On the second night, a day of driving rain had meant that a river was far deeper and faster flowing that usual. They might have made it across without accident, but that was a risk no one needed to take, so they returned early to their camp in the woods, and she said that they were right.

The third night followed a day of baking sunshine, and the river was easy to ford. They made good time, until they were almost there. Then a dog barked as they had passed within bowshot of the half dozen houses of a family farm. Perhaps the animal had scented them or perhaps it was something else.

Another dog joined in, much further away, and it was a while before angry voices hushed one, then the other into silence. By that time they were long gone, back the way they had come until they reached a hollow and lay down to wait. The people in the farms might be wary and watchful, might even be bold enough to bring their dogs and search in the darkness for thieves. Probably they would not, and probably they would simply go back to sleep if they could, all the while muttering curses at their dogs. Farmers were often lazy and too quickly came to believe that they were safe. A lot of folk lived and worked the land around here, which meant that these days there was almost never a bear and rarely even a wolf to be seen.

Just possibly the barking had carried to a sentry at the tower or even the outpost itself. You never knew. He had served in the army and was sure that most men in a quiet spot like this would pay little attention as they counted the moments until their relief. Still, there was always the chance of one being a good soldier, or simply being young and still keen, and new to this posting.

They went back and she assured them that her magic had protected them from harm.

On the fourth night no dog barked and again they hid themselves and waited. Then one, the youngest of them all, one of the Novantae, crouched and pulled down his trousers to pee. The stream seemed to go on and on, spattering down the slope, and even though the lad did his best and gave no more than the faintest sigh of relief, surely even the doziest guard must have heard. The one on the tower was closer to them than the dog had been at the farm.

They left and made their way back. This time she said that she would cast a spell on the boy's bladder and they laughed and were content. They still had faith in her, and perhaps still in him, but that might not last if they failed again. He had felt the urge to succeed at any cost this time and fought against it. The lessons of childhood helped, for recklessness was not the way of his people. She helped even more, without words, for at the touch of her hand he felt his own strength and power growing.

He was ready to turn back again if that was the right thing to do. The big raids were coming the next night and they would stir the Romans as nothing had done for years, so they must strike first, before the soldiers were truly on their guard. More than that, men needed to know what they had done.

Yet still they went cautiously and slowly and he took no greater chance than on the other nights. There was no need, for all went well and two hours before dawn they were in the gully. When the dawn came he would be able to see the path worn through the grass by the soldiers who passed each day, marking out more clearly the track used by generations of drovers taking animals down to the water. The earth was usually soft, even muddy, even in late summer.

Down by the river, about a mile and a quarter away by Roman reckoning, was the outpost, what they called a burgus. *Its walls and towers were of stone, and there were tall buildings inside, but it was a tenth the size of the timber garrisons dotted along the line of this road, and they in turn were a tenth the size of the vast legionary bases he had seen. The Roman empire was huge, and it was strong, but it was not as strong as the Romans liked to boast. Here, in the north of Britannia, it was weak. Barely a decade ago the army had kept bases several days' march to the north, and thirty years ago there had been even more troops, much further north. All were gone, and maybe these could be made to go as well, in time.*

The Romans had their road, and their bases along it, with half a dozen of the big ones and a couple of little outposts like this. Few were fully garrisoned, and the army in the whole province had shrunk in size as soldiers were sent away to fight in distant wars. Few had returned, and from what men said, many would never return, for their corpses were rotting in the desert sun. The governor of Britannia was weak and dying, as was the emperor. He had heard these things and she understood. The time was almost here, so they must begin the work. That was their task.

The Sun rose, although it would be a while before it reached into this narrow gully. His warriors had done well. Seven were in the heather, two more like him in shallow scrapes, lying flat and covered with cloaks which in turn had pieces of turf and grass on them. Only someone who was really searching and knew the signs would spot them. He was satisfied and completed his own covering. One touch reassured him that his spear was ready beside him. Then they waited.

They could hear the soldiers long before they could see them and that was a good sign, for it suggested men who were relaxed. The tower was half a mile or so beyond them, up on the ridge to the north west and every morning just after dawn, eight men marched up from the burgus to take a turn on watch. They tended not to hurry, so it took them a while, and for most of the journey they were out in the open, clearly visible to the bored sentry above the gateway of the outpost and the one on watch at the tower, who waited with less patience. Only in a few places did the path dip down so that they were out of sight for a short while. The longest was when they tramped through this gully, and even then it was for no more than a few moments.

He had spent a long time watching them earlier in the summer. It was always the same every day, the same time and the same route. The soldiers were lazy and they felt that they were safe.

The first man came into view as he watched between the long grass, closely followed by two more and then the rest. Five were in mail, one in polished scale, and he judged them to be auxiliaries. Two men in the segmented cuirasses only used by the legions trailed along a few paces in the rear. All had their shields towards him, rectangular for the legionaries and oval for the auxiliaries, but the decorations lay beneath the leather covers designed to keep out the weather. Without those, he had little doubt that they would have shown a range of different designs and colours, for outposts like this one were usually garrisoned by men detached from their units, often because the units did not want them around.

'Come on, get a move on!' the man in the lead called back at the others. In a small detachment like this, the odds were that he held no rank and had simply been appointed to command.

'Hark at the little Caesar!' one of the men called back.

'Yes, sir, no, sir, can I wipe your arse, sir? said another.

'All right, all right,' the leader said. 'But the sooner we're there, the sooner we can get the stew on.'

They kept going, muttering and moaning in the way soldiers usually did. It brought back many memories.

Then they were gone and he allowed himself a moment of satisfaction. Eight men had marched right past his warriors and noticed nothing. They only needed to wait a little longer and he thought about saying something, telling his lads that they were doing well, but decided against it. They were better than that.

It seemed an age before the men relieved from duty at the tower came back through, and for a while he wondered whether on this of all days they had decided to follow a different path. Suddenly they were coming along the trail, not talking, and most with their heads down. They were tired, and paying even less attention than the others and that is what he had wanted.

He whipped back the cloak – one of the secrets was never to put too much on top of it so that it would not come off smoothly. As he stood he readied his spear. Hearing him the others were springing up. The soldier in the lead gaped as men appeared to spring out of the earth.

Hefting the spear, he steadied himself to aim and then throw. The soldiers were just yards away, his warriors coming from their right, their unshielded side. He flung the spear with force and at this distance it punched easily through the rings on the man's mail shirt and through his ribs. The Roman gasped and was already falling.

He had told off two of the men to wait until they had seen who was left before throwing their own javelins, but only one remembered in the excitement as the spears hissed in flight. Two more men were down, apart from his own, three more staggering, and one of the others was promptly hit full in the face by the javelin thrown by the lad who had ruined things the night before by pissing.

That left one, who panicked, dropping his own spear and shield and turning to sprint back the way he had come. Two warriors sprang up to block his path. Screaming would not have saved him, but might just have given away what was happening. Instead, he dropped to his knees and pleaded for mercy in a language that was not Latin. It took three cuts to kill him, and more to finish off the other wounded. There were grunts of effort and moans of pain, but no noise likely to carry back to the tower.

The Romans were all dead, none of his warriors were injured, and although they were excited, eyes wild, none was foolish enough to shout out in triumph.

He nodded in approval, patted the youngest lad on the back and then drew his sword. There was work to do and it was best to do it quickly. Then they would leave, walking out in plain view until they went over a nearby crest. The Romans would see them if they were not asleep, and by now maybe the ones on duty down at the outpost were just starting to wonder where the men returning from the tower had got to. It did not matter. By the time anyone had started to think, and then had time to saddle some horses and roust out any troopers at the outpost, he and his men would be long gone. The farmers would see them and they would talk, but in less than an hour they would reach woodland and he had no fear of shaking off anyone trying to follow them.

He wanted to be seen, so that the soldiers and the farmers knew what had been done. He let himself smile, then swung his sword down onto the neck of one of the corpses.

I

Ten days before the Kalends of September, on the border between the Carvetii and Lopocares in Northern Britannia

'HERSELF MAY NOT like this,' the gaunt-faced man said after following his friend into the small room with its unpainted plaster walls. They were in the main house, built in Roman style with two floors, even if most of the building was wattle and daub and only the lowest few courses of stone. It was modest by the standards of the villas of the south, and even some here in the north. This room was small, sparsely furnished, but it was where his friend chose to sleep while he was alone.

'I said,' the man repeated for emphasis, 'she won't like it.'

The other man gave no sign of listening, but that was nothing unusual. He was angry, although perhaps only those who knew him would realise just how angry. Still, even a stranger might blanch at the coldness of those grey eyes.

'The queen won't want you to do this,' the first man spoke louder this time. He was the taller of the two, albeit not by much, and had the slim features and rangy limbs of his people. His name was Vindex and his father had been a chief among the Carvetii, the people of the western valleys, but since his mother was a serving girl, everyone knew who he was and knew just as well that it was not something to talk about.

'You know what she said,' Vindex continued. 'No trouble until the case comes to court.'

His companion paused as he reached for the mail cuirass lying flat on the bed. It was clean, as well polished as the small iron rings would allow and only someone looking very closely would notice the slightly different shade of some of the metal where it had been repaired after being gashed open. There were three patches like that, one so big that anyone wearing the armour must have taken a nasty wound to the side.

'That's what she said, and you and I know the lass means what she says.'

Just for a moment the other man glanced round at him.

'Well, you know what I mean,' Vindex conceded. 'When she means it, she means it. Like when she calls you by your right name.'

There was the flicker of a smile, soon gone, for that was certainly true. If his wife called him Ferox then he knew that something was up and he was probably in trouble. Whenever she called him Flavius Ferox he knew that he was up to his neck in it. She had never addressed him by his full three names. Maybe she was saving that for the day she decided to kill him.

Vindex sensed that his friend's cold fury was slackening – just a little, but that was something. 'She's a queen all right, like her grandmother.' He grinned. His face was long, the skin stretched taut across his features giving it a sinister, skull-like appearance, especially now that it was tanned and creased from years of hard service at the distant ends of the empire. Now he turned the grin into a smile. When he opened his mouth this wide and showed his teeth, it was like seeing a lecherous horse from some dark legend.

'You know that I am right,' Vindex added, hoping to reinforce his point. Many friends would have made a joke about it being bound to happen eventually, but Ferox said nothing. After all this time, Vindex knew that he would have to do most of the work when it came to conversing with his friend. Ferox was one of the Silures, the predatory wolf folk of the south west and unlike the Carvetii they raised their children to cherish silence and avoid speaking unless it was essential. Ferox was a Roman as well, having been sent to the empire for his education and then commissioned as centurion. For thirty years he had marched and fought for Rome, and for the last twenty or so Vindex had often been alongside him.

Ferox hesitated and then grunted before he moved and picked up the scabbarded sword lying alongside the cuirass.

Vindex nodded. 'I guess that means we go armed, but not armoured. That's something, I suppose.'

Ferox gripped the bone handle of the *gladius* and slid the blade free for a few inches, staring at it. There was hardly any oil on the blade, just enough to make the movement smooth when pulled with strength, and he knew this because he – and only he – cleaned the blade and kept it sharp. In the dim light of the room the iron looked dull, but still he sensed its life. These days the issue pattern of gladius was short with a stubby point. This one was old, longer and with a wicked triangular point designed to punch through mail. Caesar's men had wielded swords like this when they conquered Gaul. No, not like this, for this was special, a weapon of perfect balance so that simply to hold it like this was to feel power.

'All right, I know you haven't killed anyone for a year, but she won't be pleased if you start now.'

Ferox slid the blade back and then slipped the belt over his shoulder. 'I just haven't killed anyone you know about,' he said, his expression as flat as his voice.

Vindex laughed. 'Huh, talking are we? That's an improvement

at least.' He sensed that he was winning, but over the years plenty of folk had thought that when they were up against the Silures – and then had walked straight into an ambush. In that case the lucky ones died quickly, and the captives slowly and in great misery.

Vindex decided that it was best to appeal to the highest authority. 'You know what the queen said. Wait for her to come back from Isurium or come down there when she summons us. In the meantime do nothing. She couldn't have made it plainer.'

'She's still not queen according to the Romans,' Ferox pointed out. His wife, Claudia Enica, was from the royal house of the Brigantes, the biggest tribe in the north of Britannia, and had been promised recognition by the authorities for a long, long time, only for there to be excuse after excuse and delay after delay.

'The Romans can kiss my arse. Bastards every one of them.'

Ferox, the Roman citizen, nodded.

'Herself is Queen,' Vindex continued. 'She's daughter of kings, and more than that granddaughter of Cartimandua herself. The Romans ought to like that.' Cartimandua had been queen when Claudius invaded Britannia and had allied with the invaders and always proved loyal. 'But who cares what they think? She's my queen, and all the Carvetii say the same, as do the Brigantian clans.'

'Not everyone,' Ferox pointed out. The Brigantes had been wracked by civil war in Cartimandua's day, and she had had to be rescued by the legions. Seventeen years ago Claudia Enica had ended up fighting a war against her own brother when he rebelled, claiming that he was supporting the true emperor over a usurper, but really aiming for much more. She had won, and Ferox and Vindex had hunted down and killed her brother. A handful of leaders would never forgive them for doing that, nor would they ever whole heartedly support her for winning in the first place. Rather more waited and watched, saw that the emperor had not confirmed Claudia's rule as queen, so wondered whether there were opportunities for themselves.

Vindex was dismissive. 'Shits, the lot of them – who cares what they think! And the lass has earned it. You know it, everyone knows it.' Apart from staying loyal to Rome at the time of the rebellion, Claudia Enica had raised a band of warriors and led them in person to fight for Rome against the Dacians.

Ferox tried to explain once again. 'The Romans do not care for women as leaders, even less as warriors. Makes them nervous.' Sometimes she makes me nervous, he added to himself.

'Well, she doesn't kill any more.' Vindex winked as he added, 'Not when anyone's watching at least.' After the bitter fighting in Dacia, Claudia Enica had not wanted to see another battle. Ferox knew that she still trained, just as she had done over the years, but was discreet and whenever she had anything to do with the imperial authorities or society, she became Claudia, the elegant Roman lady, rather than Enica, the leader of her fellow tribesmen, full of old lore and magic. 'And bastards like Taximagulus have done bugger all for the Romans – or for anyone. The only ones to support him have to or he'll turf them out of their farms. Same with the rest. There's not that many of them.'

'Still means one less would be an improvement,' Ferox suggested.

'Aye, but she said no and she meant it.'

Ferox and Claudia had married back at the time of the rebellion, but had rarely been together in the years that followed. The first time it was his fault, for he had not coped well as consort to an important woman. They had argued and he had taken to drink again until she threw him out and he had gone back to the army. Then came those precious weeks in Dacia, when they were reconciled in the middle of a siege. Strange that those wonderful times had been in the midst of treachery and the imminence of defeat and death. To protect her from scandal he had left again, and been employed in one bad situation after another, officially as just another officer, but it had been the emperor's cousin, Hadrian, who pulled the strings and often employed his agent, the freedman Sosius, to arrange his darkest deeds. Vindex had been with Ferox almost all the time, and it had taken them a decade to earn release and their passage home. Hadrian had promised to help Claudia gain formal recognition and perhaps was true to his word and had tried. Or perhaps not. You never really knew where you were with Hadrian, but at least he had allowed them to return home. In the last year Ferox had seen more of Claudia than ever before and they had not had a real fight in all that time. Not so far.

'Fine,' Ferox said. 'We will just go across and pay a call on my neighbour, one nobleman to another.' Most of the time he lived here, in this small villa on one of the royal estates. Claudia said that she had given it to him, but that did not mean much. The people on the farms and villages accepted him because she said so and that was good enough. He pottered about, tried not to do anything foolish, and let those who knew what they were doing care for the animals and grow what crops would grow. Ferox was trying to learn as much as he could from them.

'One neighbour to another,' Vindex said doubtfully. 'Remember we're not in an old song, so visiting a neighbour doesn't mean burning down his hall.'

Ferox grunted, which could mean anything. 'We'll just take

Litullus and Carnacus with us,' he said. 'Make it clear we are friendly.'

Vindex was not so sure, but felt that this was as good as he could expect. Litullus was old and had lost all the fingers on his left hand in some battle years ago, but still strutted like a warrior. Carnacus was a giant of a man, with the patience, strength and wit of an ox. They were not a warband, just an escort of the sort any nobleman should take on even a short journey, and it was prudent not to go on their own. Taximagulus kept a lot of men on his estate, but probably would not want to be seen as starting any trouble. Not long ago the man had been just another petty chief of the Lopocares with little land of his own and less prestige. Yet over time he had gained plenty of land, winning contracts to supply the army, and if his prestige was still low, his influence was not. Plenty of men from older families were in debt to him for favours or coin. Taximagulus was ambitious, and his lands kept growing as folk were persuaded to pledge themselves to him as tenants or even sell him their fields. Buying and selling land was not the manner of the old days.

Taximagulus was not a good neighbour, and his men intimidated and stole freely. Plenty of unmarked cattle and sheep ended up joining his herds and flocks. So did a fair few with marks plain to see. Even people had vanished, especially the young, who were no doubt now working for their new master or had been sold off too far away to prove that they were free.

There had been plenty of provocation over the last months, and Ferox's rage had grown until this latest incident threatened to release the dammed torrent. A shepherd boy from one of their farms had been beaten so badly that he might not live and was unlikely ever to walk again, and all because some of Taximagulus' men had claimed the dozen sheep he was watching as belonging to their master. The boy had fought back, smashing the eye of one man with a stone flung from his sling, so they had taken him and beaten him. The man hit in the eye and another had lagged behind as the rest drove away the sheep, and villagers had caught them, which was how they had been sure who was responsible. They had not been gentle, but Vindex had happened by and had the captives brought to the villa. The pair were chained and shut in one of the storerooms alongside the villa itself. Ferox needed them alive as witnesses, so had given strict orders for them not to be killed. He was not worried over much if his people expressed their feelings just as the villagers had done, as long as they could still walk and talk when required.

Taximagulus was to blame, and Ferox was probably right that killing him would make the world a slightly better place, and fifty years ago – less – riding over in strength and slaughtering the little shit and his men would have been the natural thing to do. The chieftain had friends – probably not personal ones, but more important men who found him useful as an ally – so that might have led to war between and among the clans. That was the old way, but now there was the rule of Rome and the Romans did not care too much for raids and taking the heads of your enemies. The Romans liked everyone to go to court, so that trained orators could hurl vicious slanders and insults without coming to blows, and eventually judge and jury would decide whatever they felt to be an appropriate verdict. If that did not suit, the loser could take the case to the legate of the province, who might get around to dealing with it when he held assizes in one of the big cities. Or he might not, and by the sound of it the current governor was in such poor health that he was doing very little of anything.

The queen and her allies were involved in a dozen cases against noblemen and their allies working against her. Most were being conducted at Isurium, the new town she was promoting as the centre for the Brigantes. If her husband – her husband from outside the tribe, and a grim brooding man, well known as a killer – went and chopped up Taximagulus then no one would be too upset, but her rivals would unrelentingly talk of this appalling crime in any case brought against her and her allies. That would be bad, and it would be still worse in a case that came before the legate. Ferox knew all this – after all, he was the one who had explained it all to Vindex in the first place.

'No killing,' Vindex said after a while. 'Agreed?'

Ferox sighed. 'No one would know it was us. The fool often rides out with just a few followers. Easy to predict his path and get it done.'

'You would still be accused. So would I.'

'Then we don't kill anyone unless we have to.' Ferox gave one of his rare smiles. 'You know me.'

'Oh bugger,' Vindex said. 'Well, I'll go and round up the two lads and get the horses ready. The usual?'

Ferox nodded. Keeping up the habits of the old days meant that they always took food and water for three days whenever they rode out, and some hard tack and salted meat that would last a little longer. It just made them both more comfortable.

Vindex left Ferox searching through a box for his travelling cloak and the latest in a succession of wide-brimmed felt hats. The freedman Philo, once Ferox's slave and body servant, now in charge of the household he was supposed to keep as Claudia's husband, had far higher standards than his master. Over the years, plenty of garments, especially these scruffy hats, had been lost. At the moment, Philo and his family were away with the queen at Isurium, helping her to run the house there. It gave Ferox a freedom to do as he wished without facing the hurt disappointment of his meticulous servant. Yet he could not find his recently purchased hat, which suggested that Philo was one step ahead of him once again. He had noticed that the slaves polished his helmet and combed its high crest each morning, so suspected that they had been given instructions. Perhaps it would not do any harm to look official. He glanced back at the bed and changed his mind about not wearing the cuirass. Some instinct was prickling at the back of his mind and he began to wonder.

The villa itself opened onto a muddy courtyard, surrounded by a straggle of huts, barns and storehouses. Like any working farm, it gave the impression that something was about to happen and that much had happened in the past, even though it was almost empty at the moment, apart from the five saddled horses. Three had riders, and after Vindex had blinked a few times in the bright sunshine, he recognised Litullus and Carnacus, which was surprising as he had not yet called for them. The third rider was hooded and cloaked, even though there was no concealing who it was. It was more of a surprise than the fact that they were ready and waiting, but probably explained everything.

Vindex smiled, but shook his head as he stared up into the face of the nearest rider. 'Sorry, princess, but I doubt you can come.'

Senuna frowned. 'I am sure that is not the case.' She was twelve years old and carried herself with the assurance of someone two or even ten times that age and accustomed to command. 'Won't you need someone with brains tagging along?' she suggested, her expression one of patient concern.

Vindex laughed. There was so much of the queen's spirit in this, her youngest daughter. The older girls, the twins, were each the image of Claudia Enica in her youth, whereas Senuna's looks came from her father. She had the same grey eyes as Ferox, and long hair as black as raven's wing, the colour that his used to be before it became flecked with grey. Vindex often wondered whether the girl took after Ferox's mother, or other women in his family, for he could see no trace of his features in her face, even as a softer version. She would grow into a beauty, like her sisters and the queen, but utterly unlike them in the nature of that beauty.

'Sorry, lass,' Vindex said, patting the neck and ruffling the mane of her pony. It was the little bay he had helped her to train over the last months, and the mare was shaping up very nicely indeed. 'He won't allow it. Nor would the queen if she were here. There might be trouble.'

'Might there?' the girl said in a delighted tone. She pushed back her hood and laughed. Her hair was pinned up and fastened into a bun and there was a hint of rouge on her lips and cheeks. Vindex realised that she was wearing a pale dress under her cloak, and had a silver necklace around her throat. 'And do you think that even Taximagulus would risk trouble in the presence of a lady of the royal house?' She dropped her reins, and the mare did not even stir, while her rider used her hands to gesture modestly at herself. If it lacked all the elegant poise of a fashionable lady, it was not by much.

'Perhaps not,' he conceded.

Senuna leaned closer and winked at him. 'And if he does start trouble in the presence of such a lady – such a young lady, a mere girl, in fact – then would not my father have every right to fight back?'

'Shit!' Vindex said before he could stop himself. 'Sorry, princess. I forgot myself.' As smart as her mother and as devious as her father. He shook his head. 'But I doubt himself will want to take the risk.'

Himself promptly appeared, gleaming in his armour and with the even more brightly polished helmet under his arm.

'Oh, it's like that, is it?' Vindex muttered.

Ferox was looking around the yard, searching for someone or something. Analeugas, one of the older men on the estate, appeared from one of the sheds, holding a scythe in one hand and a whetstone in the other; it would soon be time for harvest and there was lots to prepare. Ferox beckoned him over and spoke for some time. Vindex could not hear what they were saying, but noticed the old man turn and look up at the slim timber watchtower Ferox had insisted they build last winter. The signs were familiar, his friend was sensing danger without knowing why.

Analeugas put down the scythe and stone and lurched off as fast as a man of his years could go. Ferox appeared to notice his daughter for the first time, even though Vindex knew that he had missed nothing. He nodded to her, then walked over to his horse, a grey called Frost who has getting on in years now like his master. Neither showed much sign of this as Ferox bounded into the saddle and the horse pawed eagerly at the ground.

The old man had routed out some of the boys who had been working, or in truth sitting and talking, in and around the villa that day. One was already climbing the ladder up to the tower's platform, while another pair went running off across the fields.

'Trouble?' Vindex asked.

'Maybe,' Ferox said, before turning Frost so that he faced back towards the others. He looked at his daughter. 'You sure?'

'Yes, father.'

'Then you do precisely what I say, when I say it. Understood?'

Senuna nodded. 'Yes, father.'

'I'll remember you said that.' Ferox spun the horse around and nudged it into a canter. The others followed. Big Carnacus trailed behind, slower than the others to start and then get his horse moving. They left the yard and then headed north rather than east, aiming for a round hill about a mile away.

As they went, Senuna came up alongside Vindex. She rode well, as she probably should, for her father was a capable if inelegant rider and her mother always seemed part centaur.

'Is father worried?' she asked.

'Aye, lass.'

The girl scanned the lands as they cantered through the pasture. Close by was a walled pen, with four cows standing listlessly in the middle. There had only been one yesterday, cut out from the herd because it was showing signs of sickness, and Vindex was saddened to see so many more there in such a short time.

'Why is he worried?' Senuna asked.

Vindex thought for a while before answering. 'Don't reckon he knows. And that's what's bothering him the most.'

II

Three hours later, further north

'ARE WE HUMPED?' Vindex asked, before realising that the girl was just behind him. He shrugged. 'Sorry, princess.'

Senuna looked up, her face apparently blank. 'I am sorry, I was not attending. Did you say something?' The lie was almost convincing.

Ferox said nothing. He was bareheaded, having relegated the helmet to hang behind his saddle, so shaded his eyes to see better. The others were back a little, beneath the crest of the hill, at least partly hidden, while he knelt down at the top. Yet even from where he stood beside his horse, Vindex could see the distant plumes of black smoke.

Ferox beckoned him forward, gesturing for him to keep low. The girl came as well, invited or not.

This was rugged country, one crest giving way to the next and hiding plenty of little valleys from view, but they could still see a long way. In the distance to the east there were three, no four, thick pillars of dirty smoke rising into the clear blue air.

'It's come then,' Vindex said.

Ferox said nothing. A fresh cloud of dark smoke appeared, a little closer and more north east than east.

'Bug—' Vindex checked himself just in time. 'Reckon there's enough of them.'

'What has happened?' Senuna asked when no one else seemed inclined to say anything more. Ferox did not reply, and just kept on scanning the lands around.

'Do you never listen to your father?' Vindex asked the girl.

'Rarely.' Senuna grinned, only a little nervous. 'But then he doesn't talk that much.'

'Aye, there is that...'

'Mount up,' Ferox interrupted.

'There is a raid?' Senuna asked as she obeyed. She was holding up the hem of her fine dress. Underneath she wore trousers and boots to make riding comfortable.

'Not just any raid,' Vindex said. 'The big one. The one your father has been warning everyone about all year.'

Again, Ferox cut him off. 'Get mounted. Litullus?'

'Lord.'

'Ride to the farms to the west and south. Tell them that there are large bands of warriors on the loose. They could be here soon. Warn everyone to be wary and to flee with all they can carry.'

'Should we go back to the house?' Senuna's voice was a mixture of fear and excitement.

Ferox gave a slight shake to his head as the only answer. 'We'll go north west. I'll lead. Carnacus, you stay with her. Never leave her side.'

'And I bring up the rear?' Vindex said. 'Fine.' They had been together for so long that no more was needed. He was already in the saddle and walked the gelding back a few paces.

Senuna's cheeks flushed with anger at being ignored. Ferox felt that she seemed to lose her temper easily, especially with him. Before he mounted he went across to her.

'Do you need a hand?'

His daughter snorted and hauled herself onto the pony's back.

'If we were back at the villa, we might hold out against ten,' he said softly. 'Maybe even against twenty. Any more than that would burn the place round our ears. You understand?'

She gave a little nod. Up close her grey eyes were glassy, but he could not be sure of her thoughts. Ferox had three daughters, and did not feel that he truly knew any of them. The twins had been away when he returned, and he had shown a knack for doing and saying the wrong thing to Senuna – or not saying the right thing. He really was not sure whether Senuna liked him at all.

'In the open we can get away. These are good horses.' He rubbed the neck of her pony. 'And you ride as well as your mother.'

Senuna did not react to the compliment. She seemed tense, and flinched when he patted her knee.

'I need you to be brave and smart, just like your mother. Can you do that for me?'

A nod.

'Good.' He smiled, never sure whether this was reassuring or disturbing to others. 'You are so much like her. But I have to ask one thing from you that she has never done.'

Senuna frowned.

'I need you to do what I say, when I say.' He tapped her knee again and this time she did not shudder. 'Just like you promised. And I if I tell you to run away and leave me, you do just that, understood?'

'Yes.' The girl licked her lips and did her best to smile. 'I can do that.'

'Good – I think.'

***

Ferox led them by a path that kept them in cover most of the time. Sometimes they could see him, scouting ahead, and sometimes they could not. He always reappeared for long enough to show them where they were heading. They trotted a little and cantered only occasionally, wanting to keep the mounts fresh. Senuna saw no one else, and could not say whether this was because her father had warned anyone he met to flee to shelter or there was simply no one else abroad. There were scarcely any sheep, which was odd, although plenty of signs that they had been in these upland pastures. The world seemed empty, save when now and again they crossed a rise and she could see the pillars of smoke. There were more of them now and some were closer, although she found it hard to judge just how close. At one point Ferox let them catch up, and he and Vindex stared at what might have been another plume of smoke, further away and to the north.

'Beacon?' Vindex suggested.

Ferox nodded. 'Near Magnis I reckon. There's one to the east of the garrison.'

Senuna was still not sure that it was anything more than a smear of cloud on the horizon. They pressed on, Carnacus riding in silence beside her. The man rarely spoke at the best of times, which was rare indeed among the Brigantes. Senuna missed Vindex's chatter.

They had gone seven or eight miles when Ferox came back towards them. He reined in beside a cluster of pines and waited for them and for Vindex to catch up.

'About fifty riders came past ahead of us, going along the next valley,' he told them. 'An hour ago, or perhaps a little more.'

'Should we go back, father?' Senuna spoke her thoughts out loud, then reddened because she had not meant to speak. 'Should we?' she added more firmly.

'No safer that way. Probably more dangerous.' Ferox rubbed his chin. 'No, they want plunder and glory. There's more of that behind us than ahead, so we keep going – just carefully. I'll go ahead and call you on once I am sure no one else is following them. When I whistle, you come on quick. There's a path leading up the far side of the valley. Follow that. You lead, Vindex, I'll bring up the rear. Just in case.'

'Who would be following?' Senuna asked, before realising the obvious. 'You think there are more of them.' Her mind was reeling. If fifty were an advance guard, then how big was the main band?

'Could be,' Ferox conceded. 'All those fires show that there are plenty of marauders out there. They haven't come this far south in this sort of strength for a long, long time. Hard to know how many parties there will be and how big.'

'And who are they?'

'Who do you think, lass?' Vindex answered. 'Novantae, Selgovae. Anyone else who doesn't like us much or just reckons we're fat and weak. It's been coming a long time and now they're here. Your father tried to warn everyone and no one listened. Reckon they just hoped another year would pass before anything really happened. Then either things would change or someone else would be in charge to take the blame. Now it's too late.' He glanced at Ferox. 'Hey, reckon the kid is with them?'

'Maybe,' Ferox said.

'Who is…?' Senuna began to ask then stopped when Vindex raised his hand in warning.

'We need to move,' Ferox told then. 'We'll get a good way on and then camp. Now come when I whistle!'

* * *

In the late afternoon they crossed another trail. Ferox, who was back in the lead again, told them that a couple of warriors had passed that way and hurried them on quickly because they were probably scouts. The spatter of dung from one of their horses was still moist, so it had not been that long ago. At the top of the next hill they stopped, dismounted and while Carnacus held the horses, Vindex and Ferox crept back up to the crest to watch. Senuna was not invited, but joined them anyway.

The Sun was already getting low in the sky, and would soon drop behind the peaks to the south. They waited and waited, and when the girl had decided nothing would happen, she felt her father's hand on hers. He raised a finger to his lips.

A moment later she heard the horses, then saw them as they trotted into view. She counted, reaching twenty, then she gave up because there were several times that many. They did not look that different from her own tribe, slim men, riding well. Half were bare-chested, almost all with faces painted in red, black or blue, and often the ponies were marked as well. Half had helmets of bronze or iron, rather fewer mail shirts, but all carried a stout shafted spear and a couple of javelins. She saw more than a dozen swords between them.

The warriors rode with assurance. Several had sheep slung behind them. A few of the ponies in the lead were clumsily painted with smears of red. Then Senuna stared more closely and understood. There were severed heads tied to the harness and it was not paint, but blood. She felt herself gagging and her father clamped one hand across her mouth and with the other turned her head to face him. His eyes stared into hers until he was sure that she was calm.

Down in the valley, the warriors rode on without stopping. Either they did not care about the marks left by a few travellers or they were not even looking for such things, for none of them checked even for a moment. Senuna was about to crawl away, when her father stopped her. They waited, and at a distance of some half a mile, a pair of scouts followed the main band.

Vindex tapped Ferox on the shoulder and drew his finger across his throat. Ferox shook his head.

At almost the spot where they had crossed the path, the two warriors halted. Senuna could not see that their four horses had left any trace at all on the grass, but her father had insisted that there were bound to be signs for a decent scout to see. One of the two men dismounted and said something to his companion. He was staring around, as if searching, until he gave up and simply lowered his trousers, bare bottom facing towards them, and squatted down.

Vindex grinned as he pointed for Senuna to look away. She found that she was trying not to giggle, and soon her whole body was shaking in silent laughter, for the warrior took a long time, and his groans were audible even up on the hilltop. Finally, he was done and pulled up a clump of grass to wipe himself. Then the two scouts rode off after the main body.

'Where are our soldiers?' Senuna asked as they went back to the horses. 'Those men rode along as if they owned the place.'

'For the moment they do,' her father said. 'The garrisons will do their best, but there simply aren't enough men up on the frontier to be everywhere, still less to stop thousands of raiders.'

'Thousands?' A thought suddenly struck her. 'Is mother safe?'

'Safer than us,' Ferox assured her. 'They may not get so far south and there are plenty of folk at Isurium. Soldiers too, working on the road and helping with that basilica your mother is always talking about.'

'She'll be all right, lass,' Vindex added. 'She knows what to do.'

'She always knows what to do,' Ferox sighed.

They kept going for another couple of hours, keeping on after sunset because the stars were bright and Ferox had no trouble finding the way.

'He likes the dark,' Vindex explained to Senuna. 'Well, he's an ugly bug— Sorry, but with a face like that what do you expect? Night's his best time.'

'Whereas you deserve to blaze in the sunshine,' she said and stuck out her tongue. She liked Vindex.

They kept a cold camp in the shadows of some rowan trees. It was a fair walk downhill to a stream for water, and Ferox and Carnacus went an even longer route when they took the horses down. As they were coming back, a fresh fire sprang up only a few miles away, reminding them of the need for caution. Ferox gave his daughter his cloak to help keep her warm, although in truth it was a sticky night, as if a storm was approaching. She slept little, feeling empty after their meagre meal.

III

That night, near Isurium Brigantum[*]

'OUR CAESAR WILL launch a new war soon, you mark my words,' Brigomaglos declared, splaying the fingers of his right hand in what he surely took to be the gesture of a practised orator. For the unpractised, it did nothing to emphasise his words and at the same time flicked a blob of grease back onto his wife's shoulder as she lay beside him on the couch. She gave a slight yelp, and brushed desperately at the spot, managing to unpin a brooch and make the shoulder of her dress flap down.

Claudia Enica sensed the man on either side of her shift his body ever so slightly as they noticed. At least their attention would be distracted for a while. She would have felt more pity for the poor woman had Brigomaglos been less of a pompous prig and his wife had ever said a kind word about anyone except in the hope of winning favour. The silly thing was pawing at the brooch and the open dress, drawing all the more attention. Fashion dictated that dress and under-tunic should be different shades. Brigomaglos' wife – who liked to call herself Ulpia even though that was not her name and she was not a citizen – was wearing an under garment in a bright red. Again, the contrast in

* Aldborough.

colour and the sheen of the material, which had some – though not much – silk in the weave, only made this trifling exposure stand out. The men either side of her, and most of the others too, were staring with more lustful interest than the desperately thin, almost contour-less, and sour-faced Ulpia could normally expect. Not that they could see very much, apart from the red undergarment.

Brigomaglos and his wife were so very desperate to be Roman. On any formal occasion, including this dinner party, he wore a toga, and spent his time clumsily balancing that most awkward of garments. He was clean shaven, very thin faced with narrow lips, and had no more than a fringe of hair left around his bald pate. Claudia Enica doubted that he was more than thirty, even though the fellow acted as if he possessed all the wisdom and dignitas – he liked his Latin words – of an elder statesman, a very Cicero reborn. The man had studied in Gaul as well as Londinium, sent there by his chieftain father who had other sons and did not know what to do with this sickly and handless individual. How much he had learned was hard to say, but he most certainly developed a fascination for the law. After that, ten years of hard work, the scarcity of experienced legal experts in the north of the province, and a willingness to treat with immense solemnity the most trivial detail of a case and embrace the widest possible meaning to any regulation whenever it suited his argument, had established him as one of the leading advocates in the tribe.

It was a pity the man was so tedious. Ignoring his wife's discomfort, and the fact that he was the cause of it, the man droned on, analysing the course of the wars Trajan had been fighting out east, and predicting future events. The man had little grasp of how wars were actually fought, even less of the mind and policies of any emperor, let alone Trajan, and no more than the vaguest ideas of the region. He spoke of Armenia as near Egypt, and only a little further from India, while half the races and kingdoms he described did not, so far as Claudia knew, actually exist.

As far as she could tell, only one other guest appreciated the sheer enormity of Brigomaglos' ignorance, although since the others barely listened at all she might be doing them a disservice. The exception was Pertacus, properly Marcus Ulpius Pertacus, who lay on the couch opposite the lawyer and continually expressed amazement at his sagacity and insight, and now and then asked facetious questions in a solemn voice and nodded, straight faced as he listened to the unconsciously absurd answers.

Brigomaglos preened himself at the attention, not least because Pertacus was a military man, just returned from serving as the prefect commanding a cohort of auxiliaries in Noricum, and certainly looked the part. He was tall, like most Brigantes, but broad shouldered and with the well-defined muscles that came from many years of effort. He was handsome, his face sardonic, his hair dark brown and like his moustache, immaculately neat. The last was an affectation, for it was narrow, unlike the thick growths normal in the old days and still grown by many of the tribe. Romans would consider a moustache outlandishly barbarian, and she wondered whether he had cultivated it since returning from his posting or whether he had paraded it then, confident that his looks, talent and swagger would carry him through.

'I understand that the Cimbri live in India, and have sent ambassadors begging the emperor to accept their submission,' Pertacus said. 'Are they a powerful folk?'

'Very,' Brigomaglos assured him. Claudia was surprised that the man did not recognise the name of the tribe who had threatened Italy itself more than two centuries ago – and been annihilated by the great – or infamous depending on your viewpoint – Marius. Perhaps the man was not really listening.

Thankfully, their hosts, Atgivios and Aunillus, called for silence as the latest course of food was cleared away and replaced with fruit and honey cakes. A boy, eight or nine years old and with the expression of someone deeply opposed to the task in hand, was ushered into the room and began to recite from Book Two of the Aeneid. Given his age, an audience mostly of strangers, and that this was a household not known for its interest in the arts, he did a tolerably good job, ploughing on regardless and removing any sense of life from the words.

'He's good isn't he?' Aunillus whispered, gesturing at the lad and letting the tips of his fingers brush against her for an instant as he pulled it back. The man was about seventy, so that the child might have been his grandson or even great grandson, even if he was more than likely to be a son. Atgivios and Aunillus were twins, so close that they had acted as joint chiefs of their clan for as long as anyone could remember. They were Roman citizens, but wore the honour lightly, taking several wives at a time as well as numerous mistresses from their household. Age did not appear to have cooled their ardour, and each had dozens of children, some even younger than this lad. The older ones lived on farmsteads of their own and were similarly prolific. Indeed, of the clan as a whole, few spoke of their great fame or achievements, but no one ever doubted that there were lots of them.

'This new stuff is all very well,' Atgivios said, after thanking the lad and bidding him good night, 'but to my mind the old songs are the finest. I am sure you agree, my dear.' He patted her elbow, letting his fingers smooth her skin for a moment.

'Here is the bard to do things the old way, so let us dream of times past.'

The man ushered in was truly ancient, decades older than the brothers, frail and half blind so that he had to be helped to the stool.

'I'm told he sang to your grandmother,' Atgivios whispered, leaning close and this time taking the opportunity to pat her leg. His speech was slurred with wine, although this made little difference to his behaviour. From the start, the Twins were free with their hands, and almost any movement, whether admiring her jewellery, showing her the latest course in the dinner, or simply illustrating any point, was followed by a touch.

'I love the old songs,' Claudia Enica whispered back, letting her voice become slightly husky. The brothers were a little bolder in their own home, although only a little, and having one on either side, who laughed, stretched, belched – and pressed closer than was necessary – at almost the same time and in precisely the same way was uncanny. She was used to her own daughters, who were almost as alike, if otherwise so different from these randy old goats. Yet they were randy old goats of influence, who had long been loyal to her family and to her. They liked her and supported her, which made it easier to bear their conduct, not least because they did not really expect to get away with anything more serious. As a child, barely older than Senuna, she had jabbed a hairpin into Atgivios' hand, and slammed a door onto Aunillus' fingers when they had become too eager. Neither had held it against her or wavered in their support, and it was good to cultivate them with the mildest of flirtation. When she wanted them to stop she would make it clear and they would stop.

The bard began to sing, the old way, through his nose, making a sound that was harsh to a stranger's ears, but stirred something deep inside all Brigantes whether they liked to admit it or not. He sang of Cartimandua, of her power and magic, and of her love for a young man who was not her husband. Claudia Enica was not offended, for how could she be offended by the truth, and as the queen and her consort argued in the verses, the old man told stories of their ancestors, or great battles and great loves of the past. She listened with pleasure, barely having to think when she jabbed her elbow down hard onto Aunillus' hand as he tried to slide it underneath her. A little later, while pretending to shift her weight, she gave the other brother a solid kick on the shin.

The tale was a long one, very long, and Brigomaglos and Ulpia did not trouble to conceal their boredom well. They were the only ones on their couch, for one guest had sent word to say that he was too ill to attend. Pertacus had a woman on either side of him, each young and plump and neither introduced as a wife, although each was clearly intimate with the brothers. They were friendly with the guest, squeezing close to him on either side. As the bard sang, the young prefect kissed and groped them both, albeit in an almost absent-minded way. The Twins kept this country house built in Roman style, and entertained guests in the new ways of Rome without forgetting the old customs of hospitality. For all the setting of a paved floor, plastered walls and the triclinium of three couches, this was as much feast as it was cena.

Pertacus would have been to plenty of meals that were more genuinely Roman, and Brigomaglos would have been to some. Having often dined in the presence of senators, and once or twice the princeps himself, Claudia could see how little resemblance this evening had borne to such a gathering. Unlike the lawyer, and perhaps the prefect, she would never voice such an opinion. These chieftains were from her tribe, her people, and she was as comfortable among them as she was with the highest-born Romans. In each case she was acting, but that was no more than the fate of any leader, let alone a monarch, and especially a queen. Whenever she appeared in public, even at a small dinner like this, duty came first. For all their vices, the brothers were good folk, and her folk. Brigomaglos was useful, and was currently advocate for more than one chieftain loyal to her, including the brothers. The man was an oaf, and only reliable as long as he felt it to be to his advantage, but remained useful. Pertacus was harder to pin down, something true of his wider kin. They had done well in recent years, even though they had backed her brother against her. Probably he was about as reliable as the lawyer, although a good deal more ambitious. As far as she knew, he had completed his spell as prefect, but had not yet received an appointment as junior tribune in a legion, which was the normal step for an equestrian serving in the army. It would be worth finding out whether this was through choice or because he lacked suitable connections. There was never any harm in knowing what someone wanted.

The bard finished, and the silence lingered for a long time. The brothers did not wish to break the spell conjured by the old verses, while some of the guests seemed stunned. It was late, and the food had never lacked for quantity and weight even if it might not match up to the standards of fashion in southern Britannia, let alone other provinces.

Brigomaglos rose and nodded his head to the brothers as hosts and then to Claudia Enica because of who she was. Neither the Romans nor the Brigantes bowed, but this slight gesture was felt appropriate to both. His wife stirred, did her best to smile, even though it did not come naturally. A servant appeared to lead them to their rooms, for all the guests were to stay at the villa, given the late hour. In the old days, if a man was able to return home on the night of a feast, then the host was shamed for not having entertained his guests appropriately. The brothers still followed this code.

Pertacus went next, paying no attention to the whispered words of one of his companions.

'I thank you for the warmth of your hearth, the meat on my plate and the wine in my cup,' he said, placing his right hand over his heart. Roman or not, he was not ashamed to be a Brigantian when the moment was right.

'We are sorry that all three were so mean,' Aunillus answered for both brothers.

'Lady,' the prefect went on. 'Your beauty is like the dawn, your hair like the rays of the morning, and the sweetness of your voice like the lark in the sky. Thank you for giving so poor a man a glimpse of the Heavens.' His dark eyes were fixed on her as he gave the compliment, his gaze earnest and worshipping, and Claudia Enica suspected that he was used to setting hearts aflutter.

'And it is good to see you, Marcus, returned safe from the wars.' There was no harm in a little mischief, in becoming very Roman, or in the compliment. One thing she did know about his spell with the army was that Pertacus had seen no active service. 'Let us not detain you from your bed.'

Pertacus gave the hint of a smile, as if he was the only one to see the full joke, nodded, and left them.

'Bit of a ponce, isn't he?' Atgivios growled.

'Father was almost as bad. No loss when he died,' his brother agreed. 'This one acts like a god walking among mortals.' He sniffed in disapproval. 'Didn't show much interest in the girls though.'

Atgivios stretched and yawned. 'More fool him. Is he married? Betrothed?'

'What, thinking of any of our lassies you don't really like?'

'No, just curious.'

'He is not married,' Claudia Enica informed them. 'Nor matched, at least publicly and families rarely keep such things secret.'

'Has he got a woman?' Atgivios asked.

Before she could answer, the other brother reminded her of another reason why these two old men were worth having as friends.

'Him?' Aunillus sniffed in disdain. 'Not a woman, that one. Maybe women, but not a woman.' He rubbed his shoulder. Reclining on a couch, propped up on one elbow, was not comfortable for long, especially to those who had not grown up with the custom. 'Oh bugger me,' he said under his breath. 'Time for bed.'

In the next few minutes, each brother in turn, judging the other to be out of earshot, suggested that Claudia might appreciate some comfort and company in the long hours of the night. Aunillus was full of concern, worried that she was missing the embrace of her husband. By their standards, and the customs of their youth, it was done with courtesy. Neither seemed offended or surprised when she declined their offers to visit her. Still, she suspected that the slightest encouragement would have brought them along in due course. Before coming to dinner, she had checked to make sure that there was a bar on the inside of her chamber's door.

'Good night, my old friends, and thank you – especially for the bard.'

'She was a woman, your grandmother,' Aunillus said reverently. Each kissed her hand, a custom of the royal house and their kin, and because she was tall, they did not have to bend far.

IV

At the villa of the Twins

Claudia Enica was tired, all the more because she knew that long weeks of work lay ahead. The court cases were interminable. She wondered whether the chief aim of Roman law was to bore people into accepting the empire. They would go on for weeks, which meant more long hours listening to speeches, even longer hours helping her friends with their cases and encouraging them, and no doubt more dinners like this one. At the same time there was so much to do at Isurium, for she wanted to make it a city worthy of being the centre of her tribe. The Romans did not understand tribes, but they understood cities, and it did not matter too much if they were small. Work on the basilica and Forum were almost complete, which gave plenty of space for the flood of legal disputes. More happily, the amphitheatre was coming on, and all were benefiting from the work party from Legio XX, who were taking on more than just the road work they had been sent here to do. That took persuasion, which was necessary if less than pleasant. The tribune in charge was almost as free with his hands as her current hosts. The next few months would be long and wearying, but they would be worth it.

Her maid was waiting in her room, which made the whole

business of undressing and preparing for bed that much easier. The girl knew enough not to chatter, and Claudia was not one of those ladies who sought constant praise and admiration of their looks from her servants. At thirty-seven, soon to be thirty-eight, she was no longer the fresh-faced girl of her youth, but the figure was still there and the skin had few blemishes or lines. Men still looked at her just as they had always done. In time perhaps only the older ones would do so, but that time had not come yet. Even her hair remained bright and thick, and did not need the slightest hint of dye, let alone the additions favoured by many ladies in the empire.

It took a while to prepare for bed. She had dressed well tonight, out of courtesy to her hosts and because she was queen, whatever the Romans might say. Apart from that, she liked clothes and enjoyed showing herself at her best. So she had donned the necklace and earrings, and amid the pins arranging her hair were delicate chains of silver bearing pearls. The girl worked in silence, carefully unfastening all of this, while Claudia herself cleaned away the touches of make-up she had used. How could Ovid devote a whole poem to such things? She tried to remember how it started and could not, drifting off into the *Ars Amatoria*, because quoting from it always made Ferox bristle. Her husband had a good memory for verse, and had read far more widely than he ever let on. It was good to have him back, especially as he seemed to have mellowed over these last years. Still, it was better that he was not here, because his temper tended to flare up at inappropriate times, or he would fall into the brooding silence that only the Silures could fill with so much menace. All in all, he was not diplomatic, so it was good that he was back on the farm. Be good for Senuna to get to know her father better as well. Perhaps then she would realise how fortunate she was.

The task was done, she was clad only in her silk shift for the night, and it was time for the girl to leave, not least because Claudia needed to employ the black clay pot under the bed. The brothers did not appear to believe in Roman lavatories, so dealt with night soil in an older way. When they had ridden here in daylight, she had noticed that the plaster below the windows of upstairs rooms like this one was discoloured, which suggested that their servants employed the simplest means of emptying them. That was a waste, since in a well-regulated house, the urine at least would be kept. Still, it was their house and they were free to run things as they wished.

'Is that all, mistress?' the girl asked.

'Yes, Calypso. Get some sleep. We leave in the morning, so be sure to be packed as early as you can.'

'Yes, mistress. Do you want one of the men to stand guard?' She had come with two warriors from the household, as well as the girl. They were less than ten miles from Isurium, so no larger escort was needed, even for a queen.

'These are friends. Just let the fellows get some sleep. You too,' she added pointedly, for she had noticed the girl flirting with the taller of the two men. 'Goodnight.'

'Mistress.'

A little later, as she lay waiting for sleep, there came a knock at the door.

'What is it, Calypso?' She was in the end room, and as far as she could tell the one next to her own was empty. Even so, she did not wish to disturb anyone, so kept her voice no louder than was necessary.

The only reply was another tap on the door.

Enica reached under the pillow for the bone-handled knife that she put there, wherever she was staying. Flicking her wrist brought out the slim blade, and a push locked it into place. She should not need it to deter either of her hosts, unless the old fools had kept on drinking, so unclasped it and pushed the blade back inside the handle.

'Who is it?' A question like that always sounded foolish, but what else were you supposed to say?

'Lady?' It was a man's voice, but low and muffled so that she could not tell whether or not it was one of her men. She did not think that it was either of the Twins.

'The hour is late, sir,' she said, going to the door, the knife held behind her back.

'Lady? Please open the door.'

Claudia Enica was a guest in the house of good friends and ought to be safe. She clicked the blade back out and kept it hidden behind her. A sensible lady would no doubt pretend to be asleep and ignore the man outside, but sensible ladies rarely made good queens. She lifted the wooden bar from its slot and opened the door slightly, ready to spring back if the person outside charged.

Pertacus smiled down at her. He was taller than she had realised, as tall as Ferox. It was a good smile, as he was well aware, and even in the shadows of the corridor his eyes were large and earnest.

'My lady – I mean, my queen – I was hoping to speak to you alone.'

'Indeed,' she said. Well, the men weren't getting older yet, although this one would probably hump a grandmother if she could help his career. Claudia stayed by the door, not letting it open any more.

'Milk white skin, hair like fire, eyes like the sea.' He chanted the lines from the song sung by the bard, and reached forward as if to touch her cheek. 'You are your grandmother reborn in all her beauty.'

Claudia Enica got the impression that the man was used to this approach working. She let his fingers brush her face, for it was either that or step back from the door which would surely appear an invitation. She smiled. 'This is not the time.'

'Night is for lovers,' he said, smoothing the back of his hand across her cheek. 'Cartimandua indeed, goddess of war and love.' He switched to chanting again. 'Breasts like round hills.'

Enica had heard the line many a time and still wondered how it was meant to be a compliment. She stepped back.

'Friendly thighs,' he intoned, coming into the room, 'and above the—' Pertacus stopped abruptly, for Enica was holding the knife's blade against his throat.

'I said that this is not the time. Do you understand?' She pressed the blade. Any more and she would draw blood. 'No need to nod.'

Pertacus stepped back. It was hard to tell in the poor light, but she suspected that he had gone pale.

'I am your queen,' she told him. 'If you have favour to ask, then ask at a more fitting time.'

He nodded, feeling the skin of his throat and then examining his fingers to see whether or not there was a cut.

'We shall put this down to drink and exuberance, but do not ever act like this again. Like Cartimandua, I choose – I am not chosen.' She shut the door and put the bar back into place. There was a little spot of blood on the knife, so she must have pressed harder than intended. Smiling, she wiped it off before folding the blade back into the handle. Then she went to bed. Sleep came easily.

***

Claudia Enica woke with a start, unsure whether the shout was part of her dream or real. Apart from a thin hint of starlight coming through the gaps in the shutters, the room was pitch black. One hand found the clasp knife. She lay still, listening. Men were talking in low voices, although she could not tell whether they were in the corridor or somewhere outside. Pulling back the covers, she felt the chill of night as she sat up.

There were men in the corridor, she was sure of it. Her door creaked as someone pushed gently at it. The bar held it shut. Claudia Enica reached for her shoes, found them near the foot of the bed where she always kept them, and fumbled to fasten them on her feet. She would have preferred her travel boots, but they were with Calypso along with most of her other things. These were no more than light sandals intended for wear inside, the patchwork of soft white bands leaving gaps to show the colour of her stockings. Not that she was wearing stockings, or anything apart from her night shift, but she did not want to wander about in bare feet if there was trouble.

The door banged as it was kicked hard. The bar held. It had looked solid when she had examined it earlier, but that did not mean that it would hold forever. Claudia went to the window and opened the shutters. The brothers had not invested in glass, and right now that seemed like a good choice. She blinked with the cold, then stood on tiptoes to peer out. Her room was at the rear of the house, above the working yard surrounded by a couple of round houses and a tall rectangular barn. There were men out there, a dozen of more, some with torches, and the red light glinted off the drawn swords and spear points of the others. Two more lay on the ground, in that shapeless sack of old clothes pose that meant that they were corpses, since no one would lie down and sleep with all this going on. The villa was under attack, and it did not really matter at the moment by whom.

Her door slammed again, the wood starting to crack. The men outside were shouting at each other. She turned and dragged the bed frame across to the window. There was a sheet, and the dress laid out for the morning. A surge of red light came through the window and she heard the soft roar as a fire gathered strength.

One of the planks shattered, and a spear point thrust through the gap. The man jabbed again, splintering more wood, and again, so that a piece fell off. Claudia tied the sheet to one of the bed's stubby legs, and tied the dress to the sheet, and looped that around her waist. She sprang onto the bed and pulled herself into the window. There was a beam above her and she jumped, grabbing it with both hands, and swung her feet up, managing to get them over the window ledge. An arm came through the gaping hole in the door, feeling for the bar. She had forgotten the knife, having put it down when fastening her shoes, and now it was too late.

Claudia Enica swung again, just as the bar was lifted and the shattered door flung open.

'Get the bitch!' someone shouted, but she was already going out, shift bunching up, so that anyone outside who chanced to be watching would have been granted a rare view of the Queen of the Brigantes. Then she was out and falling as the crude rope stretched down. She dropped five or six feet and slammed to a stop, but the material had held, at least for a moment, and there was only ten feet or so left to fall. The heat from the blazing barn felt savage, as the flames leapt high. Warriors were cheering, brandishing their weapons in excitement and no one seemed to have noticed her.

Struggling to breathe, because the abrupt stop had felt as

if she was being cut in two, she pulled free the knot around her waist and fell again. A moment later the rope was cut or unfastened above her.

'Get her!' a voice screamed from the window.

Claudia Enica did her best to keep her legs loose and to roll over and that took some of the impact. It still hurt a lot, but she did not think anything was broken. A warrior had turned, his young face staring down at her in puzzlement.

'Kill that bitch!'

The warrior raised his spear to thrust. Enica pushed herself up, then rolled again as the man jabbed at her. Her white shift was filthy with mud, but this time as she pushed up she managed to start running.

'Kill her!' the voice shouted again from the window. More warriors were reacting, some of them in her path as she headed for the wooden fence of a corral. The nearest man did not have a weapon, and had dropped his torch so that his hands reached out to grab her. If this had not been so deadly serious it was all like a children's game.

She dodged to the left, and a spear, probably thrown by the youngster, smacked into the man's belly, pitching him over. She jagged back and jumped over him because another man was coming at her and she felt the wind of his sword as he slashed down, missing her, and chopping into the one already falling. The corral was just yards away and she was going fast, and with one hand grabbed the top and swung herself over, clearing it, but falling and rolling again.

A voice was shouting, a different voice, and there was a clash of blade on blade and then the grunt of effort and that dull thud of steel sinking into flesh. She was up again, and apart from one tall horse, the corral was empty. It was a heavily built beast, and presumably old because it either had not noticed or was too weary to pay attention to the burning barn or the fighting going on nearby.

Claudia glanced back, saw that no one had followed her over the fence, and ran to the horse. She patted its neck, whispered 'Hey, boy, good boy.' Grabbing its mane, she somehow swung herself up. The horse did not move, and it was like sitting over a fallen oak trunk. She kept talking to it, but until she reached back and slapped its rump hard, the beast did not deign to move. It walked a few steps.

Back in the yard, she saw a cluster of raiders gathered around two men and recognised her warriors. One fell at that moment, a spear in his side. The tall one, the one Calypso had so obviously liked, stood alone, bare-chested. He had already taken several wounds, but still swung his long sword. A slash bit into the neck of one of his enemies, who staggered, blood jetting high and then fell, but at the same moment the tall man was stabbed from behind. He spun, slicing at his attacker without catching him. A sword cut into his thigh, and the tall man dropped to one knee. Warriors closed tightly around him so that he vanished. No one else seemed to be fighting.

'Come on, you old goat,' she said, slapping the horse again, and he began to lurch into a walk and then a trot. She took him in a circle, thinking that this old stallion was the equine match for its masters, for the creature was reviving, shaking its head, and by the time she had turned him back towards the far fence he was cantering.

'Get her!'

A spear hissed in the air and fell short, as she drove the stallion at the fence, pushing him, wondering whether his stiff muscles would balk at the last minute and leave her looking very foolish. Yet she was of the royal house of Brigantia, granddaughter of Cartimandua, and all horses loved her. She felt that oh-so-familiar tensing, then the wonderful surge of power, and she clung tightly to the mane for the big horse was rising, rising, clearing the fence with ease. There was a jolt as the big front feet landed, and she bounced more than she expected, but held on, and managed to get back upright.

'Kill her!' The voice was fainter. She had not seen any warriors on horseback, which might mean that it would take them a little time to find their mounts and give chase. Yet there could be others waiting in the darkness.

'Third twin,' she said softly to the horse, having decided to give it this name. She felt that the brothers would smile at the thought of her dressed in nothing apart from shoes and a thin, bunched up shift astride their old stud horse. 'Bear me well.'

Its big feet drumming on the turf, the stallion ran steadily into the night.

V

Dawn, nine days before the Kalends of September,
in the hill country

SENUNA HAD SLEPT little and woke feeling stiff and cold, although oddly enough not very hungry. She forced herself to eat some of the proffered biscuit and salted pork, washing it down with water from the stream.

'We need to go,' Ferox told them, once they had brushed down the horses. He hoped to reach the great east to west road by the end of the day, and ideally make it to one of the garrisons or meet up with a column chasing the raiders. Soon, they began to run into groups of fugitives, hiding in the higher valleys with their flocks and herds and whatever goods they had been able to carry off. Some were talkative, desperate to tell anyone all about their adventures and frights. Others were silent, mourning the lost ones who had not been so fortunate and the homes burned to the ground. A few men, usually the younger ones, tried to talk each other into facing the attackers, boasting that courage would make up for their lack of weapons. Ferox told them to stay and protect the others, using his authority as centurion of Rome and husband of Enica. He suspected that most were glad of the excuse.

They saw quite a few burned farms, as well as others, apparently untouched if empty of people. The raiders had gone quickly, not stopping to ransack any valley thoroughly, but pushing south. That way were richer pickings, the bigger herds, more farms, some villages and even villas like his own. Everything suggested a well-planned attack, with lots of chieftains and ambitious men putting aside their rivalries to strike together. They had seen the Roman weakness, but someone had enough sense to convince the others that it was best to go in quickly, reach the richest prizes and then get out as fast as they could before the soldiers started to organise.

As far as he could tell, the raiders had achieved complete surprise. That would give them a day with little chance of meeting any troops. The next day – today – the army would be starting to get over the first shock and panic and beginning to work out what was going on. Patrols would be out, probably not in strength, and messengers galloping from one base to the next trying to organise a proper response. That always took longer than everyone expected. Perhaps someone would seize control and begin to mount a response by tomorrow. Perhaps they would even know what they were doing. Sometimes chance put just the right person in the right place at the right time – and sometimes not. It was hard to tell, and he did not know enough about any of the prefects in command in this area to judge how well they would cope, but the raiders still had to get home, and that meant there was a chance to salvage something from this whole mess.

By noon they were steadily coming down from the higher hills and the country began to open out on either side. From one rise Ferox could see several clouds of dust. They were high and straggling, courtesy of several hot and mostly dry months. The shape meant that they were created by lots of men riding in column. More than that, it was hard to tell. He guessed, without really knowing why, other than that he had seen so many formations of cavalry on the move, that one of them was made by troopers, a *turma* or more, moving in formation. They were too far away for him to risk finding out, and were moving fast, apparently behind one of the other groups. The pursued were not going so fast, so either did not realise that they were being chased or knew very well. Probably some bold decurion was chasing after the raiders with more urgency than sense. Ferox hoped that the man was taking care not to ride straight into an ambush. Still, there was nothing he could do to help.

They pressed on, and Ferox risked taking them along one of the valleys, hoping that any raiders were a good way to the south. There were plenty of tracks of ponies and others of cows and people fleeing on foot, but none were fresh. The path was not straight, as the valley wound, following the meanderings of a brook. Soon they came across the body of an old man, lying face down on the turf. Apart from the bites of carrion birds, there was not a mark on him, nor a stich a clothing. He had likely died of fright as the raiders chased him, and they had stripped him bare because even old clothes were worth something. No one had bothered to take his head.

The ground led gently down, a clear path through the thick heather, as it opened into another, wider valley. They went slowly and could smell the ash on the wind before they could see anything. Ferox gestured to the others to halt, and then walked his horse forward where the path led through a cluster of beech trees. In a little while he was back, and beckoned them on.

One farm was close by, hidden behind the trees. Another was half a mile or so away, across the valley floor, and a third a similar distance to the south. Each had five or six round houses, drystone pens for the livestock blossoming around them, all enclosed by a ditch making it difficult for anyone to steal any of the animals unless they used the single entrance. There were dozens, even hundreds of similar clusters of houses anywhere in the lands of the Brigantes and throughout much of Britannia. Most were old, home to the same family for generation after generation, brothers, sisters, and sometimes cousins living alongside each other, twenty or thirty people and as many animals in each one.

That was in good times. Now these ones were lifeless and ruined, what was left of the conical thatched roofs no more than charred skeletons, smouldering gently. A man lay draped over one of the walls, his back bare, his neck ending in a stump where his head had been taken. In the ditch was the carcase of a calf, clumsily butchered.

The wind sighed softly through the grass and Senuna was sure that she could hear the buzzing of flies.

'Stay back,' her father told them, as he walked his horse over to the nearest farm. The animal shied as it came to the route over the ditch, and Ferox calmed it enough to cross, startling half a dozen crows that flapped lazily into the air, cawing in protest at being disturbed. Senuna had never before understood just how harsh the sound was.

A shallow ditch and the determined anger of the inhabitants was enough to hold off any but the most determined rustlers, but was little defence against a band of warriors.

Senuna felt her gorge rising. It seemed hot, hotter than even this hot summer's day. And she nudged her horse forward because seeing must surely be better than imagining.

Vindex grabbed at her bridle. 'He said stay, lass.'

Ferox had dismounted and drawn his sword. He walked into the farm, peering around the pens and at the ruined houses. They saw him bend down more than once, before straightening up and continuing the search.

'Why didn't they run?' Senuna asked, desperate to break the silence.

'Reckon there wasn't time. Probably came in the night, or just after dawn.'

Ferox reappeared, his gladius back in its scabbard, and got back in the saddle. He walked Frost across to them.

'Father, the people...' Senuna trailed off, not knowing what to say.

Vindex patted her on the arm, feeling that this was really something her father ought to have done, but had not. 'How bad?' he asked.

'Bad.' Ferox grimaced. 'They took their time.'

'All dead?'

Ferox nodded. 'The younger women and the children aren't there.'

'Have they escaped?' Senuna asked.

Ferox stared at his daughter as if he could not understand the question. 'Slaves, lass.' He said at last. He gave a quick glance along the valley, before turning back. 'Happened yesterday, but some stayed until this morning, eating and...' He seemed to notice Senuna and abruptly changed tack. 'Well, reckon they have moved on, but you never can tell. We need to go that way.' He pointed to the north, following the main valley. 'The horses are fresh, and best to get through such open country as fast as we can. We'll risk a gallop.'

'We can't just leave these people like this.' Senuna tried to sound more confident than she felt. 'They're our kin, Brigantes – we ought to cover them at the very least. I will help.'

'No,' Ferox said. 'Check your girths.'

Senuna gave him a look of contempt at the mere suggestion that she had neglected anything like that. It was insulting to anyone from the royal house of the tribe, as was the thought of neglecting their folk. 'But, father... And what about the other farms? There might be somebody hiding.'

'No.'

As so often, Vindex felt that he needed to explain for his friend. 'If they're hiding then they're safe, and we can't help them. But there won't be any, lass. And you won't want to see what's there.' He stared into her eyes. 'I don't want to see what's there.'

'Come on, we go,' Ferox commanded. 'Follow me.' He turned Frost around and with just the slightest of nudges the grey surged into life, bounding into an easy canter and then a gallop. The ground was firm and soon the horse was rushing along, so that the others struggled to keep up. Senuna kept closest behind, while Vindex and Carnacus were soon twenty or more paces behind her.

They passed one of the other farms off to the right, and she tried and failed to see any sign of movement there. The last one was closer to the centre of the valley. It seemed just as desolate, but Senuna suddenly knew what she must do. The pony felt her looking in that direction and responded eagerly as she turned and headed for the farm.

Vindex shouted something she did not hear, and the pony gathered pace, hoofs pounding across the hard earth. They were close now, and she could see naked corpses in the ditch. Her pony twitched its ears, trying to pull away, but she forced it on, until they were almost at the causeway leading across into the farm. Senuna pulled on the reins and soothed the beast as it came to halt, then swung one leg over its neck and jumped down.

'Come back!' The words were clear this time. Senuna ignored them, not knowing why and sure that she was making a fool of herself. She remembered that when she was little, her mother had once declared that it was better to be blamed for doing something than for doing nothing. Even at the time it had seemed odd advice from a parent.

The stench was appalling, almost worse than the sights, because you could not turn away from it. A raven hopped onto the top of a wall and stared at her with its beady eye. There was something in its mouth, something round and bloody that she hoped was not what it looked like.

'Senuna!' That was her father's voice. She made herself run into the yard and tripped over something, pitching forward to land with her chest in a still half-moist pile of manure. She grimaced, and, as she began to get up, saw that just ahead was the cadaver of an old woman, her guts spilled onto the ground.

Senuna dropped, just bracing herself with her hands, and vomited, coughing when there was nothing more to come up.

There was someone behind her, someone who took one arm and helped her stand up. It was her father, and he said nothing and simply stared at her, face rigid. It was worse than a rebuke.

For a while there was silence. Senuna happened to see the old woman again, and coughed up a few more trickles of vomit, some of it onto Ferox.

'We need to go,' he said.

Senuna nodded, then heard something.

'Wait,' she said. Wondering whether it was her imagination because she could not hear it any more.

'No time.' He took her by the wrist and pulled her away.

'Please.'

Ferox let go. This child usually acted as if she was already the queen her mother was not – at least officially. Hearing her ask for something was shocking.

'There!' Senuna pointed at one of the cattle pens. She strode towards it, until Ferox clamped a hand on her shoulder.

'I'll go.'

The gate lay open, ripped off its post for no reason other than that warriors liked to break things they could not take.

'Stay back,' Ferox said. 'I mean it.' A sixth month foal lay on the ground, one of its hind legs broken, which explained why the raiders had not taken it. Someone had decided to put it out of its misery and botched the job, so that the poor creature must have taken a long time to die. The ground was caked with dried blood.

Not all came from the young horse. A woman lay in the corner, half covered with a filthy cloth, and with a bundle clutched tightly to her chest. Her hair had once been a rich chestnut, before age started to fade it and turn it grey. Ferox guessed that she was around his age, although it was often hard to tell because tending crops, fields and children was not a kind life and folk aged quickly. One of her bare legs had come out from under the covering and there was a deep slash across the dirty skin. Ferox reached for the cloth, whether once a blanket or even cloak he could not tell, and eased it aside. There were more wounds on the woman's belly, as well as other marks that had come from her treatment before the men cut her about and left her for dead. Near her head was an open pit, the sort that if properly sealed would keep a store of grain good for a season or more. It was empty, and beside it was the board that had gone on top and the earth that have covered it. This woman, a grandmother probably, had been hacked half to pieces, yet had waited until the attackers were gone and then crawled to this spot to uncover some hidden treasure. Then she had died, the last of her life's blood mingling with that of the foal.

Ferox touched the bundle and understood why.

'Trouble!' Vindex shouted from outside.

Ferox had to prise apart the woman's fingers to free the baby.

It was small, less than a month old, and suddenly found voice enough to cry. He stood, trying to soothe it and not making much progress until he touched its lips with his little finger and the infant began to suck.

'Warriors coming!' Vindex called. 'Selgovae, I reckon.'

Senuna gasped as she saw her father walking out of the animal pen, a baby cradled in his arms.

'Get going!' he shouted. 'Now!'

Senuna did as she was told.

Vindex and big, placid Carnacus were outside, holding the other two horses. 'We need to go,' the Carvetian insisted. There were riders near the first farm they had found. Senuna shaded her eyes to look into the Sun and saw four, five – no, nearer a dozen men with spears.

'Get on your horse, you daft girl!' Vindex almost snarled the words. Ferox was close behind, and somehow managed to fold the baby under his arm and vault onto the back of Frost. The baby protested, and kept on protesting as the centurion shuffled to get his balance and then took the reins from Carnacus.

'Oh bugger,' Vindex said.

Ferox twisted his head, saw the warriors. 'What are you waiting for!' he bellowed.

Vindex slapped the haunch of Senuna's pony, which whinnied and set off at a run. They galloped down the valley, the baby still screaming until Frost settled into a pounding gallop, when it apparently enjoyed the motion and fell silent.

'Oh, shit.'

Vindex's cry prompted Ferox to peer back. The warriors were following, almost half a mile away, but another group as large as the first had appeared behind them. Stealth no longer mattered. Up ahead a gully led off up the hillside, as the valley curved around to the east. Climbing would slow everyone down, but was unlikely to gain them much time. He could not remember anywhere in the land up there where he could do anything. Instead, if they kept in the valley, and could keep ahead for long enough, there was an old plank bridge, wide enough for just one person or beast at a time. Even after this summer the stream ought to be deep enough and its banks steep enough to stop them fording across. If they could just get there and get over, then he could stand and hold the warriors back while Vindex took the others on to safety. The Carvetian would want to stay, but Carnacus was not bright enough to be trusted with the task on his own.

Ferox looked back. The warriors were no closer. As yet, they had not built on their lead, but at least the pursuers were not catching up. The bridge was five or six miles away, their horses were good, and fairly fresh, so they might stand a chance.

The valley narrowed, pine woods covering the slopes on either side, but the going was good and he felt that they were starting to gain.

A horn blew a rasping challenge, and Carnacus' stocky gelding stumbled into a pit hidden by the grass. Its front legs folded, head went down and the huge man was flung forward out of the saddle to slam into the ground. Senuna screamed.

Warriors appeared, riding out of the trees on both sides. One was wearing a high, gleaming helmet of bronze and armour of polished scales.

The baby started to slip from Ferox's arm, and he struggled to stop it from falling. Again it began to howl.

Warriors were all around them, spears levelled.

'What have we here?' a voice said.

'Oh shit!' Vindex said again, and began to laugh, until one of the warriors slammed a spear shaft against the back of his head.

The next morning, on the hills overlooking Magnis

THE ROMANS WOULD *call it luck, or fate, or say that it was foretold in the stars, because they saw only in a straight line, and like someone trying to see through a forest so much was hidden from their view.*

The Romans revelled in their vast empire, their provinces and their cities. They measured the lands and counted the people who lived there, so that they could tax them, and they called themselves great. He had walked and ridden for thousands of miles, had seen lands of winter ice and deserts of burning heat, and folk who were pale or burned dark, and all of them under the sway of Rome. Many even called themselves Roman, as he had once done, and exalted in being masters of the world.

Fools. The world was far bigger, far fuller than they could ever know. They counted strength in the number of their legions and the weight of their gold and silver. They did not understand the spirit or the soul, for these were the true sources of power. They did not understand the gods. Long ago, the legions went to Mona, slaughtered the druids and cut down the hallowed groves. Did they think they were killing the gods of that place? Did they not understand that the gods moved in the air and dwelt in bark and stone where they chose? They were here, in the north, and they would take back what had been theirs.

Rome's emperor was dying. Once a strong man, a warrior, a man with power in his spirit even if he did not understand it,

Trajan had let his power trickle away. Thus, he was defeated and did not know what to do, growing weaker by the day.

A man must trust his power, must cosset and feed it as a farmer tended a seed, for only then would it grow. She had shown him that, or as she said, she had led him to know what he had once known and forgotten.

She was pleased with the eight heads he and his men had brought back from the ambush. They were excited too, almost as thrilled that they had done it and done it well as they were with the swords and helmets they had taken. Two of the cuirasses were beyond repair, too badly damaged, so they had only brought back the others. She would decide who had them when there was time. The men who had stayed in the camp with the horses hailed the exploit and were eager to prove themselves.

As they were chanting a song of victory, she had reached up to put a hand on each of his shoulders. She did not need to say anything, for he knew. It was time to act.

The warriors responded sluggishly at first, as if puzzled that they needed to perform another deed so soon. Yet they obeyed, even though he did not explain, for he could not explain, and simply followed a path that seemed laid before him. His power was growing within him, blossoming, rising even higher because she favoured him.

As they rode to the north west five warriors appeared. These were men who had spoken of joining them, but had not appeared by the time they set out. He bade them follow and they did.

He began to ride faster and faster, and perhaps she filled the mind of his pony, because the beast seemed to have a sense of where it was going. They came to the wooded country, north of Magnis. There was no sign of Roman patrols out looking for them. The enemy were blind men and could not see them. On the first day their beacons had been lit, but late, many hours after the raids must have struck, let alone their own attack. More fires erupted to the south, ever further south in the days that followed, as the roving bands burned village and farm. Some of his men saw them, longing to be with them, but they did not leave him. They were not Romans, not soldiers bound by fear of punishment to obey. They were free men of the tribes, and they went where they chose. These chose to stay with him.

They came to a well-trodden track, and if his men were surprised when he turned north, still they trusted and followed, sensing that he was being led in this direction.

The path wound between clumps of woodland, rising and falling over hills and dells. They kept going, as the track bent around a dense patch of silver birch trees, and there were riders in front of them, a long bowshot away, six of them.

The men were Romans. All save one wore a hooded cloak, but he did not need to see their faces or clothes to know what they were. They rode like Romans, well enough, but somehow stiff, even formal, not one with their mount as if horse and man had become a single creature. He could not put it into words, but the way they rode, just as surely as the way they would stand and walk was different from the men of the tribes.

The leader sawed on his reins, making his tall bay rear as it started to turn. His hood fell back, showing that he was thickly bearded. He shouted something, and the others were turning, fleeing. Two of the men at the back carried heavy spears, and when he turned there was the hump of a dead boar slung across another man's horse.

The warriors charged without needing an order. They rode small ponies, hardy beasts good for long journeys through hard lands. The Romans had slimmer, higher horses, bred for speed and looks and if they had been fresh then no doubt they would have escaped. Instead, his warriors closed, fanning out, so that they could surround the enemy when they caught up with them.

His warriors were whooping with sheer joy, hunting the men who were clearly returning from a hunt of their own. Hoofs drummed on the grass as they went a mile, then another, and the lead was less than forty paces. Another half mile and a warrior flung a javelin and spitted the man whose horse carried the dead boar.

They were so close now, that he could see that the Romans' horses were stumbling, sides slick with foamy sweat, and he guessed that they had ridden hard to get here – riding straight into his arms.

His warriors were passing the fugitives, encircling them. One of the men with a spear turned to fight and was hit in the face by another javelin, the warrior yelling in delight as it hit home.

'Drop your weapons!' he shouted in Latin, and perhaps that surprised them, because they reined in hard.

'Are you scouts?' one of them demanded.

'Drop your weapons,' he repeated. The other man carrying a spear, a slave most likely, levelled the heavy shaft towards him. He had his sword out, brushed the spear aside, and rode on, smiling at the man. At the last moment he slashed, opening the slave's throat to the bone.

'Sweet Liber Pater,' one of the remaining riders gasped. 'We can pay ransom,' he added. 'In gold.'

Trust a Roman to think of money at a time like this.

The bearded man had a knife in his hand and seemed willing to use it.

'Drop it, Curius,' the other man commanded. He, and the one who was begging, were both younger than the other one,

but there were traces of arrogance under their fear. Those two each wore a silver ring on their left hand, the mark of an eques.

The bearded man dropped the knife and spat on it.

It did not take long to learn the story, for the younger men talked eagerly, emphasising their own importance. One was the prefect in command of the cohort at Magnis, the other the commander of a garrison further away. Curius, who remained silent, was the senior centurion from Magnis and an old hand on the frontier. He knew enough to know what was likely to happen, and barely veiled his contempt for the fawning of his officers. They had been on a hunting trip to the north for the last three days – which meant that they had somehow not run into any of the bands of warriors coming for the raid. Only when they saw the warning beacons had they realised that something was happening, and had left the rest of their slaves and equipment to gallop south and take charge of their men.

'If you had not come so fast, you would have missed us,' he told them. 'And if you had not worn out your steeds you would still have escaped us.'

The centurion spat again. He had probably advised them sensibly and been ignored. The man was a warrior.

They cooked the boar and feasted, letting the Romans have a share. After that they were tied and guarded.

The next morning before dawn, he rode towards the fort at Magnis. It was much like so many Roman bases, rectangular in plan with rounded corners, and packed full of long barrack blocks and even bigger buildings. This one was in timber, the roofs made from shingles, and some elsewhere in the empire were stone with grey or deep red tiles. He had seen the tracks and guessed that a couple of hundred men, most likely half the garrison in residence, had marched out more than a day before and headed south. If he had had a thousand men, he could probably have rushed the place and burned it to the ground.

Instead he walked his horse towards the darker shadow that was the fort, judged the distance and then waited. The Sun began to rise, bright red and burning, and the walls and towers were black, until it moved higher and their shape became clearer.

In front of the road leading to the main gateway, at the spot where a causeway carried it past the ditch, stood half a dozen men. That was small for the picket that regulation dictated must stand outside every gate day and night, and he guessed that the soldiers would have passed a nervous two hours when everyone knew that raiders were abroad.

They were perhaps a quarter of a mile away from him. One of them shouted as they saw him. He raised the spear aloft. The tip was pointing down, the balance poor because of its burdens. The bronze helmet taken from one of the men they had ambushed glinted red in the sunlight. His pony was daubed all in red too, and there was dark red blood smeared on his face.

'Romans!' he shouted.

One of the sentries was running back towards the fort, shouting out the alarm. Did they think one man alone would capture the fort? The others started to walk towards him.

'Your time is over!' he yelled at them and with all his might slammed the spear down. The ground was hard, but the point drove into it and stuck hard enough for the shaft to stand upright. It did not quiver, for there was too much weight fastened to the butt.

The Silures taught that what mattered was to kill the enemy, and that the best way to do this was to outwit him, to surprise him, and to kill before he understood that there was any danger. All that was good.

There was also a time for show.

He left the spear and turned his pony around, pushing it into a trot. He did not let it run, even though it wanted to pelt up the grassy slope. He did not look back.

'Shit!' he heard one of the Romans shout from behind him. They must have reached the spear. There was no sound of anyone running in pursuit.

'Bastard!' someone called after him. Tied by leather thongs in their hair and fastened to the end of the spear, were the heads of the two prefects.

He trotted on, and felt his power grow even more.

VI

Eight days before the Kalends of September, near the road

'KILL THEM, TAKE the women and anything else we can carry, and fight our way out. What are we waiting for?' The leader glared at his companions. 'I'll do it myself if you won't.' His sword grated on the mouth of his scabbard as he drew it. He was not tall, but was immensely broad in the chest and had powerful arms.

'I swore an oath, cousin,' the man beside him said, grabbing his arm. He was even shorter, slim, even slightly built, with a boyish face, but his voice was calm and flat, as if he could not imagine anyone disagreeing with him.

'I didn't!' the first one shouted, until he saw the steady look in his cousin's eyes. His was a hard face, the nose flattened and bent from some old injury, but some – most of all the man himself – would say that he was handsome. Clad in polished scale armour and wearing a high bronze helmet, he was the most conspicuous of all the warriors, for all that some were taller men, and that quite a few had been on many more raids. The two cousins were leaders, approved by vote for this ride, as much for their families as for the strength of their right arms and their past deeds. Vannus, who wished to win fame as a killer and a thief and to rise to great power among the Novantae, was determined to show the others that he was the best among them. Only slowly did he let the sword slide back and then paused before he spoke, filling the words with mockery. 'All right, then what do you suggest, Bran? Wait for them to close in on us and make a last stand – or surrender?'

There were almost fifty riders on the hilltop, a dozen of them captives with their hands tied – in front of them for the women and girls and behind their backs for Ferox and Vindex – and half a dozen ponies laden with plunder. Ahead of them they could see two Roman patrols, and knew that a third one to the east had dipped out of sight, but was also closing in on them. Those men were on foot, but there were about a hundred of them and they were moving steadily. The other two were cavalry, which made them faster and more dangerous. Each numbered about twenty or so, probably the bulk of a turma, at least the ones who could be mounted and put into the field at such short notice.

Bran smiled and let go of his cousin's arm. 'Let's use our heads for a change, Vannus, and talk. We can all get home if we are smart, and boast of our deeds and show off our spoils.' He raised his voice so that the other warriors could hear. Several murmured their approval.

'You frightened, cousin?'

Bran put his head on one side without taking his eyes off Vannus. 'Of course.' He heard one man gasp in surprise. 'Stupidity scares the shit out of me!' Most of them laughed. Hatred flashed for a moment in Vannus' eyes and he took hold of his sword again before deciding against the challenge and releasing it.

'If we fight our way out, then we will lose men,' Bran said, still staring at his cousin, although his voice carried to every warrior there. 'Oh, we'll beat them. We are Novantae!' Men growled approval. 'Who are they?' The voices rumbled louder in agreement. 'We are Novantae!' he repeated. 'So, we can kill them or drive them before us like sheep, can we not?'

'Aye!' Vannus joined in the shout, although he frowned uncertainly.

'But some of us will die, or take wounds – or lose their horses! More of them will die, far more, but their lives do not matter. I would not trade one of you for fifty of them! For a hundred!' The warriors nodded at this obvious good sense.

Bran pointed at Ferox. 'He is my friend – he is my brother! He is a great chieftain of the Romans. Even the young have heard of him, of his many fights. He is a warrior of renown. A warrior whose heart is true and whose tongue is straight.'

'He's an enemy,' Vannus cut in. 'How many of our people has he killed?'

'Many,' Ferox shouted. 'And I have killed many from other tribes in lands further away than you could ride in a hundred days. And all those men had their chance to kill me. Yet here I am.'

'That is to be decided,' Vannus snarled.

'I have not heard tales of Vannus the brave told where brave men meet,' Ferox said flatly.

'Cousin!' Bran shouted as the angry Vannus again drew his sword.

'Do all your enemies have their hands tied?' Ferox yelled. The baby had gone to one of the captive women, who claimed to know the family.

Bran rode his horse between them.

'This is not the time – and our time now is precious.'

Vannus shook his head and spat at Ferox, then wheeled his own mare away.

'We go west,' Bran explained. 'Put distance between us and the other Romans, and send him to speak to the ones on the left. He will say that we have hostages – his daughter among them. He is an important man, and his wife is Enica of the Brigantes. What Roman will wish to report that he let this girl die?'

The growling made it clear that most of the warriors agreed.

'What of those?' Vannus pointed with his sword at the other captives, at the pack animals, and then at the heads fastened to more than one horse's harness. 'Can they ignore those?'

'You will give back the women, and let us go free.' Ferox told them. 'The rest does not matter.'

'Half the women?' Bran said, ignoring a low voice that asked, 'Top half or bottom half?'

'All,' Ferox insisted. 'Take the heads, take the plunder, but all the people go free.'

Bran shrugged. 'Do you want to die for a pair of tits?' he asked the nearest warrior, an older man, bald on the top of his head, but with lank hair falling down to his waist. More than a dozen red rings painted on the shaft of his spear were testament to the men he had killed.

The man gave a gap-toothed grin. 'Maybe?' The others laughed, and then he shrugged. 'But there are always more women.'

'So be it,' Bran told them. 'They can take all the captives.'

Vannus twitched his sword, but said nothing.

'Go and tell them,' Bran said to Ferox. 'And remember what is at stake.' He nodded towards Senuna.

'I'll need my sword,' Ferox said. 'And my horse.' Bran had given Frost to one of the older warriors, as much to spite Vannus as anything else, because his desire to take the beast was so obvious. Instead, Ferox rode the warrior's piebald pony.

'Give the sword to him,' Bran told one of the warriors, 'and cut his bonds.'

'Are you a fool?' Vannus shouted and one or two voices agreed.

'Are you afraid of one man, when we are fifty?' Far more voices joined the mockery, but one man, and then two more, pushed their horses over to stand behind Vannus.

'This sword and this helmet are the badges of my rank,' Ferox shouted. 'They will add strength to my words.'

'I will go with him, to show that I trust his oath – and to honour my own,' Bran declared.

'Very well,' Vannus conceded. 'But, cousin, never speak to me again of folly.'

Ferox slung the belt of his sword over his right shoulder, for centurions wore their blade on the left hip, fastened on his plumed helmet, glanced at Bran, then Senuna, and nodded to Vindex. 'I will do my best.'

'*Omnes ad stercus*,' the Carvetian muttered. A couple of men chuckled, which meant that they knew some Latin, or at least the curses of the legions.

The Novantae and their captives started heading westwards, keeping to the hilltops. There were a few miles before the river would block their path and force them to cross at one of the fords. Ferox and Bran went down the slope towards the Romans. They were half a mile away, close enough to see the green boards of their oval shields and catch the glint off armour and weapons, and even the standard carried at their head. Ferox wondered which bright spark had decided to take the turma's flag with them when they were chasing raiders. He guessed that they were from a cohort, one of the *equitata* units, four-fifths infantry and the rest horsemen. Such troopers were not as well paid or mounted as the all cavalry *alae*, but did a lot of the army's thankless tasks. He could not make out the symbol on their shields, so did not know which cohort yet. Army units were a bit like families, each with their own little ways of doing things, and it would help to know who they were. He had been away from the frontier for too long to hope that he might know the man in command.

'Batavians?' Bran asked, obviously thinking along the same lines.

'Gone to Dacia,' Ferox said.

'Paying attention, though,' Bran noted. The turma had noticed that the main party was heading to the left and had changed direction to intercept, ignoring the two riders. 'Bold, wanting to take them all on.'

Ferox noticed the 'them' rather than 'us'. 'You know the army. Always keener to pick boldness over brains.'

They pointed their horses at the Roman patrol, but did not speed up. Ferox wanted to give the auxiliaries time to see his helmet, with the transverse plume of black feathers marking him out as a centurion.

'So, how have you been keeping?' Bran asked. 'Known you too long to wait for you to ask me?'

Seventeen years ago, Ferox and Vindex had attacked a handful of Novantae guarding the boats of a raiding party. They had killed them all except the boy who called himself Bran. He had sworn to serve Ferox, and had never broken his word. For three years he had gone north, to the island beyond the tip of Caledonia, where the strange cult led by the Mother trained boys and girls to be warriors. Enica was one of the Mother's children, having left behind her Roman side, Claudia, to learn the old ways, just as their twin daughters were now doing. When Bran came back, he had served with Ferox for years, fighting hard alongside him in Dacia, Moesia and too many other places inside and outside the empire to recall. Bran had stayed with Ferox for far more than the five years he had pledged because he had wanted to stay.

'Don't need to ask,' Ferox said. 'Heard about your kin.' When they had come back from the east, Bran had announced that he was returning to his people. When he was young, his father and most of his other family had been murdered by rivals. Bran had sworn another, older oath, to take his revenge, and the news of several deaths had shown that he was doing just that. 'This Vannus on the list?' Ferox asked.

Bran nodded. 'But I need a good reason.'

'Do you want me to kill him?'

'Best if he challenges me,' Bran said. 'Make more of a point that way. Still, if you get a chance... Put it this way, I won't feel the need for avenging him.'

One of the auxiliaries had peeled off from the main body and was coming towards them.

'Who are you?'

'Flavius Ferox, princeps of Legio II Augusta, on detached service. I need to speak to your commander now!' he added in a bark.

If the trooper was surprised, then he did not show it. 'And him?'

'My servant,' Ferox said, ignoring the groan from beside him. 'Now are you going to take me to your decurion are shall I put you on a charge?'

'This way, sir.' The trooper added a hint of doubt to the last word.

The turma did not halt as they rode up, but kept heading towards the band of Novantae. The second patrol was also riding towards them, no more than a mile and a half away.

'What's your name, decurion?' Ferox demanded.

The officer at the head of the little column had a high yellow plume on his helmet, and slightly more ornate decorations on the harness of his horse, but was otherwise wearing the same uniform and equipment as his men. His face was young and eager.

'Martialis, sir.'

Ferox was not sure whether the man responded to his symbols of rank or simply his tone. He pointed north west. 'Head that way! They cannot cross the river the way they are going, so cut them off – and give more time for those other lads to join you.'

The decurion nodded, seemingly relived to have someone else taking charge and seeing the sense of the advice.

'I'm Ferox of II Augusta.'

One of the troopers opened his mouth in surprise and the decurion gulped. Ferox could imagine Vindex sniggering if he had been here rather than with the Novantae.

'Ferox? You mean Flavius Ferox!' That would surely have prompted a comment from his friend. 'Used to be *regionarius* here? I have heard of you.' The tone suggested concern more than enthusiasm.

'Good, there is not much time.' Ferox glanced at the Novantae, still heading for the river. He and Martialis' men were riding at an angle to them, the gap widening. 'You know me, son, and you know who my wife is?'

Martialis nodded.

'My daughter is up there, a captive of those brigands. She is an eques and a citizen as well as from the royal house of Brigantia. They also have folk from my household.'

'How...?'

'It does not matter how they took us. I was their prisoner as well. The warriors are Novantae and they have killed and robbed – and probably done more – just like all the other bandits who have attacked our lands.'

'We will fight to the last drop of blood to save them,' Martialis blurted out, his face red.

'I don't need you to fight, lad – not yet, and maybe not at all, but I do need you to listen and obey. I am a senior centurion of Legio Augusta and take full responsibility. I am in charge.'

Martialis' shoulders sank a little. 'We will soon have men enough to match them,' he suggested. Whoever was leading the other patrol had understood what they were doing and shifted course to head for them.

'And who do you think they will kill first if they realise they cannot get away?'

'But my duty…'

'Is to obey a senior officer. If this goes wrong, I will get the blame. If you really have heard of me then you'll know that that's nothing unusual!' Ferox grinned. Vindex always said that this was like watching one of the big cats in the arena yawn. 'Unless your prefect or someone even higher up is riding to us with those cavalry, then I am senior and that's that.'

'Sir.'

'Good. Now, they have agreed to give us all the prisoners if we let them pass with their other plunder.'

'Sir, I do not think that I can let them get away with anything.'

'It's rubbish. Stolen clothes and tools, a few pelts. How much money do you think they have found up here? Stopping these handful of raiders isn't going turn the last few days into anything other than a disaster. Saving the daughter of the Queen of the Brigantes, a loyal ally of Rome, does matter – and not just to me. As a Roman officer I don't want them taking a distinguished hostage home. As her father, I'd wade through blood to stop them harming a hair of her head.'

'Yes, sir.' Martialis said. 'What do you want to do?'

'First thing is to get to them before they can cross the river. But keep it steady, we should do that, but don't want a race on our hands unless there is no other choice.'

Martialis waved the column on. There was a purpose about the way the Novantae rode as a group. The Romans were different, even to the more regular jingle of harness.

'Who are they, sir? Martialis asked.

'Novantae. Leader calls himself Vannus, but is not someone of account. Not yet. I would not trust him further than I can throw him.'

Martialis sniffed. 'They're all like that. Can't trust the word of anyone north of here. Kill their best friend just to steal his boots.'

Bran nodded agreement. None of the auxiliaries seemed inclined to question who he was or why he was with Ferox.

'This will do,' Ferox decided after they had gone a mile or so. The second cavalry patrol had yet to catch up, but was close now, should there be any trouble. 'Give me two of your men,' he ordered Martialis, 'and take the rest over there and wait.' He pointed to a knoll. The river was close, the ground sloping down towards it and dotted with little woods, fields of wheat and a few farms.

'Sir.'

Ferox and Bran led the two troopers towards the Novantae. They went in a steady canter, although Ferox's new mount needed constant urging to force her on.

The Novantae and their prisoners came to a halt, the warriors forming a rough circle around most of their captives, although Ferox could see Senuna was out in front beside Vannus and a handful of his supporters and bondsmen.

'Let me talk to them,' Bran said and galloped ahead, one arm raised.

Ferox sensed the movement before he could see it. He scanned the hills behind the Novantae, searching, saw a glint, then movement of spear points as another Roman patrol came over the crest, riding in column of twos.

'Sir!' One of the troopers was pointing, and before Ferox could tell him to stop, he could see some of the warriors turn, and call out in alarm at this apparent treachery.

The cluster of Novantae broke apart, heading as fast as they could towards the river. There was not a real ford to their left, but given the hot summer the water might still be shallow enough to cross without too much trouble. The bulk of them were heading directly for the river, but Vannus and his warriors broke away, galloping hard and taking Senuna with them. A few others followed.

'Give me your *lancea*!' Ferox shouted at the trooper beside him, and grabbed the shaft before the man could react. He kicked the mare hard to drive it into as fast a gallop as it could manage, chasing after his daughter.

Bran was haring after the main body, yelling at the top of his voice that they could go free if they left the captives. A woman was down, fallen from her horse, screaming even louder although she did not seem to be hurt.

Martialis' troopers were coming on, but not fast enough to cut off Vannus and his men. The mare pounded across the grass, clumsily jumped a ditch, and kept going, showing more strength than Ferox had expected. He was closing on Vannus, although he guessed that the beast could not keep up this pace for long. He passed one of the warriors who had gone after Vannus and ignored him.

'Vannus, you coward!' he yelled.

Vannus turned to glance back over his shoulder and sawed on the bit of his horse to turn it round. His men, Senuna with them, streamed ahead of him

Bran was calling something out, coming towards them, but Ferox ignored him. Vannus made the horse rear high and spat his contempt at Ferox.

'I will kill you another day!' He turned and followed his men.

Ferox had the javelin hefted in his hand. The range was long, and he would need a lot of luck, but he could feel the mare stutter under him and knew her strength was failing. He threw the lancea, aiming not at Vannus, but lower, at the legs of his horse. The missile missed by a whisker, skimming through the long grass.

Martialis was coming from the side, far ahead of his men, testament to his gelding's speed and his own horsemanship. He seemed to understand, because he threw his own javelin a moment later, and it hummed through the air and went between the legs of Vannus' horse as they stretched out. It caught between the front legs, twisted hard, the shaft breaking bones.

The horse went down and Vannus was pitched from the saddle, screaming and flying through the air to land hard. His men glanced back but did not stop.

Ferox's mare was staggering, puffing hard. Bran rode past, chasing the others. 'Tomorrow at noon, at the shrine of Cocidius. We'll trade Senuna for Vannus.' He paused only as long as it took to explain and galloped on. 'I'll get her back!' he called, using Latin this time.

Vannus lay in the grass, unmoving. Martialis dismounted beside him, sword drawn. Ferox came up alongside. 'Well done.

They'll give us back my daughter for this chieftain. I am in your debt.'

Martialis prodded the prostrate Vannus with his sword, then bent down beside him.

'Sorry, sir, I'm afraid he's dead.'

VII

An hour before noon, seven days before the Kalends of September, Isurium Brigantum

'PLEASE RECONSIDER, LADY, I beg you.' Titus Cornelius Proculus' concern was genuine, as was his nervousness. 'Please, wait another day.'

Claudia Enica gave a lavish smile, and placed one hand on the tribune's shoulder for just a moment, feeling a slight tremor and seeing the flicker of excitement in his eyes.

'My dear friend,' she said with a tenderness she did not feel, 'that is precisely what you said yesterday.' Years of pretending, of being the Roman Claudia to some, and the Brigantian Enica to others – and herself to no more than a handful – she had no trouble masking her impatience. 'And such is your virtue and sense of duty – and your fondness for your friends – that I am sure that you would say the same on the following day.

'It is time. I am sure relief will come soon, and the enemy knows this and has already fled.' Claudia Enica clasped her hands together in front of her waist, which could be interpreted as pleading if Proculus was so inclined. 'You care deeply for your friends, so understand that I have a duty to mine.' She was dressed as an elegant Roman lady, her long red hair carefully pinned up and arranged in a style that was fashionable, but also suitable for travel. Her make-up was subtle, earrings and necklace delicate, and the pale green stola under her travel cloak was appropriate for a coach ride to visit neighbours.

'Even so, perhaps I should come along... just to be on the safe side.' Proculus struggled manfully to sound enthusiastic.

'Dear friend... But you have your duties and those must come first. We are Roman after all.' Claudia Enica leaned forward to whisper. 'Thank you, but I shall be safe.' She stood back. 'You command this garrison and it is your duty to protect the city – the city of my people – and all those who shelter here. That is your task and no one could perform it better.'

Claudia had her own voice, one that came naturally, and it was not simply that she spoke in Latin. When younger, she had made sure to chatter away, talking incessantly, hiding things she wanted to learn or say in a deluge of gossip and flirtation. Now, a little older, a different manner was more appropriate, as the mother of three children, that magic number encouraged by proclamation and law by every emperor and hardly ever fulfilled by Roman aristocrats. The new Claudia was a matron, kind, interested in others, considerate and protective as a mother should be. That did not mean abandoning gossip when it was appropriate, or no longer flirting. Hinting at a fashionable wantonness rarely did any harm. Proculus was an equestrian officer, married no doubt, although he had never mentioned a wife, and at thirty-four was enjoying a reasonable, if slow career. His interest in her had been obvious from their first meeting.

'You have saved my people through your courage and swift action,' Claudia Enica assured him, making her voice a little breathy. Her younger self might have given a little bow, knowing that the man would try to peek down the top of her dress. 'Without you and your gallant men, I do not dare to think what might have happened.'

In truth Proculus had been slow to understand and timid throughout. Claudia Enica had ridden hard to escape from the villa, fearing pursuit, but knowing that her duty was to do everything to protect the town. She had reached the army camp by the river in the middle of the morning. She was muddy, wet and cold, for it had rained on and off during the night and she had had to cling to the stallion's mane and swim beside it as they crossed the river to reach Proculus and his men.

The vexillation of Legio XX Valeria Victrix had set up its tent-lines in the decayed ramparts of the old fort built decades ago to protect the river crossing and long since abandoned. The legionaries were there to improve the road and Proculus had not wasted time on restoring the defences or building new ones. After all, no one thought that there was any real danger so deep into the province. The legionaries had set to work, and, after plenty of dinner invitations, letters sent to him by Claudia Enica's many highly placed friends and acquaintances, and more than a few wide eyed pleas, the tribune had come to interpret his orders as including the roads within the nearby town and even some of its buildings.

By the time Claudia Enica had hauled herself back onto the old horse's back and ridden up to the picket outside the camp, the Romans must have been aware of the pillars of smoke rising in the distance, for the rain had not been heavy enough to extinguish them. Yet when she was ushered into the camp, her long hair plastered flat, her pale skin even whiter than usual from the cold, she had found Proculus unconcerned at first. He was out of the camp when she arrived, but a centurion recognised her and had her taken to the tribune's tent, where she sat on a folding chair, wrapped tight in the cloak they had given her.

'Just the farmers,' the tribune had explained when he arrived. 'They burn the stubble after harvest.'

'It is a raid,' she said, not bothering to explain that the reaping would not begin for another ten days at the earliest. 'One villa is burned, farms as well, and the people slaughtered!' She had jumped to her feet, losing the cloak. This was not deliberate, but a simple accident. She was very tired and angry at a fool determined to deny the obvious. Her wet shift clung tightly to her body, and was almost transparent in places. Proculus stared, open mouthed.

Lust quickly turned to panic. 'Hercules' balls! Are you sure?' He did not wait for a reply. 'Claudius, sound the alarm!' he bellowed at the centurion waiting outside the tent. This prompted more shouting, and in moments a *cornu* horn blared out, calling the camp to arms. The centurion reappeared.

'We're under attack!' Proculus informed him. 'Barbarian raiders. Thousands of them!'

Claudia Enica gathered up the cloak and sat down, marvelling at the tribune's imagination, but deciding that it was better to let him call his officers together before intervening. She had spent long enough at an army base back during the Dacian War to know how soldiers did things. Time enough to add a dose of sense to proceedings when Proculus started to issue orders. She wished that Ferox was here to take charge – whatever his rank, he had a way of asserting himself – for she doubted that the tribune had ever seen any real action. The thought brought back the worries for her husband and Senuna. If there were a lot of raiders abroad then the villa would be a tempting target. During the night, she had wondered whether to head there, before deciding that it was too far, most likely would have taken her towards any other marauders, and that the first duty should be to ensure the safety of the town. That proved harder than she had hoped.

Proculus' instinct was to call all his men back to camp and do their best to restore its defences. 'They'll think twice about facing the legion,' he assured them.

'What of the townsfolk?' Claudia Enica asked. One or two of the officers had seemed surprised when she was included in their hasty *consilium*, until Proculus explained that she had more information than anyone else. 'What of my people?'

'They can come in and shelter with us,' Proculus said.

Claudius rubbed his chin. 'Best be careful to make sure that they are the queen's folk when they arrive though. Don't want enemies slipping in alongside them, do we?'

'What of my town?' she said. The cloak refused to stay in place and kept parting in front where the slip still clung tightly, leaving little room for imagination. Perhaps that would help. 'Do you want to be held responsible for the burning of the civitas capital of the Brigantes? The *legatus* himself has taken a keen interest in the project, and even talked of visiting. I am told that he has written to the princeps himself to praise what we are doing, so...'

In the end she had persuaded them, and Proculus issued orders for the vital equipment and supplies to be packed away and carried into the town. She left them as they were arranging matters, although there had been time to change into a borrowed tunic and trousers.

A crowd had already gathered in the half-completed Forum, for more than a few had spotted the smoke and then several folk had rushed into town telling of the attack. Several chieftains were shouting at each other, arguing that they should all hole up in their own houses, that they should mass to fight the enemy in the open, or that they should flee to safety. Several were her enemies, but all seemed relieved when she rode among them. Claudia Enica was still bedraggled and dressed in men's clothes far too big for her, but she was the queen, whatever the Romans said and whether or not everyone liked her. More than that, she brought purpose and a clear plan – and the news that the legionaries were coming to help. From then on, she kept them busy.

Perhaps two thousand people were in the town, about a third of them visitors for the market and the on-going legal disputes. A couple of hundred more came in over the course of the day, folk who had decided that the town might be safer than their farms. Among these were travellers caught up in all this, and these were separated from the others and put with the other wayfarers and merchants. The Brigantes were a numerous people, but even so they knew their own folk, at second or third or even further remove, so that locals vouched for all save a few of the strangers. The remainder were kept apart and watched by a few men from her household.

'Be kind,' she told them. 'We do not wish to make them enemies.'

The town's walls were unfinished, barely three-quarters of the circuit marked out at all, and often only to the height of a few feet. A splendid gateway with its twin timber towers stood on the route leading to the main road, but did not yet join onto the rest of the wall. She stationed some boys up on the towers, feeling that their keen eyes would give them the earliest warning of any trouble, but otherwise could not include it in the defended area. Instead, she marked out a perimeter protecting nearly all the houses and on two sides making use of the outer wall. Everywhere else, men were set to barricading the streets, and turning any solid wall into as much of a defence as time allowed. Once the legionaries arrived, Proculus took over much of the task and progress was good. Every hour she sent someone to check with the boys on the tower and the other lookouts. No one had seen any bands of armed men, only the fugitives coming to the city.

Claudia Enica worked hard, for apart from defences there was food and drink to consider. Somehow she managed to find the time to eat a little, and all the while Ferox's freedman Philo and his wife Indike hovered around her. She put Philo in charge of organising the food supply, for the little man delighted in order and was relentless in his determination to impose it wherever he could. Eventually, there was time to retire to a backroom and dress in the clothes Indike had brought. They could not take long, but she was able to wash, fasten her hair back into a suitably Roman bun behind her head, and put on a dress. It was oddly refreshing, although she was not sure whether the people looked at her in quite the same way. Times were changing, and even some Brigantians were less sure of a warrior queen wearing men's clothes and giving orders.

Another sign of a different world was the lack of gear for war in the town. Barely a quarter of the men had anything remotely like a proper weapon, and only the household warriors of the visiting chieftains were turned out in armour and with shields and swords. The rest would have to make do with whatever they could improvise. She toyed with the idea of splitting them into groups to concentrate the best equipped, before deciding that it was better if men fought in the old way, alongside their relatives and among their clans. Only the townsfolk with no such connections needed to be grouped together by their districts.

It was not much of a force, and she knew that all the most threatened spots would have to be held by the legionaries, not that Proculus' men were the finest. Almost all of them had been detached on various building projects for two or three years, so that they had rarely drilled or trained as soldiers. She spotted men missing bits of equipment and a lot of them moved with an awkwardness that suggested that the burden and feel of arms were strange and unfamiliar. Even so, they were by far the best she had – not that she was officially in charge, for she had made a show of handing the defence of the town over to the tribune. Proculus was puffed up with all the flattery, although still proving amenable to her suggestions.

'Come, lady, come!' A boy started tugging at her dress as she was talking to a group of women helping to sew bags to be filled with earth and built into the defences. He let go and flinched as she turned and looked at him. The youngest and smallest of the lads put up in the towers, the others had obviously chosen him to run with a message.

Claudia Enica smiled. 'All right, show me the way.'

The boy bounded off, waving his arms in excitement. She had to lift her skirt to walk as briskly as she could to follow him. He kept surging ahead, then realising that he had left her behind, turning around and bouncing up and down and calling out. 'Please follow, lady, please.'

At the towers he shot up the stairs onto the stub of rampart beside the gateway, then bounded up the ladder to the top of the turret itself. Claudia Enica went far more slowly, for negotiating a ladder while wearing a long dress required care. It made her think back to the fort in Dacia, when Ferox had chided her for climbing while clad in the short tunic and the felt boots she wore for fighting. A party of legionaries and townsfolk were coming in carrying timber they had felled for the work, and she saw that almost all, more or less openly, were watching her every step of the way as she climbed. At most they would see her shoes, ankles and shins, perhaps once or twice the thrill of a bare knee, and presumably they felt this was worthwhile. One dropped a bundle of faggots and was bawled at by the man in charge. Not for the first time Claudia Enica marvelled at the strangeness of men.

The boys were excited, although only one or two were old enough to be awkward and tongue tied around her simply because she was a woman.

'There!' The little lad who had guided her was panting as he gestured over the parapet.

'And there!' A bigger boy interrupted. 'And there!'

'I saw them first,' another declared and shoved at the small boy.

There were four more plumes of smoke rising in the distance, very dark against a sky that had cleared and was a now a blue so vivid that no dye could have captured it, even in silk.

'Well done,' she said. The closest was still a good few miles away, and the others near the Twins' villa or even beyond it. 'Have you seen any enemies?'

'I did!' shouted a plump lad whose face was a patchwork of freckles and his hair as red as her own.

'You never! They was cows!'

'They weren't. Who rides a cow?'

'Your father – and your fat uncle!'

Fists were raised, so Claudia Enica slapped her hand down hard on the top of the parapet. She had a vision of one of her tutors doing the same thing when he had lost patience. It took an effort not to giggle.

'Now then,' she told them, 'I placed you here because I need my keenest eyed warriors keeping watch. You have done well, but we all rely on you doing your duty.' They were all preening. 'Are you hungry?'

'Yes, lady,' her guide said.

Another kicked him on the leg. 'No, you mean, "yes, my queen"!'

She smiled again. Children, especially boys, always seemed to be hungry. 'I'll have some apples sent up. And some water.'

'How about beer?' one of the oldest and boldest whispered, provoking laughter.

'Only when you kill your first enemy,' she told them.

The journey down the ladders was slower, for it was always more awkward descending. Almost a dozen men, a mix of soldiers and civilians, had found some reason to hang around the gateway, so once again she was scrutinised every step of the way. Once her dress snagged on the head of a nail, but she noticed it as soon as it began to tug away from her and lifted the material off easily. All the while she felt the men watching. Presumably it was worthwhile for them at a time when they could be toiling to make themselves, and everyone else, safer.

No more new fires were seen that day, and although one or two claimed to have seen a pair of riders armed with spears, there was no sign of any band of enemies. That did not mean that none were out there, so Proculus set double guards throughout the night. An alarm went up in the fourth hour, but after trumpets sounded, and everyone rushed about shouting, it was discovered that it had been started by a farmer climbing out over a barricade because he wanted to check on his farm. A legionary saw the movement, threw his pilum and brought the man down. The victim screamed, men called out, so the panic began. Claudia Enica learned all this only later, when the farmer was brought in. The heavy javelin had gone through his thigh, so that he had to be carried. They managed to cut off the tip and pull both it and the narrow shank away, and stopped the bleeding. There was still a good chance that the man would lose his leg.

The next day there were no fires and no clear sign of the enemy, although sentries reported movement and glints off weapons in the woodland three-quarters of a mile away. No attack came, and Claudia Enica was now certain that none ever would come. Proculus was still wary, as were most of the chieftains.

'They're waiting out there,' the tribune said. 'I can feel it.'

No more than a handful of fugitives arrived, but just before sunset a tall figure staggered towards the town. He was bloodied, barefoot, with his tunic ragged and a bandage around his head, but kept walking, swaying without ever falling. He manged to raise a hand when he was close, and by this time a crowd had gathered.

'That is Pertacus,' Claudia Enica said, shading her eyes against the setting Sun. No one else who had been at the Twins' villa had appeared so far.

'Hercules' balls, so it is,' Proculus said. 'You men, help him in.'

Two soldiers ran out obediently through the little gap kept in the barricade. Pertacus held his hands up, palms outwards and gave a wry smile as he refused their aid, so the legionaries walked one on either side of him as he lurched towards the barricade.

'Pertacus, reporting for duty,' he rasped. His eyes flickered and he fainted forward.

He slept through the night, helped by a draught administered by the *seplasiarius* attached to the legionaries.

'Rest is the best thing,' he assured them. 'Jupiter knows what the poor lad has been through.'

Claudia Enica remembered less sympathy when she had arrived, but then, she had not asked for it. Pertacus' dramatic entry to the town had struck her as a performance rather than genuine exhaustion. He woke late the next day, and spoke a little of the night attack.

'I don't know how I got away, I really don't know.'

When she asked him what had become of the others, he simply shook his head. There was still no sign of any enemy, even when the tribune permitted a few men to ride out and scout. They reported nothing, and even said that folk were going back to some of the farms.

On the day after that Claudia Enica would wait no longer. 'I need to take a look.' She had her carriage prepared, for she must still play the part of a Roman lady. Three of the men from her household would go with her, one to drive and the others mounted and armed.

Proculus had argued and begged, but did not dare to order.

Now that his last effort to dissuade her had failed, it was time to leave in case he gathered the courage to test his authority.

The *raeda* was ready, and Philo opened the door for her and pulled down the folding step. He had wanted to come along, but she preferred to leave him here to supervise the household as well as the massed food supplies.

'If you are sure,' Proculus said.

'I am.' Claudia Enica put one foot on the step. No doubt Proculus and the others noticed that she was not wearing shoes, and instead had on a pair of her boots, the type the Alans and other Sarmatians wore. They would not see that she also had tight breeches underneath her dress – a trick she had passed on to her daughters. Her warriors led a couple of spare horses, and if necessary, they could all abandon the carriage and escape more quickly. Still sore from her bare-backed and bare-skinned flight from the villa, she was not about to have another uncomfortable ride.

'I thought you could use another sword,' a voice called. It was

Pertacus, mounted on one of the few other horses in the town, clad in mail and with a gladius on his hip. His head was still bandaged and he was pale, but he had that familiar wry smile.

Claudia Enica got into the carriage and closed the door. Let the man have his stage and let him perform to the admiring crowd. 'Only come if you can keep up,' she called back and banged on the roof to signal her man to set off. A few people were cheering, no doubt for Pertacus. After a while, when they were out of sight of the town, he rode alongside the carriage, looking in at the window.

'How did you escape?' she asked, for it was as well to know as much as she could.

Pertacus sighed deeply. 'It is not very heroic, I am afraid.'

'How disappointing for you.'

He grinned as he did so often. 'I did not fancy using the pot they put under the bed. The food had not agreed with me, and I suspected there might be quite a task ahead of me – sorry to speak of such things... So, belly rumbling, I headed out into the night, and was behind some bushes when I heard riders. Then within moments there were warriors everywhere, armed with weapons and torches. I could not move, I was – well, you know how it is when you are in the middle of something. There was nothing I could do. By the time I was finished, the place was on fire. As I got up, one of the warriors saw me, shouted and... Well, I ran away and hid. That's all there is.'

'And you saw no one else escape?'

Again the shake of the head. 'Just hope they have all cleared out. Not that I wouldn't like to see them again, this time with a sword in my hand.'

'And do you know who they were?'

'Northerners, I think. Maybe Selgovae, maybe not. There were a lot of them. Fifty or more, at the very least.'

'Well, I am tired,' she told him, 'and think a nap is in order'. She closed the leather blind on the window and ignored whatever it was he tried to say. She did not sleep, but rested, for she had no doubt that the danger had long since passed. Partly that was instinct, but also it was the evidence of her eyes. In just this first part of the journey they had seen a drover with a dozen cattle and a couple of farms, empty, but unscathed. This was no longer a land in fear of marauders.

The journey took several hours, for the raeda could not go quickly, especially once they left the main road and weaved along the tracks towards the villa. They saw a few folk abroad, and after initial wariness on both sides, came close enough to speak. No one had seen any raiders, although most had heard that they were running amok a few nights ago. Since then there had been no sign.

They passed a few farms where the thatch had been burned and the houses more or less collapsed. There were no corpses or sign of struggle, so most likely the families and their animals had fled long before any warriors arrived.

The villa was a ruin. If Pertacus had not joined them, she might have dismounted and ridden with the warriors the last few miles. Instead she had them drive her there. There was no need for caution, since the only living things left at the spot were the ravens and other carrion fowl. Half collapsed, the remaining timbers charred black, the house and the out buildings looked smaller. In the yard was a circle of stakes, each topped by a man's head. The eyes were long gone, as were the tongues, while the skin was heavily tinged with green, but the Twins were easy to recognise, as was Brigomaglos the lawyer. There were other faces she knew, members of the household and kinsmen of the brothers, and some she could put a name to and some she could not quite recollect. That lapse of memory bothered her, for she was sure that she ought to remember. As far as she could tell, every single man who had been there that night had died and been decapitated. She stared for a long while at the heads of her two warriors, who had died fighting, and given her the chance to get away. She touched each one on the forehead, feeling that strange cold flesh. One of her escort took them down and they would carry them home to be placed at the spots where their families took the dead.

The women were separate from the men. She could not see Calypso, but since one body was burned beyond recognition in the ashes of a hut, she could not be sure. Perhaps the warriors had carried off a few, perhaps not. All the others they had killed. Most were stripped, several still tied down, and there was no doubt that they had raped them before the murder.

War was never pretty, but this was especially foul. As far as she could tell the warriors had destroyed more plunder than they had taken. This seemed a murder raid, intended to kill rather than despoil.

Pertacus turned away and made choking sounds when they found Ulpia, the lawyer's wife, tied down and bent over the top of a fence.

VIII

Earlier, the evening of the eighth day before the Kalends of September, near the road

VANNUS WAS NOT dead, although for a long while it seemed just a matter of time. He would not wake, and his breath was weak. There did not seem to be any bones broken.

They made him as comfortable as they could, setting up over him the only tent the auxiliaries had brought with them. Four men were left to guard him, not that there seemed any chance of an escape, but in case his warriors came back or others intervened. Ferox, Vindex and two more troopers galloped to the nearest base, one of the outposts between the main forts.

'His is bigger,' Vindex observed as they rode above the stream and stared across at the little stone fort on the high ground on the far side.

Ferox said nothing. The local centurio regionarius was based here, an officer detached from one of the legions and tasked with keeping the peace in the area. It was a job Ferox had performed for many years, back when he and Vindex had first met. This stone burgus was new, and he had operated from a smaller, rather poorly built post to the north east, closer to Vindolanda. This outpost was larger, better fortified and gave off more of an air of permanence.

'You're Ferox! *The* Ferox!' The centurion in charge was no more than thirty, only recently appointed and desperately keen. 'Well, this is an honour, a true honour. Everyone in these parts speaks of you.'

Inevitably Vindex chuckled.

The centurion in charge was named Titus Felicio. 'Ah, you must be Vindex of the Carvetii,' he added. 'Yes, just as I imagined.'

Ferox let himself chuckle, but then got to the point. It made a pleasant change to deal with someone so eager to help. Half to his surprise, the garrison was able to provide a two-wheeled mule cart, but while that was being prepared Felicio asked a favour. 'I would like your opinion on something. It should not take long. I realise that you are tired and deeply concerned about your daughter, but I really would value your opinion, sir. And you have plenty of time, if you need to be at the shrine of Cocidius by noon tomorrow.'

The centurion explained that eight of his men had been ambushed and killed early in the morning of the day when the raids came in. There was no reason not to follow and see whatever it was the man wanted to show. In the distance was a watchtower, stark against the red sky of a setting Sun. They rode out, in order to get there before it was dark.

'We were sloppy,' Felicio explained. 'Did not think there was any danger and we were wrong. Just like the threat of raiding, I suppose.'

'Do you know how many bands came across?'

'Not really. Reports are coming in, but everyone is still chasing their tails. Doesn't help that most garrisons sent more than half their men, and the pick of them too, down south for the summer's manoeuvres.'

'No, it doesn't.'

'Well, anyway, I reckon at least a dozen bands, and probably more… I should have read the signs better and been more forceful in my reports of the danger.'

'They would not have believed you,' Ferox assured him.

'They'll probably blame me though.' One of the regionarius' jobs was to talk to the tribal leaders and keep the legatus down there in Londinium informed about their mood.

'That's the army for you. Doubt it will ever change.'

They came to a little dell, where the path dropped out of sight for just a short stretch. Felicio told him all that he knew of what had happened and pointed out where the bodies had been found. Sadly, his men had trampled the ground as they cleared up afterwards and removed the headless corpses of their comrades for cremation. Even so, Ferox was able to tell a lot.

'You're right to be worried,' he said eventually.

Felicio laughed. 'Pity, I was hoping you would tell me I'm wrong. Well then, this was not chance.'

'No, it wasn't. They knew what they were doing. They were good too.'

They left even though night was falling, for the sky was again clear and the stars bright. Ferox wanted to return to the campsite, so that they would have plenty of time to reach the shrine before noon the next day.

Vannus was now snoring noisily, but had not stirred in any other way. At least he was alive. Ferox fretted, pretending to sleep when he could not, and glad when the time came to take a turn on watch. Vindex joined him halfway through and they sat in a silence rare for the Carvetian. If anything, he was even more worried.

'Bran's a good lad,' he said eventually. 'He'll keep the lass safe.'

Ferox knew that his old friend would try.

⋆⋆⋆

They set out early, with Vannus still unconscious and lifted into the back of the cart. Carnacus drove, for the big man was good with all animals, and especially horses. Ferox sensed that in some strange way Carnacus felt responsible, as if he had failed Senuna.

They travelled warily, Ferox scouting ahead, the troopers escorting the cart and Vindex at the rear. There was always a chance that warriors coming back from the raids would stumble across them and decide to do a little more killing, especially if they were not being chased. From what Felicio had told him, there were too few troops in the field to do very much. It was only luck that the Novantae had run into all those patrols. Still, luck could change and turn quickly sour, so they went carefully. Ferox was glad when they were about three miles from the shrine of the war god Cocidius. It was a place of purification and no one would be willing to fight this close to it unless bound by an oath. When they were barely a mile away from the shrine a dozen warriors rode past, trophy heads hanging from their saddle horns and bouncing against their legs. They glared at the Romans, doing everything to suggest that they could kill them, but simply did not feel like doing so at the moment.

One of the Novantae was waiting for them.

'Is my lord dead?' he asked, seeing no sign of Vannus so guessing that he was being carried.

'Hurt by the fall,' Vindex told him. 'He'll be fine, but won't be dancing for a while.'

'Come,' the warrior said.

⋆⋆⋆

Senuna had grown to hate the darkness almost as much as she feared the light. They had brought her to this place the day before. After a bid to ride to freedom, she had gone the last few hours slung over the front of one of the warrior's horses. She had been terrified, although she did her best to hide it. This was not an adventure any more and she dreaded what might be in store – slavery, degradation. She was a child still, in body, but doubted that that would be any protection. The men were gruff, their speech hard to understand for the accent was so strong even though the Novantae lived just a few days' ride from her own people. She had ached, and though she had not wanted to, she had wept.

The warriors had simply laughed.

Bran appeared suddenly, having got in front of them somehow. Senuna could not see, for her hair had long since come loose from its pins and hung down in front of her eyes. She could imagine his smile, and remembered the young warrior coming home with her father just a few months before. They all were weathered by the Sun, utterly confident as if they owned the world, and with a stare that hinted at men who had seen a vast country and were not afraid.

'They'll do a deal, boys,' he said to the warriors. She wondered whether he had picked up this direct way of speaking from her father.

'What deal?'

'Vannus for the lass,' Bran had told them. 'Tomorrow at Fanum Cocidius.'

'The chief all right?'

'He is. Will stay that way as long as she is.'

'I am going to gut that bastard Ferox,' one of them said. 'Pretended to deal then led us into an ambush.' The other three warriors murmured agreement.

'Fine,' Bran had told them. 'Trade first, then gut. That's if you want Vannus in one piece. If you only want some of him, then you can get nasty sooner.'

They liked that, laughing and joking about various parts of their chief's anatomy and how much each was worth.

The mood had changed, and Senuna no longer wept, although the fear was only a little less. Bran paid little or no attention to her.

'Our spoiled little princess been any trouble?' he had asked at one point.

'Not much.'

'Good. Still, if her arse needs slapping, then I'd better do it. I'm almost family.' The warriors liked that as well and roared with laughter. Indeed, they were jollier now that Bran had joined them.

Senuna thought that her bones would stretch and break and her belly burst before long, and was relieved when they stopped. Yet the shrine was a grim place, a centre for worship of the war god Cocidius and other, even older and darker gods, all enclosed within a ditch and a circular stockade. She had once been told that there was a stone inside where sacrifices had been made for a hundred lives of men or even more. If it was there, she did not see it.

Instead she was led away into a hall, the Great Hall in the centre of the sanctuary, a vast round house with a high conical roof. Priests took her, silent unsmiling men, for mere warriors were not allowed inside unless to dedicate spoils or trophies. She was neither presumably, not yet, and instead it was the same as when Romans deposited their gold or coin in the keeping of a temple for safety. The priests took her to a wooden cage and shut her inside. Afterwards a young girl came with water and bread. Senuna had forgotten how thirsty she was and drained the bowl straightaway. Though she was hungry, she could not bring herself to eat. Too many faces stared at her.

The Hall of Cocidius was a place of battle and death. Everywhere, on the walls, or on stakes set into the floor and hanging from the beams of the ceiling, were heads. There were surely not hundreds of severed heads, but thousands, the fruit of long ages of warfare. These were the heads of the famous or taken by the most famous, for the priests judged whether or not a man's deeds were sufficient to accept the trophy he had brought. Many were old, some no more than skulls perhaps with a few wisps of hair, some with traces of black and shrivelled skin, some oiled and preserved as grotesque memories of the man they had once been. Others were more recent, no doubt recognisable to those who had known them, although as time passed they rotted away, skin shrinking as they dried in the smoke from the central fire that burned during the hours of day.

The Hall stank of decay, and crawled with the vermin drawn by its ghastly display. All thatched houses drew insects, but this place of death was alive with constant noise, the movements and buzzing of the tiny creatures, the flapping of the birds. Senuna heard it even after the priests had extinguished the fire for the night, as she sat or lay down in pitch darkness, always knowing the heads were watching, and always hearing the little noises of the feeders. She was bitten by lice and fleas, and often flies landed on her hands and face and she could not help thinking of what these had eaten. It took an effort not to scream and go on screaming until madness came.

That night, in the western marshes

THE ROMAN WAS *brave, just as he had sensed at that first encounter. This man had the heart of a warrior. Some centurions were like that, men you could have accepted as brothers had the world been different.*

The Roman had not flinched when the prefects were killed, only turning away when one of them was forced to kneel and began to beg for mercy. A man being shamed was not something any warrior wanted to see. The centurion turned back when the stroke was made and the headless corpse slumped down, gushing blood. Then he had looked at the other officer and given him some of his own strength. The second prefect died like a man, learning courage from the centurion.

After he had gone to Magnis to deliver his message, he found the Roman bound to a tree and badly beaten. In his absence, the centurion had somehow slipped free of his bonds, grabbed a short knife they used for cutting meat and had gutted one warrior. They told him that he would have got away, had the wounded man not clung closely to his legs and tripped him. Even so, it had taken three of them to pin the Roman to the ground.

Tied to the tree, one eye so bruised it could barely open, the centurion had still stared defiance at him. For the rest of the journey, all the warriors were more careful to watch the man even more closely.

'Where are you from, Curius?' he had asked the centurion.

If the man was surprised to be addressed in Latin, he did not show it. Nor did he reply. Instead, he waited and he watched. There was no doubt that he would have put them all to the sword given the slightest chance. This was a man.

The Roman was wary around her, it showed in his one good eye, but that was not surprising. Even so, he held her gaze when she stared at him, and that was no mean thing, for her power and her cruelty were obvious to anyone, even a Roman. The man could surely guess that he had not been spared, but was destined for something more important.

'Where are you from, Curius?' he asked the question each night and each morning. No answer came. It was clear from his dark skin and hair that he was not a Gaul or even a Spaniard.

She seemed to understand why he asked, as she seemed to sense everything, and did nothing to stop him. She was as silent as the Roman, for at the moment she had nothing to tell them. She rode, sat or slept in her long black cloak, the hood pulled over her head so that her face was in shadow. When awake she carried her staff with her everywhere, its shaft painted black and mounting a ram's skull. When she slept it was thrust into the ground just next to her head. No man would ever dare to touch it.

He did not know her age, and it might have been fifty or it might have been five hundred. She told him what he needed to know and guided him and he followed. She would guide him as long as she trusted him to enact the will of the gods. From the first moment he had met her, and had answered her call to follow, he had known that the path led wherever she chose. There was no turning back.

'Where are you from, Curius?' he asked one last time when they had reached the lake. It was small and surrounded by peat bog save for narrow, labyrinthine paths known only to few.

She had brought them through, and they stood beneath the withered oak tree. No one knew how old the tree was, or why it had sprouted in such an unlikely place, and no one could remember it when it was alive. It was long dead, the trunk hollow and black, with just a single heavy branch still reaching out above them.

One of his men tossed the rope so that it hung over the branch, while another took the end with the noose and pulled it down. The Roman watched in silence, and said nothing when they stripped him.

'Eat!' she commanded, holding up a bowl to the centurion's mouth. The man turned away, so two men grabbed him and another one forced his jaws apart.

'Eat!' she said again and pushed the beans into the Roman's mouth. A warrior clamped the jaws shut and another held his nose, forcing him to swallow.

She drove her staff into the ground and took the club from him. That was a surprise, for he had expected to deliver the blow at the right moment, for it was important that it was heavy enough to kill.

'I am from Utica,' the centurion said. The words sounded like a challenge.

'The Africans are a brave people,' he replied in Latin.

A warrior checked that the centurion's hands were tied behind his back and then slipped the noose over Curius' head and tightened it.

The Roman began to froth at the mouth.

'Very brave,' he added in the language of the tribes. Two men hauled on the rope, pulling the noose tight. Curius stood on tiptoes, but even that was not enough. He began to choke.

She watched, face shadowed in her hood as always. Still the men pulled and still the Roman did all he could to fight them, even though he struggled to breathe at all. Froth dripped down his chin and onto his bare chest.

'Now!' she said, when he thought the Roman must soon die, and the men let the rope down just a little She raised the club, waiting, waiting, and then swung. It was a heavy hardwood, polished and old so that it looked black, and its weight and the remarkable strength still in that old arm smashed into the skull.

It was done.

They wrapped the corpse of Curius in the skin of a deer, sewing it closed around his body. Then they lifted the remains and took them into the marsh, pressing down on it with beams until it vanished into the mud.

'Very brave,' he said again, and felt his own power soaring high.

IX

Noon, at Fanum Cocidius[*]

FEROX AND THE others followed the warrior, the hills behind them. This was bleak country, the farms half a mile or even a mile apart from each other. A chill wind gusted from the north, buffeting their faces, then fading in an instant and instead they felt the hot sun.

The warrior walked his horse towards the circular stockade set on a gentle rise. This was the shrine of Cocidius, place of war and celebration, and also the place where the leaders of the tribes met to speak of their disputes. The priests did not arbitrate, but they imposed the rules of truce in this place. Men could argue, but they could not come to blows unless they took an oath to fight within a circle of spears. Such fights were always to the death, and the death of all involved if there was no clear winner, the priests using a stone axe to crush the skulls of any wounded left unable to fight each other any more.

The shrine was busy. Apart from the men who had passed them earlier, other warriors, as groups or as men riding alone, were going to the sacred place or returning, their offering made. Few of them spoke. This was not a place for light words. They said no more than was necessary and went about their business.

---

* Bewcastle.

Tracks in the grass and piles of spoor made it clear that very many had been here in the last day or two.

Ferox reached down to check that his sword slid easily from its scabbard. Vindex noticed the gesture, for they were now riding close together, and sighed. His instincts were telling him the same thing. This was not going to be simple. Yet a fight seemed unlikely, for the priests and all warriors who responded to their command, would slaughter anyone who broke the truce of this place.

They dismounted beneath the path leading up to the main entrance to the stockade. Bran was waiting for them, a white-robed priest beside him. One side of the man's head was shaved bare, the other side had long hair reaching down to his waist.

'No animals, unless for sacrifice,' the priest told them, when they explained what was in the cart. 'If you want to take him in, you have to pull it yourself.'

Carnacus nodded and jumped down from the driver's seat. One of the troopers helped him unharness the pair of mules. Then he took the yoke while two of the auxiliaries pushed from behind. The slope was gentle, but even so it took effort and the soldiers grunted as they urged it up the track. Carnacus made no sound at all.

The others walked ahead, apart from one soldier who stayed with the horses and mules.

Most of the stockade was empty around the Great Hall, with just a few smaller huts and three or four yew trees. In the grass were circles of spears, each topped by a fresh head. There must have been eighty at least, with more being set up as they spoke. The harvest from the raids had been great.

There was order to the display, men going to where their families, and their clans and their tribes had gone in the past, so that some circles were small and some very large. The priests would decide which ones had earned a place in the Hall of Cocidius and would send word to the tribes so that they could sing of the killers' deeds.

One ring of eight spears stood apart from all the others, circling one of the trees and closer to the central track than the others.

'Recognise that mark?' Ferox whispered to Vindex as they passed them.

'Oh shit, not again,' the Carvetian replied, for on the forehead of each one someone had cut a symbol with a knife. 'Thought we killed them all.' Only once had the two of them visited Ferox's homeland. As so often, the journey led to blood and slaughter.

'Except one.'

'Maybe,' Vindex conceded. 'Just maybe. But why here?'

'Who knows? We have enough to worry about for the moment.'

'That we have.'

The path took them around the Hall, with it on the right. Men who came in peace always walked or rode past a strange village or farm or any dwelling on the other side. That way they showed their right side, the side never protected by a shield, to signify that they came in peace. At the shrine of Cocidius there was no peace, and even when men came to talk they came as warriors armed and strong, as equals before the god, and only the courage and the might of their arm set any above another.

The track was well trodden, hard after the summer, and the wheels of the cart rolled so smoothly that Carnacus pulled it along without needing any help from the troopers. Behind the Hall they came to a field without any trophies on display. There were a few huts, pens for beasts waiting for sacrifice, and four tall silver birch trees forming a square. Between them, the earth was bare, every blade of grass or other growth removed, and the dirt as level as one of the army's parade grounds.

'The Circle,' Vindex muttered.

'Yes,' Bran said, and something about his tone made Vindex stare at him.

Senuna was waiting, flanked by two priests, and several yards away four warriors. The girl gave a little smile when she saw her father, then did her best to make her face rigid and unafraid.

'You have your captive?' one of the priests chanted as if in song. He was tall, desperately thin, and if this was within the empire a man might have guessed that he was a eunuch, for his voice was very high pitched. Whether in strength or manner, he seemed an unlikely guardian for the war god. The other one was shorter, broader and had only one eye in his wizened face. No doubt in his youth he had been a warrior of renown, but now his bare arms were wasted and thin.

'We have,' Ferox replied. 'He is in the cart.' He gestured to the men and they untied and pulled away the leather cover over its back. Perhaps it was the suddenly brighter light, perhaps something else, but at the moment Vannus sat up. He looked around, blinking and confused.

'The feast is set,' he said, and then slumped back to lie down.

'So be it,' said the one-eyed priest.

'These men challenge the one who calls himself Ferox.' The tall one's voice seemed even higher pitched, almost a squeak. 'Although that is not his real name. He is a Roman, but he is of the tribes and understands our ways.'

'Which is he?' his companion said, his one eye fixed on Ferox and obviously knowing who he was. 'Speak.'

Ferox put his hand, palm flat, over her heart. 'I am.'

'Do you accept the challenge and the cost?'

'I do. I swear by the god my tribe swears by and by Sun and Moon.' There was a strange sense of returning to his youth as he spoke the formula. Even after so many years of living as a Roman, this felt natural.

'Sound the horns, cast the lots and prepare the circle.' The thin one's voice had settled again and was less piercing.

Senuna struggled to judge the passing time, but guessed that it was almost an hour before all was ready. Thankfully, she was not taken back into the Hall, but only Bran was allowed to come near her, for her father and Vindex had to stay with their hostage.

'I do not understand,' she asked, when the priests led them over to the four birch trees. 'I thought I was to go free. I thought... I thought it was over.'

'Trust your father, princess.'

'But why do they need to fight?'

Bran considered this. 'Pride, and anger... and reputation. This is not really about Vannus or you for the moment. Esupas and his brothers are sworn to Vannus as his shield guard – it is a practice of my people. They must protect him, but they let him be captured. That is a stain on their honour, which they must remove or be despised.'

'Just that?'

Bran smiled. The noise around them was growing as horns blared out. A large crowd had gathered as news of the challenge spread. Duels at the shrine were rare, and bound to become famous. There was honour in simply watching.

'Esupas is ambitious. He is gaining a reputation and lusts

after more fame. If I do not kill Vannus, then one day I should not be surprised if the brothers slay him to take his power.'

The crowd parted for the priests, who took them to stand under one of the trees, the one closest to the Hall. The one-eyed man raised his staff in both hands and held it above his head. With one last blast of the ceremonial horns, silence fell on Fanum Cocidius. The priest waited, staff still held high, for what seemed an age, until a raven gave its harsh call.

'It is time,' the thin one sang. 'Know that Esupas and his brothers Lossios and Gavus have blood grudge against the one called Ferox and he has accepted. Do all understand?'

The crowd grunted. It was a strange sound, something Senuna had never heard before, almost like the cry of a boar.

'The lots are cast. All three brothers will fight, youngest first.'

'Three!' Senuna gasped before she could help herself, but the sound was lost as the priest continued.

'None may leave until the enemy is dead. That extends to all who watch. This fight ends in death, and only death permits a soul to leave before it is over.'

Senuna glanced behind her and saw that there was another priest, this one younger and with a shaven head, and carrying a brightly polished axe in his hand. She glanced around and saw several others, standing a little back from the crowd.

'If the one called Ferox lives, he takes his daughter, the lady Senuna, and may do as he wish with Vannus of Lakeside.'

Senuna did not remember anyone ever asking her name, and wondered how they knew it. She had not heard Vannus' title before, but then before all this had happened, she had never heard of Vannus at all.

'If any of the brothers live, then they will take to wife the lady Senuna and take back in friendship their own lord. Is this understood?'

'Not by me,' Senuna said, although it was lost in the massed grunt of approval. This time it reminded her more of a bark.

'No armour or helm may be worn,' the priest sang. 'For this is the place of Cocidius and the brave fight to kill and worry not about their own safety. Is this understood?'

'Aye!' Senuna was surprised that this time they spoke a word.

'Be ready!'

'Why three?' she whispered to Bran, for there seemed to be a pause. 'Do they hate father? Or do they hate Romans?'

'Yes and yes.' Bran patted her on the shoulder and grinned. 'But it not about that. It is about reputation, and your father has a great one. Plenty of people hate him, anyone with sense fears him, and a good few want vengeance for their kin he has killed or for the times he has defeated them. There's even a few misguided souls who like him!'

'But it's unfair.'

'So is the world... And your mother would say that even if it is unfair, there is no time to wait for the brothers to find more help!'

'Is he really that good?'

'We'll see, won't we.' Bran smiled. 'Either way, you either get to go home or you'll soon be married. Isn't it every girl's dream to be a bride? And your father's a grumpy old sod, so who'd miss him?'

'Mother, and she would never let me hear the end of it.'

'You see?' Bran assured her. 'You're more frightened of the queen than what might happen to you. So is your father, although he'd never admit it. So he can't die otherwise she will kill him.'

'Does that make sense?'

'It's just the world, princess, just the world.' Bran gripped her shoulder. 'Trust him, he is good.'

Senuna nodded. 'I hope you are right. Still, the middle brother is quite handsome in a way...'

Bran refused to be shocked. The girl was a lot like her mother.

Ferox stripped off his mail shirt and the padded *subarmilis* that went underneath it. He wondered about keeping his tunic, but without a belt it would hang down well beneath his knees and was likely to get in the way. Apart from that, it was hot. Little things mattered. He had read manuals written by Greeks and Romans on the art of generalship and war, some of the texts even written by men with knowledge and experience. All recommended getting every advantage on your side, no matter how small, because even the smallest edge might make a difference.

Clad in only boots and trousers, he was ready.

'If I die, you know what to do,' he said to Vindex.

'Challenge whoever is left and slice 'em up?'

'Or wait and snatch Senuna back as soon as they leave. Up to you.'

'Fine,' Vindex told him. He did not bid his friend good luck, but when Ferox stepped up to the edge of the circle, Vindex drew the wheel of Taranis from around his neck and kissed it.

Gavus stood opposite. The top half of his face was painted red, the bottom half black. His hair was long, almost as black as the paint and was plaited behind him. He was barefoot, his only garment a pair of trousers ending at the calf.

Each man was empty handed for the moment. They turned to face the Great Hall and touched their forehead and their chest in honour of Cocidius.

'Two weapons!' the priest chanted.

Gavus had a long sword, the blade notched in a couple of places. It was a slashing weapon, the sort the tribes of the north loved, although someone had given this one a point as well as an edge. In his left hand he had a square shield, studded with iron circles and the central boss extending as a sharp spike. Shields were counted as weapons, and this one was designed to stab as well as deflect.

Ferox chose his gladius, smiling as he felt it in his hand, and the *pugio* dagger he kept on the other side of his belt. Legionaries were still issued with these, although few used them for anything other than cutting meat. Most auxiliaries did not wear them at all these days, but Ferox had always liked them. With the dagger in his left hand and the sword in his right, he felt balanced.

The trumpets rasped.

'Begin!' intoned the priest.

X

Fanum Cocidius

'I AM GAVUS, son of Essus, grandson of Cunomoltus!'

Ferox said nothing in reply.

'My family are strong men, red-handed men, reapers in battle.'

Some of the crowd murmured their approval. Ferox waited.

'We are foremost among the eagle clan of the Novantae. All know of us, and where strong men meet and feast, they sing of us, of our fame and our deeds.' Gavus lifted his shield and sword high to emphasise his words and the murmuring grew. He paused, and men glanced at his opponent, who simply stood there.

'I am Gavus. When I was fifteen I slew a boar on my own, driving my spear into his belly, and thus my people knew that I was grown and was a man in truth.'

This was the way that heroes spoke and prepared to fight. Ferox drove the long point of his gladius into the ground while he waited.

'Three times already had I ridden to war, as the boys of our people do, to carry food and to tend the horses, and all said that I did these things well.' Men nodded. It was the way among many tribes. Ferox toyed with the pugio, and men were barely bothering to glance at him since he was refusing to answer his opponent.

'From then on I rode as a warrior, and fought and killed. I burned the farms of our enemies, killed their men, took their women.' Gavus was enjoying the admiration. 'What is this?' He pointed his sword towards Ferox. 'Who are the Silures, but dogs of the south?' There was plenty of agreement, since apart from Ferox there were no Silures there.

Gavus turned his head, looking at each of his audience in turn. 'Who is this old man, to be worth my time in killing? A cur who fights for the Romans and takes their gold?' Men roared approval. 'How can he dare show his face here? What deeds of his are sung were deeds of many years ago? Huh! I think he must have killed only men whose backs were turned or who slept! He is weak and old! His soul has died and he cannot speak! See how he stares numbly, lacking the wit to know that death is at hand!'

Men laughed and many shook their fists in the air in triumph, for the Romans and their soldiers were not loved and most of these men had just come back from plundering the Romans and their allies.

'I do not know whether to laugh or to weep, that I should need to slaughter such as this, to put an ageing hound, with weak breath and blind eyes out of his—'

Ferox moved quickly, whipping up the pugio, held tip first in his right hand and throwing it hard and straight. Gavus was looking away, revelling in the acclaim, but saw the movement and turned only for the knife to bury itself in his throat. He dropped his shield and sword, blood seeping from the wound. Gasping for breath, choking, he grabbed the hilt with both hands and pulled it free. Thick blood jetted in a fountain from his throat. His knees sagged, and he fell forward, still gasping, eyes wide in horror.

The crowd sighed, as they watched the warrior pitch forward face first into the earth reddened and wet with his blood. A few men shouted in anger. The priests said nothing. Senuna found herself gagging, and could not stop from vomiting. Bran patted her on the back.

Lossios took his place in the square, seeming to pay no attention to the last few gasps of his younger brother. He had chosen a shield, round and plain without spike or ornament and a spear about six foot in length, with a spike on the butt and a larger, jagged-edged iron head. He was a lean, wiry man, as tall as Ferox, but slighter and perhaps fleeter of foot. He was also naked, his hair limed and combed back into spikes. He wore no paint, but his chest and legs were a network of whirling tattoos.

Senuna giggled, for Lossios was a big man and every movement emphasised this.

Taking his sword out of the ground, Ferox turned to one of the auxiliaries. 'I'll borrow your shield, if I may?'

'I am Lossios and I have come to kill,' the warrior said in a matter-of-fact tone. He twitched his right arm as if to throw the spear. Ferox did not react. Lossios nodded, and took a step forward. Ferox matched him. His borrowed shield was oval, with a dome-shaped boss in the centre. Cavalry shields tended to be lighter than the ones carried by infantry, and he guessed that this was made of two layers of wood beneath the calfskin covering instead of three.

Ferox moved to the right and Lossios matched him, going to the left and for the moment keeping the distance between them. The circle measured some ten paces across, and each was now a couple of paces in. It was not good to be pressed back into the circle of watchers, for the slightest step across the line marking the arena meant death.

Lossios came forward, for going more to the side would bring him close to his brother's corpse and he did not want to trip. Ferox took a step towards him. In this contest between spear and sword, distance was not on his side. Lossios feinted to the right and then went left, darting forward even quicker than Ferox had expected. He caught the spear thrust on his shield. The blow was hard, there was a crack and the tip of the point burst through the back of his shield. Ferox yanked it away, hoping to catch the spear and pull it out of his opponent's hand, but Lossios was too quick. Ferox risked swinging his unshielded side around so that he could lunge. The warrior dodged just in time and jumped back. Then both were ready again, watching, shields up and weapons poised.

The crowd grunted in approval. This was the way warriors fought.

Lossios attacked again, the same move, but, instead of thrusting, swung his spear blade low, under Ferox's shield in the hope that the big spearhead would slash his leg. The Roman went back, and the warrior followed slashing again, and then Ferox bounded forward and thrust. Desperately the round shield came up, but the blade was past and Lossios jerked his head to the side so that the triangular tip struck only the side of his face instead of driving through his mouth. His cheek was ripped open, spraying blood and spittle, and he dropped his shield, but swung the shaft of his spear with all his might and pounded it against Ferox's leg. It felt like a hammer blow, and the right leg was numbed and sluggish as the Roman went back.

The warrior spat, most of one tooth coming out with the mix of blood and carved flesh.

'Bastard!' he tried to say, although his voice was a strange mumble. He spat again, glanced at his fallen shield, decided against it, and took the spear in both hands, ready to thrust under arm.

Ferox forced his leg to move. He could feel the sweat running down his back and this was no more than the beginning – if he lived long enough to see it through. Nothing seemed broken. He could not yet judge whether Lossios would be weaker or wilder from now on.

The warrior surged forward, if anything faster than last time, and he was screaming, the noise distorted. Ferox took the first thrust on his shield, saw the point burst through the back of the board, creating a bigger rent this time. He lunged forward, turning, gladius low, but his right leg almost folded as he stamped forward and the blow did no more than slice the edge of his enemy's thigh. They sprang apart, and now all at once his leg seemed fine.

Lossios was bleeding freely from the face and from his gouged thigh, but was far from defeated. As he hefted his shield, ready for the next attack, Ferox could feel that it was coming loose, both of the layers of boards broken and held together by little more than the outer cover.

The warrior charged, but as he did so instead of lunging forward he hurled the spear two handed. Ferox had his shield ready, expecting a higher attack, and the heavy head slammed into the wood and shattered it, and drove through, the spinning point hitting him on the body, cutting into the flesh.

Ferox threw down the ruined shield and with it the spear. He felt the pain in his side, and the hot blood flowing. Lossios glared at him, not trying to flee or reach for his spear.

'My brother will end you.' The words were only just intelligible and flecks of blood sprayed across Ferox's cheeks.

Then he stabbed forward, driving the long triangular point of his sword through the warrior's right eye.

There was a murmur of approval for the bravery Lossios had shown in the face of death, and for Ferox as victor, as he twisted the blade to pull it free and let the dead man drop. The Roman felt his side. The wound was not deep, but he was losing blood and that would weaken him in time.

'I'd be obliged for your shield now, trooper,' he said to the other cavalryman.

'Make him sign for it,' advised the auxiliary whose shield had been shattered.

Esupas chose a Roman cavalry *spatha*, a two-edged sword longer than a gladius and with a stubby point, and an axe with a haft about eighteen inches in length. Like his brother, his hair was stiffened with lime, although in his case the front of his head was bald, whether from choice or necessity was hard to tell. He had painted his face and all the skin above the belt of his trousers a pitch black. It gave him an unearthly appearance, with his bright blue eyes, making him seem one of the *lemures*, the dead spirits so feared by the Romans.

Ferox noticed Bran tap the top of his left arm twice, which meant that his opponent was left handed. That was worth knowing, although was surely something he should himself have noticed during their captivity. He must be getting old.

Praying that he would have the chance to get older, Ferox took the shield and stepped forward.

'Greet your brothers for me,' he said. 'They were brave men.'

Esupas' eyes widened, the whites very bright against his painted skin. Perhaps he was surprised by this sudden burst of conversation from the Roman, or perhaps he was angry. The man must have been about thirty, and moved with the proven confidence of a warrior who had fought and won. He was clearly the most dangerous of the three. After a moment he spat as the only reply.

The warrior came forward, each weapon moving a little as he kept his arms loose and ready to strike. Ferox advanced, more slowly than last time, because although the spatha was a little longer than his own blade, the difference was slight. They closed, Esupas trying to hook the axe head over the top of the shield and yank it down. Ferox raised the shield, punching the axe away, but was waiting for the slash from the sword and parried with his own. Sparks flew as blade met blade. Neither broke.

Esupas slammed the axe hard into the shield, breaking through just as his brother had done and trying to pull it away. Ferox bounded forward into him, feeling his side scream with pain, but surprising his opponent and pounding the shield into him, knocking the warrior back. He jabbed, but the aim was poor and the blade caught on something, then was free, and somehow a wild swing from Esupas caught him on the right thigh and there was a fiery pain.

Ferox pulled away, panting hard, but sadly the axe blade came free of his shield. There was a gaping hole not far from the boss. He glanced down at the cut and for all that it felt like the touch of a hot iron, it was neither deep nor bad. Yet he was bleeding from there as well as the other wound.

Esupas examined his own leg. A stretch of wool was ripped away from the leg of his trousers, hanging down as a flap. The skin was grazed, nothing more, and the warrior laughed. Men smiled from the crowd as they saw it, and began whispering, so that soon all were grinning.

They closed again, and this time Esupas led with his sword, dealing big slicing blows. Ferox met them with his shield, left leg forward, gladius back in the low guard taught by the army instructors and now so familiar that it required no thought. Blow after blow pounded against the shield, more than once clanging on the dome-like boss. It took a dent, numbing his fist, and the shield was weakened, but held, and all the while Ferox was waiting for the axe coming in the left hand, knowing that this would be the real attack.

It came, faster even than he had expected and lower, past the shield and into his side almost at the same spot as the earlier wound. He had swung away, robbing it of much of its force even though the agony was fierce, but he turned the move into an attack, slashing hard. Esupas was quick, but not quite quick enough and the blow sliced down his right arm like a butcher's cleaver. The warrior shrieked, dropping his own sword. Ferox punched with the shield, striking the face, crushing Esupas' nose, but the warrior swung his axe again, and the blade bit into the Roman's left thigh. Another punch with the boss of the shield, and this time the warrior gave back and hacked hard, the axe head biting through the brass edging on the top of the shield. The boards split apart.

The two men staggered away from each other, both panting hard for breath, blood flowing from their wounds. On Esupas' face, the blood gushing from his nose was bright against the black paint. Ferox pressed his left hand against his leg, which was not too bad, but the wounds to his side were gushing blood.

Esupas struck like a snake, flinging the axe with all his might, and Ferox was caught off guard. He flicked up the gladius as fast as he could, only managing to take some of the force from it and the axe slammed into his left shoulder. Half running, half staggering he went forward, charging at the warrior who came to meet him. Esupas' one good hand clamped around Ferox's throat and as they met the Roman's leg gave way under him and he fell, his opponent on top. There was blood on Ferox's face, Esupas' blood from his slashed cheek and broken nose, and the fingers were like a vice on his neck.

Ferox could not breathe, but he still had a grip on his sword and his left arm still worked even though his shoulder blazed with agony. He was the taller of the two by a whisker and the heavier by a big margin, and grunting with effort he managed to push and roll over so that the warrior was on his back. There was not room to aim his sword, so Ferox smashed the pommel down into Esupas's face. The pommel was shaped like an egg and made from a heavy wood to help balance the sword.

Still the fingers held him like an iron trap, and Ferox's eyes were failing him, the world going black. He pounded down with the pommel again, smashing an eye, and then struck again and again, more blood splashing onto his face.

At last the grip was loosed as Esupas' hand fell back limply. Ferox hit him once, twice more, but as his vision came back he saw that the man's head was a shattered ruin. He tried to stand and could not, until he used his sword as a prop. His hand was sticky with blood and gobbets of flesh. Staggering to his feet, he ignored the roaring crowd and stared at his opponent. Somehow, incredible though it seemed, the left hand reached towards him, fingers grasping. He lurched around to the side, managed to balance and pressed down with the point, opening Esupas' throat to the bone. The hand fell back and there was no more movement.

Ferox felt his leg give way, and landed hard on his bottom, but he sat and did not drop altogether. With his remaining strength he raised his gladius high as the trumpets blared. Servants of the priests came for the corpses and Senuna ran to her father and then was not sure whether it was safe to touch him.

'The challenge is answered,' chanted the thin priest. Servants beheaded the dead men, but their heads were treated with honour and would be taken to the Hall, for this was the place of Cocidius.

XI

Just over a month later, three days before the Kalends of October, Isurium Brigantum

Ferox was alive and Senuna was safe, and that was what really mattered. Yet Ferox was getting old, and he felt it all the more in the weeks that followed. He had been wounded before, many times, and some hurts were worse than the ones from the fight against the brothers. These days it just took him longer to heal, and he knew that it would take longer to regain his full strength, and that knowledge made him chafe all the more as he was forced into idleness. At least now he could sit out in the small, walled garden, and could walk with a stick into the town if he wanted. He began to feel less like a prisoner.

They had brought him back from Fanum Cocidius in the cart, for he could not stand, let alone ride, and much of the time he had slept. Vannus was gone, released to go home for Ferox had not wanted him as a captive and there was not good enough reason to kill him. Bran had gone too, and no doubt one day he would deal with his cousin. For the moment what credit Vannus had gained from leading the raid had taken a blow from the defeat of Esupas and his brothers, all his shield men.

Ferox was taken first to Magnis, and spent a few days in

the hospital at the garrison, having his wounds treated and sewn. He had always felt that army doctors could be more of a danger than any open enemy, so was glad when he was judged well enough to move again, and Claudia Enica came with their carriage. Sadly, she chose to ride alongside rather than stay in the raeda.

'Huh!' she had scoffed. 'As always, just like a rutting pig, and me a poor defenceless woman.' She was wearing her two swords openly and dressed in her travelling and fighting gear. 'Shame on you. You would just open your wounds and go and die on me.' He thought that her eyes were glassy, but could not be sure.

Perhaps he was hurt worse than he chose to believe, for the journey was uncomfortable, even with the sprung wheels of the raeda. Alongside Vindex, there were ten men from the royal household, all armed and all proven fighters. There had not yet been any fresh raids, but that did not mean that more would not come. Apart from that, there were other dangers in the world.

To Ferox's disappointment, they did not go to the villa where he usually lived, and instead kept going south to the house at Isurium. Yet the villa had not been touched in the attack, nor any of their folk lost, although a few cattle were missing.

'It's more comfortable and the doctor I have hired will stay with us,' she explained. 'You'll just have to put up with being polite to people.'

Before they reached the town, the queen changed back into a dress and took her place beside him in the carriage.

'Calm down,' she told him, 'this is for the people, not for you, so do not get any ideas.'

'And is it for the Romans?' he asked, for most Brigantes were happy enough to see their queen as a warrior.

'We are Romans, dear, or had you forgotten?'

'You know what I mean.'

In answer she smiled, leaned over and kissed him, only pulling away when he put his arms around her. 'Remember what I said. Wait until you are recovered – I said wait. That's better. Now how is my face?'

'Beautiful.'

'You would say that, but what do you know? I'll have to get the girl to check. Now sleep, Flavius Ferox – and get well.'

He was recovering, gradually, day by day, and, as always, she had probably been right to bring him here. It was frustrating having nothing to do, but if he was at the villa, he would surely have tried to ride out before he was ready. Here, there was nowhere to go, or at least nowhere interesting, and certainly no way of slipping off unnoticed.

Autumn was coming, he could feel it in the air, even in the little garden. Leaves were brown and soon they would start to fall, while over his head, he saw the birds whirling in great clouds, preparing for their long journey. He had always wondered where they went and how they knew the way and when to come back. The druids had known of such things, but the druids were gone, for the guardians of the shrine of Cocidius and all the other holy places were priests, just priests and did not have the decades of study required for a druid. The world was changing, as it always changed, and some seasons and moods were predictable and some were not.

Ferox was alive, but the princeps, the Lord Trajan, the man whom he had sworn to serve these last nineteen years, was dead. It turned out that the emperor had died back in August, before the big raids had come in. News, even big news like that, took a long time to travel from Cilicia all the way to Britannia.

'Did you know him?' Claudia Enica had asked when she told him, and the two of them sat for a while in the garden.

She looked tired, as she so often did these days, for she was still pressing on with the works in the town, and also trying to help folk find relatives and possessions and rebuild homes destroyed in the raids.

'Not really,' Ferox said. He remembered a younger Trajan as a loyal supporter of the hated, and since his death formally damned, Domitian, but that had really been no more than an officer doing his duty to the best of his ability. Ferox had done the same, and had lived with the nightmares ever since. 'I met him a few times, but I did not know him as such.'

'I met him in Rome,' she said. 'I don't think he cared much for the devastatingly beautiful and wonderfully witty young Claudia, now isn't that absurd? Silly man. Until he happened to overhear me talking about swords and gladiators with one of his tribunes, some pretty fellow from the praetorians.'

'Do I need to be jealous?'

'I should be disappointed if you were not – and even more angry if you doubt me.'

'I'm confused.'

'You're a man so what do you expect. But I was talking before you so rudely interrupted. There I was, discussing the length of blades and the virtues of different thrusts and cuts and the princeps was behind me grinning as he listened. "You are just like a man, lady," he told me, which I presume he meant as a compliment. He did not really take to women, I'm afraid.'

'So they say.'

'Don't pay heed to gossip. He was a good man, and a good emperor, and now he is dead, poor fellow. They have declared him a god, so I am sure he is pleased with that, and we have a new emperor.'

'Hadrian,' Ferox said flatly.

'Yes, and we both know him.'

Ferox sighed. 'Anyone else making a bid?'

'Not so far, at least not openly as far as we know. There have been a few arrests, but no real trouble. The army is getting a bonus to encourage them to renew their oaths.'

'That's nice for us,' Ferox said.

'You are on furlough, so you probably won't get anything.'

'Just my luck.' They sat in silence for a while, and that was rare, for even if she did not chatter as much as when she acted the part of Claudia, his wife talked a lot, as did all the Brigantes. The flow only tended to slow and then stop when they were in each other's arms. Ferox was feeling better, a lot better, so he decided to take a chance and put his hand on her knee. It was lifted off.

'I am tired, and you're still recovering, so button up your breeches you old goat.' This time, she was the one to sigh. 'Men!' she said fondly. 'Hadrian has decreed that Trajan will celebrate the triumph over the Parthians voted to him by the Senate.'

'Even though he is dead?'

'Even though he is dead. I suppose Trajan cannot really refuse, in the circumstances, can he?'

Ferox made another attempt to smooth her leg. The silk of her dress was wonderfully soft. 'Never been done before,' he said.

She slapped him away. 'Well, that is true of a lot of things. Now I came with purpose and you are distracting me with your lechery. Now what was it? Ah yes. Tomorrow we will have a visitor, an old friend – well a young man, but one we have known for a long time – and I wanted to discuss something before we speak to him.'

He waited, and after a while she slapped him hard on the

wrist. 'Your manners are atrocious, so I had better conduct both sides of this conversation.' Affecting a deep, gruff voice, she went on, 'Well my dearest, sweetest, most beautiful wife, my true queen, alongside whom I am as graceless and witless as Polyphemus, and see less than he did even after his eye had been put out by Odysseus – where was I? Huh, oh yes, may I beg to know who this guest is?'

She switched back to her natural voice, 'Well, my poor, pathetic and witless husband, you will never guess.' 'No I won't for I have no curiosity at all, so must plead for enlightenment. I beg you, end my misery, look down from the Heavens where you dwell in the glorious beauty of divinity and tell me who is coming.' She paused to draw breath.

'It is Titus, Cerialis' eldest boy, and dear Lepidina's stepson.' She frowned. 'You used to be a bad influence on him and all the children. Perhaps it was fortunate that you were not around much to corrupt your own daughters?'

'That was not my choice.'

'I know.' She reached over and clasped his hand. 'But Titus is all grown up and aged twenty-five, soon to be twenty-six, and one of the last actions of the late princeps was to appoint him as *tribunus laticlavius* to II Augusta.'

'He's a little old.'

'Yes,' she conceded, 'but given that his father is an eques and only his mother a *clarissima femina*, this is a great honour.' There were six tribunes in each legion, five of them equestrians, and the senior one a young man who could expect enrolment in the Senate in due course.

'His father must be pleased.' Ferox had known Cerialis and his wife for a long time, since they came to the fort at Vindolanda back when he was the regionarius.

'They are both delighted.' Sulpicia Lepidina was a remarkable woman, and she and Ferox had had a brief affair. Claudia, who was one of Lepidina's closest friends, knew all about it and had never held it against him. Cerialis knew nothing, at least as far as Ferox could tell, and that bothered him over the years for he had come to like and respect the man. He was also very fond of the children, not least Marcus, the youngest, for he was the boy's father.

'Marcus is fine.' Claudia Enica did not have to ask what he was thinking. 'Lepidina writes that he talks of the army and only the army as a career. She says he wants to be a centurion and nothing else. Silly boy.'

'It will be good to see Titus,' Ferox said.

'It will, but he is coming under orders to prepare a response to the raids and we must help him, and that means I need to see what is in the twisted mind of a child of the Silures!

'There is no surprise that the attacks came. They have been brewing for years. If memory serves me, some obnoxious lout of a centurio regionarius was reporting years ago that we seemed weak. Rome has abandoned its garrisons in the far north, and sent unit after unit off to distant frontiers, never to return. When I was born – which as anyone must see cannot have been more than sixteen summers ago – there were four legions stationed in Britannia and now there are two.'

'The men of the north look at Rome and they see a once mighty empire that is now weak and in retreat. Why should they be our friend when they do not fear us and when we are too weak to help them?' Ferox said.

'Quite – and though it may amaze you, the women notice it as well, some of them at least. And though few women lead openly, there are many chiefs and kings who are guided in all that they do by their wives.'

'What about queens?'

She sniffed. 'We pretend to listen to men – especially when the Romans are watching.'

'Are you forgetting that we are Roman?'

Claudia Enica ignored him. 'So it was just a matter of time, but what's strange about all this?'

'It was planned,' Ferox said. 'You would expect the odd raid to come in, and when the warriors get away with it they will want to come back and have another go, and the story will spread and others will try their luck. From all I hear it's been quiet for the last year or so. Somebody has had an idea, and convinced lots of others to share it. That's never easy among the tribes.'

'Any idea who?' she asked.

'Not really, I've been away too long. But there is something bigger going on, and this will just be the start. After all, hearth fires for a hundred miles or more north of the frontier will ring to songs of this raid. They took cattle, and heads and captives, and anything else they wanted, and burned at will. And most of them got home to boast. There were too few soldiers in the area, and the ones who were there did not respond quickly or all that well. Too many officers away at the manoeuvres with the pick of the men, or permanently posted to comfortable jobs elsewhere.'

'Two prefects were out hunting when the raid started,' she told him. 'Their heads were left outside Magnis.'

'Bad luck, as well then. But the point is that from looking weak, we now look helpless. They'll be back. So that's the background, but other things don't smell right. They didn't touch my farm, although it was ripe for the plucking.'

The queen nodded. 'I have read that Hannibal deliberately did not let his men touch the villas of the great Fabius Maximus. He wanted to make the other Romans think that Fabius was a traitor, secretly in league with the enemy.'

'Little girls shouldn't read books meant for boys.'

She slapped him again. 'Pig! ... Sometimes I do not know why I bother. But you are all I have, and I do not have the patience to train another husband.

'They worry about you – and probably me,' the queen went on. 'We're a threat. I do not think that the attack on poor Atgivios and Aunillus was just chance – or part of the wider raids. More likely someone from within the tribe.'

'They were after you,' he said, eyes serious. 'Kill you probably, perhaps take you captive, but probably not.'

Claudia Enica showed no trace of surprise, so had already reached the same conclusion. 'Why?' she asked.

'We will know that if we can work out who. I don't think it was a band like the rest, but whoever was in charge knew that the raids were coming and used them as cover. Everyone would think it was just chance, but you would be gone, one way or another. But why? Was it someone wanting to take your place as head of the Brigantes – there are a few of those out there. Or someone who fears that you will unite the tribe? I do not know.'

Claudia Enica nodded, and for once, had nothing she wanted to say.

Ferox brushed her cheek with his fingers and she let him. 'There is one more thing. Before it all got started, eight soldiers were killed outside a burgus on the road. It was done very well, very carefully – just as my own people would do such a thing.'

'The Silures?'

He nodded. 'Just so.'

'But up here?'

'Why not? I am up here, blinded, clumsy cyclops that I am.'

'But what does it mean?' Her own hand clasped his and she smiled.

'Perhaps that one of my nephews is not dead as I had

thought. There were signs, do you see, that only my family use. It may not matter, but he is clever and ruthless – they all were, but one even more than the rest. They called him 'the bastard' and it wasn't because of his birth. And my family are...' He ignored her broadening smile. 'If he is training men in our way of fighting it could lead to things. The tribes are dangerous enough in the first place.'

'Then we have much to ponder,' she said, 'but I must go, for I have spent too long tending to an invalid.'

He held on to her hand for a while, before letting go. 'I love you,' he told her.

'I should think so!' She patted him on the shoulder. 'Make sure to rest. Everything is healing well, so do not mess it all up at this stage.'

'Yes, my queen.'

'That's better.' She pressed her teeth into her lower lip for a moment, a rare child-like gesture, that he always found irresistible. 'So Hadrian is emperor.'

'Did you ever doubt it?' Ferox thought for a while. 'He will be a good emperor. He's a nasty little shit, but he'll probably make a good emperor.'

'I'm always surprised when you swear. What is it your people say – "a waste of good anger".'

'Some people are worth swearing about.'

She laughed at that. 'Shall I send Senuna to keep you company?'

'That would be nice.'

'No swearing though – I don't want you picking up any more bad words from her!'

'She'll just want to talk about Bran.'

***

The next day Titus Flavius Cerialis, tribunus laticlavius of Legio II Augusta, arrived. With him came an escort of cavalry, and a freedman from the governor's office.

The tribune brought news of orders for Ferox, and with them a promotion. The freedman had a letter explaining that Ferox was charged with murder.

At Sahmain, far to the north

THE BONFIRES BURNED *in the valley beneath the old fort. This was the night when souls came back from the Otherworld to walk among the living. You could feel their passing in the chill air. Throughout the night he stood on the ramparts, with sword in one hand and spear in the other. She had told him to listen and he listened. The breeze was the whisper of his ancestors, and of the warriors who had lived, fought, and died in this place in ages uncounted. They accepted him and he felt their strength feed his own.*

They had made a start and it was good. Men were calling him 'The Wolf' and that was as good a name as any he had carried over the years. They spoke of what he had done, of how they had snapped out the lives of eight soldiers in an instant, before they realised what was happening, and of how he had killed the two prefects and taunted the Romans with their heads.

Men were coming to join and take the oath. They came from many tribes, and some were from the peoples of the south and some were deserters from the army. All were welcome as long as they passed the test and swore the oath. She had refused five, and their bodies were impaled on stakes and left to rot at the entrance of the valley. Almost two hundred had joined him, so that they could learn from him and follow him to war. They were drawn by his fame and reputation and by the power she bestowed. More still came.

He had led one more raid against the Romans, preparing

with the same care as before. He took twice as many men this time, and they ambushed fifteen Roman cavalrymen. Half the horses broke their legs on the traps he had prepared, but they took the remainder and killed all of the soldiers.

Just a few days ago, she had sent him to punish the Votadini for beating a servant she had sent to them. They burned three farms, killing people and beasts alike and leaving nothing alive. When the Votadini mustered a band to pursue them, he drew them into a trap. They were surrounded in a glen and all eighty men slaughtered.

She had brought them to this place, once a fort built by giants in ages past, but long since abandoned. They were building huts as they needed and repairing the defences when there was time. There was very little, for each day he took men out and showed them how to hide and how to wait. This was no army, and none had to obey, but many came and learned and those would be the pick of his warriors.

She drew others to her, priests and some who said they were druids or the dreamers of visions. The tests she gave them were harder, and half died, but the others moved among his men and inspired them. Each raid added to their supply of weapons, for whatever they did with other trophies she had told him that the gods did not want swords and spears and armour gifted to them – they wanted all these things used to drive out the Romans and bring back the old ways. Almost every man had a sword, for among the deserters was a man who had been a smith in the army's workshops, and he was producing blades as fast as they could bring him iron and coal. Some of the men came from nothing, labourers on the estates of Romans or the pigs who joined them and lived like Romans, and men from the fringes of the tribes, the beggars, the outcasts, the thieves. Anyone who stole from their own was flayed alive, but he had only had to inflict the punishment once. The men of the fort, the followers of the wolf, kept their oaths and lived in harmony, for the punishment for raising a hand against one another was also death.

The rules were simple and the warriors followed them, for they were becoming a warband the like of which the lands had never seen.

Come the spring, it would be time for the wolves to howl.

XII

Night, the third day before the Ides of November, at Nicomedia in the province of Bithynia

Hadrian lay down in bed and stared at the carved wooden beams of the ceiling above him. This was a nice room, in a nice house, with a fine thick mattress, and he was exhausted. Yet he could not sleep.

He was forty-one years old, would be forty-two in January, and now he was princeps. The stars had foretold his rise for those with the skill to see, and he had laboured for it – the gods, should they ever pay attention to the affairs of mere mortals, knew how much he had laboured for it.

The army had accepted him, and so had the Senate, more or less willingly, so that only a few men had needed to be removed. He knew that many resented that, and would resent it more if they ever learned that Sosius and other agents had helped arrange a few illnesses and a couple of accidents. So far, only one man had been executed, and that was an old fool long since exiled to an island for conspiracy, who had taken it into his wooden head to leave it. The punishment for that was just and well established, but that did not matter for the circumstances would soon be forgotten. Other senators would resent it. It may be necessary to pass some of the blame onto his advisors, and at some point to place Sosius out of harm's way. The methods he had used in the past would not all be fitting for a servant of the princeps.

He had wanted this and now he had it, which meant that every day up until his death would be filled with work or with worrying about work. Hour after hour during the day he had listened to petitions, or retired to the chambers he was using and worked with his staff and household, listening to letters, reading letters, and dictating replies. There was no end to it and could never be an end to it, not if a man took his responsibilities seriously. Already he felt that he understood how Tiberius had been ground down by the unending demands and requests. Great or small, everyone in the empire knew that the princeps held supreme authority, and thus if they had a problem – or had been offered a solution for which they did not care – they came in person or wrote to him.

Today, among one hundred, perhaps two hundred, little decisions, he had dictated a letter thanking the 'Young Men of Pergamum' for the pleasure they expressed when he became emperor. He had nothing against the aristocratic youths of Pergamum or anywhere else – indeed if he had the chance to make their acquaintance informally some were surely delightful – and he was glad of their support, but it took such time and effort to listen to their praise. No Greek ever used ten words when a hundred would do the job.

Tiberius had not coped well, having waited too long to succeed. He had left Rome, forcing the petitioners to come to him, and eventually secluded himself on Capri. Hadrian had no idea whether or not the old man engaged in all the rumoured debauches on that island. He did know that Tiberius had kept on working, for there were plenty of his replies to requests preserved in the archive, many of the rulings still in force. The problem was that a secluded emperor could only see and hear from those people allowed to reach him by his subordinates in Rome, chief among them the commander of the Praetorian Guard, Sejanus – a man the emperor had eventually been forced to kill. That was the dilemma, if the emperor did not plough through all these requests and questions, or read all the reports from throughout the empire, then many problems might fester because no one did anything about it. Or worse, others usurped the task, and unless all were utterly loyal and highly competent – neither of which could be assumed – then even greater dangers could emerge.

Tiberius had said that leading the empire was like holding a wolf by the ears. All a man could do was grip hard and do everything to stay on the beast's back. If he let go and fell, then he would be ripped asunder. Men remembered Tiberius as cruel, as a man who had ordered many deaths on trumped-up charges. Yet he had led the empire well, and most provinces had prospered as a result. Domitian of accursed name had not been a bad ruler in his way, and had tried to work hard and make the right decisions. He had been hated from the start, and all the executions only meant that the hatred was hidden until after his death. What was it he had said though? 'Do I have to be murdered before you believe that they are plotting against me?'

Hadrian did not believe that he was ever cruel simply for the sake of it, but surviving in this world, let alone helping the empire to thrive, required more than a little ruthlessness. There would probably have to be some deaths, for men were ambitious and there were bound to be some who wanted to take his place. He feared that some deaths might have to come soon, for he sensed that senators were waiting to see whether anyone else was inclined to challenge his rule. The divine Augustus had once told Tiberius not to worry about what anyone said or wrote about them – worry only about what they did. If they were not given the opportunity to rise against him, then perhaps he would not have to kill them. An emperor clinging to the wolf's back needed a hundred eyes to watch in every direction at once.

He was determined to govern well. Ambition was natural in the able, but he had always believed that he wished to rise to the summit because he was the best suited to lead. Now, he must prove it, most of all to himself, so he would work the long hours and endless days and formally thank the youths of Pergamum and anywhere else, so that they would be satisfied and could spend hours reading his words, make speeches thanking him for his thanks, and no doubt carve most of it onto stone to be preserved for ever.

Trajan had tried to be a good emperor, but lacked dedication, and too often sought relief in the simplicity of war. Hadrian would fight no wars save the ones he could not avoid. There were bound to be plenty of those. There was already trouble in Dacia, the kingdom his cousin had seen fit to destroy and turn into provinces, and just a few days ago news came of serious problems in Britannia. Rome would never be short of wars, and the army must be kept efficient and well prepared. That way there was a chance that prospective enemies would not start a war. If they did, then at least we were more likely to win, and win without too many embarrassing defeats.

Hadrian would not hunt for conquest and glory. Almost all of Trajan's provinces in the east were already gone, evacuated by the garrisons scattered around them. He suspected that some of the Dacian conquests would also need to be abandoned. Instead they would return to the old way, relying on allies to keep a measure of control, with the threat of the legions to keep them honest.

There was so much to think about, and he was finding sleep

difficult because there was always too much on his mind. That was his fate and he had chosen it.

At the moment Hadrian was worried about his wife. They did not get on, and had never really got on. Some of that was the differences between them of simple nature, and of desire. Yet he had to confess that he had made things worse, and had said and done things right at the start which had soured their marriage forever. In the hope of sparking love in himself as much as her he had gone too far, getting badly drunk, losing his temper and becoming brutal. She was terrified throughout, and afterwards sobbed as she lay beside him. He could never take back that hurt.

The other women of Trajan's family had always adored him, but Sabina could not and he could never look at her without secret distaste and some guilt. Before he became princeps that had mattered less, because they could arrange to spend almost no time in each other's company, and for the most part she lived quietly at one of their villas. That was no longer possible, for she was the wife of the emperor and must be seen. To her credit, she was doing her duty to the full, listening to almost as many petitions as him, even if most were of a trivial nature. He knew that she hated every moment of it, of being stared at by strangers and having to greet and thank so many folk from senators and their wives to the humblest of people. There had been times in the last months when if he could not love her, at least he admired her. Yet he wondered how long it could last and feared that she would do something foolish or embarrassing. She had never been a good judge of character and so many people now wanted to seek her favour. Hadrian worried about this, and about many other things, until at long last sleep came.

ACT II

XIII

The consulship of Hadrian and Cn. Pedanius Fuscus Salinator, the Kalends of April, at Fanum Cocidius*

WIND BLEW WAVES of drizzle under the canopy. This was the place of council, employed by the tribes for generations whenever these wished to debate a matter without the use of threats or arms. In spite of this, no one had ever built a hall to provide proper shelter, and instead they sat under a huge tent, the material from patches made by each tribe and clan and sewn together. It was in the far corner of the shrine, away from the Great Hall and the circle, and on one side the stockade offered some cover, at least as long as the wind blew from the west. Today it was fitful, and changing, so that every now and then a damp spray washed over the Roman delegation.

This was their second visit in a month, and Ferox was feeling happier. His wounds were healed, his strength and stamina were coming back at long last, and the meetings kept him busy. He was never at his best when he had too much time to brood.

'Tell them that we understand their concerns, and take them to our hearts.' Titus Cerialis put his hand over his chest and waited for Ferox to translate. As time passed, he was more

---

* 1 April AD 118.

naturally framing his words in the manner of these councils. At the start, Ferox had needed to embellish everything, but young Titus was paying attention to his translations of what the chieftains were saying and learning from them. 'And tell them that Hadrian, Lord of the Earth and Great King of the Romans, feels their sorrow. If wrongdoing is discovered, then fair punishment will be dealt and recompense made.'

Titus was still referring to Hadrian. For Ferox, it took an effort not to assume that Trajan was still emperor. However, for the tribes it was better to say Caesar, one deathless, all-powerful Caesar, with all the might of Rome behind him. Still, that meant convincing everyone that Rome was still mighty.

'We thank him. The truth is not in doubt,' the old man said. He must have been eighty or ninety, and needed a young warrior to hold him upright when he stood. More than seventy leaders had assembled, so that the space under the canopy was crowded with men sitting cross legged. That was the way in these parts, unlike in the south, where the tradition was to sit on your haunches. Ferox remembered bringing one newly arrived prefect to a similar council some twenty years ago. The young pup had declared that breeches were effeminate and refused to wear them, so made a fool of himself trying to sit cross legged in his tunic.

'Not in doubt?' Titus whispered when he heard the translation.

'It is the custom to claim that,' Ferox explained. The old man had accused the Romans of stealing seventy sheep and a score of fat milk cows during the attacks made back in the autumn. Punitive expeditions was what the army called them, although they were in essence not much more than raids launched by the Romans as vengeance. It was precisely what a tribe or clan would do in response to an attack from neighbours.

Punishment was all very well, but it helped to punish the right people, and the Roman expeditions had only the loosest ideas who that was. Thankfully, with troops only slowly returning from the training manoeuvres down south, and no one having thought to prepare for major operations by massing supplies and transport beasts and vehicles, only a few small columns had gone out. They had burned some farms, perhaps even a few where some of the raiders lived, rounded up animals and driven them away, and demanded local leaders submit to Rome and hand over weapons as a mark of good faith. Ferox had seen the small piles of rusty spears with rotten shafts, and notched and broken swords, back at Vindolanda and not been impressed.

A couple of the columns had pressed further than the rest, the commanders bold in their eagerness. One had got into serious trouble, and had to fight its way back, warriors dogging its heels all the way, and losing a tenth of its men and a third of its animals and baggage. The other had lost a patrol, a dozen or so troopers massacred, and the commander was foolish enough to count himself lucky. This was the column that may have taken the old man's animals from him.

'Unless it was one of the other clans,' Ferox explained quietly to Titus, using Greek for there was a chance that some of the gathering knew Latin. 'Assuming the animals existed in the first place. I would be surprised if there were so many.'

All in all the Romans had achieved little, but at least had shown a willingness to strike and that might just be enough to persuade everyone that it was better to take the glory and loot from last summer and be content, waiting for the Romans to be less on their guard once more. Now that it was spring, the Romans were assembling a much stronger field force ready to strike. Troops were coming from all over the provinces, and were training hard. Ferox was in charge of organising several thousand volunteers from the tribes to serve alongside the regular soldiers and bolster their numbers. That should have meant promotion, but the murder charge continued to hang over him, not that it had come to court, for the accusers had no evidence, merely suspicion because Taximagulus was dead and Ferox was known not to have liked him. So that meant he was left to help prepare a war, if a war needed to be fought. The Romans were mustering in a strength not seen for decades.

The tribes knew it, for such things could not be kept secret even if the Romans had wished to try. A repeat of the great raids was unlikely to do well. The question was whether or not the Romans would attack regardless of what the tribes said and did. That doubt and uncertainty might help young Titus, Ferox and the others convince the chiefs to accept peace, but also ran the risk of convincing them that they had nothing to lose.

Ferox had worked to keep the peace up here all those years he had served as regionarius, wanting to avoid the bloodshed and destruction of war which so often fell on those who had nothing to do with the conflict. In the process he had killed a lot of men, so many that he had long since lost count. At bleaker times this made him wonder whether he was just like the empire itself, preaching peace at the point of a sword. The Silures would have laughed, for was not war natural for men? There would always be war, so fear us, because we are the most savage.

'Should we make a gift now?' Titus asked. 'To show goodwill.'

'If we do it for him, we will have to do it for all of them,' Ferox replied. 'Do you have enough to do that?' The tribune shook his head. 'Then the coin will do.'

'Take this gift as token of the Lord Hadrian's goodwill,' Titus declared, holding out a silver denarius in his hand. 'This is his symbol and his bond.' Actually, the coin showed Nerva, the man who had adopted Trajan, but that did not really matter, especially as Ferox continued to say Caesar and not Hadrian.

The young warrior reached out to take the gift, almost losing his grip on the old man, who swayed and nearly fell.

'This is the gift of Caesar, and he is a generous and mighty lord, king over more kings and more lands than you can count. He is generous, open handed, but strong in anger.' Ferox was not sure about the generosity, but then he had laboured for Hadrian for a long time and got little in return. The new emperor was certainly strong, and even more cunning, in his anger.

'He thanks us,' Ferox translated, as the old man was helped to sit. He was one of the lesser chieftains of a clan of Selgovae who lived in a little glen amid the Novantae. Both tribes were well represented, as were the Votadini from the east, and there were also Damnonii, Venicones from the north and a few from the little groups in the region who did not fully belong to any tribe. Plenty had come, but Ferox worried about the men who had not, for they were likely to be the most determined. Most of the ones who had come were old, if few quite as ancient as the man who had taken the coin. Older men tended to be cautious, ready to hear if not to pay heed, their famous deeds already done and reputation long since made. The young were hungry, eager and reckless. Few had appeared, although Bran and Vannus were among them to speak on behalf of their kin. Each of them took a denarius, and in the end almost all had found some grievance that needed a token of the emperor's faith or had made a pledge of their own goodwill.

'They seem happy enough,' Titus suggested. They had met after dawn and it was now barely an hour until sunset. Food and drink had been brought to them on platters during the day, and now and then men left to relieve themselves. No one had failed to come back, and a few latecomers had joined over time.

'Perhaps.' Ferox was wondering about the last man to appear, a travel-stained lord of the Venicones, whose face looked familiar, although, since the man was not yet twenty, perhaps he had met his father in the past. So far he had sat in silence, but it was obvious that he was being treated with respect.

'Are there words still be spoken in this council?' The priests of the shrine took no part in the discussions, apart from declaring that the time for talk had arrived at the start and when it was over. Ferox was glad, for the thin one with the high voice was present today, and it kept reminding him of the fight with the brothers.

The young man stood, waiting for the priest to nod, and then spoke. 'I am Divixtus, son of Divixtus, and I come as envoy of Tincommius, High King of the Vacomagi and Venicones, Lord of the Caledonii and many others. I come to speak to the envoys of the Lord Caesar and would wish all gathered here to be witness to my words.'

That was it, Ferox had known the boy's father years ago, when he had accompanied another young tribune to see Tincommius. That tribune was dead now, some four years past, while Tincommius, just like Ferox, was getting old, which did not mean that he was weak. The Vacomagi and Venicones had never had a High King before, as far back as anyone could remember. As a boy, Tincommius' entire family had been massacred, and he had been a hunted fugitive, yet he had returned, and somehow beaten or won over every rival, building on each success to make the rest possible. Some chieftains and lesser kings liked him, for he had a charm and a way of inspiring others. More came to fear him, and obeyed as long as he was strong, and as the years passed got used to the idea because the High King never seemed to be weak.

Ferox liked Tincommius, and respected him too much ever to trust him. The High King was ambitious, very ambitious. His rise was helped a lot by Rome's retreat from the Highlands of the north. The Romans had humbled kings and tribes, disturbing the balance between them, which made it easier for one leader to grow. For twenty years Tincommius had sought friendship and alliance with Rome, and got it, largely because the Romans did not have the strength to challenge him. For successive legates of Britannia, it was easier to deal with one High King who, more or less, kept his word than lots of different leaders. Tincommius never provoked the Romans, and if his power kept growing it was never openly as a challenge to Rome. Yet as the Romans drew back ever further, more and more leaders to the south were convinced to acknowledge the High King. Ferox had done his best to explain all this to Titus, although he had not gone into detail. He had not expected Tincommius to want anything.

'On behalf of our legate, and on behalf of the Great Caesar, I welcome you to this council and would hear your words,' Titus said, and waited for Ferox to pass them on.

Divixtus smiled. 'May I first pass on the High King's sadness at the death of Trajan Caesar, and joy at the accession of his cousin, Hadrian Caesar.'

Titus darted a quick look at Ferox as a reminder that the centurion had assured him no one would know who the emperor actually was. Ferox shrugged. Of course, Tincommius would know, he thought to himself. The High King always knew.

'I thank you for your sympathy and congratulations, and will pass both on to the legate who will convey them to Rome.'

'My Lord Tincommius also wished to extend his greetings

to you, Titus Flavius Cerialis. Your father earned a great name in the north at the head of his gallant Batavians, and his wife was as famous for her grace, beauty and courage. He trusts that your father and the rest of your family are well. He is also glad to see Cerialis' son embarking on such a distinguished career.'

Again, count on the High King to know, and to make everyone aware that he knew.

'Again, I thank your lord, they are all well. My father spoke often and in great praise of the High King.'

Liar, thought Ferox, but a good liar and that was such an advantage when sent on tasks of this sort.

'And also...' Divixtus coughed with an embarrassment that appeared genuine. 'And also my lord bade me speak in these words and no others, and bade me... told me to say that... that he was pleased to see that old rogue Flavius Ferox was not yet dead, to congratulate him on his victory won in this very place, and once again to marvel that so fine a woman and great a queen as Enica of the Brigantes would stoop to wed such a one.'

This was not a place for light speech, nor one for much laughter, but there were exceptions. As the amusement died down, Ferox rose beside Titus, and nodded. 'Assure your lord that I am not yet dead, and thank him for his concern.'

'My lord is also sure that you did not kill this Taximagulus and his men.'

'That is kind of him.' It was also typical of Tincommius. The gods alone knew how he had found out about the murder charge. Taximagulus and several of his men had been found dead in the aftermath of the raids.

Divixtus smiled. 'My lord says that you would not have been foolish enough to leave any trace behind.'

Titus coughed. 'While such talk is good and fair, the hour is late and we would hear what the High King wishes to say.'

Ferox sensed that Divixtus understood the Latin, even though he waited patiently for the translation.

'The High King is vigorous and mighty, and though he has seen more than fifty summers, he remains sharp of mind, hale of body and strong of arm.' There were murmurs of approval from most of the leaders sworn to Tincommius.

'Yet one day, like all men low or high, his days will end and his soul will travel to the Otherworld, where he will live in honour and glory.' The chieftains nodded for this was no more than the truth. 'When that time comes, Tincommius will pass the rule to his cherished son, the mighty Epaticcus. You all know of his deeds in war!'

'Aye!' The chorus of agreement was immediate and seemed genuine.

'The kings loyal to him and the chieftains and all the people love Epaticcus and trust him.' Divixtus did not wait for agreement this time, perhaps in case it was less enthusiastic. 'Tincommius trusts that the goodwill and friendship he has always shown to Rome will flourish as strongly as ever with his son. For that reason, he wishes the Caesar Hadrian to grant recognition of Epaticcus as the High King's successor and as a friend. So that when he is acclaimed as High King, the Romans will join the celebration and recognise him and take him as their friend, aiding him, as he will always aid them.'

That was it then, the point of all this. Tincommius wanted the Romans to accept his kingdom as permanent, to be ruled by his heirs after his death.

'I am sure my legate and my lord Hadrian will consider the High King's proposal with great interest,' Titus said, speaking carefully and slowly. 'Such a matter is too great a thing for me to decide, but I will carry your words to my governor.'

While Ferox was translating, Divixtus produced a scroll from inside his tunic. Papyrus was rare and expensive in the north of the province, let alone beyond its borders, but the piece was obviously of good quality, and was even sealed in the proper way. The High King's spokesman waited politely for Ferox to finish, before walking forward and handing it to Titus.

'My lord felt that the Roman way was to write such things down,' he said, in accented, but clear Latin, before switching back to the language of the tribes. 'And also, the High King asks that you two be chosen as surety for the agreement, when in the course of time, the great Caesar accepts it. You, Titus Cerialis as your father's son, from the royal house of the Batavi, and as future senator of Rome, and you, Flavius Ferox, who in his first battle acclaimed the courage of the great Epaticcus and hailed him as a warrior. You are both friends and men of honour.'

'I thank the High King for his courtesy and suggesting so great a privilege, although again I do not have the authority' – Titus glanced at Ferox wondering whether the tribes had such a word – 'to accept on behalf of my own lord.'

'Of course, that is why the High King has set everything down in his letter. Carry this to your governor so that he can carry it to his Caesar. My lord knows well that this will take time.' Divixtus inclined his head, and sat down.

'Are there words still be spoken in this council?' the thin priest trilled. No one answered. 'Then it is done.'

'Did you really acclaim this young fellow in his first battle?' Titus asked as they were leaving, using Greek to be on the safe side.

'Epaticcus? As far as I can recall I hit him and told him to go away – not very politely,' Ferox explained. 'Didn't know who he was. But everyone took it as admiration. He'd fought a famous warrior – me if you'll credit it – and come away with his life. Of course, I played along when I found out. No doubt Tincommius knew the truth, but what does that matter?'

'Quite. So what does this High King want now? Don't think he has ever been formally recognised as *rex et amicus* by the Senate, has he? And they do not usually get the right to name a successor unless they are truly favoured.' He caught Ferox's expression of mild surprise. 'I do read books, you know?'

Titus tended to hold his head right back. His spine was not straight, although his cuirass was designed to hide the way his shoulders arched forward, which made him appear more solidly built than was really the case. He had learned to cope with the deformity, although it gave him an oddly stiff gait. He could walk well enough, for as long as required, and rode excellently. Running on foot was another matter, and something he did his best to avoid.

'If this fellow is as smart as you say – and that means relying on the judgement of an old rogue – then he is up to something,' the tribune went on. 'But is he seeking advantage over us, or over his own subjects and neighbours?'

'Both probably,' Ferox suggested. 'You can trust Tincommius as long as it is in his interest to be faithful to us, no more and no less. He's much like us, really.'

Further conversation became impossible as they came through the gate and were greeted by a great roar of delight. A huge man, a head taller even than Ferox, bounded forward and clapped the centurion on the shoulders. It felt like being hit with a hammer.

'Ferox!' the giant boomed, in a strange accent that in some ways reminded Titus of his Batavian homeland. 'Ha, you old dog!'

Ferox grinned. 'This is Gannascus,' he explained. 'He's a friend – and Tincommius' best warrior.' The man was as old as Ferox, his long hair and beard dyed a vivid red, no doubt because he had gone grey. When they first met, Ferox had fought him and been amazed at the big German's speed as well as strength. Help had arrived in time, otherwise he was not sure he would still be here, and more than once afterwards they had fought side by side. Even after all these years he did not fancy crossing swords again. The German had a big belly, for he had always eaten and drunk as if there was no tomorrow, but his arms and legs remained huge and strong.

They talked for a while, the big man explaining that he and half a dozen others had ridden as escort for Divixtus. 'Good to see you,' Gannascus kept saying. 'Like the old days.'

'How is your sister?' Ferox asked, for she had been the woman, if not the wife, of Tincommius and his most trusted advisor.

The German frowned and spoke quietly by his standards, although he still must have been audible fifty paces away.

'Last winter, the fever,' was all he said.

'I am so sorry.'

'She was good sister,' Gannascus rumbled. 'She saw far and deep. Things are not the same now.'

Divixtus appeared, smiling and friendly, but the conversation was at once less natural, and the Romans were keen to depart, wanting to ride at least some of the journey before night fell.

'Ready to go?' Titus asked, glancing back at the dozen troopers acting as escort.

'Yes, sir,' the senior soldier, a double pay man or *duplicarius*, replied.

'Then let's go.'

Ferox lagged a little behind, waving back when Gannascus raised his hand. He wondered what his old friend had meant when he said that things were not the same.

XIV

Three days before the Ides of April, in the hill country of Dacia

A STROKE OF the pen made a tattooed king of the Roxolani a Roman citizen, with the outlandish name of Publius Aelius Rasparaganus, confirming in writing a decision made some weeks ago when they had met near the banks of the Danube. In theory the king was subject to Roman justice, which would preserve his rights against others, and could marry a fellow citizen if he chose – and she was willing, of course. He would not be the first or last barbarian without a word of Latin to be welcomed as a member of the res publica, the glorious Roman commonwealth. More practically, the man was no longer demanding such a big subsidy to protect the Roman traders visiting his lands, and had accepted recognition as king as a far better prize.

The Roxolani were superb horsemen, and their leaders and warriors moved with the seasons, trailing their families in waggons. Such folk were rarely too reliable, for they lacked the stability of settled communities, but for the moment he should be happy and that, alongside all the deals with all the other leaders, and the threat of reprisals, should help settle the area for the moment. Life was lived for the moment, for after all it was as impermanent for a princeps as it was for a slave, or a long-haired bandit who now carried Hadrian's family name of Aelius. He wondered whether anyone had ever counted how many new citizens were made by an emperor and took his name, and suspected that there was probably some clerk at Rome who did keep track and would be eager to tell anyone with authority the answer.

The work continued, growing rather than shrinking, as each fresh decision led to a dozen more, but he still clung to the wolf's ears – an apt description this morning, as the restless hounds were barking away, eager to be let loose.

The eastern frontier appeared to be stable for the moment, the Parthians too busy squabbling with each other to seek trouble with Rome. Dacia needed to be sorted out, for Trajan had taken all of the old kingdom of Decebalus, and some of that was simply not worth keeping, given the cost of maintaining garrisons. Which meant that some land and some tribes would be given up and left to fend for themselves in the future with the threat of the legions returning with fire and sword a cheaper way of keeping them under control. That in turn meant that more than a few senators would lament the loss of vigour of the old Romans, that drive to expand Rome's *imperium*, to make its greater power ever greater, a spirit that had flourished under Trajan.

They would not say it to Hadrian's face, of course, not yet.

Avidius Nigrinus came over to join him. 'The huntsmen tell me that all is ready, my lord.' He was a tall, slim man with grey eyes, tanned skin and a hawk-like nose. His hair was greying, but had once been that mousy fair colour that usually meant that someone in the family was from Cisalpine Gaul.

'Good,' Hadrian replied. The readiness was obvious to anyone, although Nigrinus' tone suggested a level of uncertainty rare for the man. Hadrian had appointed him legatus of Dacia as one of his first decisions after becoming princeps. His task was to deal with a crisis as various bands of Carpi, free Dacians and Sarmatians had attacked the province. Nigrinus had done well, fighting through the winter to expel the raiders and then punish them.

'Shall I give the signal?' Nigrinus asked. The legatus of the province grinned rather stiffly. 'The huntsmen say that there are reports of boar, wolf and bear. We should have a good day.'

'Good.'

'I reckon the weather will stay fair.'

Hadrian nodded. They were high up, and it was not long after dawn, so that their breath steamed. He was stiff, for they had camped up here so that they would not need to ride any distance before the hunt.

This would be a rare treat, the first he had allowed himself this year, for when hunting no one was likely to start an oration for his benefit or beg leave to submit a petition. For just a day he could be Aelius Hadrianus again, the hunter not the emperor. It was freedom of a sort, the closest he would ever get, and he longed to kick back his heels and give his stallion its head, galloping fast and far, the wind in his hair so that he lost himself in that moment. Was it really so much to ask?

'My lord, I realise this may not be the best moment, but have you had a chance to consider my cousin's case?' Nigrinus asked quietly so that no one else would hear.

They were as small a group as was possible when the princeps did something. Thirty or so were there as hunters, grooms and to handle the dogs, with half as many again other slaves to cater for them when they returned, hungry and thirsty. Nigrinus had six riders from the governor's bodyguard, auxiliary troopers seconded from their units and under the command of a centurion. Apart from a brace of tribunes from the Praetorian Guard, Hadrian had a dozen of his own horse guards, the *singulares Augusti*. All were in armour, and as usual it gleamed so brightly that he had to wonder how long it would take to wear through the iron and bronze by subjecting it to such vigorous cleaning. His own men carried hexagonal shields, apart from the two archers, who had little bucklers slung behind their saddle. The cavalrymen were to stay close, just in case there was any danger. With all that weight of equipment, they could not expect to keep up with the hunters, all but a few of whom were provided by the legatus and knew these mountains well.

'... so although we all regret his youthful impetuosity, they are the mark of an eager, passionate nature, and I am sure that he will control it, indeed that service with a legion would help to give him greater discipline...'

Hadrian turned to stare at Nigrinus.

'My apologies, lord,' the legate said. 'It is unbecoming in a friend to spoil a day of relaxation. I am truly sorry.' The man was tense. 'Shall we go?' He raised his arm, and his senior huntsman lifted the little brass horn he carried.

'A moment,' Hadrian called, louder than he had intended. He sighed inwardly. Sosius had kept him well informed of what was afoot, but a little part of him had hoped it was not true. If the legatus had not been so uncharacteristically nervous, he might just have convinced himself that the man was innocent.

Hadrian shrugged, perhaps too theatrically, but the moment was not a pleasant one. 'I'm sorry, my dear fellow, but whenever I see an eagle before a hunt, it is my custom to pour a libation to Artemis and another to her brother Apollo. Will you humour me?'

Nigrinus could not help glancing around at the skies. He saw no eagle, but then neither had Hadrian. 'Of course, my lord, of course,' he almost stammered the words.

'Thank you. A foolish habit from Italica, no doubt – I am the bumpkin still,' Hadrian added, tone a little harder, for so many senators had dismissed him as a vulgar provincial. He held up his hand and clicked his fingers.

Two slaves came with cups. Less obviously, Sosius followed them, his shaven head covered by the hood of a long cloak.

Hadrian took the cups and gave one to the legatus. 'Nigrinus, my dear friend, let us face the rising Sun.' The sky to the east was a brilliant spray of reds, pinks and dark smudged clouds, with the ball of the Sun blazing in the middle. Both men blinked as they raised the cups. 'Dazzling, isn't it?' Hadrian said softly, brightness greater than any earthly gem. He paused before adding, 'I suppose as princeps I had better go first.' He poured the wine onto the grass. Some of it splashed onto his boots and legs. 'Now you.'

Nigrinus was about to do as he was bidden, when Hadrian turned and clasped his shoulder.

'Old friend, as of this moment you are stripped of office, expelled from the Senate and in disgrace for attempting to murder the princeps. I am so sorry.'

Nigrinus gaped in surprise, then felt something prod his back. Sosius was standing right behind, and from under the cloak had produced a sword. One of the legatus' singulares shouted a warning.

'As you were!' Hadrian commanded, his voice booming. 'Tell them,' he added softly to Nigrinus. He could see the man's grey eyes darting from side to side, considering. Nigrinus knew that he was dead whatever happened, for the sword in his back would end him even if his men somehow managed to overcome the emperor and his guards. There was a moment's determination, the thought of noble sacrifice for the greater good.

'Think of your family,' Hadrian whispered. 'There is no going back for you, but they do not need to suffer.'

Steel grated on bronze as the centurion in charge of the governor's escort drew his sword. 'With me!' he called. Not only the auxiliary cavalrymen, but eight or nine of the hunters hefted spears and walked their horses forward. One, a broad-chested German with a scar on his cheek, pushed up beside the centurion.

Nigrinus' jaw was clenched, his body straining so hard to keep still.

'It is up to you,' Hadrian told him.

The legatus' shoulders sagged. 'Obey your princeps!' he called, his voice cracking with emotion.

Hadrian patted him on the shoulder. 'I really am so sorry,' he said and then strode towards the centurion and the horsemen clustered around him. Several of the huntsmen were big burly men, obviously former gladiators or wrestlers. Nigrinus had been careless to choose them, and as he walked forward Hadrian had the idle thought of how he might have planned the assassination better. His own men were fanning out in a circle around the other horsemen.

'It's Viator, isn't it?' Hadrian called affably to the centurion. 'From Legio IV Flavia – the Felix?' He had taken the trouble to find out beforehand.

'Yes, sir.'

'This is a sad day, but your legatus has plotted to murder me and – well, I'd rather he didn't.'

'Sir?'

'Now I know honourable and tested soldiers like you would have nothing to do with anything so disgraceful, but those fellows are not soldiers.' He gestured at the huntsmen. 'They're slaves who have to do what they're told.'

Hadrian sighed. 'Now I don't know what madness caused your legatus to plan this dreadful thing. It's a pity, because he used to be a good man, as you know. All I need from you is what I expect from any true soldier. Be true to your oath, be true to your units, and do your duty. Will you do that for me?'

Viator gulped, licked his lips, and then nodded. 'My lord!'

'Excellent. Now these slaves need to die.' Hadrian pointed in turn at the five men Sosius believed were the key assassins. 'Right now.'

Viator swung his spatha into the neck of the German slave beside him. Blooded jetted high, as the man's head fell to one side, the neck almost severed. It was not a fight, but a swift massacre, as only one of the men fought back, managing to spear the horse of an auxiliary. The other huntsmen and slaves stared as much in surprise as horror at the slaughter

'Take him away, and keep him guarded,' Hadrian ordered a couple of the singulares Augusti to lead off Nigrinus.

One of the tribunes slammed to attention beside Hadrian and saluted, arm high. 'I'll keep a close eye on him, my lord.'

'No need, some men will be here soon to do that.' The tribune frowned, obviously puzzled, and Hadrian wondered how the man had ever reached this far. Still, perhaps too much imagination could be a drawback in an officer commanding a cohort of the Guard. 'We have still have a day's hunting ahead of us!'

'My lord?'

'Didn't you hear? Plenty of boars and perhaps other delights.'

'But...' The tribune did not seem to know what to say, until his face suddenly filled with resolve. 'I will stay by your side.'

'Thank you,' Hadrian lied, dreading the day when his safety might depend on this buffoon. Sosius appeared, waiting and not drawing attention to himself. 'Be a good fellow and tell the chief huntsman we are ready now,' he told the tribune.

'Nigrinus' man?' the tribune asked, frowning again.

'I am told he is excellent at his job,' Hadrian assured him, wondering briefly whether to give the officer some advice before deciding that it would be a waste. 'Get him moving – and have my horse brought over.'

'Sir.'

Sosius presented a list of names.

'Yes, yes, no,' Hadrian said taking them in order. 'Not yet anyway. Then yes, yes... What do we think about Spurius in Britannia?'

'He's very sick, my lord. Everyone is surprised he has lasted this long.'

'Then yes, if nature does not beat us to it. No to all the others.'

Sosius did not comment. He never did unless asked his opinion. There was something disturbing about the man, and the only time he seemed mild, even affectionate was when he was around Sabina. That rarely happened these days. She did not seem to have the slightest clue about what this man was capable of doing, of the things that needed to be done for Hadrian and for the empire.

The deaths were necessary. If Hadrian had thought the tribune capable of learning, he would have explained that, just like a surgeon, he must cut away the decayed flesh in the hope of preserving the rest and letting it become healthy again. The assassins brought by Nigrinus to murder him somewhere out on the hills, when they were able to catch him alone or almost alone, had to be killed. Slaves had no choice but to obey, but even so to accept that they would kill the emperor meant that there could be no pardon.

The same was true for Nigrinus. He must die, but he was a senator and had accepted the futility of resisting so had earned the chance to write a few last letters and to take his own life if he preferred that to the executioner's blade. The man was smart enough to know that the letters would only ever be delivered if he wrote nothing inappropriate in them. As long as he understood and acted sensibly, his family would keep all his property. The same was true for Lusius Quietus and the other men who had corresponded with him. How far each had been involved in the plot was hard to say and did not really matter. They had encouraged and incited one another simply by sending each other messages written in code and delivered surreptitiously. So a few would die and be publicly condemned, and a few more would perish without formal disgrace, and the rest of the res publica ought to be able to live on in greater health.

Hadrian enjoyed the rest of the day as well as he could. This was a precious rest from his labours and he did not know when he would get another opportunity. Nigrinus' fate saddened him, for he had hoped that able men would accept him as princeps and continue to serve him as he served Rome. It really was a pity.

The haul was good, with several boar, and Hadrian always liked them both as challenging, dangerous quarry and because their meat made such good meals. Only the truly desperate could eat bear or wolf, and the latter's skins always kept too rough a look to be really useful.

The chase was long and hard for the last one, and he got his chance to ride, if not quite to forget. The plot was over, but there might be others. By the sound of things, he would soon need to find a new legatus for Britannia, and that was too important a post to be filled lightly. As he galloped, hounds braying ahead of him, he thought of men able enough to do the job and loyal enough – or pragmatic enough – to be trusted with it.

Hadrian also worried about his wife. Poor Sabina was still trying so very hard to be a good Augusta. If anything, the more she tried the worse she did, saying the wrong things at the wrong time. One of her most foolish and unthinking comments, readily misunderstood, had reached Nigrinus' wife and helped spur him along. She had meant no harm, would probably never understand that she had done harm, but he doubted that it would be the last time. All her letters were now opened and assessed before they were sent on. For the moment that was the best that could be done. He did not involve Sosius or any of his men in this. That might test the man's loyalty too much, for he genuinely appeared to like the Augusta. Hadrian had never had reason to doubt Sosius' loyalty in the past, nor did he now. He did wonder whether the man had done and seen too much, and worse, might even one day tell too much to the wrong ears. For the moment Sosius remained useful, but there were other agents and those could watch Sabina and her household.

The princeps rode on, trying not to think and failing. Still the horse was magnificent, and a stag ran them a wonderful chase until it was cornered and killed. That ended the day. Tomorrow they would ride back to civilization and the full weight of his duties would resume. After all, there was an empire to be run.

Beltane, in the vale of the Wolf

AT IMBOLC SHE had told him to travel for three days and climb to the peak of the great mountain. At each noon and midnight he was to run a flint knife across one arm, making the blood flow. At noon it was to be the left arm, and at midnight the right. He was not to bind the wounds, but let them flow until the blood hardened. He was not to wash.

As he had ridden through the lands he had seen the folk preparing their sacrifices for the festival. Soon the first lambs would be born, steaming as they came out into the cold air. At Beltane men and women made offerings and prayed to give the ewes an easy time, and most of all to prevent any polluting spirit from entering the new lambs, or worse still, be released to wander in the world.

No one troubled him, nor did they offer hospitality. Strangers were dangerous on these days, for who knew what malevolent spirit might be hiding in human form. He had left his horse outside a farm near the foot of the mountain, knowing that no one would dare to take it, not until three days had passed and by then he would have returned.

The climb was hard, and as he went higher there was more and more snow on the ground. Yet he did not notice the cold, even when he bared his arm at noon and made another cut. Near the end of that short day he reached the top, and just below it was a hut, the glow of a warm fire coming from its open door. A girl appeared as she had said. She was young and lovely, with long golden hair down past her waist, and was clad in a brilliantly white dress.

He ignored her and climbed the last few yards. His body was weary, but his soul soared as high as the mountain itself and then higher again into the air. Throughout the night he kept vigil, sometimes singing, sometimes silent when he would dance as the first men had danced back at the beginning.

At dawn he did not cut himself and instead went down to the hut. She was waiting, standing beside the fire, the dress gone so that she was naked, save for a red ribbon tied around her head like a crown. They lay together and, when they were sated, he slept. Dreams came of galloping horses, hundreds of them, and cattle running among them, and of tents burning with fire. The tents were clear, and they were not houses.

When he had woken she was gone. He stirred the fire to life, took one of the branches and left the hut. With the fire he set light to the thatch, waiting to be sure that it had caught even though he knew that it would. Then he left and returned to the old fort.

Now it was Beltane and the bonfires blazed again on the walls of the fort, and in the valley, and throughout the land. The spring was here, and in the next days the flocks and herds would be led to the uplands, where they would feast on grass grown long after all the winter's rain. Before that, they would be driven between the fires, to cleanse them and make them healthy. Some folk made their children run between the flames for the same reason. Beltane was a time of hope, for the world was renewing itself and life could flourish again.

She killed a man that night, for as always life and death were intertwined. The man had claimed to be a druid and to do magic. Before she killed him, she cut out his tongue, just as the first druid had done at the very first Beltane after lighting the first bonfire. Fifty men accused him of sacrilege and all claimed to be druids, although they spoke falsehoods. He cut out their tongues and burned them on his fire and the story says that they could not scream as they died. The one she killed made odd, choking sounds and struggled against the bonds that tied his legs and arms, the body twitching far longer than he had expected. When the man was still at last, she led him away and they stood, alone in grove of pine trees, their rich scent mingling with the smell of the fires.

'My granddaughter is with child,' she told him as the first red glow of dawn split the black sky in the east.

She was the daughter of Acco, the last druid, one who had lived on Mona before the Romans came and the last to know all the great secrets. He had taught her much, but not everything. Much she had learned for herself, because there were things no one could teach. The girl he had coupled with at Imbolc was her granddaughter. He did not know her name, nor anything else about her, and had not seen her since that night. He did not need to know these things.

'You will have a son,' she said a little later. The sky was ablaze as the Sun edged higher.

'You will not live to see the boy grow into a man, but he will be mighty.' The clouds were fading from vivid pink to a softer shade.

'Before you die you will win fame and glory, you will win great victories and gain vengeance.' The sky was turning blue, the Sun yellow rather than red.

He said nothing. What man could ask for more than that.

'Now go back to the fort. A stranger has come with a request. You will meet him and agree to do what he wants for then he will help you in turn.'

He did as he requested, walking alone, for she remained in the grove, softly chanting verses he did not understand. The guest was there, just as she had said, and this did not surprise him, because she always knew.

The guest was a great prince and he sought the death of kin.

He had smiled when he took the prince's hand and agreed. That night he slept and again dreamed of burning tents and running horses.

XV

Twelfth Day before the Kalends of June, in the praetorium at Vindolanda

FEROX SAT ON the edge of the bed and put his feet in the legs of his trousers. There was a musty smell in the air, mingling with a faint aroma of fresh plaster. Both suggested that the room had not been used very much, as did the dust on the chest in the corner. The prefect of cohors III Tungrorum was rarely with his unit, being required for duties down south. Both the commander and his family preferred the milder climate of Londinium, and were delaying as long as possible their return to the fort. Claudia Enica knew them – she seemed to know just about everyone – and had secured a letter instructing the few members of the household in residence to make them welcome.

'Remember,' she said, 'this is your duty.' She lay on her back, long hair spread out around her head. Against the white of the bedclothes and in the dim light creeping through the gaps in the shutters her hair seemed very dark. 'So do it well.'

Ferox glanced back, and was at once even less enthusiastic about leaving. 'It's a pleasure. Was for me at least!' He made a lunge, and half slipped off the bed.

'Pig!'

They grappled, kissed, kissed again, until she put a finger to his lips.

'No time,' she told him. 'Even for you!'

'I am in command,' Ferox declared with mock seriousness. 'Let 'em wait.' His hands were on her, peeling back the blankets. She was so soft, so perfect, and for some inexplicable reason she loved him.

'Said the tyrant.'

Somehow he managed to kick off his trousers. 'I must do what is best for the state,' he declared, pulling her close.

'Said Nero. Now...'

For a short while, neither of them spoke in words, until she pulled away.

'No,' she said. 'There isn't time.'

'Even for me?'

'Especially for you!' She slapped him playfully on the cheek. 'Now run along like a good little boy and play soldiers for a while.'

'This is what soldiers most want to do,' Ferox assured her, then began to suck at her right breast, before nuzzling the gap between them. His tongue felt the little scar that was the mark of her training with the Mother.

'Have you heard anything?' he asked, pulling himself up. He linked his fingers with hers, pushing gently down, so that her arms were above her head.

'They are fine.' Their twins were still training there, where all the young pupils were called Brother or Sister. Somehow, they found ways of passing messages to each other throughout the rest of their lives. 'The Mother is pleased with them.'

'Good.'

Claudia shifted her head to one side. 'Are you surprised? They're a lot like you, in many ways, poor things.'

'But is it safe?' Ferox feared for these children he had never really known. 'War is coming.'

'That's not what everyone is saying they want.'

He thought for a moment. 'That's just how it smells.'

'Huh! Surprised you can smell anything over your own stench! Now get that fat bulk off me, and get about your business. If war is on the way, then you have a lot to do to make them ready. Get up, you lazy soldier!'

'I am comfortable. And learning to wait is one of the first lessons a soldier needs to learn. That and hurrying, of course. ... And moaning. Speaking of which.' He leaned down to kiss her again.

She dodged. 'No.' Pulling her hands free, she took a hold on his throat and glared up at him. 'Remember that I am queen, and a Sister skilled in arms.' Her face stared intently, until her lips twitched and she started to giggle and then could not stop.

Ferox was puzzled, and the blanker he looked, the more she laughed, her body shaking. Without really understanding why, he pushed himself away and sat up.

'Oh well,' he said, and she laughed all the more. 'I don't understand.'

'It's...' the laughter took over again. She had gone red in the face, tears streaming down her cheeks.

Ferox searched around and found his bunched-up trousers on the floor. He began to dress. By the time he was finished, Claudia had almost recovered.

'Is there anything to drink?' she asked, then started giggling all over again.

Ferox found a jug of water, sniffed it to make sure that it was just water and fairly clean. Satisfied, he poured some into a cup and took it over to her.

'Thank you,' she said, drank and coughed a little. 'That is better.' She was sitting up, bare to the waist where the blankets still covered her. She noticed his expression. 'I said no.'

'You did,' he conceded. 'Then you fell about laughing. A fellow might not take that too well.'

She almost cackled, spraying him with water, and then punched him lightly on the chest. 'Ow. Forgot you are wearing armour. Don't you feel safe?' She laughed again. 'You don't see, do you? When I put my hands on your neck, the thought came to me that we had become one of those debauched aristocratic couples – the sort who mix fighting and pain with their love-making.' She giggled again. 'I found that funny.'

'I noticed,' he said.

'Well, you have always been observant, and I suppose there were some subtle clues that only a husband would notice.

'Now,' she went on, suddenly serious. 'Do you really think a war is likely – a big war, I mean?'

He nodded.

'And you do not really know why you think that? I see… Yet Tincommius seeks friendship and alliance that is in Rome's interest, and though the tribes to the north have some leaders determined to fight, they are not united, and as many or even more want to take no risks. The natural prediction is that there will be only a little fighting… You sense more.'

'Yes.'

'Then all the more important that the Brigantes are prepared – and the other tribes of course, for the Romans probably will not distinguish one Briton from another. Can you do it?'

With so few troops left in Britannia, the legatus had responded enthusiastically when Claudia Enica offered to raise a unit from her own people to serve as allies. Indeed, within a short time, the idea gathered a life of its own, like a rolling boulder stirring up a landslide. Orders went out to half the communities of the province to raise a levy, and instead of one unit of a thousand men, there were now six being organised. At the same time, the proposal that Ferox take charge of the Brigantes also grew and grew, until he was tasked with supervising the organisation and training of all the others as well.

Ferox thought for a while before answering. 'I do not know... Depends a bit on what they are asked to do.'

He was no nearer knowing the answer after three hours watching the unit organising here at Vindolanda undergo training. Someone had decided to base the units on a *cohors milliaria* of auxiliaries, setting down the ideal size as about a thousand men, divided into ten centuries of a hundred. They could not call it a cohort, because a cohort implied a regiment in the regular army, and no governor was authorised to raise those without express instructions from the emperor. Instead, each of the six would be a *numerus*, a band, because the term was so helpfully vague that it could mean almost anything.

This one was the first one he had formed and the best, precisely because it was the least regular. It was also the only one wholly consisting of Brigantes or their kin. Ferox had kept the clans together as far as possible, forming centuries all from the same areas and groups. There were two centuries of Carvetii, three of Textoverdii, three more of Lopocares and two of Gabrantouices. To support them, and taking advantage of the ambiguity of his instructions, he had added one hundred and fifty horsemen in three turmae. Two were Carvetii and the other mostly Textoverdii.

Having the queen at Vindolanda helped encourage them. These were all men whose leaders were loyal to her. A fair few had served in an earlier numerus raised from the Brigantes, the one Claudia Enica had led in person to fight against the

Dacians. Those desperate days had turned even some former enemies into her devoted supporters. Ferox knew that plenty of them expected her to don her war gear and join them if it came to a real fight, and they might even be right. As far as most were concerned, their queen had called on them and their chiefs had answered, as was right and proper. The cause did not matter, nor did the enemy. She had agreed that they fight alongside the Romans, so that is what they would do

Better still, Ferox had picked them not just from the northern clans, but from the folk who still lived closest to those old ways, from the times before the Romans came. They still lived a hard life, with the risk of sudden attacks by men wanting to murder or steal. Such things were rarer these days, but not so rare that men no longer took care to be ready. These were men who knew how to fight, because that was what it meant to be a free man among the Brigantes.

Almost all of the warriors now camped across the road from the fort at Vindolanda had brought their own weapons, a shield, and sometimes a helmet or armour, while the cavalrymen had ridden in on their own horses. Ferox had managed to find swords for everyone who lacked them, using the money set aside for their pay. Men like this did not come for the money, but because of the bond with their chiefs, and the disgrace among their neighbours and punishment from those same chiefs if they did not. There had been no shortage of volunteers, and he doubted that anyone had been compelled. Any man issued with a sword would keep it, and the rest could choose a bounty in silver or keep one of the helmets or cuirasses he had managed to gather and issue. The chieftains got gold and prestige, whether they led their men in person or simply sent them, and were content.

Called *Numerus Prima Brittonum* for the benefit of the

Romans, this was a muster of the Brigantes raised as they had always been raised at the command of king or queen. They carried two standards, and one was a square vexillum flag with their Roman name and nothing else. The other was a bronze figure of a rearing mare, the shape vague, but clear if you understood. It was the totem for the queen of the Brigantes from ages gone by.

Ferox knew that these men would fight, and would fight best in the way they understood. He gave some basic drill to the infantry so that they could form up in rough line alongside Roman units and wheel to the left or right. Employing an old army trick, he had each centuria compete with the rest, to see who could keep formation better, who threw javelins better, marched faster, or bested the rest in mock fights. The prize each night was a pig to roast in addition to their ordinary rations. They boasted and did their best to cheat, and apart from a few injuries when fights became real, it helped improve the already good mood.

He was lucky in the centurion sent to take command. His name was Claudius Amminus, and although serving with Legio XXX Ulpia Victrix on the Rhine, he had chanced to be on furlough visiting his family, who were well-to-do aristocrats of the Atrebates. He was young, eager because he had not yet seen much active service, and appeared able. More importantly he spoke the language of the tribes, albeit with a rather flat southern accent. Vindex was in charge of the cavalry, and like the other officers, understood how to act as a chief and not simply a Roman commander.

All in all, Ferox was satisfied with numerus I, and reckoned they should be more than their match for a similar or even larger force from any of the tribes. They were not regulars, but they were not going to face any regular, well drilled and heavily armoured foes, and as long as no one expected them to labour they should do well. He could not say as much about any of the others. The III and IV were the pick of what was left, both containing some Brigantes, although even they were a mixed bunch. Some were from the northern clans, and still warlike enough not to need much training, but most of these had been raised by leaders who were none too keen on the queen. Ferox had wondered about mixing them in with the others, until he decided that it was better to keep them separate, as the last thing they needed was infighting between the groups. More Brigantes came from the Latenses and Setantii to the south, folk whose lives were much safer and more settled under Roman rule. Barely a quarter of these mustered with any sort of weapon at all, and even some of those did not give the impression of having practised with it.

All of that was even more true of most of the recruits for the other units, who came from the peoples of central and southern Britannia. They lived in an ordered province, where hardly anyone owned, let alone felt the need to carry, arms. Some were keen, some not, and some units shrank as desertion took their toll. They needed six months of hard training, just like other *tirones* joining the army, and needed to be fully equipped and well led. Ferox could provide none of this. Everyone seemed to have assumed that the Britons were born warriors, who just needed to be called out to be ready for simple service, so no one had thought to prepare equipment. Half the men in one of the numeri did not even have boots, and were clearly the poor and desperate that some of the southern towns had decided they could happily do without.

Ferox used some of his own money, and even more of the favours he was owed or his wife's friends could supply, to ensure that within a month every man in the II and V had a spear, some sort of shield and clothes on their back. He could not find anything like enough officers able to speak the same language as their men, and had to make do with what he could get. Some were decent enough, many meant well, but lacked experience or talent. Some simply shouted at their men and then hit them until they obeyed. A few died when they tried the same techniques with the Brigantes, or men from any of the other tribes who still carried themselves like warriors, and that led to punishments and resentment. Ferox did his best to sift these men, and inevitably the already better units got the pick. His last visit to see numerus V had been extremely depressing, for the men were cowed and spiritless. They also seemed underfed, and although he had found out who was selling off their supplies and got rid of the offenders, it was not much. Now they were adequately fed and sullen rather than hungry and sullen.

Numerus VI he had written off in his mind altogether, and was simply waiting for formal approval to make it official. Just a couple of hundred of the worst leaders and least enthusiastic recruits were left on its books, assuming the officers had actually completed the books, which was doubtful. Of the others, none mustered more than five or six hundred men. Numerus III, currently training at Coria to the east of Vindolanda, also had about seventy horsemen and the most distinguished commander. Ferox did not care for Pertacus, although the man had obvious charm and the experience of commanding a cohort. For all his public enthusiasm and eagerness to please, Ferox could sense that the former prefect despised him, and resented serving under someone not of his social class. His family were rivals of the queen, in the sense that they believed that the weaker the royal house became, the easier it would be for them to grow their power locally.

Yet the man was unusually affable in person. 'I'll help as long as I can,' he had kept on assuring Ferox during the last inspection. 'But when my posting comes through, I shall have to hurry off to whichever end of the empire I am sent.'

For the moment, there was no one better available, and all the other numeri were led by seconded centurions. Numerus II at Magnis had an old sweat from Legio VIIII Hispana, who had risen from the ranks and spent thirty years as a centurion before retiring in his last station. The man was sixty, if he was a day, red faced, fat and quick tempered, swearing at his men in a mixture of their tongue and camp slang. Even Vindex reckoned he had learned some new expressions from the man.

'Most fun I've had for years,' the old man admitted. 'Good to be back with the army – any army, even this shambles of yours. Farming makes a man old before his time. I'm getting soft... Move you idle buggers!' He yelled as a centuria on the drill ground was ordered to charge. 'Move! ... Where was I? Oh yes, glad to be here... Jupiter's holy toga what do those mongrels think they are doing? Excuse me, Ferox.'

'There's a voice on that man and no mistake,' Vindex observed. 'Reckon they like him.'

'Maybe,' Ferox said. 'At least they know where they stand with him. He's predictable, and he's on their side, whether they like it or not.'

Things might have been worse, a lot worse, which did not mean that they were good. More and more troops were arriving and setting up temporary camps if they could not squeeze into empty barracks in the forts. It was hard to believe that so many soldiers would concentrate without something happening.

'You may be right,' the queen admitted when he joined her back at the commander's house, the praetorium.

'Oh well, it was bound to happen one day. Still, can I have it in writing to show to the children?'

'They'd assume it was forged. Now stop talking nonsense and listen, for I have received word from dear Lepidina.' She saw his look. 'Yes, yes, they're all well. Apparently Titus has written home telling them how helpful you have been, so the poor lad may be sick.'

'Just a splendid judge of character.'

The queen ignored him. 'Hadrian is busy touring the provinces and has not yet returned to Rome. The legate of Dacia tried to murder him, so he has got the chop along with several of Trajan's other favourites. He has not said anything openly, but he plans to put a new man in charge over here.'

'How does she know if he has not said anything?'

His wife gave him a pitying look. 'You know Lepidina.' She sniffed. 'I forgot, you have known my old friend rather too well, haven't you. Yes, for all your act of being a brutish, unthinking and uncaring soldier, you have had your conquests. Shocking really, and I waste my time with you.' She shook her head. 'If you must know, I suspect her source is the princeps' wife. They are quite friendly, you know, have been for years. Well, the world of the Senate is a small one, and even smaller for their womenfolk. Everyone knows everyone else.

'And if Lepidina knows, there is chance that our most noble Spurius Ligustinus knows. Remind me again, wasn't the original fellow with that name famous for something?'

'Complaining, I believe. He was a centurion after all.'

'Oh dear, as bad as that. Well our legate may well want to make his name as a soldier before he is replaced. As far as I can tell from my sources—'

'Should I know about them?' he interrupted.

'Better not – you might get jealous. But these secret, highly placed – and no doubt handsome – sources tell me that the governor believes that Tincommius' appeal is a sign of weakness, and that that presents us with an opportunity to assert Rome's might in the far north. He is talking about a show of strength – to show that even the High King must take what Rome chooses to give, and to make it clear that a Roman army may march at will wherever it wishes. No enemy will be safe, no matter how far away from our province he lives. It is bold, I suppose...'

'Stupid, more like.'

Claudia Enica ignored the interruption. 'He wants to be seen as a bold, decisive leader, and to hand the new princeps a victory right at the start of his rule. Look, he will say, under Trajan there were raids and turmoil, but now there is Roman strength and peace, all from my actions. This is the moment for a man of quality to strike with an iron hand, to be a hero and glorious servant of Rome and the princeps. That is what our governor thinks... When he is well enough to rise from his bed, that is.'

Ferox sighed, and decided to change the subject. 'Odd being here again.'

'We are married – we are supposed to be together, although the gods seem to have had other ideas. Or do you mean Vindolanda?' She pulled a face. 'Are you having wild fantasies about my old friend?'

'There is something about a blonde,' he said wistfully and ducked a thrown cushion. 'Actually, I was thinking how strange the army is. Here we are at Vindolanda, but it's not the Vindolanda I knew, because they have pulled that fort down and built this one on top of it. It's the same place, almost, and the fort is like all army bases, basically on the same plan. Yet it's different, only a little, but still different. Almost like a dream, when it feels real, but part of you realises it isn't.'

'That's more words than you have spoken in an age. Is something wrong?'

He chuckled. 'I was just thinking. This was – or the old fort was – the first place I came across you. Didn't know it at the time. You'd broken in and ended up diving into a latrine to search a corpse.'

'Don't remind me. It was months before I really felt clean again.' She shuddered. 'Do you remember how I escaped the guard afterwards?'

'Yes.' After tipping as much water over herself as possible, she had torn her dress open, distracting the young sentry who happened to chance on her.

'Well, be a good boy, and be polite at dinner to our guests, and later on I'll give you a chance to catch me.'

Ferox remembered that she had invited the centurions from the garrison and some of the officers from the numerus, the ones she felt most likely to enjoy a Roman-style meal. It promised to be a long evening, for Philo was with them and had thrown himself into the preparations.

The next day, Ferox led Vindex and a dozen of the cavalry off on a long patrol. He wanted to sniff the air, and get a sense of what the tribes were expecting. They did a long loop, taking several days, first west past Magnis to the little village at Banna, then up past the biggest fort of the Selgovae, around to Fanum Cocidius and then back in a big circle.

He did not like what he saw, even though no one challenged them, still less threatened them. Folk were restless, worried, and sometimes excited. Even the Votadini to the east were carrying more weapons than usual. War was coming. Everyone seemed to sense it, even if few knew why.

XVI

Seven days before the Kalends of July,
in the lands of the Selgovae

'IS IT EMPTY?' Calpurnius Priscus shaded his eyes with his hand as he studied the hilltop. A single rampart ran around the crest. There were a few ragged gaps in the timber palisade on top, but no more than he would have expected from these barbarians – too lazy to keep the place in proper repair. The gate was open, whether deliberately or because the timbers had rotted away.

The slope up was steep, which made him wonder whether a direct assault would be costly, which in turn might mean settling down to set up *ballistae* and pound the place before sending in his legionaries. He did not want to waste the time, but nor did he want to risk the slightest check so early on.

'I cannot see anyone,' Titus Cerialis ventured. 'No movement or glint of weapons.'

Priscus suspected that his senior tribune was right, but clung to the thought for a little longer. He could see it in his mind, the legionaries pushing stubbornly up the hill, rectangular shields forming the roof of the testudo over their head, each one bearing II Augusta's symbol of the Capricorn. Behind them light *scorpiones* shooting darts with deadly precision, and the bigger engines hurling heavy shot. Long-haired and moustached barbarians falling beneath the deluge, wavering, rallied by a frenzied chieftain, then slaughtered as his men broke in, oval-shielded auxiliaries and archers in support, perhaps even a few of their own ragged arsed barbarian allies to add colour. It was perfect, a scene or set of scenes for paintings in a triumph, much like the great monument they were still preparing as the centrepiece of the divine Trajan's new Forum. Not that a mere senator could celebrate a triumph these days, or even be commemorated on a monument unless the new princeps permitted. Discreet pictures for display at home would pass, unless Hadrian proved to be particularly suspicious. There would be no harm having the artist add the emperor as a dominant figure, watching from the distance.

'No, I think it is abandoned,' Titus concluded.

The dream faded, and Priscus, legatus of Legio II Augusta, silently cursed his tribune and second in command.

'Just like the villages and farms,' Titus went on. 'They are frightened of us.'

'As they should be, as they very well should be.' Priscus felt the wonderful dream fading. A glorious victory required enemies willing to stand long enough to be beaten.

'Wait, I see something!'

Titus obviously had good eyes, because Priscus could not make anything out, until he saw movement at the gateway and one, no three riders trotting out.

'It's Ferox!' Titus said.

Once again Priscus marvelled at the tribune's eyesight, because all he could see was the dark shapes of the horsemen against the green of the rampart behind them. They were half a mile away, a handful of officers on a gentle rise and their escort a short distance behind them. The riders were closer now, and there was something about the way the leader sat his horse, and worse that appalling felt hat that made the fellow look like a farmer, that meant that it really was Ferox.

'No one home?' Priscus called out, trying his best to be jovial. Up close, you would never mistake Ferox for a mild farmer. The man was a killer and no mistake, although sometimes Priscus could imagine his face to be that of a particularly grim oracle, the sort that always predicted disaster and had a nasty habit of being right. Still, he was useful, knowing more about the area than anyone else, and raising all these irregulars for the campaign.

Ferox reined in and saluted. 'No, sir. Not many live up there, these days. They use it as a refuge when there are marauders at large – there's space for hundreds of sheep or cattle, at least for a while – but hardly anyone lives there. Those that do left a couple of days ago. Not sure what we intended, I suspect.'

'Hmm.' Priscus considered this. 'Guilt, do you think? Hiding from us for a reason, perhaps? Do you reckon men from this valley went on last year's raids? Thought this local fellow had a treaty with us?'

Ferox was sure that the answer was yes, the clan chief was an ally of Rome, and yes, at least some warriors had almost certainly gone raiding. He was far less sure how to make a Roman understand that a free man of the tribe was just that, free to do as he wished. If warriors went off roving, it did not mean that their chief was any less true to his pledges to Rome. These were his fellow clansmen, not slaves to obey his every whim, or even soldiers.

'Not as far as we know, my lord. They're hiding because they are afraid that we might be angry, even if they do not understand why. You have brought a lot of soldiers, more than anyone has seen in these parts for years. It makes them nervous.'

The legate liked that. 'As I say, so they should be, for Rome's arm is long and powerful. Should we burn the place to make the point, do you think?'

Ferox kept his face wooden. 'No point. There is not much up there to burn. They can see your army marching at will through their lands. If you want to burn everything to ashes you can, and they see that.'

'Yes, yes.' Priscus nodded to himself. 'That makes sense. Better to show them that we are kind and worth keeping as a friend. They can see well enough that they won't want us as enemies.' The legate stretched, the sudden movement startling his horse, so that its head shot up and ears twitched before calming again. 'Well then, no fight today. Let's see whether the Novantae have bigger balls, eh!'

Titus and the other officers laughed, for it was only polite and tactful to share a commander's joke. Priscus was a decent enough man, thirty-five years old and had already commanded the legion for two years. He had a round, very Roman, face, that in time would no doubt turn jowly and resemble those grim busts glaring out from every tomb along the Via Appia. He was still young enough for the lines around his eyes and mouth to be soft, and when he smiled, he was handsome enough. Yet it required care and experience to read his moods, for joviality could turn to anger in the blink of an eye. Life was far easier for all of his staff and senior subordinates if the legatus remained happy. Fortunately for everyone, he was still so excited to be leading this campaign that bursts of anger tended not to last too long.

'Let's see who will be the first back to camp!' Priscus shouted to them, and set his horse racing off the hill and down the valley. He was a competent, if not elegant, horseman, but the others understood that it was better to stay with him, and keep a little behind. The legatus liked to win.

Ferox found him typical of so many senators. He looked like so many others, was of medium height, in reasonably good physical shape, without being truly athletic, and could be charming when he wished or a nasty piece of work. He was neither smart not stupid, but moderately capable and fairly serious in his approach to his duties. He was ambitious, as they all were, for a man would not get even this far in a public career unless he craved success. Ferox did not sense the driving, often dangerous, ambition he had seen in a few aristocrats over the years, and suspected that in normal circumstances, Priscus would have been content to see out his years in command of a legion peacefully enough. So far, he had done the job competently enough to give him a decent chance of a consulship and maybe even a provincial command in due course. That was enough for most senators.

Then his luck changed in less than a year. Thanks to the raids, Britannia went from a quiet backwater with a run-down garrison, to a place where the prestige of Rome was being challenged. There was a new emperor, eager to secure his rule, which meant that he had to be seen as a true imperator, a leader under whose guidance Rome was mighty, and, as Virgil would have it, the subservient were treated with mercy and the arrogant beaten down in war. In Britannia's north, there were some proud needing to be made humble again, or simply killed, and Priscus was in the province at the head of one of a mere two legions, and the one closest to its proper strength, so bound to be involved in any serious operations. A routine spell as legionary legate had suddenly turned into an opportunity to fight and win in a manner that was fitting for the ancient Calpurnii whom he claimed, with a certain degree of mental flexibility, as his direct ancestors. Not only that, but it meant a chance to catch the eye and win the favour of a new princeps.

The Romans took luck seriously, especially when it came to politics and war. That utter swine and gifted soldier, Sulla, had named himself 'Lucky', and the divine Julius, who was a far more charming and even more able scoundrel, boasted of his good fortune. Ferox suspected that Priscus now felt the same thrill. Legio II Augusta formed the most important single element of the main field army formed by the governor for his great summer expedition. Naturally, Priscus was put in charge, although Spurius Ligustinus planned to go with the column. At that stage, Priscus' colleague, the legate of Legio XX Valeria Victrix, had an independent command, but one less than half the size and given a minor, supporting task.

Then fickle Fortuna gave another twist to the story. Spurius Ligustinus, for a long time weakened by a succession of illnesses and his own high living, fell seriously ill at Eboracum, on his way to take command. He was still alive at last report, although no one would be surprised in the slightest if the next letter to arrive announced his death. There was certainly no question of a recovery rapid enough to let him participate in the campaign. Yet his orders stood, and the expedition had already been prepared at great effort and expense, which meant that it was difficult to call off, which also might be perceived as weakness by the watching tribes and hence achieve the exact opposite of its intended purpose.

Priscus, commander of the main column, was the obvious choice to take over as overall commander and act in the governor's place. Thankfully, the old fool had been well enough to confirm this in writing before he collapsed and began to rave in his fever. Titus Cerialis became the head of the main column, although since Priscus would be with him, the tribune would always be under close supervision. Some of the legate's cohort, his staff of officers and clerks on attachment had come over to join Priscus, even if most seemed unsure whether their new head was someone influential enough to advance their careers.

Thus, in just a few months, Priscus' prospects had gone from moderate, to good, to perfectly splendid, with the chance of impressing the princeps and becoming one of the trusted handful who got all the plum jobs over the years to come. Fate was taking a hand, and the legate's brimming self-confidence made very clear that he sensed it and knew that this was just the start.

'Our new princeps is a man of action, like his cousin, the divine Trajan,' Priscus had declared one evening while entertaining senior officers in his tent. 'They expect a true Roman to see the problem and solve it, without waiting around for instructions or all the men and supplies they might want in a perfect world! No, act now and strike hard!' The legate had drunk well that evening and his words became louder and louder, if a little slurred.

Claudia Enica, who accompanied the expedition for the moment, had glanced at Ferox and rolled her eyes.

'You wanted to come,' he whispered to her. He could sense that she would prefer to dress as she had done in Dacia, but for the moment remained the respectable Roman lady. The legatus had a mistress along with him, and the queen treated her with courtesy, which had helped to persuade the legatus to let her come. Much to Ferox's amusement, the commander's woman was also named Claudia and had her hair dyed a vivid red. Claudia Enica wanted to remind the legatus – and more importantly Hadrian – that she had once again loyally raised soldiers and done her best to inspire them. 'Think of yourself as an honorary man,' he suggested.

'Huh!'

Drunk or sober, Roman aristocrats loved to orate and

Priscus was no exception. 'Why, just a few short years ago, our valiant princeps, then a private citizen, was made acting legatus of Syria, saw a crisis in the making, and scraped together the few troops available to storm a city in the east!'

Claudia Enica put her hand on Ferox's knee and squeezed tightly. He had been one of the men scraped up for that expedition. Though he had not said much to her about it, she had learned more from Vindex and Bran before he left, so understood enough to realise that the ambitious Hadrian had created a war, leading to a grim siege and the sack of a place whose folk had played no part in the political games that led to the war. Nor had Trajan been pleased, although the whole thing was kept quiet, and evidently he was persuaded to forgive Hadrian in the long run.

'You should go back,' Ferox said quietly. 'I cannot, but you can – and I'll do everything to look after your lads.'

She smiled and squeezed his knee again. 'I know you will. But I am queen, and they are here because of me. I cannot leave.'

Ferox was not convinced, but at least so far his wife had stayed with the main body and not felt the need to buckle on her swords and ride out with the patrols. Hopefully the desire to be a queen and at the same time a proper Roman would help to keep her back – and he had to admit that it was wonderful to have time with her, when for a change he was the busier of the two. They even had their own grand tent, pitched with its back to Titus Cerialis', which in turn was pitched to the side because even though he was the commander of the field force, Priscus was the overall commander and had precedence, and in practical terms issued nearly every order that was required. If Titus was offended by this, he made no protest, since after all, II Augusta was Priscus' legion.

It was also the heart of the army, having provided seven

cohorts, including cohors I with the legion's eagle at its head. Altogether there were some three thousand two hundred men from II Augusta, along with one cohort of three hundred and fifty soldiers from Legio XX and, gathered by prising just about everyone still in the old depot of VIIII Hispana, they had assembled another cohort, some six hundred strong, half of them *veterani*, men excused fatigues and doing five more years after their initial twenty. The gods alone knew where the rest of the legion was, for Ferox did not, and they were certainly not in Britannia. The last time he had seen them was in Osrhoene, where they had formed the heart of Hadrian's private war.

In support of his legionaries, Priscus had three and half thousand regular auxiliaries, a third of them cavalry. They were from a number of cohorts, and only the two alae who provided the most dashing, and perhaps even the best, of the cavalry were present at anything like full strength. Then there were Ferox's men, with numerus I, II and III, together making up more than two thousand, for he had been made to detach a couple of *centuriae* on one task or another. The other two numeri were with the secondary force, which mustered fewer than four thousand fighting men, even including the irregulars. Its job was to advance in the east, into the lands of the Votadini, where no real trouble was expected. The intention, so Priscus had assured Ferox, was to distract any enemies since they would not know which was the main attack. They were also to act both as reserve, and to be ready to move and guard the frontier line along the east to west road in case some large body of warriors managed to get past the field army and threaten the province.

Ferox felt that it was a wonderful plan, as long as the enemies – whoever they proved to be – were blind and stupid. Priscus' army fell just short of the ten thousand soldiers that he

– and poor, sick Spurius Ligustinus – had hoped to muster. The *calones*, the army-owned slaves who performed many practical tasks and supervised the baggage train, along with the other *lixae*, slaves and freedmen owned by individuals, and a ragbag of other camp followers, took the total to almost thirteen thousand.

That was a huge number of mouths to feed. Ferox had been asked his opinion back at the start of the year, and advised that as much transport as possible ought to be carried or drawn by mules, or failing that by ponies and horses. Inevitably, there were nowhere near enough mules available, for the army in peacetime never kept more than a fraction of the numbers needed to move each unit if it was required to take the field. Feeding mules was expensive, keeping them healthy took time and effort and the attention of a lot of calones or even soldiers, and the contrary beasts had a tendency to die before they were needed.

Each *contubernium* of regulars, whether legionaries or auxiliaries, was supposed to have a mule to carry the tent, and other heavy equipment, including some of the tools and cooking pots. There were supposed to be eight men in a contubernium, and a lot of shuffling and reorganising in the run-up to the campaign meant that this was just about true, although a fair few still had just seven or six. Another way to reduce the burden was to say that not all the *contubernia* in a *centuria* needed to have a tent of their own, since at any time either a fifth or a quarter would be acting as sentries or performing some other duty. So the manuals said that a thrifty commander could take just three-quarters of what was needed, and let the men coming off guard slip into the tents and bedrolls vacated by the men relieving them.

No one ever liked that way of doing things. A soldier might

not carry much with him on campaign, but what he had was his, and only his and he did not care for the thought of someone else going through his pack or sleeping under his blankets. As far as Ferox could tell, only a couple of cohorts had adopted the practice, and on the warm and dry nights you could see the men without tents bedding down in the open, so that they had a little patch of their own. His own men had not been issued with tents, so slept out regardless of the weather. That made Ferox all the more guilty because he slept dry, with a beautiful woman beside him. She said – and so did all the men willing to speak – that this was only right, for she was queen and he was her consort, outsider though he might be. If the queen lacked a tent, then each night her tribesmen would have to build a shelter for her, so at least the tent made it all faster. Ferox was still not sure, and feared that age was making him weak to let himself be with her every night. Perhaps a quarter of the warriors had brought wives and families along with them, husbands and wives coupling under the stars in plain view and hearing of all around them. That had always been the way in time of war, unless a man was wealthy enough to bring a waggon, and only a handful of chieftains had done this.

So many tribesmen gave each night's camp a wilder feel than was usual. Priscus had assigned them one corner to themselves, which worried Ferox for his men were not familiar with Roman ways. There were a fair few warriors who could not be brought to understand that the army insisted on a man relieving himself into a latrine trench, and only a latrine trench. Thankfully, Priscus had been persuaded to let the irregulars reinforce the outside pickets rather than man the rampart. Even so, Ferox made sure numerus II camped behind the others, furthest from the rampart and the *intervallum*, the open area kept behind it to allow troops to form up. The men might manage to perform well enough in daylight and with time to work themselves up, but he was sure they would panic if a night attack came in.

Priscus had a big army, even if elements of it were as much for show and to add bulk as anything else. Big armies moved slowly, for that was simply the way of things. If they formed a column it was longer, which meant the contingents at the back had to wait a long time before they could even set out for the day's march. Every time the advance guard met some obstacle – a place where the valley narrowed into a defile, a gully or there was a stream to cross, let alone a river, or even just a steep slope to climb – it slowed progress. While those in front made their way past whatever was slowing them down, it meant that everyone behind had to stop and wait. A delay of half an hour for the leaders became greater as it rolled like a wave back down the column. Those in the rear soon found that they arrived at the night's campsite three, four or even more hours later than they would have done had progress been steady.

The commander of II Augusta was an active man. Although he often rode ahead with the patrols, especially if they reported anything interesting, when he was not doing that, he went up and down the column encouraging and cajoling. Priscus took his job seriously and had read about the actions of famous commanders. He even learned a few words in the language of the tribes so that he could call out to the numeri. Being a Roman, he was not too particular about pronunciation, and failed to understand the difference between the various tribal groups, so would tell Carvetii how proud he was of the Setantii or just mangle his words.

'Just give him a cheer,' Ferox told all the warriors. 'He'll go away happy and not bother you any more if you do that.'

Some of the warriors started grinning and waving enthusiastically at the legatus while shouting nonsense or insults, until Ferox assured them that, even if the legatus did not understand, he did. They were more careful after that.

The army plodded on, heading north day after day, although not going in a straight line because the landscape did not run that way. This was not a land of roads, but of tracks. Some were well marked, and wide enough, and the best were the ones followed in the past by other Roman armies, when the empire had asserted itself to the north. They were the best because past experience had proved that an army could negotiate them and get to where it wanted to go without too much difficulty. They were also the best because they were known, their details set down, such as the distances between staging points, the rivers to cross and hills to climb, and the access to water and food and forage at different times of year.

Priscus' staff had been able to pull all these details from existing records. He had planned to march from one established point to another, for that was the army's way. Whenever campaigns were fought in the same area over the decades, successive columns would halt and set up their night's camp on the same site used by earlier armies. Only rarely did this mean that they built on surviving traces of defences, but it gave the assurance that what had been a good position in the past was likely still to be one. Yet it had not worked.

'Why are we so slow?' Priscus demanded of no one in particular when for the fourth night in a row they had gone nowhere near as far as he and his staff had planned. 'Agricola had twice as many men when one of his columns came this way.'

'Maybe he was luckier with the weather?' Titus Cerialis suggested.

The weather was certainly not ideal, for it rained every other day with an uncanny regularity, but Ferox suspected that the bigger army was simply a far better prepared army. Back in those days, almost forty years ago now, there had been some twice as many regular troops in Britannia, and more importantly, they were still used to acting as field armies nearly every summer. For back then Britannia was one of the best postings for anyone keen to see real fighting. There were lots of eager officers who quickly gained experience and even more soldiers who were old hands at campaigning. They knew what they were doing, and on top of that were geared up for marching and fighting, with well-prepared baggage trains for each unit and more to move the supplies needed by the army as a whole. Ferox did not feel that 'They knew what they were doing,' would satisfy the governor, so said nothing.

This was a makeshift army, but that was most obvious when you looked at its transport. Most of the regulars had their tents, but only two-thirds had mules to carry them. The rest made do with horses, who tended to be very delicate, or ponies, which were fairly delicate and could carry less. It did not help that there were not really enough soldiers or calones with recent experience of caring for pack animals, and the training tended to assume mules who needed a rougher hand. Quite a few horses had already gone lame, and Ferox saw and smelled ponies whose backs were a mass of sores. Even some of the mules were suffering, not least because the insatiable needs of this campaign meant that plenty of beasts that would normally have been rejected as too small or unhealthy had to be used.

There were enough mules for some of the transport waggons, and all the *caroballistae*, light catapults mounted on carts. Horses pulled a few more, but well over half of the many vehicles were drawn by plodding oxen, because it was simply easier to find oxen in Britannia than any alternative. Priscus had not been strict when it came to personal baggage, not least because he had his mistress and plenty of luxuries to make campaigning comfortable. Many of his officers followed his example, and even Titus Cerialis had brought along a couple of slave girls as well as his other servants. When it came to military supplies, Priscus was similarly keen to be prepared for any possible occurrence. They had more heavy ballistae than Ferox had ever seen taken into the field in Britannia.

'Good!' Priscus had declared, when Ferox had asked about the allowance for machines and stones as ammunition. 'No one up there will ever have seen anything like this before. Let 'em see our engines smashing down their houses and their ramparts and they'll realise what they are facing. A few well-placed stones and it might all be over.'

There was no sense trying to explain, so the army went north with a lavish siege train, and also waggons full of shiny gold coins, some so new that they carried the bearded face of Hadrian on them.

'Rome can be a good friend as well as a terrible enemy,' Priscus declared. 'A gift of a hundred aurei immediately will be worth ten times the value of gold promised in the future. Let them see the glint. We might need more for this High King, if he has the sense to show proper respect.'

Ferox doubted that the arrival of an army, and presumably one lobbing stones at anything substantial enough to offer a good target, would give the High King much chance to be submissive and still keep face with his lesser kings and chieftains.

'He may be a barbarian, but he is still a politician,' the legatus pointed out. 'A man who knows how to make a deal and accept reality.'

So the army trudged north. The oxen were slow and stupid, which meant that the carts had to be well spaced out to stop them barging into the one in front. That stretched out the army on the march, even when the country was wide and flat enough to allow more than one column side by side. The oxen had to be fed and they had to rest, and most certainly could not walk for more than seven hours in a day otherwise they would barely move at all on the next day. The rain made the grass slippery and the ground soft, and all the boots and hoofs and wheels churned it into mud, and once again those at the back suffered the most. Carts bogged down and took much swearing and sweat to free. Slopes became a nightmare of skidding teams and vehicles.

Once, back at the start of the campaign, Priscus' army covered almost ten miles in a day. The gods must have realised that they were not paying sufficient attention for this miracle was never repeated. A march of eight miles or so was wonderful, seven abundantly satisfying, but five or six were good enough. On the really bad days they did less.

Thus the might of Rome crawled its way north to face enemies who were not yet enemies.

XVII

Four days before the Nones of August, among the Damnonii

'WE HAVE ALWAYS been friends of Rome,' Epaticcus said. 'Always,' he repeated, 'and that is my father's wish for as long as he lives, and my own deepest wish when I follow him.'

Ferox thought back to facing the young warrior in battle all those years ago. He had fought the Romans that day, alongside his foster father, a king of the Selgovae. Still, he understood precisely what the prince meant. He had fought for his foster father, even staging a lone attack on Ferox when the king was beaten to the ground, because that was what any good and free man would do. Oaths and pledges had to be respected or a man was nothing.

'We are truth speakers and our word is good,' Epaticcus continued. 'We have always kept faith with our Roman friends. Is this not true?'

The prince spoke decent Latin, just like his father, so Ferox was not needed to translate. Instead, he sat on a folding chair, a little behind Titus and a couple of other favoured officers. He had met Epaticcus and his escort the night before, and shared their camp, sending word that he would bring them to the Romans the next day. The result was that Priscus gave his army a day of rest, something that was becoming more and more common as the march continued. The legatus had ordered a tribunal to be built, although with most of the wood already carried off to fuel the soldiers' fires and nearly all the thin turf used for the rampart, all that could be managed was a square platform little more than a foot high, for attempts to go higher tended to crumble. Roman commanders were supposed to greet foreign embassies from a high place, to make absolutely clear to everyone that Rome was mighty and they were not, so this would have to do.

Epaticcus was a tall man, much taller than his diminutive father, and because he alone of the envoys had been given a chair, he was almost at eye level with Priscus.

'We are friends, faithful friends, who protect your merchants when they come to us, and are always true. Is this not so?'

Priscus gave no answer. He had begun by asking the prince to speak, and say all that needed to be said, promising to listen and make no interruption. 'Trick I picked up in the courts,' the legatus had explained to his staff. 'Be polite, show no emotion, listen solemnly and with every courtesy. Then when they have finished you tear them apart, point by point.'

Epaticcus matched the governor in dignity and solemnity. He was clad in mail, and wore trousers and a long-sleeved tunic so bright in colour that they must have been expensive. On his shoulders was a cloak, patterned in simple tartan and stained from travel to show that he was not some pampered weakling but a warrior. The iron helmet he had placed on his lap was well polished, but also showed signs of wear, including a small dent on the top.

Ferox had recognised him immediately when his men had approached the band of horseman. There was the same boyish enthusiasm and pride, made stronger because he was a man now, and had accomplished a good deal on his own. There was a scar on his chin and another on the back of his left hand to tell of battles fought. His dark hair was starting to get thin, especially on top, but was so wiry that it stuck up without needing to be stiffened with lime.

'What do you want, Ferox?' Epaticcus had asked as soon as they met. 'Or should I say what do they want?'

The prince had inherited a lot of his father's shrewdness, and might well make a very good high king, and like his father be a friend of Rome – as long as it remained in his interest.

'Do they want a war?'

'They want a victory,' Ferox had tried to explain. 'They want to be seen as strong.'

'Well they are, aren't they?' Epaticcus seemed genuinely baffled. 'They have marched through the lands and no one has dared to face them.' Much to Priscus' disappointment, the Novantae had shown no more inclination to display 'balls' than the Selgovae, and the same was true of the Damnonii to their north. There had been a few tiny skirmishes, some stragglers from the column had vanished, perhaps to attack or simply through desertion. Nowhere had a chief rallied his clan to war, let alone a king called out the muster of his tribe. People had fled, and it was easy enough to get away in plenty of time. Now and then chieftains and kings rode in to talk to Ferox and the other scouts, swearing loyalty to Rome. Priscus had met a few, and even if he was not there, his standard demand was that they hand over swords and spears as a mark of good faith. All had promised, and some had even delivered. There was a joke going around the camp that the new emperor had come up with a brilliant way of ensuring that the provinces never ran short of scrap metal.

'What more do they want?' the prince had demanded to know. 'Do they want my father to hand over hundreds of swords? ... They gave them to us in the first place as part of the treaty!'

'And you bought even more, keeping very quiet about it.'

'Huh! What has that got to do with it?'

Ferox did the best he could to help. 'Make it a chance for the High King to show off his generosity. Give them more than they ask for and show your welcome by your humility. If your father comes himself before they – we – push deeper into his lands, that will count for a lot. The governor needs to be able to write back that everyone respects and fears Rome and that peace is restored. Give him that and he will be happy.'

Epaticcus had not been convinced, and Ferox could not blame him. 'I think he wants a war, this Roman of yours. I think he wants it with us because we are big enough to let him boast. Huh! Like a young fool challenging a famous warrior.'

'We are both still here,' Ferox said.

'So far... But my father is not well, and there are others, loud voices who want war. There is not simply Roman pride and vanity to consider.'

Ferox had grinned. He liked Epaticcus more and more, and was proud of the prince as he faced Priscus and his tribunal, with a couple of dozen standard bearers formed up behind it, the aquila of II Augusta foremost among them. He spoke well, choosing his words carefully, staying calm and very respectful.

'My father asks why you have come to our lands with so great an army. Are there enemies here for you? There are none at the court of the High King.

'My father is old and frail, but still would meet with you to show once more his love for Rome if his son is not enough. He will bring whatever gifts would be proper to honour Rome, its princeps and his legatus. These are the words I bring.'

If Priscus was surprised, then he did not show it. Ferox knew that the legate had expected the prince to raise the question of Roman recognition of him as the High King's heir. Priscus had mentioned more than once how he planned to explain that the honour of choosing a successor was something Rome rarely granted to even the greatest ally. Such matters were for Rome to decide, when the time came, for that was only proper and did not imply any hostility to a ruler's heir or heirs.

'Young prince,' – Priscus was a similar age to Epaticcus, but assumed an added air of superiority – 'it makes me very happy to see you come today and speak of your love for Rome.' The legatus was gripping the arms of his folding chair, clearly restraining himself with immense effort from standing and gesturing in proper oratorical manner.

Ferox struggled to listen, for the speeches made by Rome's leaders tended to be long and tiresome. There was a lot about the greatness of the empire, more about the many virtues of the princeps, the noble Hadrian, who according to this version mixed the wisdom of Socrates and Aristotle with the decisive vigour and heroism of Alexander. It had always amused him how often Romans boasted of the achievements of Greeks.

There was more, much more, before the legate reached his point. 'Let your father come to meet us within fifteen days. We will press on towards him. Let him speak as you have spoken, and act as you have acted, and let him give to us one thousand swords and spears as symbol of friendship, and two thousand head of cattle or sheep to feed my soldiers. Then he will have Caesar's friendship forever, and a gift now of gold to seal it.' That was it, then, the demand at last, and twenty times greater than the demands made on any other leader. The High King was wealthier, far more powerful than any other tribal king, but the amounts were outrageous. Unless Tincommius was truly desperate for peace, then Ferox doubted that he would accept. Even if he did, the humiliation would be severe, and many would believe that the man who had united so many tribes was no longer so strong.

'Please take these words to your father, lord prince, with my greetings and my hope to see him within fifteen days.'

Ferox doubted that even Priscus believed that the deadline and the demands were practical. He was not sure whether the commander wanted to provoke a war, or whether he wanted to show how serious he was.

'Try to get half, if you can,' Ferox advised Epaticcus. The prince had come with just a dozen men to the Roman camp, and Ferox and Vindex escorted him back to rejoin the bulk of his warriors. 'He might be willing to do a deal. All he wants is a symbol, and he really has brought lots of gold and is desperate to give it away in some grand gesture.'

'I suppose that we could always take the gold and buy new swords to replace the ones we have given away,' Epaticcus suggested. 'But I do not know whether anything will be possible in so short a time… Father really does not want a war with Rome, and nor do I.'

'Nor does anyone, apart from Priscus and a few,' Ferox said. 'And they are in charge so the rest of us do not have any choice.'

The prince frowned. 'Thank Taranis and Cocidius that I am not a Roman.'

'I agree,' Vindex added. They were close to the score of riders forming the rest of Epaticcus' entourage. One of them waved happily, and rode his horse to meet them.

'Well I'm buggered,' Vindex said as he saw the man, for he was huge and looked exactly like Gannascus when they had first encountered the German.

'It's Aesucus,' Ferox explained, having gone through the same surprise the day before. 'Our lad's son.'

Vindex drew breath. 'Look at the size of him. Wonder there's any beer or meat left in the whole north, with two of them like that!'

Introductions were made, and farewells bidden. It was later afternoon, but Epaticcus wanted to go as far as he could today.

'Time is not on my side. Nor is much else, but I have to try,' he said as they parted.

Vindex nodded. 'Good lad, that. The pick of the litter.' Tincommius had several wives and more than a dozen children. His daughters were wed to kings as soon as they were old enough, the sons kept at court and served as leaders whenever the army was called out.

'Yes.'

'So is the donkey set on war?' The two of them were riding a little behind the rest of the Carvetii, so free to talk.

'Donkey?'

'Himself, the high and mighty legatus of Legio whatnot. He keeps asking us how our donkeys are keeping. Reckon he doesn't know the word for horse.' Vindex considered this for a moment. 'Daft bugger. Bloodthirsty too, by the look of him.'

'Tincommius might turn up with everything,' Ferox suggested.

'Yeah.' Vindex's tone made his opinion of that clear.

'Or he might come along with some of it, or send the prince back and promise the rest. Might satisfy the legatus. After all, summer's getting on and it is a long way home.'

'If not?'

'Then maybe Tincommius calls out his army and we find how good it really is... Or maybe he doesn't, and he does what all the chiefs and kings have done so far and keeps out of our way and waits. We march up and down, Priscus gets less and less patient and more and more angry. He'll probably start destroying things then.' Up until now, the Roman column had been under strict orders not to damage anyone's home unless they were resisted and so far no one had resisted in that way. The Romans took animals, grain and straw to consume, but the lack of wider devastation made this whole expedition even stranger.

'You reckon that's what he will do?'

'It's what I would do,' Ferox said.

'But you're a clever bastard,' Vindex observed. 'Tincommius is just clever.'

'It would make life difficult. By the time Priscus has got fed up with marching up and down and setting light to things, August will have gone, and we're even further from home.'

'Doesn't bother me,' Vindex said. 'I can always resign and go home. Wasn't me who lugged all this rubbish up here. Now if you…' He stopped as Ferox held up a hand in warning. The centurion pointed. There was a rider, half a mile away or a little more, silhouetted on the ridgeline.

Vindex squinted. 'That's you, isn't it?' The horseman was riding a grey, had armour that was drab at this distance, and wore a broad-brimmed hat. 'Yes, the daft hat, the dumb expression. Must be you.' A couple of auxiliary cavalrymen rode up alongside the lone figure. 'At least they've got helmets like sensible folk. Hate to think of the entire army dressing like you. Do you want to go over and talk to yourself?'

Ferox was tired. 'No.'

'Very wise. You're not the best of company. Oh, they've gone.' The horseman had ridden off and vanished over the crest.

'Then let's take a look. Bring a couple of men, but the rest can go back to camp.'

Vindex shook his head. 'Silures and Romans, neither make any sense.'

That night, five miles away

THERE WAS NO *mistaking his uncle, or that Brigantian cutthroat who was usually with him. They were looking back, but what would they see – a Roman officer going about his business while wearing a disreputable hat.*

He had three men close by, a dozen close enough to call and fifty he could summon in less than an hour, and they might be able to outstrip Ferox and his men before they reached the security of other Roman patrols. The temptation was strong, and she had promised him vengeance, although she had not said whether this would be for the deaths of his brothers. There were so many wrongs demanding payment. As a boy Silures were taught to cherish hate and nurture it so that it grew and grew and gave you strength. They also taught that it was wise to wait for the right moment, and trust the gods that it would come.

This was not the right time. 'Come on,' he told his men and led them away.

They were all dressed as Romans, as were the dozen others close by. The uniforms were not perfect, for they were trophies scavenged from the dead and other bits and pieces he had been able to find. They had shields which did not match, and he had found no one able to paint designs in a way that was convincingly Roman. Instead they had found or made leather covers for each one, and since patrols usually kept the shields protected in this way, that was convincing enough. Men had

had to lose long-cherished moustaches or at least have them cut to be neater.

Anyone who really knew the Roman army would not be convinced, at least not close up. He had tried to show them how to sit in the saddle, how to carry and wear their kit, how to have that resigned expression of a man who was tired and fed up, but who was used to hiding his feelings to avoid rebuke and punishment. A man had to have been a soldier, or lived around them for a long time to understand and his warriors did not. Still, they would do, for the deception did not need to last long.

They had to ride hard to catch up, driving the horses on. If anyone saw them, then they might have wondered what reason these Romans had to hurry. That did not matter, for he wanted to be seen, and half the time he had to use his hand to clamp the felt hat on his head as the wind threatened to take it.

The horses were struggling by the time they arrived, but as they reached the edge of the valley, he could see Epaticcus and his escort trotting along beneath them, barely a long bowshot away. The woods were ahead of them, clustering on either side of the track.

'Go!' he told four of his men, the ones who best passed as Roman troopers.

He watched as they kicked their horses hard to make then canter, and saw more than one beast stagger as it went down the mossy slope. His job was to sit up here and be seen. He raised his arm and waved. He could see the prince at the head of his men turn back to look.

'My lord!' one of his warriors was shouting just as he had been instructed. 'My lord!'

Epaticcus and his men stopped, the prince walking his horse back towards them.

'What do you want?' Epaticcus called in Latin. He was

staring and even at this distance it was obvious that he was puzzled.

The Wolf kept waving, and the prince saw him, saw the hat, and a big man in uniform riding a grey. He smiled and waved back.

'What is it?'

Of the four disguised warriors, only one spoke enough Latin to understand. 'You are needed,' he called back.

A huge warrior, so big that his tall horse looked a mere pony by comparison, trotted in front of the prince. He must have seen something, or sensed something, because he drew his sword.

'Halt!' he shouted in the language of the tribes.

Epaticcus seemed confused, uncertain, and the troopers were close to him now.

There was movement in the trees up ahead, although for the moment no one in the prince's party noticed it. The Wolf gave a thin smile, for the Silures did not show more emotion save when they were with true friends and it was time to celebrate, but he was satisfied because his warriors were there, just as he had planned, twenty of them on either side. He could not yet see the other ten who were to act as reserve.

One of the prince's warriors shouted in alarm as he spotted the ambush. The leading trooper hefted his spear and threw in one motion, the spear driving into the chest of Epaticcus' horse, which reared, screaming in agony, and threw him from the saddle. His helmet must have been untied because it fell, glittering in the air, and rolled away. The big warrior surged forward, swung his sword, and the 'trooper' who had thrown the spear was a headless corpse, torso still upright and blood jetting high. Two more of the disguised warriors closed with him, while the third tried to go round and reach the fallen prince.

Forty men charged from the trees, spears ready, little square shields held up. Ten riders came to the edge of the woods behind them. The men on foot hurled their throwing spears, as the prince's men wheeled around, trying to form some sort of line. Some horses were down, another bolted, and three riders lay in the dust.

'Come on!' he called and he and the others did their best to get their horses moving. Ahead of them, another of the 'troopers' slid off his mount, his mail split and chest ripped open by a savage cut from the giant's blade. The third man thrust with his spear and caught the giant on the leg, but then had his right arm cut clean through just below the elbow. He stared at the stump and the fountain of blood.

The last of the four disguised auxiliaries was past, heading for Epaticcus. The prince was staggering, but managed to rally himself and drew his sword, a long spatha. He waited as the horseman bore down, the trooper's spear poised to thrust or throw. At the last moment he swung his blade, cutting into the horse's mouth. It reared, but not before the rider had thrown his javelin. Some of the force had gone, but the distance was so short and the missile went low, beneath the hem of the prince's mail coat as the tip bit into his groin. He shrieked, swayed, but just managed to stay on his feet. The trooper was down, thrown from his mount, and Epaticcus limped across and stabbed down once. The prince's trouser leg was dark with pumping blood.

'Javelins!' the Wolf shouted as his men bore down on the big warrior. Behind them he could see that his men, outnumbering the enemy two to one, were killing the escort. A few tried to reach their prince and died.

The huge warrior had red hair and a shaggy beard. He glanced back, saw his prince in danger and began to step his horse backwards to help. Half a dozen javelins sailed through the air towards him. Two missed, another bounced back from his shield, but two more struck his mount and the last one hit the man in the side. Horse and man both staggered, and both were bleeding, but somehow they stayed upright.

'Take him down!' The Wolf needed to make sure of the prince, much as he wished to win fame by killing such a great warrior. Another spear hit the man's horse, and its front legs folded, so that it kneeled. The big man stepped away and then was lost from sight as the other disguised warriors surrounded him.

The Wolf saw the prince swaying as he tried to stand. His face was already pale, a pool of blood seeping into the ground around his drenched boot. He stared at the Wolf, frowning.

'Who are you?' he asked. His eyes seemed unable to focus.

The Wolf threw his own spear, and somehow the prince had enough strength left to hack it away with his sword, but the movement unbalanced him and the effort was too much for he fell.

The Wolf jumped from his horse and drew his sword. One of the prince's escort, bleeding from half a dozen wounds, tried to block his path. The Wolf feinted with his sword high, let the man raise his shield and then kicked him hard in the belly. The man fell, and one of his own warriors appeared to finish the job.

Epaticcus was flat on his back, staring at the sky, yet still he somehow had a grip on his sword and raised it feebly.

The Wolf stared down at him. The prince was brave, a good man who happened to be in the way. Even faced with death he showed no fear. His lips moved, although whether in an effort to speak or simply to spit at his foe, he could not tell. The Wolf stabbed down.

It was over. The last of the prince's escort were dead or

wounded. He wondered for a moment whether to leave one alive to spread the word, but decided to be cautious. Enough of the locals must have seen the 'Romans' chasing the prince and murdering him for the story to spread. Better not to take the risk of a man surviving who might just have seen through the deception, as his prince had surely done.

The huge warrior was dead, body hacked about so badly that he was barely recognisable. He had wounded two more warriors before he had fallen. One of them was too badly injured to be carried away so would have to be killed. Some Roman dead would help to sell the lie.

'No!' the Wolf shouted when he saw a man readying his blade to take the great warrior's mutilated head. 'Remember what I said. Now make sure that they are all dead and we can go.'

It was done, and soon the war would start.

XVIII

The Nones of August, among the Venicones

THE TOWER BURNED well. It was like a lot of the chieftains' dwellings hereabouts and further north, a tall round house with stone walls and timber thatched roof, so that there were several floors as well as smaller houses and animal pens joining on to it and around it. The shape was much like a stubby amphora, and now that the roof was gone it acted like an enormous chimney, flames shooting high.

Priscus was impressed by the heat, and was happier than he had been for days.

'Splendid!' he kept saying. 'Splendid! First blood to us.'

Half a dozen prisoners sat huddled together and guarded by a couple of cavalrymen from II Augusta. They were all of them very old, and all save one were women. No slave trader would want to buy them, but they were the legatus' prisoners and he had dismissed Ferox's suggestion of letting them go free.

'We'll keep 'em, and see whether the chieftain comes to talk now. You said one of them is his grandmother? There you are then. Should think he would want her back – assuming he likes the old bitch.' The legatus' roar of laughter was drowned when a beam fell and part of the tower collapsed.

Ferox was not paying attention. Seeing the tall house made him remember the time he and a handful of others had held out in a similar tower on an island far in the north. There had been a good reason for that fight, unlike now. A Roman patrol had gone to seize a flock of seven sheep watched by a boy. The boy objected, and with his sling put a stone into the eye of the decurion in charge. His shouts for help brought over some drovers, so as the troopers attacked it was not as easy for them as they had hoped. Then a party of warriors who had been shadowing the Romans, trying to avoid fighting while keeping an eye on them, decided to join it. The end result was a cavalryman dead, two more seriously wounded, the decurion blinded and standing a good chance of joining the dead in a day or so, as well as a number of injured horses. They claimed to have slaughtered far more of the tribesmen, and perhaps they had, even though they had most certainly been driven away without taking any of the sheep.

The rest of that day, several other patrols had stones and even a few arrows hurled at them, always from cover and always by attackers who fled after the first volley. A couple of horses were injured, and another decurion had the big toe on his left foot broken by a pebble by some bizarre fluke. They saw a few figures in flight and killed one young lad who was too slow.

Priscus decided that such open resistance could not go unpunished, especially when a day passed and no local leader appeared to beg for forgiveness and make a show of submission. A couple did send envoys explaining that they had had nothing to do with it, and blaming the kin of the chief Anavionus. That was sufficient for the legatus, who personally led a cavalry ala, two cohorts of his legionaries, and numerus II to punish the culprits. Ferox was half surprised that he did not bring up a ballista or two, but the outcome was some twenty farms burned, along with the chief's own house, and these six prisoners taken. Everyone else had fled, taking most of their goods and all their animals with them, so that there was little plunder, although the irregulars were very enthusiastic in looking for it.

'Sometimes a lesson is required,' Priscus assured them. 'We may need to repeat it and we may not, but soon they will realise that we are serious.'

Ferox was still surprised that similar incidents had not happened frequently over the last months. It did suggest that the tribes really did not want to fight, at least when the Romans seemed so strong. Now the mood was changing. At the start Priscus had issued strict orders to his men not to provoke the locals, and most certainly not to rob, molest or destroy. He had ordered several severe floggings to soldiers who had disobeyed, including a couple of men from his own legion. This, combined with a refusal to let anyone, even patrols, go ranging too far from the main column, seemed to have worked. The army was like some lumbering monster, so ponderous and noisy in its approach that everyone kept out of its way.

That had been back when the legatus was brimming with confidence and had a baggage train amply provided with food. Both his enthusiasm and the army's supplies were now greatly diminished. A letter had arrived, sent on by Spurius Ligustinus, who apparently still clung to life, to say that Hadrian's response to the report of his planned expedition was lukewarm at best.

Claudia had also received a letter when this despatch came up, and Sulpicia Lepidina informed her that the princeps was actually livid. Her wording was careful, but the two women had a code of their own, informal, and based on many years of friendship.

'He's really angry,' the queen had told Ferox two nights ago in their tent. 'Thinks this expedition is dangerously rash and out of all proportion to the problem. There is a new legatus on the way to take over. Do you wish to know who?'

'Does it matter?'

'Tiresome man. It's Falco. He's good, by all accounts, very good, but is coming all the way from his current command in Moesia, so won't be here anytime soon.'

'Pity.'

'Lepidina wants us to keep Titus safe – and out of serious trouble. You know what happened with her brother?'

Ferox had nodded. Sulpicia Lepidina's older brother was one of the biggest fools ever to don army uniform, and that was no mean feat. He had had the knack for getting himself involved in scandals, even to the point of suffering exile for a few years. 'What can we do?'

'Whatever we can,' she had told him. 'That's all any friend can do.'

Priscus had said nothing, but it was obvious that the summer was waning and he still had not achieved a great victory, whether through battle or the High King and others coming in to pledge loyalty to Rome. A really big success would surely please the princeps, even at this late stage.

Yet no word came back from Tincommius. News of the slaughter of Epaticcus and his party had spread faster than the wind. Everyone said that the Romans were the killers and nearly everyone added that the soldiers had been led by Ferox, husband to the Queen of the Brigantes.

'You didn't do it, did you?' Priscus had barely been able to conceal his amusement. 'I mean I know that you are often accused of murder, but you are still walking about so I guess there is nothing in it... Though after a while, everyone's bound to think that there is no smoke without fire!'

Ferox told him about the horseman dressed up to look like him. 'He's a man who calls himself "The Wolf". A renegade from the Silures.' He did not need to say more, for Legio II Augusta was based at Isca Silurum, in the heart of tribal territory, so Priscus ought to know them fairly well.

Priscus shook his head. 'Thought we had quieted you lot down at long last. But are you certain?'

'Near as I can be.' The traces left by the ambush showed a degree of care and planning that few war leaders displayed in these parts. On top of that, who else would dream of pretending to be him?

The legatus had sent a centurion, Felicio the regionarius, with an escort to Tincommius to tell him that the Romans were not responsible for the ambush and explain that Ferox – the real Ferox – was sure that the Wolf had killed the High King's son.

'If you're not careful, I'll send you next,' Priscus had told Ferox. 'Doubt you will be all that popular at the moment.'

Vindex was not there at the time, so Ferox found himself imagining the 'So what's new.'

Three days passed without word from Felicio, and then the trouble broke out over the sheep, and the legatus enjoyed himself setting fire to things. In the meantime, folk were saying that the High King was assembling an army, summoning all the kings and chieftains to bring their warriors and have them ready for war. It was hard to get close enough to talk at the moment, given the understandable wariness of the locals, and all Ferox was able to manage was a few shouted conversations. All told the same story. Tincommius would stand no more provocation from the Romans. Instead, he would fight.

'Hope he does!' Priscus declared when Ferox told him what the tribes were saying. 'I truly hope he does. If we hammer his army into the ground then it will be the best possible demonstration of Roman might. Make everyone think twice.' The legatus sighed. 'But sadly I do not think it will come to that.

He will bluster and threaten, and back down in the end. My only fear is that he will take his own sweet time about it. I want to head south again before the end of the month, so the sooner he fights or backs down the better.'

The army still struggled to move with any speed, and now it was beginning to struggle to feed itself as well. The flour had long since gone, and the sacks of grain waiting to be ground by the soldiers' hand mills were running out. What biscuit was left was hard and wormy, needing to be boiled for some time before it could be eaten, and the remaining salted meat was not much better. Priscus had embarked on this campaign with a generous, even lavish allowance of food, and now most of it was gone, which was just as well because there was far less transport to carry it. Behind the army there was a trail of animal carcases as ponies and horses and oxen died or became incapable of working any more, which amounted to the same thing. Some of the mules had died, but contrary in this as in everything else, most were doing well enough and kept plodding along, even though some had backs worn raw by badly made and badly fitted harness and packs. Their sores oozed pus and stank, and there were not enough men who knew how to treat them properly.

By this time something like a quarter of the draft and pack animals were dead, all of them butchered, which at least provided plenty of meat. The oxen were the most popular, tough and lean though the meat was, because the carcases were the largest; only some of the auxiliaries had a preference for horse meat. The dead transport animals helped, as did the periodic arrival of tribute in the form of sheep or cows, for the herd of cattle for slaughter had almost gone. They could take more, but that would mean sending out raids much further from the column. Tribesmen who did not fancy facing the main army were likely to be bolder when it came to a small detachment, a long way from immediate help, especially when they were defending the animals they needed to feed everyone through the autumn and winter. The same was true of the almost ripe wheat and barley. If the Romans swooped in and took the harvest, that meant days or weeks gathering it in, and as many or more soldiers guarding the ones working.

Priscus was bound to start gathering grain and cattle before long, for otherwise the army would no longer have enough to survive. Already they were on three-quarter rations and half for the irregulars and followers, but the legatus was not ready to give the order to start wholescale plundering.

'That's the last threat and the last punishment we have. Once we have done it, we have nothing left to convince them, so we will wait a few more days and pray that the High King sees sense or offers up his army for slaughter. What we do now is press him, make it abundantly clear that we will march all the way to his fort and burn down his Hall if he doesn't give in.'

Priscus decided to split the army into two. He took a little over two-thirds of the regulars and some of the numeri forward with just basic equipment for fighting and entrenching the camp. Each unit was told to bring tents for half of their effective numbers.

'Everyone will have to cram in if it's raining or sleep out if it is not,' Priscus told them. 'We are going to advance and do it quickly for a change.'

They did, covering seventeen miles and building a new camp. Over the next five days, the bulk of the remaining transport went back and forth, ferrying everything else in stages to the forward position. Two of the numeri along with other troops went with the train as escorts and to help clear the way when the path was poor or blocked.

Titus Cerialis expressed a concern about the plan. 'Should we divide ourselves when the enemy may be close?'

'They won't fight,' the legatus assured him. 'Wish they would, for if the High King sends his army, they would have to get past me first and I have enough men to rout whatever rabble he has mustered.' He leaned closer. 'And even if by some ill fortune they get around me, you have four thousand men, and that is more than enough to see off any attack. Mind you, I'll be jealous if my tribune gets all the glory, I surely will!'

Titus kept his remaining doubts to himself. Ferox was busy, sometimes riding with the advance patrols, hunting for news, and sometimes back with the convoys. Almost to his surprise, no one tried to attack the supply train while it was stretched out and vulnerable and eventually the army was reunited in the forward camp, which had been laid out with space for everyone.

'Well, that was exciting,' Claudia Enica said. She had waited, in her own words 'as part of the least important baggage' and only come up when Titus brought all his remaining troops forward with the last convoy, arriving just before sunset. 'What's this place like?'

There was little time to judge, for the next morning Priscus announced that they would begin the operation all over again, for tomorrow he planned to lead another rapid advance. He was delighted with the choice of the new advance camp site, for his maps and itineraries informed him that the army had used it before.

'One of Agricola's do you think?' the legatus asked, though he did not wait for an answer. 'What a splendid omen.' They were well into the territory of the Venicones, and the arrival of two local chiefs offering submission and promising to deliver fifty head of cattle in two days' time cheered the legatus even more.

'They say that they are too old to fight,' Ferox translated. Both chieftains and their half dozen followers did appear truly ancient. 'But they say that the High King has mustered an army and is coming to meet you, but that he still hopes to come to an agreement.'

That made Priscus even more delighted.

'However, they say that their young men have gone to answer Tincommius' call, and that they have killed the bull several days ago.' Ferox had explained many weeks ago, but it appeared that the legatus and his immediate staff had forgotten for their bafflement was obvious. 'It is a ritual test for the new warriors and I suppose a sacrifice. Picked men who have never fought in battle before have to wrestle a bull to the ground and kill it with their bare hands. Once it is done, the army is ready.'

The chieftains were happy to tell more. 'They say that the young men almost all want war, as do the half-brothers of Epaticcus. They talk of vengeance and of how the High King will eat up the Romans. They say he has fifty thousand men.'

'Unlikely,' Priscus said.

'I think it is just a great number. They say that it is a big army. I would judge that Tincommius could readily field twenty thousand, even thirty if all his subjects and allies appear. If some of the other tribes only loosely under his rule decide to show up, then who knows, perhaps a lot more. I doubt fifty thousand, but it would be wise not to underestimate his strength.'

'Hah!' Priscus remained unimpressed. 'Scum most of them. Farmers dragged unwillingly from their fields at harvest time.'

'Like the men who beat Hannibal,' Ferox thought, as he strode away from the meeting. Priscus wanted him to take out some cavalry and scout out the route for the coming advance. He took Vindex and thirty of his Carvetii, along with a turma from an auxiliary cohort.

'If we run into any real trouble, we run, understood?' he told them all.

For the moment the army was concentrated in the one camp just beneath a strange rocky outcrop, difficult for anyone to climb. It was a long bowshot from the rampart, but offered a useful landmark. The camp itself spread down a slope, a slightly skewed rectangle because of the shape of the ground. It was big, and for the moment full. Priscus had refused to abandon any of his siege train even though he was yet to find a use for it, so parts of the interior were given over to lines of waggons and piled equipment. For the moment, most of the draft oxen were grazing outside, protected by reinforced pickets. It was a peaceful scene, and even Ferox had to remind himself that there was a good chance a large enemy army was approaching, and could already be nearby.

The planned advance would move down a shallow valley, stretching for a good five miles. On his left, to the north west, the hills rose sharply, dotted with copses and some larger stretches of woodland, while to the right the land was open, the nearest hills several miles away. A stream chuckled merrily, winding back and forth in the shallow valley. There was the clear line of an old road, most likely an ancient path for traders and herds, improved for a while by the Romans when they garrisoned the lands up ahead for a few years. In most places the stream was easily fordable whenever it crossed the track. Ferox noted two spots where there would need to be some work done to make it easier for the carts, and three miles out they came to the remnants of an old bridge. That would either need to be repaired or the banks made less steep to improve the ford used in recent years by man and beast.

A little further, a neatly round hill rose on their left from the otherwise gently rolling ground, separate from the ridge.

Ferox took Vindex, the decurion and a couple of scouts up to the top. The camp was still just in view, more from the smudges of smoke from its camp fires and because of the rocky outcrop.

'Sir!' the decurion was excited.

'I see them.' Ferox had already spotted the movement. Ahead of them the wide valley curved to the right and began to narrow a little as it met a series of ridges. On one there was a dark patch, just like shadow cast by a cloud, except that there were few clouds today and none in position to cause this.

'What is it, sir?'

'Couple of thousand men, I should guess.'

'Is it the enemy?' The cavalry officer was so excited that he forgot the 'sir'.

Ferox made an effort not to sigh out loud. 'They will be warriors. Who else would wander around in such numbers? Whether or not they are enemy has yet to be decided. But unless Legio XX and the rest are more than a hundred miles off course, they are not our men, are they?'

The decurion grinned. Ferox sent him back with a note for the legatus. He would have preferred to keep the officer and send a reliable trooper instead, but was not sure that the legatus would pay sufficient attention to an ordinary soldier. There was more chance that he would question an officer, even a junior one, which meant that the report would be supplemented. 'Tell him we have not had a chance to scout the hills to our left,' Ferox added as the man was about to leave. The land up there bothered him, for the hills meant that he could see nothing beyond them.

'Want me to take a look?' Vindex offered, as the decurion galloped off. It was August and the days were getting shorter, but there were still more than four hours of good daylight left.

Ferox shook his head. It was tempting, but his duty was to

find out as much as he could about the bands of warriors they had spotted. 'We'll do it tomorrow,' he said, 'now let's push on.'

They kept to the open, which should mean that they ran into no surprises in these wide fields. The mass of warriors up ahead had moved and disappeared down the far side of another crest. That could mean that they were moving around to Ferox's left or moving back to hide.

'More?' Vindex asked, three-quarters of an hour later when they saw men spilling over another of the heights ahead of them. They were a little over a mile away, and there were fewer, perhaps a few hundred. 'Or the same ones?'

They waited, resting their horses. The warriors came closer and they could see that they were horsemen.

'Different buggers then,' Vindex decided, as the distant horsemen halted, presumably having spotted the Roman patrol. The two sides watched each other for a while, as two troopers headed back to camp with this fresh information. 'I wonder if we moved to the side a bit whether they'd do the same?' Vindex asked, then glanced behind him. 'Hey, do you see what I see?'

Ferox turned. There was a formation moving up the valley towards them along the track. They were kicking up dust in a line of thin, patchy clouds. That meant cavalry, several hundred as far as he could judge.

'Oh well, it'll give those buggers up there something more interesting to watch than us, I suppose,' Vindex decided.

'No, it won't.' Ferox saw that the warriors up ahead had turned and were riding back the way they came.

'What do we do now?'

'Push on a little,' Ferox told them. 'Very gently.'

They saw no more sign of the warriors up ahead. No doubt there were scouts watching them, but at this distance one or two men would be impossible to see unless they did something very stupid indeed.

Half an hour later, the commander of the approaching reinforcements came galloping up to join them, accompanied by a standard bearer with a white vexillum carrying golden letters with ALA AVGVSTA GALLORVM PETRIANA bis torquate civium Romanorum. White was an odd colour for an army flag, and it was rare to spell out the titles in full rather than abbreviate, but then the Petriana had always thought of themselves as special.

Ferox knew the commander, Caius Camurius Clemens. He was a gruff man, very aware of his eminence as one of the most senior equestrian officers in the province, and apt to stand on ceremony. He was not particularly likeable, but the man was capable and that was what really mattered.

'I hear you have some trade for us,' the prefect said as he reined in. The flanks of the standard bearer's horse were foamy with sweat, but his commander rode a neat little mare who looked as fresh as the spring. Some four hundred men from the ala were coming on at a steady trot to join them, and some way behind there was a column on foot.

Ferox reported all that they had seen and what he had deduced. 'They've moved back under cover now, my lord,' he said. 'I am not sure just how the valleys beyond run, and whether they can go around on either side without us seeing them. We have not seen any sign of them for a good half hour.'

Vindex was pointing, as some warriors came riding over the top of the nearest hill to their front. Even Clemens grinned. 'Unreliable fellows, aren't they.' He stared at the hill top. 'About a hundred?'

'That we can see,' Ferox confirmed.

'Quite. However, the legatus wants us to pin the enemy and

keep them here. He's worried that they might slip away before he has a chance to smite them like one of Jupiter's thunderbolts. I have my splendid rogues – oh, and there are a lot of your tag, rag and bobtail coming up behind – so I do not think we need to worry.'

When they arrived, Clemens formed his ala into two lines, each two deep and about one hundred and fifty paces between them.

'You watch my flanks,' he ordered Ferox. 'Don't think anything will appear, but no harm in being careful. And sort out the numerus when they deign to join us. We might need them to beat the quarry into the open.'

Ala Petriana advanced at a walk towards the hill, but before they were halfway, the warriors turned about and rode off. The auxiliaries followed, still at a walk, and when he was nearer, Clemens ordered one turma to push forward and reach the crest. They obeyed and signalled that all was clear. The prefect reached the top and stopped, beckoning Ferox to join him.

'You just missed them,' Clemens told him, pointing across to the ridge in front of them. This was pasture land, the long grass rippling in the wind. There was a clear path where it had been trampled. Ferox suspected that more horsemen had been waiting behind the hill, but whoever was leading them had decided to withdraw rather than fight. They must have gone back quickly, because no one was in sight any more.

'Well, that's all the fun for today,' Clemens announced. 'We'll camp up here, keep the horses down slope and post plenty of sentries. Should be safe enough.'

Ferox was surprised. 'Are we not returning to camp, my lord?' There was little proper daylight left, but the track was easy to follow.

'Not my orders. The legatus wants the enemy pressed. I'm

not going into those hills up ahead with night falling – no one can expect cavalry to do that – so we will rest and can start out in the morning. Who knows, we may well get fresh orders before then.' Clemens unfasted his helmet and then lifted it off his head for a waiting trooper to take. The prefect ran his hand through his thick black hair. 'I'll need these scouts of yours, but if you want to go yourself and take one or two back as an escort then I've no objection.'

Ferox was tempted, but the Sun was setting and numerus II was loping into the position, the men giving every sign of being tired and confused as their elderly commander alternately cursed and encouraged them. None of them were carrying blankets, few had cloaks and he doubted that they had brought any food. He could not provide them with any of those things, not tonight, so felt that the least he could do was share their discomfort.

It was a cold camp, and Ferox was relieved when Clemens gave the order forbidding fires, for there was no sense in making themselves too conspicuous. Then the wind blew in clouds and brought almost two hours of driving rain. Everyone was drenched and many huddled together to share what little warmth they had.

'You off then?' Vindex asked as he stood beside his horse, cloak drawn tightly around him and water dripping from the hood.

'Just taking a look,' Ferox replied. The Silures raised a man not to fear the dark, but to embrace it as an ally. They learned to move silently, to find their way, and most of all to wait and watch. Ferox was as cold and uncomfortable as anyone else, but wanted to make sure that there was no one watching them in the dark. The rain made it easy to get past the sentries without being noticed, for few were able spare much attention from their misery. He went out about fifty paces, lay down on the sodden grass and waited. Before long the rain stopped, and soon the sky cleared to reveal a field of bright stars and a waning Moon. He crawled a little, moving as slowly as he could, then stopped and watched. The Moon had risen higher by the time he was sure that there was someone else out there doing the same thing. At least one man, and perhaps a second.

An hour later one of the guards shouted out a warning on the far side of the camp, near the horses. That was closest to the stream and someone coming back from fetching water was mistaken for an enemy. The warning was taken up as an alarm, and a musician from the ala sounded his trumpet. The cavalry stood to arms and most of the irregulars fled in screaming panic. There was chaos and confusion, orders shouted, men trying to rally others. The old sweat in charge of the numerus had a great booming voice and employed a remarkable range of insults.

During the panic Ferox saw a figure move forward fast, past his front before lying down close to the camp. 'Got you,' he thought. Now that he knew where the other man was he would spot any fresh movement. He still was not sure whether there was another out there, but if so, he doubted that he was close.

Eventually some sort of order was restored, and after a while even the swearing stopped. Peace returned, and lasted for a while until once again an alarm went up and there was a fresh stampede. This time, the fleeing irregulars must have got among the grazing horses because a lot of them were also swept away.

Once again the watching man took advantage, coming forward at a crouch. Ferox stood as he came close, took three paces, saw another dark shape further off, so when he clamped his hand across the closest man's throat he thrust up hard with his pugio, driving the dagger underneath the ribcage. The warrior gasped, there was a stink as he fouled himself, and the body went slack.

The other man fled into the night and Ferox was not inclined to follow. Slowly, the panic died down.

XIX

The morning, at the Roman camp

PRISCUS ADVANCED BEFORE dawn, taking five cohorts of Legio II Augusta with him, the eagle at their head. They formed the centre of the column. The vanguard consisted of ala Augusta, two cohorts of auxiliaries and half of numerus I. With the legionaries went half a dozen carroballistae and a small baggage train. Two more auxiliary cohorts, both equitata with their own cavalry, and a couple of centuries of numerus III formed a rearguard.

'Not that there really needs to be a rearguard with you behind me,' Priscus assured Titus Cerialis, 'but there is no harm in doing things according to regulation.'

There were all the usual rituals of marching out, as units formed up, and then the legatus himself called out asking the men three times whether they were ready for war. After a long summer of campaigning, it was all routine, but, for the first time since the start, Priscus did not use a herald and the rumours of action made the men bawl out 'Ready!' with immense enthusiasm. The noise meant that no one could sleep, but then the activity had long since ensured that the whole camp was awake and up.

'I do not know whether or not we will get a battle today,' Priscus explained.

Titus had heard all this before, first at the consilium three hours ago and then again privately from the legatus. He could sense that Priscus was excited, even nervous.

'If they will not be drawn, then we will set up the new camp just as planned. Have a convoy ready with tents and food to send forward as soon as I call. The lads from Legio XX can escort it, along with some of the irregulars. That should be enough, I think. Yes, that will do. And even once they are gone you will have five cohorts, including the auxilia of course, a couple of hundred cavalry and the rest of the numeri. Oh, and enough artillery to besiege Carthage!'

Titus smiled dutifully. 'We will manage.'

'And better yet, you are in charge again – free from having me breathing down your neck. Not that I think anything will happen back here, but it is a relief to know that I can trust you if it does, and trust you to support me.'

'Of course.' Titus Cerialis saluted. 'Good hunting!'

Priscus gave a cross between a salute and a wave. 'Remember, send that convoy as soon as I call. And see you in a few days' time when we have finished the move to the new camp.'

The column had marched away, and even the rearguard was only dimly visible by the time the Sun came up. There was a lot of cloud and a strong wind blowing from the west, so that the clouds hurried across the sky. Titus kept his force formed under arms for an hour, and then let all save the units on guard dismiss to eat *prandium*. There was plenty to do and this time he was determined to get a tower erected next to the main gate. He did not want anything fancy, simply a raised observation platform. It was something he had missed in the last camp, so this time men would go to that woodland to the east and fell enough timber.

Titus ate well, something that was rare for him so early in

the day. For once he felt hungry, which was just as well given that the day was likely to be one of long waits and sudden frenzied activity. The first time he had enjoyed the thrill of being in charge of his own force, even if his task was largely that of a muleteer on a grand scale. As the days had passed and his force diminished, he had grown more and more nervous. No doubt he would feel the same this time around. For the moment, he felt content and free. Priscus had been difficult company in recent days, worried that the campaign would not achieve anything worthwhile. That was one advantage of being a subordinate. The plan was not his and he could only be tarred up to a point if it did fail.

His senior officers appeared – a tribune, two prefects, the senior centurions and Pertacus and Claudius in charge of the numeri all or partly still in camp. It was not a bad little army. They had just begun their conference when a soldier arrived with a message. It was important enough for them all to get up and tramp over to the rampart by the main gate, the one pointing up the valley. Grooms were waiting with horses, but he shook his head. A walk would keep everyone alert. There was something very satisfying about trailing a gaggle of officers wherever you went.

'There, sir!' A centurion pointed up towards the valley side on their left. Titus wished for his tower, because the walkway of the rampart was barely five foot high and did not help very much. 'Can you see it?'

Titus saw one of the low peaks turn darker than the others as a cloud's shadow passed over it. He stared at where the man was pointing, and the dark shadow was as clear as anything, especially when the sunlight rolled over it. There were sparkles of light, like the tiniest stars in the sky. There were men there, quite a lot of them, and perhaps a mile and half away.

'Definitely not ours?' he asked, sure of the answer, but wanting to check just in case.

'Not up there, sir.'

'Fetch me a writing tablet,' he ordered.

A *cornicularius*, waiting behind the officers, stepped briskly forward, a folded wooden tablet and stylus in hand.

There was a pleasure in authority. 'Take this down,' Titus ordered. 'Warriors in strength on heights to north west. Add the time. Got it? Good. Send a trooper and three men as escort to gallop after the legatus.'

'I think they're going,' Pertacus said. 'Yes, I am sure of it.' The former prefect gave one of his wry smiles. 'As sure as one can be at this distance of course.'

'He's right,' a centurion added.

'Send the despatch anyway,' Titus said firmly. 'The legatus needs to know.' He was wondering what to do. Getting patrols up on that ridge to see how many folk were up there and what they were doing was the obvious thing, but he had to be careful. Priscus had taken most of the cavalry with him, and he would need to keep some in hand to react if there was a threat, particularly a threat to any convoy or reinforcement heading down the track to aid the legatus. One could see as well as fifty, his father had often said, but he did not like the idea of sending a handful of troopers so far out on their own. He would need a couple of patrols to search the land up there. He had been told that there was something of a plateau, but there had not been time to see it for himself. At least two patrols, each of twenty or more men to be safe, and suddenly a fifth of his horsemen had gone, surely for several hours at least. Would not many more than a hundred and fifty be enough to escort any convoys and keep communications open with the legatus? When it came down to it, how reliable were the irregulars? They made up almost half of the horsemen available. If only he had more—

'Good morning, my lady,' Pertacus said, startling him from his thoughts. 'You are...' the suave officer hesitated, although it sounded deliberate and controlled... 'most striking this morning.'

Claudia Enica gave a gleaming smile as the tribune turned around.

'Good morning, especially to you, dear Titus.' Her long red hair was plaited and coiled up on top of her head and she wore no obvious make-up. Instead, she had a shirt of mail over a short tunic and a tartan cloak flung back across one shoulder. Her legs were bare apart from felt boots, the sort the Steppe peoples wore. In her left hand she carried a bronze helmet, and on her belt there was a gladius on the left and a curved sica on the right.

Someone coughed, more than one muttered something or grunted, for though several of them were younger than her, they were not used to seeing so handsome a noblewoman not only clad in this way, but walking with such obvious confidence. When he was nine, Titus had fallen in love with Claudia Enica as the older sister he did not have, and when he was past twelve he had fallen in love with her again, this time in a different way. Back then seeing her legs like this would have been a dream come true, so long, so shapely, so full of possibilities.

'Good...' his voice cracked and he coughed to clear it. 'Good morning, dear lady – or should I say, fair Athena.'

'Minerva, I suppose, although perhaps I am disloyal, for the Greek Athena is usually shown cutting a better figure.' She gave them all another lavish smile. 'And good morning to you all. Have we a battle on our hands?'

'Do you plan to lead us, lady?' the centurion Claudius asked.

'Oh this.' She glanced down at herself in mock surprise. 'I just fancied taking a ride. A stola is not really suitable at such times. But, of course, I do not wish to get in the way.'

There were a few stammering gallantries, until Titus cut them off. 'It may not be safe out there...' he began.

'How thoughtful, but I have my own escort. Twenty strong men, most of them former soldiers, ought to keep one little girl safe, don't you think? I have a mind to ride up on top there.' She nodded at the ridgeline. 'My husband is a worrier, and was keen to take a peek up there, but doubted that he would get the chance. I promised that I would do my best. As I say, he worries so, like most older men.'

'I'd be happy to take my cavalry along as well,' Pertacus said enthusiastically. 'Cannot let a lady take risks, after all.'

'That is sweet,' she replied, before Titus had a chance to say anything. 'But you are needed here. And don't forget that many of your men are my own folk, so they need their commander here to guide them.

'I do not wish to cause inconvenience, but if you could spare a few troopers and a centurion, and perhaps a score of men from numerus prima? I know there are a few left behind – and they're also my own folk, of course. Well then, that would be wonderful, quite wonderful, and more than adequate.'

Titus remembered his stepmother telling him about how well Claudia Enica had led and fought with her men in Dacia. He had wondered at first, for it was not how Romans expected women to behave – or for that matter how Batavians expected women to behave. Yet he loved and trusted Sulpicia Lepidina, almost as if she was the mother he barely remembered, and knew that she spoke the unvarnished truth.

Titus Cerialis made his decision. 'I am sure we can oblige.' He nodded to his staff. 'See to it.' It was not perhaps the orthodox way of doing things, but at the cost of a single officer, a handful of troopers and some irregulars, he would get scouts up on the hills, with enough spare men to send messages back if they found anything while the rest kept looking. That left a hundred and eighty or so horsemen at his disposal should anything happen. He would have liked twice that number, but this would have to do. 'Thank you, lady.'

'My pleasure,' Claudia Enica assured him and trotted down the bank of the rampart. Titus could not help admiring her legs, even though the cloak blocked his view.

'Well, gentlemen, there is much to do. Each of the legionary cohorts will take a turn standing to arms two hundred paces in front of the camp to reinforce the pickets. Two-hour shifts for the moment, and then we shall see how the day goes. Well then.' Titus was still not quite used to giving the orders, for nearly all the time Priscus had acted as column commander and left him with little to do. He gave what he hoped was an encouraging smile. 'Let's get to work.'

XX

The second hour of the day, with the advance guard

PRISCUS RODE AHEAD of the long column winding its way down the track, appearing with fifty cavalrymen from II Augusta as his bodyguard. He barely listened to the reports of the last night.

'Anything this morning?'

'A few scouts. We saw a herd of cattle driven across that hilltop,' Clemens pointed, and moved his arm to show the direction they had gone. 'They vanished down there. Guess that was an hour ago.'

Priscus frowned. 'You did not take a closer look?'

'Cattle are tempting, my lord,' Ferox explained. 'A very tempting lure if you are planning an ambush.'

The legatus dismissed the concern. 'You have nearly a thousand men, what have you to fear?'

Clemens did not flinch at the commander's impatience. 'Not any more. We lost quite a few of the irregulars during the night. No idea where the little sods have run off to... My judgement was the same as the centurion's. It was too much like a trap to take the risk. Once you sent word that you were bringing up the army – we got that message before dawn – then it was my duty to stay here and wait. No sense in bringing on a battle so far ahead that it will take an age for everyone to come up.'

Priscus glared at Ferox for a moment, as if blaming him, before his face softened. 'Yes, well done.' He was silent for a while, as if preoccupied, and Ferox wondered whether he had received another letter from Spurius Ligustinus expressing Hadrian's concern about what was going on. Even more than usual, Priscus came across as a man desperate to get the war won in a day. Yet still he was a senator, and senators loved to talk, so soon the legatus was explaining in great detail how he was bringing up the pick of the army, and would push forward, either to fight or prove once and for all that he was set on marching to Tincommius' stronghold and dictating his terms there if the High King did not submit beforehand.

'Have we patrolled the heights?' Ferox said when Priscus asked if there were any questions. Ferox had turned to face back down the valley. There was a thin mist rising off the ground, so that the ridge seemed to rise like a row of islands in a milky sea.

The legatus was unconcerned and glanced back only for a moment. 'I am sure that Cerialis will do that when he has time.'

'Would you like me to ride up there, my lord?' Ferox offered. He was tempted to point out that they had divided their force when they did not know how many warriors were out there, where they were and what they planned to do, but doubted that it would do any good. With senior officers you had to nudge them towards working it out for themselves. It was a bit like a shepherd and his dogs, handling sheep.

'No, I need you.' Priscus waved an arm expansively to take in the hills ahead of them. 'That is where the enemy are. I can smell 'em! They're up there, watching us. Probably too frightened to fight, but they may just be fool enough to think that because we have only part of the army, they have a chance against us. That is our hope, and all of you need to pray to all the gods you worship and promise them anything if they make the enemy believe that.'

Ferox went over to join Vindex. None of the cavalry had gone missing, although at least a quarter of the men from numerus II had failed to come back after the second panic. The rest looked nervous, unhappy, and most of all hungry.

'There's supposed to be food coming up with the army,' Ferox said.

'Aye, and who'll get it first?' Vindex asked. 'Not us, and certainly not those poor buggers.' He stared at his friend. 'You worried?'

'Always.'

'Aye. At least the horses have had a rest. Reckon we might need them.'

'We might need to eat them the way this is going.'

An hour later the advance guard had arrived and cohors I with the eagle at its head was close behind. There was also a despatch rider, feather tied to his spear for II Augusta liked traditions, the older and less intelligible the better.

'From Cerialis. Sent during the first hour,' a tribune explained after breaking the seal on the folded tablet. '"Warriors in strength on heights to the north west." That is all, my lord.'

'Hmmph,' Priscus snorted. 'What strength? He needs to learn to word his reports more precisely. Still, no matter. The tribune has ample forces to protect the camp and support us. How long before the rest of the troops join us?'

'An hour at the most, my lord.'

'Splendid,' Priscus replied. 'After that give them an hour to rest and take some food, then we will form *agmen quadratum* and march straight up that hill over there. That should stir something, and if not, we will keep going until we reach the new campsite. Better send someone back to Cerialis to send us the convoy as soon as he can.'

'Yes, sir.'

No one else said anything, so Ferox felt obliged to ask the obvious question. 'These warriors in strength to the north west – there might be a lot of them up there, perhaps even the bulk of their army. Everything we saw yesterday that moved off went in that direction. And we haven't looked so we don't know how many are up there.'

'If any.' The fingers on Priscus right hand clenched and unclenched as he kept his temper. It was clearly a struggle. 'Cerialis can handle anything that comes from that direction. He has half a dozen cohorts, and the camp itself, in the extremely unlikely event of a heavy attack.' He grinned, trying to turn it into a joke. 'Don't fuss man, or we'll be starting at our own shadows!'

'But the convoy? It has a long way to go.'

'Quiet!' It took the legatus a moment to regain his composure. 'I am glad that my officers think, but I hope that they will credit their commander with a thought or two of his own! There are risks, but they are small, and bring greater opportunities. If the convoy is attacked, then we have the enemy between our two forces and we can crush him in a vice. Once again, if they are foolish enough to attack then I will be delighted, truly delighted. But remember we are not talking about Alexander's Macedonians, or Hannibal's motley crew. These are barbarians, pure and simple, and not from the great martial tribes, but hill brigands.'

Ferox gave in, hoping that a better moment would come.

He might be wrong, and after all did not know anything, but the legatus' very assurance made him all the more afraid that Tincommius' army was close. They might walk into a battle they could not win, or find that the enemy was past them and threatening the camp. Cerialis had a decent enough force, but not enough men to defend a huge camp and all the baggage if the attackers were strong and knew what they were doing.

The man he had killed last night was not his nephew, nor a Silurian, but someone had taught him the ways of the tribe. If the Wolf as he called himself was here, which seemed certain, then there was one leader on the other side who would not come at them in a straight line. Nor was Tincommius anybody's fool. He had not built up and trained this army to hurl it to destruction without trying to get every possible advantage. Instinct, the instinct that had kept him alive all these years, screamed out to him that the legatus was searching in the wrong place.

'Is there any food for the numerus?' Ferox asked one of the narrow-stripe tribunes of II Augusta.

'Doubt it. We have half rations for ourselves for the rest of today, but that's all. I thought they had their own. Maybe there will be something when the convoy comes up, but not before. You could try asking one of the prefects though, they might know?'

Ferox got nowhere, so went to see the legatus, who was mounted alongside his escort.

'Good man, I see they found you – that was quick. We're going to take a look up those hills ahead of us and I need you with me. Some of those mounted rascals you call soldiers as well, if you please.' He frowned. 'You had not got the order had you?'

'No, sir, I came about the food.'

'Food?' Priscus spoke the word as if he did not know what it meant.

'Yes, my lord. The men of numerus secunda have not eaten since yesterday morning when they left camp.'

'I see. Do we have anything to spare?' His staff's faces made clear that there was nothing. 'That's a shame. Better send them back to camp. We don't need them any more up here, and it will be quicker for them to walk to their food than for their food to walk to them!' The legatus chuckled at his own wit and was joined by his officers. 'Give the orders, somebody. Now, Ferox, fetch your rogues and follow me!'

Claudia Enica was enjoying herself more than she had for months, even if that thought seemed a mild betrayal of the times spent with her husband. She was free of the bustle of camp, of its stench and the sense that nowhere was private, for at best the leather of a tent separated her from the rest of the world. On top of that she was riding a horse in the clear morning air and doing something truly useful. The temptation was to kick back her heels and let the animals run for all they were worth, an urge that became all the stronger as they started up a defile leading up the ridge. The horses had to be held back not to race up the smooth grassy slope. This was good ground, sure underfoot, and she allowed them a canter when they reached the top, before slowing down again. They might have a long way to go and she wanted the horses to stay fresh.

The centurion took his party to the left, peeling off to search in that direction, as she led her own escort along the ridge top. There were plenty of little rises, and all the time the ground rose and fell so that it was hard to see more than half a mile or so in any direction, except back into the valley. The camp was like a child's toy, with several small clusters and one thick line made up of the pickets and duty cohort in front of it. From up here, they all seemed tiny. She stared in the opposite direction, but could not make out the legatus and his men, only the hills where they had gone.

They kept close to the edge of the valley for a mile or two, and she took care to spot all the places where the ground led easily downwards. There was no sign of life, apart from a few sheep, dotted like white flowers in the distance. In normal times she would have expected the land to be covered in the animals, for this was good grazing, but perhaps all that meant was that the folk here were as nervous about the Romans' intentions as everyone else.

'Here will do,' she told the old warrior in charge of her shield-men. 'Let's see what's over there.' He nodded and shouted out to the riders they had sent out as scouts, who were hundreds of paces in front of them.

They began to climb again, saw the scouts vanish, realised when they got there that this was a false crest and that the top of the hill was still ahead of them, came to the peak and saw nothing. There was a shallow valley ahead of them, more hills beyond, so they kept going.

It was hard to see very far in any direction, even though the land was almost bare of trees. It reminder her a little of the mountains around Dacia.

'My queen!' The old warrior reined in and stretched out his hand to stop her. They were on the far slope of another little valley, but the two scouts leading the way had stopped on the hilltop ahead.

'Stay here!' she said, and almost smiled as the man obeyed,

although he signalled to one of the warriors to make sure that the man followed her. She let her gelding surge up the slope.

'*Omnes ad stercus*,' she heard one of the scouts say in an awed tone as she came close. The man was one of the former soldiers, hence the curse, but neither he nor his companion seemed to notice her as she stopped alongside them. Then she saw why.

Ahead of them, in a wider valley than any they had seen up on this high ground, was an army. Thousands upon thousands of warriors were sitting or standing in the fields below them. There were lots of horses, some chariots, and so many people that it reminded her of the crowds coming out of the Flavian Amphitheatre at Rome.

The closest were not much more than a quarter of a mile away, a cluster of a few hundred men slightly apart from the rest. Several were standing, staring up the slope at them. Only one seemed to be armed, so perhaps he was their sentry. At the moment no one seemed particularly impressed by their arrival. There was a low hubbub of noise, not quite conversation, but the sound of men moving, eating, grooming horses and polishing weapons.

Claudia Enica turned to the former soldier. 'Ride to the legatus up the valley. You know the way?' He nodded. 'Good. Ride as fast as you can. Tell him what you have seen – you know how they talk. Tell him that the army is here, behind him, and tell him of its size. Now go!' She sent the other man back to the camp, telling him to ride his horse to death if need be, to warn Cerialis. No Brigantian ever said such a thing lightly, and the man understood the urgency, as he galloped away.

That's it, then, Claudia Enica thought to herself, now time to go. She knew that Ferox might have stayed to watch them, but then her husband would never have sat silhouetted against the crest for so long. As the thought came, so the camp beneath her started to react. Horns and trumpets sounded, the murmur of sound grew to a roar like breakers on a beach, and suddenly all the little figures were moving, rushing here and there like ants when a child had poked their nest with a stick.

She turned and went down the hill. It was time to go.

XXI

The fourth hour, at the camp

TITUS CERIALIS WATCHED the convoy set out with mixed feelings. The summons had come sooner than he had expected, but that did not matter because everything was ready and it did not take too long to form up the escort and the train itself, with twenty waggons and one hundred and fifty pack animals. By the sound of it, they ought to catch up with the legatus in three hours or so, perhaps more if he kept pushing ahead. Again by the sound of it, Priscus was content and making good progress, which suggested that everything was going to plan. No reports had come back from the patrols up on the high ground, which was surely a good thing. He smiled as he remembered his mother often saying that if Claudia Enica said nothing, then there could not possibly by anything to say, however trivial.

The work party had come back with timber and were even beginning work on his tower. Cerialis had lost two cohorts from his force, and a turma of cavalry to help them, and he would have preferred to have kept them, but all in all the day was calm and quiet and there seemed no great cause for worry.

Half an hour later, a Brigantian riding a lathered horse came splashing through the mud of the main gateway, calling for the tribune. Titus listened as the man explained in strongly accented

Latin that the queen had found a vast enemy army camped up on the plateau. 'Tens of thousands,' he said. 'Cavalry, chariots, the lot.'

'Were they moving?'

'No, they were waiting, but they must have seen us.'

'Quite,' Titus said. He gestured to the cornicen on duty outside the principia tent. 'Sound the alarm. Then sound stand to arms and officers to me.'

The notes rang out, each call repeated once, and there was something about the brazen messages than filled Titus with energy, even as his head was flooded with questions. It took time, it always did, to explain the changed situation, deal with questions and make decisions, but somehow it seemed easier now that there was less chance to think.

'Should we recall the convoy, sir?'

'No. The legatus has called for them, and for all we know his need is greater than ours. Just because there are warriors up on the ridge, that does not mean that there are none facing him and he'll need that food, and the tents and tools if he is going to entrench his own position.'

'Shall I take my cavalry and warn the convoy?' That was Pertacus, who seemed to feel that a sardonic smile excused him from saying 'sir'. However, the idea was not a bad one.

'How many do you have, fit to ride?' Titus resisted the urge to say 'acting prefect'.

'Seventy, sir.' That was better.

'Fine, take them out – and use your discretion. Fulvius is in charge of the convoy, so only tell him to come back if he feels that he cannot get through.'

Pertacus nodded, and ran off excitedly. A slave was waiting, holding the reins of a tall grey so pale that it was almost wholly white. That was an affectation typical of the former prefect, who always wanted to be noticed. Titus smiled at the thought. After all, the dour Ferox favoured a similar grey over his other horses and that had nothing to do with appearance. He forced his mind back to the present as there were more questions.

'Do we meet them in the open, sir?' The sole narrow-stripe tribune to remain in camp asked the question.

'Only if they come to us. They may not, we just don't know, but the army doesn't fight from behind walls unless it has to. We'll defend the camp in the plain outside. Give me that papyrus and a pen. Thank you.' He sketched a quick plan of how he wanted the units to deploy. 'Calones and anyone able to hold a stick can man the ramparts as best they can. Even if we brought everyone back inside we could not line the walls, so they will just have to try as well as they can. I doubt anyone will come past the rocks behind us – too hard to climb. The irregulars can watch our left, but the main threat will come to the front, so that's where we'll be strongest. The right is wide open, but we'll see any threat there in plenty of time to do something about it. Any more questions?'

'What about the animals? Do we let them graze, my lord. The oxen need it.'

'Yes, but only for the moment, then we had better herd them all into camp. There'll be space once we have taken down and packed the tents and gear of the legatus' force. That should only take a couple of hours. After that we bring them inside.'

'How about using some of the artillery?' the senior centurion of VIIII Hispana asked. 'That could spoil their day.'

'Yes, if there is time. Yes, that is good. Right, all clear.'

'Yes, sir.'

'Then let's get on with it.' Titus Cerialis felt more alive than he could ever remember.

***

Claudia Enica turned for a moment, before she followed her warriors down off the ridge. All of them were ahead of her, apart from the leader and the man he had told to stay with the queen at all times.

'We should go, my queen. There's nothing more we can do here.'

No one had tried to chase them, at least not with any real urgency, although whether this was because there had not been too many cavalry nearby or because no one felt that they were important was harder to say. It was not that the great army was not coming, it was just that they were not bothered any more about having been seen. More than once she had glanced behind and seen large masses of horsemen, and far, far more warriors on foot coming, all advancing steadily.

'Wait,' she told them. This was the most open part of the plateau, so that she could see a good half a mile, as far as a low ridge. As they watched row after row of brightly painted shields appeared over the crest and headed on towards them. They were in groups, no doubt clustered together by clan and tribe, but these were strangers to her so she could not tell who they were. Years before, she had led an army of her tribe and faced another raised by her brother. The warriors over there did not look very different at all.

'There! Are some going to the left?' It was hard to see, as the ground meant that no one went for long in wholly straight line.

'Perhaps, my queen,' the old soldier allowed. 'But they might just be heading for one of the slopes down. We need to go, and tell the tribune that the attack will strike soon.'

They followed the others, who against her instructions had

stopped and were waiting for them some fifty paces down the slope. Though many were old soldiers, they were here as her men, her bodyguard, and no orders would change that.

As they rode down the slope, she could see the regulars forming up in front of the camp. There was a body of horsemen a long way ahead of them, following the trail, and in the far distance a column of troops and carts plodding along. They rode on, keeping at a brisk walk until the slope opened out into the plain, when they started to canter, heading towards the troops drawn up in front of the camp. There was a line of four distinct bodies, each a cohort probably, with auxiliaries on each flank and legionaries in the centre. Their shields were grounded, the men standing at ease, until suddenly trumpets blared and there were ripples along the ranks as they stood to attention.

'My queen!' a man shouted. There were horsemen, lots of horsemen, surging down the slope after them.

'Come on!' she called, and urged her gelding into a gallop. The Roman lines were close now, and she could make out the ornately decorated blue shields of the Tungrians, the cohort from Vindolanda.

There was a strange thrumming sound, louder than the thumping of hoofs on the grass, and a dark grey stone bounced a few yards away on her left, throwing up a great plume of earth.

'No!' she screamed. 'No! It's us!'

Another stone followed, and the warrior riding beside her, the man told off to stay with her at all times, was grinning, and then his head was smashed to ruin and she felt hot blood spattering over her face.

'No, you stupid bastards!' she screamed, but the sound was swamped by a blare of trumpets.

There were no more stones, and she saw Titus Cerialis on horseback next to the auxiliaries, waving to her.

'You've brought friends, I see,' he called cheerfully, then noticed the blood on her face. 'Hercules' balls, are you hurt?'

'I am fine.' There did not seem much point telling him now that they had just killed one of her men. The rest had all made it back, and there was too much to do. 'You have a battle on your hands. They will be here soon. Thousands of them. It is hard to tell with such numbers, but I should think that there were ten or twenty thousand in the camp, and for all we know there might be others.'

Titus Cerialis did not seem convinced, and she could not altogether blame him, for numbers were so very hard to judge, and the Romans always prided themselves that discipline and skill mattered far more than mere quantity. 'Well, we shall have our hands full.'

'I think some might be trying to work their way around behind us.' She pointed and the tribune turned to look, but neither of them could see anything apart from the hills. 'Where do you want me?'

'You've done enough already, and I thank you,' he said. 'Although if you are willing, have a word with the irregulars over there, and keep an eye on that flank for me.'

'Of course.'

Titus turned back to survey his little army. Most of his cavalry were on the far right, some one hundred and forty men, a third of them irregulars and the rest from the *cohortes equitatae*. He also had scraped together twenty-five men under a decurion as a reserve and his own bodyguard if he needed it. Next to the cavalry, cohors I Tungrorum had just short of four hundred men, and on their left were the two cohorts of II Augusta, each a little smaller at around three hundred and fifty effectives, and on the far left cohors II Asturum, new to the north, for their usual base was down south. They were the strongest unit in his first line, and, with four hundred and fifty men, almost at full strength.

The army preached the importance of reserves and that it was better to have depth than let a line get too thin. All of the four units in his front line were deployed just three deep, the minimum considered safe, and his second line was far weaker. He had the VIIII Hispana, the strongest cohort he had, and someone had found almost a hundred and fifty men left behind by the units with the legatus, to form a second formation. That, and his little turma of cavalry, were the main fighting units. He had about fifty archers as skirmishers, and between each cohort were two scorpiones, while behind the first line he had a row of six bigger ballistae, able to lob stones over the heads of the men in front. Anyone coming straight at the camp was going to have a tough time of it, shallow formations or not.

His left flank was more of a worry, but he had little choice save to trust the numeri to hold on. There were almost a thousand of them, most of them from numerus prima, which was obviously the best of the lot, and since they were Brigantes the queen's presence ought to help encourage them. None of the easy slopes down from the ridge led in that direction, so if his luck held they should not be pressed too heavily.

Titus dictated another message to Priscus and sent it, wondering about giving the man an escort but deciding that he could not spare anyone. He did give the trooper one of his own horses, so at least the man was as well mounted as could be. Just then he realised that the oxen and other beasts were still out grazing behind the camp. He sent another trooper to round up some calones and tell them to start driving the animals into the shelter of the ramparts. That would take a long time, but it would take hundreds to hurry it up, and he did not want to pull hundreds out of the fighting line.

Then everything slowed down as the enemy took their time arriving, but by the time he was almost ready to change his mind, they were already too close. A few hundred horsemen swept down the nearest ravine, coming in little clusters. As they reached the open plain, they spread out to cover the front of the Roman line, keeping well back. After the unfortunate incident with the Brigantes, Titus had given strict instructions for the ballistae only to shoot on his specific order. The warriors fanned out and stared at the cohorts. There did not seem much point in tiring out his own cavalry by risking a charge, so Titus let them be.

Behind them came chariots, skimming across the grass and Titus marvelled at their agility, even though his father had often spoken of his own amazement when he first saw them. Then great masses of infantry, warriors grouped in hundreds, followed them.

It was a shame that they did not rush. Titus would happily have faced a charge by men already tired from running for miles to reach the field of battle. That was what you expected of barbarians, or so all the books said. They were wild, more animal than human, filled with passion, and the tribes of the north liked to boast and show off, rushing at the enemy and relying on brute force and courage. Titus had never really believed those tales, not least because as one of the Batavian royal house on his father's side, he was as much a barbarian as anyone out there. So were a good many of his soldiers, apart from the irregulars, and the army had drilled them to think as well as fight. Ferox had told him that Tincommius had crafted something different from most tribal armies, and as he watched them deploy, he could believe it. There were distinct units, some of them with shields of one colour, and a few helmeted and mostly in armour. This was no mob, but something resembling a proper army, and that gave him cause for thought. Already, his men were outnumbered, and more and more enemies kept debouching from the defiles to join them.

It was so tempting to attack, to strike hard and quickly. These men might be a lot more soldier-like than most warriors, but they had never faced the iron fist of a Roman charge. He reckoned legionaries and auxiliaries alike could carve through the men in front of them like a hot knife through butter. Then let's see how their confidence held. A lot might run, and he could start wheeling his cohorts to sweep the rest away, his little force of cavalry covering the flanks. The army encouraged boldness, and this was bold, even reckless, so perhaps his barbarian side has its blood up.

Without the camp to protect, he would have done it, taking the fight to them and not giving them a chance to build up their courage, gambling that his men were better than even the best tribal army, and striking before the numbers turned too far against them. Yet that risked driving deep into the enemy masses and leaving the camp exposed. He could not expect the calones to hold long on such a huge perimeter, and if the enemy took it, even for a while, then they were bound to lose a lot of supplies and equipment that could not be replaced. The stomach of the army was guarded in that camp, and if it was lost, then there was no knowing how the army would cope, so far away from the frontier.

There was no real choice, and Titus knew that he had to fight here, and hit each attack only when it came close. He rode behind the front line. Faces were drawn, some pale and silent, some chattering away, probably only dimly aware of what they were saying. The lines of soldiers reassured him.

'Look at that daft sod!' one man said, suddenly.

A chariot had come forward, within long bowshot, and the warrior riding in the car leapt down and began to posture and shout at them.

'What's he selling?' another legionary asked.

'Bollocks by the look of it.' The warrior wore a bronze helmet with a tall red plume, carried a shield, and had a sword slung from his belt, but otherwise had no clothes. He was covered in weaving patterns of woad or perhaps just paint.

'Tell him we've already got some.'

Titus Cerialis grinned. He knew that some commanders believed it was good for the men's spirit to let a few soldiers go out and meet the enemy in single combat – assuming our men won, that is. His father always condemned such posturing with a vehemence that made Titus wonder whether the old man had done that very thing in the past. More chariots were driving into the space in front of the armies, and other warriors came forward, singing their own praises and mocking the enemy.

Titus rode past the cohort to the gap between it and the next unit. He stopped by a scorpio, and happily remembered the name of the soldier in charge.

'Bitus, isn't it?' The man nodded and seemed pleased to be recognised. 'Now when you hear my tubicen sound a blast, I want you to kill that naked fellow. Just him. One shot, and an amphora of wine if he goes down. Then save your bolts for later, because we are going to need them. But wait for the signal. Understand?'

'Yes, sir.'

Titus told the crew of the next bolt-shooter to aim at another warrior, a stocky fellow with a bright red shield and gleaming scale armour. He kept going, walking his horse behind the next cohort to give similar orders to the crews of the two machines beyond them. He rode back to the centre of the line and then told the trumpeter to give the signal. It was clear and sharp, in spite of the hubbub of the massing enemy and the near constant braying of their horns.

Each scorpio cracked like a whip as it spat the heavy dart at the enemy. One missed the warrior and threw off splinters as it broke the spoke on the wheel of the chariot waiting behind. Another made a warrior yelp, as the iron head burst through his shield and drove into his arm. He staggered, but somehow did not fall. The other two warriors were down, one screaming and the naked one lying still, a bolt sprouting from his left eye. Bitus and his men had earned their amphora of wine.

Horns fell silent as the Roman line cheered. The centurions let the men shout for a while, then raised their hands, and the *optiones* behind the line bellowed for silence. This was the army, after all.

The masses of warriors facing them began to hum like a swarm of bees, as the horns redoubled their strident enthusiasm and the harsher calls of the carnyx trumpets joined in. Individuals ran forward, screaming at the camp, so that the line of shields facing the Romans seemed to ripple and move like a live thing.

It would not be long now, and Titus was glad. There were five big masses of warriors on foot ahead of him, on a front only a little longer than his own line. Each group was deeper than his own men's formations, at least twice as deep and perhaps more although there were no neat ranks. The cavalry outnumbered his own, but nothing could be done about that. As far as he could see, the warriors were on quite small ponies, and very few of the riders wore any armour. Even their shields were small, so hopefully that would give his troopers an advantage.

With a great roar the mass in the centre of the enemy line

charged, the men breaking into a run as if racing to be first to reach the enemy. Trumpets and horns called wildly as the men playing them tried to charge and blow at the same time. The other groups came forward less quickly.

Titus Cerialis turned to the line of heavy ballistae and waved his arm in a circle over his head. The sound of the heavier engines was different, less a cracking whip and more the thump of a heavy hammer. The stones sounded different as well, thrumming over his head like a cask rolling. Ahead the archers and scorpiones were shooting as well. Titus craned to see over the cohort of legionaries lined up ahead of him. Warriors shook as arrows struck home. Other men slowed in their charge to lift their shields protectively. The bolts from the scorpiones pitched victims over like children's dolls. Then the heavy stones landed, ploughing through the massed formations, shattering shields, flesh and bone. The bands of warriors quivered and slowed.

The archers shot the fastest, the bolt shooters sent one missile for every three or four arrows, and the ballistae for every dozen. There was time for two more volleys of stones before he circled his arm again and the men in charge of each team screamed at them to stop.

'Now!' Titus shouted and the musician sounded the advance. The cornicines with each cohort repeated the command.

'Cohors VII will advance!' the senior centurion of the unit in front of him bellowed. Somehow the enemy's noise seemed reduced. All along the line there was a rattle of armour and shields as the men stiffened to attention. 'Forward march!'

The line stepped forward. This cohort was quickest off the mark, but only by an instant. Opposite them, the bands of warriors had paused, reeling under the barrage of missiles, but then started to come on again. Their lines were a lot more ragged than the Romans, except on their left, where the two groups were some of the more organised and better equipped troops.

Javelins hissed through the air towards the Roman lines, landing short and either skimming along through the grass or sticking into the ground. The auxiliary archers were still shooting, and the scorpiones cracked one more time before they stopped, for as the cohorts advanced it was too difficult for them to shoot without risking striking one of their own.

'Steady, boys! Wait for the orders,' the centurion called. He was a pace ahead of the centre of the unit, where the six signa were clustered together in the third rank.

The warriors surged forward and there were more javelins. The legionaries raised their shields, bracing them as missiles thumped home. A soldier shrieked as a spear came low and the head drove into his calf. He dropped, and the ranks went past and closed up again.

'Front rank, ready!' The warriors were close, less than twenty paces away.

Each man in the first rank raised his pilum, ready to throw.

'Now!' More than a hundred of the heavy spears were thrown straight and level at the onrushing enemy.

'Second rank!' the centurion yelled as the pila struck home. They were long weapons, and all their weight was concentrated behind the small, pyramid-shaped points. These met shields and the wood cracked as the iron heads went straight through, sliding quickly because the long shank was thinner than the head itself. The points still had the power to pierce mail or scale and even flesh.

Titus watched in awe as the enemy line shook, men falling, men screaming, and then the second volley of pila came in, and the chaos was renewed.

'Third rank!'

Some shields were pierced by two or more of the missiles as they thumped home. Warriors were screaming, some on the ground writhing, the lucky ones untouched by the points and trying to shake the heavy missiles loose from their shields.

'Charge!' the centurion led the way, his gladius already drawn, and he turned the command into a screaming war cry. The soldiers reached down to the sword on their right hip and pulled the short blades free, and as they did they yelled. Few of the warriors came to meet them, but they managed to put together a ragged line. Shield thumped against shield. There were grunts of effort, rage and fear, rare clashes of sword on sword, more of iron biting into flesh.

The band to Titus' left did not even stand to meet the charge, but broke and streamed to the rear. The Romans followed, killing at will anyone they could catch. The warriors ahead of him and the ones on the far left of the Roman line fought briefly, then folded, the men in the rear running away first and then the rest. The slaughter was greater because more of them were slow to flee and some were injured and could not go quickly. Younger legionaries and auxiliaries forgot their drill and hacked and slashed with all their might. The older soldiers killed economically, saving their strength and delivering neat, carefully aimed blows.

The two more-organised bands held on for longer, fighting hard, especially the one facing the far right of the Roman line, for the Tungrians had the lancea spear, much lighter than the pilum and less devastating at close range. The warriors fought hard, meeting the charge, using their shields to batter and overbalance the enemy just as the Romans did. On the flanks the Roman cavalry made a few charges, making the enemy gallop away only to come back after a while. Most of the time individuals or groups closed with the enemy, threw a javelin or two and then turned away, always to the right so that their shield protected them.

It seemed a long time, but could only have been short before the two bands of warriors gave way. They went back slowly, sullenly, but they did retire. Titus had the recall sounded and brought his cohorts back to their original position. As they passed, men finished off any wounded enemies. Titus guessed that there were five times as many enemies down as Romans, and that was good, even though more and more bands of warriors kept coming onto the plain. The flow seemed endless. A new line was massing two hundred paces ahead, a mix of the defeated bands and fresh ones. There seemed to be more of the organised units, distinct groups one with yellow shields and two more with blue. The cheeky fellows were even forming a second supporting line, as if they were Romans.

A rider appeared behind him, one of the Brigantians from the royal escort. 'Queen's compliments, sir,' the man reported just like the soldier he had once been. 'And she has held the first attack, but is worried that they are extending to her left and she cannot stop them.'

With great reluctance Titus ordered the scratch unit to reinforce the irregulars. It was probably wise to have disciplined troops on his extreme flank, even though that left him with just the men from Hispana and his little escort as reserves.

Some calones were manhandling carts out from the main gate. He could see the stacks of pila and lancea spears. A man could only carry one in combat, certainly only one pilum because it was so heavy and cumbersome, but an army carried more in the train. He wondered whether there would be time to issue them to the men in the fighting line, but then a blare of horns and carnyxes answered that puzzle.

'Here they come again!' someone shouted. The archers and

scorpiones began to shoot, and he waved his hand to signal to the ballistae. Stones whizzed over his head and went to spread ruin in the enemy ranks.

Titus wondered what Priscus was doing, whether the legatus was fighting his own battle or driving his men to march back here as soon as they could. It was hard to hold out much hope for the convoy. There was dust in the distance, far too much to be caused by those men or Pertacus' little band of cavalry.

'Cohors VII will prepare to advance!' The centurion's shout brought his mind back to the moment. There was nothing he could do to help them. Nor was there any point sending another messenger to the legatus. Priscus would send help or he would not. What mattered was holding the enemy.

'Come on the Capricorns!' Titus Cerialis yelled at the top of his voice.

'Forward march!' The line of red shields with the Capricorn symbols of the divine Augustus above and below the boss went forward. Javelins slammed into them. A man dropped, a throwing spear in his throat.

XXII

The sixth hour, in the hill country

PRISCUS HACKED AT the air with his riding whip. Why was the old fool taking so long? Ferox had his uses, and knew the country and its people better than anyone, but he was so cautious, seeing threats everywhere. It just made everything take an age. There was a perfectly clear path heading straight to the High King's envoys – if that was who these men really were – and the centurion was looping around in a wide arc. The gully did not seem boggy from here, and the man was just wasting time, time that was precious.

'Is that all he says?' the legatus asked the tribune who had questioned the Brigantian messenger. Priscus had been silent for so long that the question came as a surprise.

'Yes, my lord. Our scouts came across a huge encampment up on the ridges north of the camp. Tens of thousands of warriors, he claimed. Did not say what time this was, though.'

'Hmmm. Not sure the ignorant bastards can tell the time,' Priscus said, forcing himself to joke. 'Or count past twenty once they have finished with their toes!'

The laughter was muted, for the staff sensed that the commander was worried.

'And Cerialis?' he snapped.

'Large forces of enemy advancing on the camp. He has

formed to meet them. Says that he is heavily outnumbered.' The tribune thought for a moment. 'Time was the fourth hour, my lord,' he added. The legatus had heard the message several times, so surely already knew, but thoroughness was the safer option given his current mood.

'I know, man, I know.'

'I could take the alae back,' Clemens offered for the third time. 'Almost a thousand prime cavalrymen coming in behind them would ruin anybody's day. We could be there in a couple of hours, less if we're lucky and don't spare the horses.

'And strip me of all my cavalry!' Priscus snapped, face red, before he managed to control himself. He shrugged rather than apologise. 'No. Cerialis has more than four thousand men and a good position – and there are those ragamuffins from the numerus who must be back with him by now. There isn't an army in these parts that could shift him. He will have driven them off long before you could get there, and I don't want to split my forces again. If we all go back there then we could not possibly do any good. All we'd be doing was chasing our tails for a day and losing time. Those fellows over there are from Tincommius.'

'So Ferox says,' Clemens growled, then realised that he had spoken aloud. 'Apologies, my lord.'

'We will know very soon. If they are, then Tincommius is ready to talk, which means he will give in. Oh, we might have to ease up a little on the public submission, but he'll do it, dead son or not. He's smart enough to know that Rome is better as a friend. No, no, he'll see reason because it is to his advantage.' In recent days the legatus had come to sound more and more like an advocate presenting his case. He knew it, and did not care, indeed was happy, because there was a logic in such a case that helped cut through the confusion and uncertainty of war.

'If they're here, then their army must be back behind them somewhere – just like we believed all along.' He felt the 'we' was a nice touch, for his officers seemed worried and that was not likely to make them do their jobs well. Certainty was what a soldier needed, that absolute faith that he was right and would win.

'Oh, I know we've seen some. A few hundred here, a few thousand there, but nothing really big.'

'But the reports from Cerialis, my lord?' Clemens was the most experienced man there, which added to his already substantial self-confidence.

'Advance guards and strays, nothing more. Remember that this is not a real army. This Tincommius calls on his tribal and clan leaders to root out their fellows, get them armed and bring them to meet for a battle. All we have seen is ones coming from different directions. The main body, and all the royal troops, all the good ones, will be coming from Tincommius' capital – and that is up there, ahead of us. There won't be enough to put Cerialis in real danger. The fellow should be glad. He'll get a neat little battle and an easy victory. How many young sprigs get that in their first posting? Help to get a career going that has started late. Once he has won, he'll realise how lucky he has been.'

Priscus beamed. The case was clear, the evidence good and the conclusion simple and obvious. No one chose to contradict him.

'Now let's hope Ferox gets on with it.' He could see that at long last Ferox and that brigand who always seemed to be beside him were close to the barbarians. Ferox was sure that the staff one of them carried was the mark of a herald, and since they were waiting and showing no hostile move, he appeared to be right.

After so many delays, there was progress. Priscus had given up any thought of a real battle today – these hills were so clearly empty, and, of course, logic dictated that envoys precede an army rather than follow in its wake. Some of these barbarians could talk, oh how they could talk, but even so he ought to give them his message – condescend to soften his terms a little – and send them away happy in an hour or two. There was still time to reach the new campsite, and the convoy ought to arrive before darkness. Cerialis could have his scrappy little fight. A victory, however small, was useful for the campaign, and there was no harm in having done a good turn to someone starting out in public life. Priscus was already planning how to give plenty of credit to the young tribune, as the promising officer given a chance by the careful strategy of his commander.

Everything was falling into place. He just wished it would fall a little faster. His stomach agreed. He had planned to ride and take a look and return to the main body in time to eat. Now, there would be talks, probably long talks, and his hunger kept gnawing at him. Pity they had not seen any animals up here. Sharing roast mutton or venison with these envoys would have been a nice touch.

The legatus' stomach gurgled. His staff made sure that they did not hear it.

Ferox and Vindex dismounted and walked towards the men waiting beside the smoking fire. Gannascus towered above the rest, but of the half dozen others he thought he recognised chieftains he had met in the past. Ten horsemen stood their horses some distance back, and the only other man he knew was the strangest, a thin, bare-legged man, who was famous for knowing every path in the lands. He had been ancient twenty years ago, but here he was, as spry as ever. People called him 'the Traveller' because no one remembered his real name.

'Well I'm buggered,' Vindex murmured and pulled out his wheel of Taranis. Some folk said that the Traveller was a wandering god with deep, perhaps dark, purposes of his own. He and Ferox had met him before, another time when the old man had agreed to help Tincommius.

'Better let me do the talking,' Ferox said, and glanced behind him. The legatus and his escort were half a mile back, a patrol either side of them at a similar distance. There was a gully in between, and he and Vindex had taken care to ride around it rather than going through, because it was thick with heather. There was a path leading through, but anyone could be hidden in there. He kept thinking about the man he had killed and the other one who had run off.

They were close now.

'Do you think they know we did not kill Epaticcus?' Vindex whispered.

'Probably. But you can see the herald's staff. They'll respect the truce of that.'

Vindex sniffed. 'Would you if someone had killed one of your kids?'

Ferox was not sure, but if the High King wanted to talk then there might just be a chance of avoiding a fight and still giving the legatus what he wanted.

'Greetings, Flavius Ferox,' the Traveller called out. 'Greetings Vindex of the Carvetii. Do you speak for Rome?'

'We do,' Ferox said. 'On behalf of Priscus, great general of Rome and envoy of the emperor.'

'Then come and talk in peace,' the Traveller said, beckoning.

Gannascus moved past the others and strode towards them. He was not smiling, but instead seemed sad.

'I am so sorry,' Ferox began.

The huge German swung his fist. It was like being kicked in the head by a dozen horses. Ferox dropped, eyes flickering, struggling to see and to breathe.

'Hey!' Vindex shouted, jumping back.

Gannascus reached down, his hand open. Ferox managed to focus, saw the grin and took the hand. His cheek was throbbing.

'That was in case we are wrong,' the German rumbled, pulling him up.

Ferox swayed, tried to speak and it hurt, so spat out some blood instead. He could see some of the legatus' escort cantering towards them, so raised his arms and waved. Eventually, they understood and halted.

'Someone else will talk now,' Gannascus told them.

Ferox rubbed his face. He was not sure whether a tooth had come loose. 'Good,' he muttered.

An older man began. 'We are sent by the High King. He does not wish for war with Rome. He is ready to fight, if he has no choice, but he does not wish for it.' He paused, waiting so long that Ferox was about to reply, then continued. 'Many want war. Some of the High King's sons want war and are with the army massing now. They will fight and fight soon, if older, wiser heads cannot agree.

'Some are near our camp down the valley,' Ferox said. 'There may be fighting already for all I know.'

The chieftain sighed. 'The High King ordered everyone to wait until we had spoken to the Romans. He wants peace.'

'Volisios doesn't,' Gannascus rumbled.

'That is true,' the older chieftain admitted. 'He craves war and reputation, but he is young, king's son or not, and there are plenty of wiser heads with the army. They will wait – unless you attack them.'

'Let us hope,' Ferox said. 'I will call my general, so that you may give the High King's message to him.' He turned and waved as they had agreed.

The legatus and his party trotted forward. There were seven officers, a couple of cornicularii, and eight troopers from the legion's cavalry. Priscus pushed his horse into a canter, surging ahead, and the others speeded up to match him. They were coming straight at them, the gully in their path.

Ferox waved at them to go around. Priscus ignored him.

'No, not that way!' He drew his gladius.

The legatus was going down the slope, the others jostling to follow because the path through the heather was only wide enough for one at a time.

'Come on!' Ferox shouted at Vindex and ran, not quite sure why he felt so very certain. 'Ambush!'

Priscus disappeared as his stallion quickened pace again, Clemens just behind him.

Ferox and Vindex were thirty yards away, more than half of the staff already invisible as they went through the low ground. Priscus' plumed helmet appeared, then his horse's head as it jerkily bounded up the slope this side, both rider and mount unscathed, and Ferox wondered whether he was just nervous, but did not stop running.

Priscus' stallion reared, neck arched, a spear buried deep in its side. The legatus struggled, then was falling, arms high. Horse and man vanished into the gully as the air was filled with shouts and screams.

Clemens came up the side, his horse bounding, blood slick on its shoulder, and the prefect was fumbling to draw his sword and at the same time to steady the animal. Ferox ran past, Vindex close behind. He wished that he had wrapped his cloak around his left arm as a shield, but there had been no time. As he came over the lip of the gully he saw a frenzied battle amid the heather. There were horses down, plenty of riders too. Two warriors stood over a body, slicing again and again. It was Priscus. The warriors were wearing drab tunics and trousers and had their faces painted half black and half dark blue.

Ferox rushed down the slope, almost tripped in the heather, and that gave a chance for one of the warriors to turn and face him. The man's long, blunt-tipped sword sprayed drops of blood as he raised it to strike. Ferox dodged, felt the wind of the other man's blade as it sliced past him, and drove forward with his gladius, taking the first warrior in the throat. Vindex hacked through the arm of the second man, then hit him with his left fist to knock him over.

The last of the legatus' escort were coming down the far slope or up onto the lip. A legionary cavalryman threw his spear and impaled a warrior, but another jumped past, found a tribune trapped under his dying horse and slammed a short-handled axe into the Roman's face. Most of the officers were down, for they had been the ones caught in the gully when the warriors had sprung up from nowhere, hurling spears and following them up with swords and axes. A senior centurion sat in the heather, clutching desperately at the bottom of his mail, his hands red with his own blood.

With the bellow of some great beast, Gannascus ran down the slope into the middle of the fight. He reached down with one great hand and pulled the centurion back just before a warrior could reach the man with his spear. Letting the wounded man go, ignoring his moans of agony, the German grabbed the spear shaft, wrenched it aside and swung down, his sword biting into the warrior's skull. The blade stuck, so Gannascus left it and took the spear in both hands, swinging it over his head like a staff, driving back a pair of black-painted warriors coming towards him. Vindex was beside him. He lunged to kill one man, and the German slammed the spear into the side of the other warrior's head, once, twice, then turned the shaft in his hand and stabbed the swaying man in the belly.

A man erupted from the heather beside Ferox, who tried to turn, tripped on a low branch, falling hard against his hip, but somehow keeping a grip on his gladius. The warrior had the top of his face painted black and his chin bright red. He tried to stab with a long spear, only for the butt end to catch in the heather. Ferox slashed hard into the man's leg. The warrior screamed, dropping the spear and another cut went through flesh and bone, so that he fell. Ferox tried to push himself up, tripped again, because his foot was still caught, then narrowly rolled out of the way as a sword hacked down beside him. The man came closer, teeth bared and very bright against his painted skin. He cut again, and Ferox barely manged to block it with his sword. There was a shout, and a horse came rushing through the heather.

'Bastards!' Clemens croaked the word. 'Bastards!' He sliced down with his spatha, missed, but the warrior was distracted and Ferox had the chance to lunge into the man's stomach, twisting the blade because from this posture it was hard to drive it in very far. Clemens cut again, missed again, and yelled in frustration, 'Mongrel!' The warrior dropped his sword and grabbed at Ferox's sword, trying to pull it free, so he pushed himself to his knees and leaned with all his weight behind the blade. Clemens' spatha slammed into the warrior's shoulder, sending up a gout of blood, but coming away with the iron blade bent at an angle. 'Shit!' hissed the prefect, and hit the man again and again on the head.

The fight was over, as suddenly as it began. Ferox scrambled to his feet, leaving the gladius buried in the dying warrior, and ran up the slope. He saw the High King's envoys clustered in a circle, and on either side of them the Roman patrols were closing.

'Stop!' he yelled, but his mouth was full of blood and still sore from the punch and the word came out as a croak. He sprinted towards them, spitting as he went, waving his arms to attract attention, and managed to shout, 'Stop! Not them!'

A decurion was far ahead of his men and threw a spear, which flashed as it went through the air and thankfully stuck harmlessly into the ground. Hoofs pounded as Clemens galloped past, waving his bent sword in the air.

'Halt! Halt!'

The troopers obeyed, and contented themselves with forming a circle around the chieftains.

Clemens sawed at his bridle to turn his horse. The animal was panting and wild eyed, its sides slick with blood.

'Tell me why I shouldn't kill them?' he asked.

'Because it wasn't them, or Tincommius.'

'Save it. I'll sort things out over there. You see what you can do.' He nodded back towards the gully.

There was not much. Priscus still breathed, although no one could understand how. His right arm had gone below the elbow, his face was unrecognisable, mutilated beyond repair, and there was a spearhead with a broken stub of a shaft driven clean through his cuirass and into his chest. His breathing was noisy, red bubbles on his lips, and even a surgeon could have done nothing to save him. The centurion was a different matter, if only he lived long enough for them to bring the surgeon.

There was no question of moving him. Apart from Clemens, all the other officers were dead, as were the clerks and two of the escort. Several more were wounded.

There had been seventeen warriors hidden in the gully since the night before, and Ferox wondered whether other ambush parties were concealed in likely spots. Otherwise, the warriors must have known that the envoys would come this way and wait just where they did.

The last warrior squealed in torment as Gannascus lifted him in the air, a spear driven through his body. The German shook him like a fish, and the man kept shrieking, arms and legs flailing, until he was slammed down into the ground. Gannascus ripped the spear out savagely, spilling the warrior's innards, and the man gasped a few times and then went silent.

'These bastards killed the prince,' Gannascus said, his voice softer than Ferox had ever heard him in the past. 'And my son.' It was sometimes easy to mistake the man's vast strength and strong accent for stupidity. 'Volisios told them to do it.' His voice was bitter now. 'I'll kill the little shit. Kill them all.'

It took longer to convince Clemens, but in the end he understood, and then after a lot more discussion with the envoys, they agreed to go back to the High King to say that the Romans also wanted peace.

Vindex reached up to pat Gannascus on the shoulder. 'If you need any help,' he offered. Gannascus stared at him and then at Ferox. Ferox nodded.

'Bastards need to die,' the German said. 'And this Wolf. All of them.'

'Watch him, he's clever,' Ferox told him.

'He's dead. He just doesn't realise yet.'

At the rear of the Roman camp

HE WAS AMAZED *that the Romans had no one on top of the rocky hillock next to their camp. It seemed an obvious vantage point, and he and three of his best men had taken a long while inching their way up, crawling from cover to cover, ready to kill the sentries. Only they were not there, so the four of them lay flat on the summit and watched as the battle began. They had ridden hard to get here, driving their ponies because they did not plan to fight from their backs. They had been on the edge of the great encampment, a little apart from the others, for no one was too keen on their company. That suited him and his men. He took forty riders and rushed with them here. Now it was time to send one man back to bring the rest up to the shelter of the hill. Five hundred more warriors were following on foot, and ought to arrive before too long.*

The rest of his men were hiding in the path of the main Roman force. Volisios had told him about the High King's embassy and his hope to snatch peace back at the last minute. With luck some of his men would kill the envoys, or the Romans sent to meet them, or both. No, it was not a matter of luck and he knew it. She had told him how things would be and he had dreamed it.

There was something familiar about it all as he watched. In front of them they could see the Roman line, bent back at an angle on the left, with mostly Brigantes and other tribesmen covering that side of the camp. The regulars were at the front, facing the main attack in thin, somewhat ragged little lines of tiny figures, and beyond them the darker blocks of the tribesmen. There were far more of them, far more, but for the moment the Romans were holding on. Patches of colour on the grass, the dead and wounded, helped tell the story of the fight so far. He watched as some warriors made a charge, not so much the whole band of five or six hundred men, as a dozen rushing forward in a knot, some more coming behind, attacking, but without the same enthusiasm, and the rest shuffling forward. It was like jabbing a stubby finger at the enemy. The Roman line did not come forward to meet it, which suggested that they were tired. For a moment the cohort's line bulged back as if it was one, solid thing.

'They're here, lord,' the man beside him whispered.

There was the glint and flash of steel as men fought. They were too far away to hear properly, and the sound was like the rustling of many fallen leaves blown by the autumn wind. The cohort seemed to shuffle back a pace or two, the tip of the finger of tribesman did the same, and then both sides straightened their lines and stared at each other.

The Romans were giving ground, slowly, but surely. He could see that the High King's army and its allies were fighting well, especially Tincommius' own men, who were the best armed and equipped of the whole army. They were attacking hard, and persisting each time they failed to break the enemy. He watched as a cohort went forward and the warband facing it gave way, going back ten, even twenty paces before both sides stopped. Yet the Romans looked weary, as if staggering rather than running forward. They were fighting well and stubbornly, but that is simply what you would expect. He hated and despised the Romans, but there was part of him, the part that remembered the good times of service, that was proud of the regulars as they fought so very stubbornly.

It did not matter. Numbers were against them. Already the Roman reserves had been sucked forward to maintain the fighting line. On their right more and more enemies were gathering, threatening to come around that flank, and the pitifully few Roman horsemen were being worn down. The same was happening on the left, albeit slower, because it was harder for the warbands to get around that side. Still, the defenders were mostly irregulars and although they were doing well, they rarely had the sheer bloody-minded persistence of disciplined soldiers.

Further out in the plain he could see smoke rising, and wondered what that was. A wing of the army, at least ten thousand men, half as many as were attacking here, had swept down into the valley further along from the main camp. He guessed that they had met Romans, and unless the Romans were in great force, the odds were that they would be swamped. Most of the High King's cavalry were there, and a lot of the chariots. A dark mass was coming at some speed towards the camp, which meant that they had killed or passed any enemies out there and were on the way. When they arrived they would sweep around the Roman right with ease for there was no one to stop them. The other wing of the army, as many men although few on horseback, was coming up behind him, and it was anyone's guess whether they would arrive before or after the left wing, but when they did they would come around south of this hillock and close on the rear of the camp. That would be that. Thetatus *to use soldier's slang.*

'Come on,' he said and led the others down the slope, no longer needing to worry whether or not anyone was watching. As they reached the bottom and the waiting warriors standing

next to their weary ponies, the rest of his men jogged down from the ridge to join them. It was perfect. He remembered dreaming of burning tents and running beasts and now he understood.

They went forward one by one, for there was still time. Something like a thousand animals, mostly oxen, but some ponies and mules, were grazing behind the camp, the dumb creatures oblivious to the turmoil of their masters. There was shouting as some of the slaves herded them into the camp, but the men's hearts were not in it and they were clearly paying more attention to the fighting.

He led them forward, mingling with the cattle, using the beasts as cover, and it was so easy. They crept or walked forward behind an animal, hunching where necessary.

'Get a move on, you idle bugger, Achilles!' a voice shouted.

'I'm trying, I'm trying. The sodding great thing doesn't want to move!' This one was even closer. He crouched, peeking under the belly of the ox, and saw army boots and a pair of stocky legs just ahead.

'Hit the bastard and shout!' the first voice said.

The man did as suggested, and there was a deep moan of complaint from an animal.

He stepped into the open. He had mail, a gladius in his right hand and an oval shield in his left, although he had left off his helmet, for he wanted his men to know that he was unafraid, and to see his long black hair, for that was a rare colour in these parts.

'Oi, who are you?' the stocky man snarled. He had a grubby tunic and an old-style bronze helmet, the ones with a stubby point as a crest, although in this case the crest had long since been ripped away. One of the cheek pieces swung loosely, fastened on by nothing more than wire.

Another head bobbed up over a pony's back, a little way ahead. This one had a similarly old helmet, which gleamed from obsessive polishing. He guessed the men were calones, and they were usually like that, either as slovenly as the mules they cared for or more spick and span than the most eager legionary. 'Shouldn't you lot be fighting?' He waved an arm. 'Over yonder. That redheaded bint is in charge I reckon.'

'No she's not, she's in the camp. Wouldn't get a woman fighting, would you?'

'Fausta fights me all the time!'

He smiled, strolling towards the nearest man. 'Angry woman, is she?' he asked in his best camp Latin.

'Not compared to Vesuvius,' the scruffy slave answered. 'Know anything about cattle?'

He nodded. 'A fair bit. The secret is to yell and hit them with a stick.'

'Nah,' the one with the shiny helmet suggested. 'That's women.'

He smiled, coming round behind the animal as if wanting to help, and then stabbed the scruffy one in the belly.

'Shit!' the other slave gasped, until a warrior stood up behind him, pulled back his head and slit his throat.

The recalcitrant ox decided that this was a good time to walk briskly back to camp. 'Get them all moving!' he told the warrior, and started slapping another beast with the flat of his sword. 'Come on!' he called. 'Get them moving. And keep low!'

First a few, then more and more of the beasts began to lumber towards the gateway.

'At last!' a voice shouted and there must have been more calones among the herd. 'Clear the way there!'

One of his warriors laughed out loud and he was tempted to join in, but that was not the way of the Silures. There was no picket in front of the open gate, and no one had bothered even to extend the rampart around to cover it. That was sloppy, and he felt almost disappointed because it was so very easy. There were calones on the rampart either side of the opening, trying their best to look like soldiers.

He was through, even though a cow chose that moment to barge against him, pushing him into another beast so that he almost lost his footing.

'Watch out! Take 'em over that way! Left, left – into the empty space.'

He saw the man giving orders, a calo with three feathers for a crest, would you believe, and punched him with the boss of his shield. The man tottered, slipped in the mud and fell. A quick thrust down ended his cries of anger. There were screams as his warriors began the killing. No soldiers were anywhere in sight, just the calones and other riff-raff from the camp and none of them were expecting any trouble. A few ponies bolted in fear and the cattle started to run, ploughing straight through a line of tents. Some men were running along the ramparts on either side, killing anyone in their path, and warriors were pouring over the turf wall to join them because the gateway was crammed with animals.

A pony came past and he dropped the shield and grabbed hold of its mane, hauling himself up and riding with the herd into the heart of the camp until at last he managed to break away. Flames were rising, from fires knocked over by the animals and then as his men helped them to spread. Screams were everywhere, women and children's cries mingling with the shouts of men, but no one seemed to be bringing any order to the place or organising resistance.

He jumped the pony over some tent ropes, got onto the main road, with the centre of the camp ahead of him. A sentry stood on guard outside two tents, pitched side by side and one smaller than the other. There were some of his men behind him, he had not seen them arrive, but there they were.

'That way!' he pointed his sword at the largest tent and let them run past him to deal with the sentries. He was looking around, saw the confusion, saw no sign of any threat, so followed his men.

The sentries were already dead, although one of his warriors was clutching at his side. It did not look too bad. A woman screamed, loud and piercing from within the big tent. He jumped down and pushed his way through the flap, saw tables, chairs, the luxuries of an aristocrat, and a partition wall separating off the back of the tent. The woman screamed again and it came from the back.

'Come on you bitch!' one of his warriors shouted angrily. Two men held a sobbing woman by the arms, forcing her down on her knees. Her expensive dress was torn open, her breasts exposed, and her long red hair was dishevelled. The warrior fumbled with his belt.

They went silent as he appeared.

'We take the camp first,' he said. The woman stopped crying and gave him a look of utter desperation. 'Are you Claudia?' he asked her gently.

She nodded. So this was Ferox's wife, the queen of the Brigantes, skulking in her tent. He had heard that the Romans frowned on her fighting as a warrior, so perhaps she had no choice. She was younger than he had expected, shorter too, but in spite of the tears, very pretty and beauty often hid the years.

'Tie her up and bring her,' he told them. 'She's mine.' He did not need to say more or go into detail. These were his men and they were good ones. He felt a stirring, not simply of joy at the thought of hurting his uncle, but of sheer desire. He

had not been with a woman since Beltane, as those were her instructions. That vow would soon be over. 'You two watch her,' he told them. There was a lamp burning on a round table next to the bed, its flame hardly giving off any smoke which meant that the oil was expensive. He found a chest, half open and full of clothes, so dropped the lamp into it and waited as the fire caught. 'Let's go.'

He led them out, the woman trussed and over the shoulder of one of his bigger men. It was all there in front of him, the flames, the rushing animals – the dream of victory.

XXIII

The seventh hour, in front of the camp

TITUS CERIALIS KNEW that they were being ground down, that the enemy were pushing further and further round both flanks and there was nothing that he could do about it. There were so many enemies, and a lot of them were good, with a determination that all the books said barbarians lacked. There were no more reserves, for even his escort had gone to help his cavalry stem the tide for just a little longer.

'Come on, boys!' he shouted as loud as he could to the legionaries in front. 'Keep it up! They're hurting, they're hurting!' His voice was hoarse, little more than a croak.

The men were magnificent. They had beaten back four all-out attacks coming from the whole enemy line and so many attacks by one band or just a group that he had long since lost count. There was nothing to choose between the legionaries and auxiliaries, for citizens and non-citizens alike kept going, finding strength from somewhere. The third big attack had been bloody, for he had managed to issue new pila and lanceae to the front rank, and that added punch had cost the attackers dear. The fourth attack was only stopped by sending in all of VIIII Hispana, half to extend his right wing and the rest to reinforce the fighting line.

'Come on, lads!' he shouted as best he could. 'Up the

Capricorns!' He did not know the nickname of Hispana, and wished that he had bothered to learn. 'Come on the Ninth!' he called out as he rode behind a knot of men from the legion.

At the start of the battle the optiones took post behind each formation, each with a long hastile staff. It was not a weapon designed to fight the enemy, for its top was ornamental and blunt. Their job was to keep the ranks in order and discipline, and when the pressure mounted to stop anyone from trying to run away. Then they ordered, cajoled, embarrassed the men into going back to join their comrades, or failing that, bodily shoved them back into place using the staffs.

By now all the optiones were down or at the front of the cohorts, replacing centurions who had fallen, or simply drawn forward by the need to fight and set an example. These were no longer neat formations. Ranks were thinned by the dead, and by the many, many more wounded. Some of these kept going, others came back after their wounds were bound, and the rest staggered or were dragged away as best they could for whatever treatment was possible. At the start, men had been carried to the hospital tent in the camp, but soon there were far too many and the *medici* and their assistants did their best for them in the open space in front of the rampart.

There were no more ordered ranks and neat formations, but clusters of men, the most determined at the front, and those simply holding on behind them, and a few drifting back without actually running away altogether. A row of these groups, like little islands, made up the Roman battle line, and there were big gaps between each of them. Those archers with arrows left sometimes ran forward in these places, shot a missile or two, and ran away, but ten more enemy spears or sling stones came back in return. Most of the crews of the scorpiones were down, and now that the line kept edging back, there was not the space for the ballistae to shoot over their heads. He had ordered the crews to find shields and join the fighting.

Something slammed very hard into his right knee as he walked his horse past one of the gaps. The horse stirred, trotted a few steps until he stilled it. He did not want to go fast, just as he had forced himself to go slowly across the gap, in case men thought he was nervous and that made them worry.

'Sir? Are you hurt, sir?' one of the archers called, running over to him.

'I am fine,' Titus lied. The pain was immense and he suspected a bone was broken, but as long as he was on horseback he would manage somehow.

With a distinct clang a stone hit the back of the archer's tall helmet. The man's eyes fluttered, he swayed and then pitched forward, onto Titus' leg. The tribune bit his lip, feared blood was coming, but somehow managed not to scream in agony. He grabbed the man's shoulder and supported him.

'Help this man!' he called to another archer, who ran across and took his comrade. 'Get him back!'

He made it to the end of the line and saw that the Brigantes and other irregulars were still just clinging on, although they were now barely fifty paces in front of the camp. He wondered whether they could get back behind the rampart without being slaughtered, any more than his men could do the same. There was no real ditch, which made it easier, just as it weakened whatever protection they would gain. The enemy kept pushing forward and there were so many of them that eventually the Romans must break, unless something changed.

Titus could not see Claudia Enica at first, then movement caught his eye and he saw a horseman – no, not a man – a rider, with what he had thought was a streaming red plume. It was the queen's hair, and she must have taken off her helmet to be seen.

He did not want her to die, but the thought that she was here, enduring all this, made him think that there must be a way to keep going and survive. For a moment he was tempted to ride over, but another surge struck against the big clump of Legio Hispana in the centre of his line, and the veterans gave way for a few paces. He cantered over, yelling encouragement, and then saw to his amazement that the legionaries were going forward again, fighting all the way, and this time the warriors facing them dropped or stepped back a pace, then another. Men had died and others been maimed so that the Britons could take a foot or two of nondescript grassland and it seemed so absurd and so admirable.

'Sir!' A trooper appeared, helmet gone and head bandaged, the chest of his horse and his hexagonal shield daubed with drying blood. 'Cavalry coming down the valley towards our right. Lots of them.'

'Ours or theirs?'

'Don't know, sir.' The cavalryman did not sound optimistic.

Titus shaded his eyes and saw dust, lots of it and a dark mass coming quickly towards them. There was a smaller group some way ahead, and a lone rider streaming in front of them. He strained to see better, his eyes blurring for a moment then focusing and he was sure. The man at the head of all those horseman was riding a grey. He desperately wanted it to be Ferox, come in the nick of time at the head of two alae and all the cavalry the legatus could spare. A thousand men charging into the back of the enemy would scatter them for sure, snatching victory from the mouth of defeat. Memories flashed through his mind, of how Ferox, that gruff, almost mythical Ferox who had played so freely with them when they were children, was the same man who had bloodyhandedly won so many battles and fights, and saved people time and again, among them his stepmother, and had kept the whole family safe in the fort in Dacia.

Titus sighed. It was not Ferox, but the swaggering Pertacus, fleeing faster than his own riders because he was better mounted. Behind them came not a thousand prime auxiliaries, but thousand upon thousand of Britons. He could even see chariots racing among them, for they were close now. Pertacus was waving his arms as he rode around the flank, shouting a warning even as he all but led the enemy into the attack.

As the realisation sunk in that this was the end, a deluge of trumpets and horns blasted from the rear, behind the camp. His head snapped around and there was black smoke rising from the tent lines. There were screams, some of them in women's voices and for an instant he thought of his slave girls, but knew that there was nothing he could do to save them. The camp was falling or had fallen, so they could not hope even for its modest refuge. The trooper was still beside him.

'Tell the cavalry to retreat,' he said.

The man's face showed a mix of relief and stubborn determination not to quit.

'That is an order, do you hear me! Everyone who can get away should go. Try to find the legatus, or make your own way south if you can. Go!'

'But, sir!'

'Go!' Titus turned his horse. She was a good one, and could not be that tired for they had walked more than they had hurried anywhere. The battle was lost and most of his army would die for he doubted that the tribes were in much mood to take prisoners. A quick death might anyway be preferable to the sort of fate likely for anyone falling into their hands. Most of his men were going to die and there was nothing he could do about it. He turned to his tubicen. Beside them, the clusters of men were wavering as a great roar of triumph went up from the enemy ranks.

'Sound Form Orb!' he yelled over the din.

The trumpeter nodded, spat to moisten his lips and then blared out the signal, repeating it. 'Now go, you're no more use here!'

Titus galloped over to the men from Hispana. 'Let me in,' he called, as the legionaries, more than a few of them grey-bearded veterans, shuffled aside to let him come into the centre of the rough circle, before closing up so that a wall of shields was presented in every direction. Mounted, he could see other similar groups forming, and although it might have been more fitting to join one of the rally circles formed by his own legion, this one was closest.

'Reckon we've got the bastards worried now, sir!' a centurion called to him. The man's transverse crest had taken a blow earlier in the fighting, and half of it dangled down, somehow still attached by threads of horsehair. It bounced every time he moved.

Titus Cerialis laughed and for a moment barely felt the pain in his leg. 'Too true!' His dry throat suddenly seemed clear and he shouted easily. 'Now, lads' – most of them were much older than him, but what did that matter. 'We're going to fight our way out! Home is that way!' He had his sword in his hand although he could not remember drawing it and used it to point.

'Yeah, about a hundred miles that way!' a voice called.

'Then we'll do it step by step!' he shouted and they laughed, a grim, frightening laugh, but somehow they laughed. Spears and stones thumped against their shields and the warriors followed with a charge.

'Hold them!' Titus bellowed. Men fell, pulled back into the circle whenever possible, but sometimes dragged into the enemy mass. More of the Britons went down, bludgeoned by shields and stabbed by swords whose edges were long since blunted and the points not much better. The warriors gave way, stepping back a few yards.

'Right, lads, that's the way we're going!' the centurion ordered. They grunted as one as the men at the rear took a short step and everyone tried to match it, going sideways or backwards.

'That's it!' Titus called out. 'One step, now another.'

They grunted together and shuffled along. A man sighed as a javelin slammed into his face. Another swore as he was nicked on the leg.

The warriors charged again, clashing into the orb.

The men of the numeri fought harder and longer than anyone had expected, including themselves. They fought because this was what their chieftains had sent them to do, and because many stood beside kinsmen and did not wish to be shamed in their eyes. Few had seen battle before, almost none battle on this scale, and at first that inexperience helped, for they were confident of victory and unable to imagine anything less.

That mood did not last long, so they found other reasons to fight. The queen helped, not simply encouraging the Brigantes, but the other tribes. There was something about the sight of a woman dressed as a warrior, and her shouts of encouragement, high pitched, even shrill sometimes, that stirred something within them. Even for men from the settled communities it evoked memories of stories told by grandfathers, of songs of great deeds and terrible battles that had nothing to do with Rome. They were proud men, or they discovered their pride, so they fought and died, gradually giving ground, but somehow holding together.

Their opponents were just as proud, and kept on coming, and as time passed, more and more bands of warriors edged around onto this flank. If there had been an easy path down from the ridge at this point, Claudia Enica suspected that no amount of courage could have held the position. They were lucky, but could not hold on forever. The battle needed to be won somewhere else.

It was not. The northerners were coming on again, slowly this time, not the wild charges of earlier, but a determined step by step advance. Then men were shouting, turning to stare in amazement back at the camp so close behind them as the tent-lines started to burn. The clumps of warriors seemed to shake as if they were caught in a strong wind. Moments later came that great blaze of noise as thousands of enemies appeared on the left, coming down some wide defile a mile or so in the rear of the camp.

The irregulars broke, each man streaming away from the fight, now like so much cut straw carried on the wind.

'We must go, my queen!' The old warrior gestured to the other escorts to cluster around her.

'No!' she said, but her heart was not in it.

The old man slapped the rump of her horse with the flat of his sword, and the beast sprang forward.

'That way!' he shouted, and took them close to the corner of the camp and then in front of the rocky hill to go south. Some of the men were running in the same direction, although most were trying to get around the other side of the hill, even though that took them straight towards the masses of enemy closing in. Some were slow, confused and uncertain, but the sight of their panic inspired the main enemy line who rushed forward, all order gone, and hacked and stabbed at the fleeing, helpless men.

'Clear a path!' the warrior thundered, letting his horse barge anyone who got in the way. The others wielded flats of swords and spear shafts to push men aside, and soon the speed of their mounts took them ahead of the mob.

The queen made herself look back once, to see the fleeing men and the vengeful enemy in pursuit. She owed them that much, even if she could do nothing to save them, and had brought all too many of them here in the first place to serve her ambition. There were tears in her eyes, and she blinked to clear them. After Dacia she had never wanted to fight another war, yet somehow this had happened. She wondered about Ferox, about poor young Titus, and many others, but most of all at that moment she wondered whether they could escape at all.

They came around the rocky hill and the warrior led them off towards the opposite side of the valley. There were northerners to their right, coming on at a run. She could not see any on horseback, none at all, but they were close, less than a hundred paces and they needed to go nearer to get to the open ground.

Hoofs drummed, her horse was running smoothly, pushing to the front, and only the old warrior was ahead of her. A javelin skimmed through the grass nearby and a stone hummed past her head. The old warrior was staring the other way. There were riders coming towards them, dozens of them, and further back thousands of horsemen swarming around the remnants of the Roman army.

A man streaked ahead on a grey, and she recognised Pertacus. A rider was with him, one of his own warriors, but the man's horse stumbled and he was thrown, landing badly. Pertacus did not even glance back, even when the man pushed himself up and begged to be carried. She shifted her horse towards him, until the older warrior nudged his mount against hers to force her on.

'No, my queen.'

Another of her escort went to the man, arm reaching down, and managed to haul him up to ride double. They kept going, leaving the infantry far behind. The horsemen were close, and one of her men arched his back, arms wide as a javelin struck him. She heard a cry as another horse went down, ridden by someone she did not recognise. He was too close to the pursuing enemy to save.

They rode on. There were a dozen men left in her escort for several had fallen in the fighting, and as many more fugitives. One was a tubicen, his thin bronze trumpet slung over his back and clanging as it bounced against him. She saw no officers apart from Pertacus. More missiles fell, killing a horse and pitching another rider down. A trooper was in their midst, blood dripping from the bandage around his head and more seeping through the rents in his armour, and suddenly the man wheeled around and drove his horse back the way they had come. He was yelling something, but she could not catch the words, and as she turned to watch she saw the first few pursuers shear away rather than meet his lone charge. Then one did face him, and was thrown down, the auxiliary's spear driven clean through his body. The man kept going, struggling to draw his sword, and several riders closed around him, cutting him from the saddle.

They rode on. Their horses had gone a long way during the day, but so had the enemy, who had rushed down the valley chasing Pertacus and his men and then on to envelop the

Roman line. Her Brigantes all knew how to ride and all had taken care of their horses. These were mounts from the royal household, and she doubted that there were many half as good anywhere else in Britannia.

A few of the other fugitives dropped behind and were caught. Pertacus and a handful stayed with them, and over time they built up such a big lead that after a while the enemy gave up. They were miles from the camp, too far away to see more than the smoke as it burned.

'Do we seek for the legatus, my queen?' the old man asked when they eventually stopped to rest. 'And your husband?'

If Ferox was right in his guesses, then she reckoned most of Tincommius' army had attacked the camp. That might well mean that Priscus was on a fool's errand, but had not fought or lost anyone. They were probably still up there somewhere, perhaps fifteen miles away, some five thousand well-trained regulars, even if they were without supplies.

When the tribes won a victory the army tended to melt away, as each warrior went home with his loot and his stories, the task complete, the war won, and needing to purify themselves properly before they sat again around their own hearth. There were things a man needed to do after a battle, and fighting another battle was not one of them.

Claudia Enica reckoned that there was a good chance Tincommius' army would disperse like this, although she could not be sure. The High King had created something new for these parts, so perhaps some of the troops would stay in the field to fight again. Priscus might well be able to cope, and if he did, or found that for the moment there was no enemy to fight, he was a long, long way from safety. The Romans would have to find food, and keep together, and all the while they would be under attack. In time some of Tincommius' men might return, but before that any warrior hearing of the Romans' plight was likely to think that it was worth harrying the column and being part of the great victory.

Claudia Enica made up her mind. 'No, we go south.' That was the only way she could see to help.

The old man did not question the decision and simply nodded. 'Then let us make a few more miles before we tend to the horses and sleep.'

They saw no one, and slept in the cover of some woodland. Pertacus vanished during the night.

XXIV

The day before the Ides of November,
on the Palatine Hill, Rome

HADRIAN OFTEN THOUGHT about the divine Augustus. When he was young, he had read that the first princeps had thought more than once of laying down his powers and retiring to private life. He had decided, or had been persuaded, not to do this each time, because there was always so much work or some crisis that needed his attention.

His younger self had never really believed any of this, for surely supreme power was its own reward. Now he knew different. It was a burden, an endless task, like Sisyphus and his boulder, but it needed to be done, and it was best for the res publica and the provinces if it was done well. Augustus had certainly been good at it, and Hadrian felt that he was just as good.

Before Augustus there had been chaos and civil war, and it was almost incredible that so many aristocrats still believed in their hearts that those years were noble, because the senatorial class competed for power and distinction and the right to take a turn guiding the state. It did not matter that most of the Senate these days were not actually the descendants of Rome's ancient aristocracy. Those families were nearly all long gone, and it was hard to miss them.

Even so, these offspring of men who joined the Senate under the Flavians, or even in a few cases under Augustus and his family, preened themselves as the sole inheritors of ancient virtue. These were the fools who revered Brutus or Cassius, neither of whom had ever done anything very worthwhile for the common good. The libertas they proclaimed, as their knives dripped with Caesar's blood, was the freedom for their class to squeeze every ounce of gold from the provinces and to put their own selfish pride and honour before the interests of everyone else. Caesar was just as selfish, just as precious about his own honour and status, but at least the man had talent, rare talent, and did whatever he did well. Give me a Caesar in charge before a Brutus, any day, and better yet give me an Augustus, who did a dirty job well and just went on doing it.

Hadrian had been back in Rome since July and was well aware that most of the Senate loathed him. There was not too much he could do about that. Nigrinus and Quietus had had to die after what they had done. Let some men who may think they have noble intentions start plotting to murder the princeps and it opened the door to everyone else. Both were brave men, Lusius Quietus especially, and had known the risk they were running. If you stake your life on a roll of the dice, you cannot change your mind when the roll is bad. No one had made them plot.

None of that would ever matter, for he had ordered the death of senators – and even worse got the Senate to apply the law and give the order – and that was all that they would remember. He executed the sort of men who ought to be indulged, even when they plotted murder, so the irony was that he would be remembered as the killer. Senators would remember that, and perhaps only that, for generations to come, when there was no one at all left related to the senators of today. For the moment they would hide it, but that part of his story was already written, before the stylus had touched the page.

Hadrian glanced at Suetonius Tranquillus, the slightly flabby, smooth-skinned North African who was in charge of his Latin correspondence. The man was using his access to the imperial archives, including the most private collections, to write biographies of the divine Julius and Augustus and all the rest up until Domitian; the man was pedantic, naïve in many ways, but was not fool enough to write about Nerva and Trajan so soon. He had not asked permission, perhaps because everything was rough, but Hadrian knew about it and knew that the fellow was organising it by topics, so had chapters on failures, defeats and executions during the reign, as well as on the admirable things.

'Is that from Britannia?' Hadrian asked.

'Yes, my lord.' Suetonius had a surprisingly gruff voice, making everything he said so much less refined than anything he set down on the page. It was his duty to read all correspondence – apart from the highly confidential messages which came from other sources – and his gloomy expression did not augur well. Apart from him being good and thorough, Hadrian usually enjoyed having the man around for his cheerfulness.

Hadrian took the scroll, saw the seal of Falco, in his official role as legatus Augusti of the province.

'There is another from Ligustinus, my lord. It is...' Suetonius struggled to find the right words, '... something of a curious document in which he seeks to make clear that he was in no way to blame for the mishap suffered in the summer.'

'Mishap!'

'So the former legatus terms it, my lord. Apparently he was ill, unaware of what was going on, and others made all the significant decisions.' The words dripped with irony.

'Don't overact,' Hadrian told him. 'We both know the man's a fool.'

'Was a fool, my lord.'

'Of course.' Hadrian skimmed the lines. There would be time enough to study every little detail later. This was not the first news of the disaster in northern Britannia, but the initial reports lacked detail.

At the very end of September Falco had reached his new province and written to say that his predecessor had not only started a war, but was doing his best to lose it. An army had marched north, far beyond our settled garrisons, and had not come back. The tribes were telling stories of an army slaughtered to the last man, but Falco had no details.

A few weeks later Falco reported that some of the lost army had reappeared among allied tribes and was on its way back. The senior officers were dead or wounded, and the man leading the remnants was a centurion called Ferox.

Hadrian could remember his feelings when he read the name, a deep inward sigh that dampened the full flush of relief. Ferox, it would have to be Ferox. That was good because the man had a talent for survival, and by the sound of it had saved plenty of others in the process. It was bad because if ever any man had the knack of attracting disaster and intrigue and somehow walking out the other side, it was Ferox. At the very least, it meant that the whole unfortunate affair was likely to be even more complicated than he had feared.

The story seemed simple. Spurius Ligustinus, abetted by the eager commander of II Augusta, this fellow Priscus, had over-reacted to some nasty raiding by deciding to start a war. They reckoned that they could win before the news that it had started had reached him and given him chance to remind the man of his official mandata as governor and forget the idea. So they dragged everyone fit to take the field out of the garrisons dotted around Britannia, supplemented them with thousands of poorly trained levies to make up the numbers, and picked a fight with a powerful allied monarch, who had always done his best to avoid conflict with Rome.

All that was bad enough, and what the divine Augustus had called fishing with a golden hook, where the catch could not possibly match the risk. What made it all truly unforgivable was the stupidity from then on. Ligustinus collapsed into illness, and spent the summer somehow not dying as everyone expected. Priscus charged off north – or did not so much charge as crawl – not catching any enemies because he was so slow, and also because no one was particularly minded to fight the Romans in the first place. He kept on going, provoking the king, then when the two armies closed, his military ineptitude was such that he split his army into two, widely separated parts.

Suetonius seemed to sense the point Hadrian had reached in the letter. 'There are reports of the unfortunate legatus of II Augusta in the archives. He had not made similarly grave, or indeed even noticeable errors in the past.'

'He'd never had the chance,' Hadrian said bitterly. 'He must have been waiting all these years to cock-up in the grandest style.'

'Quite, my lord.'

Priscus had gone looking for the enemy, not realising that they were already behind him. He wore himself out, then got himself killed in an ambush, along with most of the senior officers. A prefect named Clemens took over, but by that time the Britons or Caledonians or whatever they were, had poured down out of the hills and wiped out the rest of the army, sacking the main camp. There were at least four thousand dead, probably more if you included all the followers. Some of them might be prisoners, not that that mattered. Nor would it matter to the gossip that a third of the dead were those poor, hastily raised local troops. This was a major military disaster – one that Suetonius or someone like him would collect and list if ever they wrote Hadrian's biography.

That he had been thousands of miles away and not authorised the war was irrelevant, as was the fact that the garrison of the province was so weak in the first place because Trajan had drawn men from all over the empire for his wars, leaving so many regions thinly protected. Ligustinus the sick fool, and Priscus the active fool, were both his legati, his representatives; their right to issue orders and be obeyed delegated from him. The princeps took the credit if they won, and the blame when they failed; that was the deal, so this disaster was his disaster, like the smaller one in Dacia last year. Oh, people would understand, and they praised successful commanders and muttered dark things about the failures, but each was appointed by the emperor, so their competence reflected his wisdom in choosing them in the first place.

As princeps this was all his responsibility, which did not mean that he could not hint at where the true blame lay. Priscus was dead, which in some ways was unfortunate, as the man sounded such a fool that he was bound to have drawn attention to himself by trying to blame everyone else. Ligustinus was as great a fool, and Hadrian had changed his mind and sent instructions to Sosius not to dispose of the man. He did not know whether that order had ever arrived, for the former legatus had been found dead at the *mansio* in Londinium, during his long journey home. That could be chance or it could be Sosius, and either way the man was gone. Perhaps it was for the best. Sometimes people felt so sorry for an obvious buffoon that they began to believe him.

At least he was confident that Falco was the right man to restore the situation in Britannia. Orders were on their way to Hispania Tarraconensis and to Germania Superior, requiring the legions there to each send one thousand of their best men as a vexillation to Britannia.

'Here are the orders for Pontius Sabinus, my lord,' Suetonius said, passing the document over. That was the name of the tribune who would command this vexillation, and Suetonius had anticipated his next request. Hadrian signed and sealed the letter. Falco would get three thousand legionaries and almost as many auxiliaries, so that instead of the Romans becoming weaker they would be even stronger than before the disaster.

Yet it was the less dramatic, least glamorous aid that truly mattered. Ligustinus and Priscus had scraped together just about all the draft and baggage animals from the entire province, and then proceeded to lose almost all of them. Without transport, it did not really matter how many soldiers went to Britannia, because they would not be able to march anywhere. Provincial governors never much liked sending vexillations of their soldiers away for years on end. They were even less keen to give up the assets that allowed their remaining troops to operate, so any request for animals and carts would be unlikely to yield much. They would scrape together the worst of everything, because they would feel deep down that the chances of ever getting them back were slim. Individual units tended to be even more reluctant to give up something they might just need one day, which meant that there was resistance all along the line. It was better to start from scratch, buying new animals and having the carts, harness and saddles made, but after Trajan's spate of wars, the price was high throughout the empire.

Hadrian sighed. If he had any sense he would quit being

princeps and breed mules. He would make a fortune. 'What are those?' he asked. A slave was waiting behind Suetonius, carrying a basket full of scrolls of one size or another.

'A request from the Augusta, my lord.'

'Indeed.' Hadrian waited.

'She requested several books of the poets. Horace mainly, some in his own hand no less, and Ovid, a little Virgil. Also, she is interested in the divine Livia, seeing the wife of Augustus as the perfect model to emulate.'

Hadrian stared at him, until Suetonius grew nervous.

'There is nothing too secret, I assure you. I chose them myself from her letters. They talk of family matters, of proper comportment and dress, that sort of thing.'

Poor Sabina, she was trying so very hard, especially now they were back at Rome. 'Do you think he loved her, Augustus I mean?' Hadrian mused.

Suetonius thought for a while before answering. 'It is hard to know, so much is said of her, so many crimes attributed to her... but, yes, I think he did. She lost their only child together, you know, a very bad stillbirth, and that was when they were both young. Augustus wanted children, well a son, anyway, to follow him, and he could so easily have divorced her and found another wife. Men do so readily, and yet he did not.'

'A princeps cannot just do what other men do,' Hadrian said.

There had never been a choice for him. The marriage to Sabina was one of the few things Trajan liked about him, one of the few favours. He could never have divorced her then or think of it now. They were together, until one of them died, and that was that, and the last thing he wanted was for her to die young because he was bound to be blamed, even if she was struck by lightning. His attention drifted, and he wondered what it would be like to be in love again, to feel that excitement, that desperation only salved when in the loved one's company. Perhaps one day. Yet there was a worry, for his agents were reporting dangerous conversations and secret notes between the Augusta and people who should know better. There was even a question about her closeness with Sosius and a rumour – impossible to check after this time – that the man was a bastard sired by her father, and that she had a particular fondness for him for that reason.

Suetonius coughed. 'My lord, do you require anything else tonight?'

Hadrian smiled. 'No, that is all. Leave these with me so that I can study the full horror.'

'Falco is a good man, my lord. He will do what needs to be done.'

'Yes, there is that consolation. What was it Augustus is supposed to have said, after news came that that idiot Varus had lost three legions?'

'"Quinctilius Varus, give me back my legions!" or "where are my legions?" depending on the source. I believe he had nightmares and wandered the palace, banging his head against the walls.' Suetonius shrugged. 'He was very old by then.'

'Well, it's a thought if I cannot sleep tonight. Thank you, Suetonius.'

'My lord.'

'Oh, and Suetonius. About the things for the empress. Take her the poets, but forget the letters. Say that you could not find any and put these back in their place.'

'I understand, my lord.'

Hadrian wondered whether he did. He would know that Livia had aided Augustus as secret advisor as much as consort, and had travelled with him on his many tours of the provinces. There was a good chance that she had influenced many of the decisions during those long years when he governed the empire. He dreaded the thought of Sabina aspiring to do the same.

That was a small problem, at least for the moment.

'What is the time?' he asked a slave waiting in the corner until needed.

'The fifth hour of the night, master.' That was later than he realised, which made him feel guilty for keeping Suetonius at work so long. There was simply so much to do.

He could not change what had happened in Britannia, and no amount of head pounding would make him feel any better about it. No doubt the divine Augustus had realised that in the end. Hadrian, the killer of senators, had also become Hadrian, the princeps who had lost an army. Neither could be changed. The best he could achieve was to keep on toiling and hope that in the long run Suetonius or some other author at least judged him Hadrian the diligent, and Hadrian who governed well. If the fools never realised that then at least he would know it. The gods did not care, but he would do the right thing and keep doing it whatever the cost.

It was time for bed. Hadrian stood and left the chamber, the slave trailing behind and another who had been outside following as well. He barely noticed them.

ACT III

XXV

Three days before the Ides of February, in the consulship of M. Annius Verus and Cn. Arrius Augur[*]*,*
at Isurium Brigantum

FEROX WOKE WITH a start, his back slick with sweat, even though his face was cold. He pulled at the bed covers, for the night was bitter and he seemed to feel it more as the years passed. The covers moved a little, but were firmly wrapped around the softly snoring queen lying beside him. He shifted, trying to bring all of his body into the warmth. His cloak was on the table nearby, left there deliberately because it was thick wool and this was not the first time this had happened. Getting it meant leaving the bed altogether, so he tried for a while to get comfortable. It did not work, there seemed always to be a draught somewhere. He got up, retrieved the cloak and returned to bed, where even more of the blankets had shifted to the far side, without his wife appearing to have moved at all. There was a magic to the line of Cartimandua.

He was awake now, fully awake, and lay staring at the dim outline of the ceiling. The dream had been the same one as usual. He almost did not want to return to sleep in case it came again.

* AD 121.

Ferox had seen plenty of battlefields, far more than most soldiers or warriors, seeming to find battle and slaughter wherever he went. He was still young when the dreams started, those nightmares of horror, the moments when he had so nearly died, and worst of all the times when friends suffered before his eyes.

When they were first married, he had warned Claudia Enica, telling her that sometimes, when he writhed and called out in his sleep, it was best to wake him and free him from the visions. She was a warrior, if a far less experienced one, and she understood. If anything his confession had brought them closer.

She rarely woke him, and that was not because he did not have nightmares, but because she slept so soundly. His wife had a knack of deciding that she wanted to sleep and passing out in a matter of moments. She rarely seemed to dream, and that was a novelty in Ferox's experience, for the women he had slept with in the past tended to wake and immediately recount every detail of their many dreams. Instead, and much to his amazement for she was so talkative and so restlessly energetic by day, Claudia Enica passed out beside him, breathing through her nose or open mouth, and often snoring, sometimes remarkably loudly. Sleeping was the only thing she ever did without elegance and poise. The only movements she made, slight if very effective, were to burrow and wrap herself ever more deeply in the bedclothes.

The queen snorted in her sleep and he smiled. He had never been fool enough to hint to her that she was an inveterate snorer. It was well into the night and only a faint gleam of starlight came through the gaps in the shutters. Dawn must be several hours away, so he lay there and waited, eyes closed and his body fairly warm under his cloak. There was no desire to leave the bed, for it was a reminder of how fortunate he was, lying beside this glorious, snoring woman, who in spite of all reason loved him as much as he loved her.

An hour or so later he was jerked awake again. He must have drifted off, even though he had thought it impossible. He had been back in the valley, marching with the column heading to the camp. It was the day after the battle, for they had spent a nervous and wet night up in the hills, lacking tents, but sheltered behind a feeble rampart and ditch. No one attacked them, but they heard singing and taunts during the night as the rain pattered down steadily.

The next morning the sky was grey, the rain a steady drizzle, and the hills around them empty of enemies, or indeed anyone else. Only a few thin plumes of smoke rose from stubborn fires still burning in spite of the rain. The only enemies were dead ones, and there were plenty of those, even though there were marks in the grass showing where hundreds had been carried off or dragged away on their shields. No Roman was alive, and the fields were scattered with pale humps, corpses stripped naked and always beheaded. The rain had washed away much of the blood, so that up close they seemed to be broken statues.

They passed the scattered corpses of numerus II first. There were several small clumps of bodies suggesting determined resistance, but on the whole the tired, hungry and untrained men had fled and been slaughtered as they ran. They were on foot and the enemy were mainly on horseback or in chariots. The convoy had put up more of a struggle, but the man in charge had tried to do his duty and protect the waggons, the pack animals and their precious supplies, so had stretched his units out thinly. They were always too few to stop the attackers, and by the time anyone tried to rally them together into bigger groups it was all over.

At the site of the main battle the dead again told their story, of the heavy fighting where the main lines had met well in front of the camp in a back-and-forth slog, the collapse when the wings of the High King's army had swept around both flanks and overrun the camp, and the slaughter that followed, some men running in terror, while most of the regulars stood back to back and tried to fight their way out. The path of each knot of soldiers was marked by a trail of corpses, and a final dense cluster where they stopped at last, overwhelmed by numbers and unable to cut their way past. One group of about seventy had made it half a mile, which seemed incredible, but that was where they lay. Titus Cerialis was in the centre, easily recognisable by his humped back and oddly angled legs, even though his head was gone. His knee had been smashed, and there were wounds on his body.

Every time he had slept for the last month he came back to that moment and that place, the horrible certainty dashing the feeble hope that the lad might somehow have escaped. Sometimes the corpse was Marcus, the son he could not acknowledge openly, and half-brother to the dead tribune, but in truth his sadness was as strong for Titus, the eager young man he had known since he was a boy. Worst of all he felt again the flood of despair at the sight, as the truth sank in that his wife was likely among the dead or carried off. Sleep renewed all the fears for her in vivid and brutal reality, of torture, rape, murder and sacrifice. The slow death of a queen could work great magic, especially the granddaughter of Cartimandua. In his dream he searched and searched through the dead just as he had done, finding a few women, reliving that stab of pain at the sight and the relief, that guilty relief when he realised that it was someone else.

Ferox had seen plenty of disasters, but never quite known a fear like this. Yet he was one of the few officers left, and Clemens was relying on him to help get the army home. Somehow his dreams never included Vindex's muttered 'Oh shit' at that announcement. There was so much to be done, searching for the little food left behind and unspoiled by the looters, finding anything else of use. There was not much. The tents were gone, artillery and carts burned or dragged away. A few pack and baggage animals had somehow escaped and decided to wander back and graze amid the ruin. They were caught, and orders given for men to butcher the far more numerous dead horses, mules and oxen. Any man carrying even a small amount of salt found himself very popular in the next few days, for there was none otherwise.

They had marched a few miles and made another camp for the night, for no one wished to sleep amid the dead and there was no time to bury them. The next day they started to see a few bands of men on foot and on horseback shadowing their progress. They stopped in the afternoon, to gather as best they could ripe barley from the closest fields. There were few sickles, for most had been in the camp and something so useful had inevitably been stolen. Men did their best with knives or whatever else they could find, even breaking the stalks with their bare hands. Patrols caught a few prisoners, who spoke of the great victory and said that the army had mostly gone home. One claimed that the Brigantian queen had escaped, another that she was dead, and a third that she was a captive of the Wolf. That brought an even deeper chill, for since boyhood his nephew had gained a reputation for cruelty exceptional even among the Silures, who prided themselves on their skill at making enemies suffer.

The attacks started as they foraged more and started to pass through the narrower valleys. Men who straggled from the main column, or wandered too far in the desperate search for food, were caught and killed and some were tortured first. The warriors gradually became bolder. Patrols were ambushed, and whenever they went to gather grain from the fields, they needed to deploy a strong covering force and expect to fight. Losses mounted, from wounds and from sickness brought on by lack of food, or from eating stuff that was rotten, half cooked or raw because there were not enough axes to chop sufficient firewood. Men died of dysentery or became so weak that they had to be carried, and the near constant rain drenched everyone and brought on fevers. The *primus pilus* of Legio II Augusta had his horse killed in an ambush, and then his leg crushed when the beast rolled on top of him.

They lumbered on, going slowly because they refused to abandon anyone still breathing. The men were frightened, angry and savage, so they burned farms and villages after they had searched every inch for anything to eat. Any locals they met were killed unless Clemens or Ferox were there in person. Orders stating that the folk here had nothing to do with the battle were so much wasted breath, and Ferox could understand that, while still hoping that they could avoid turning absolutely everyone against them. There was still a very long way to go.

He worked well with Clemens, not becoming friends, but understanding that each was capable and wanted to get as many men home as possible. Often one was at the rear and the other in the lead, but they both rode hard each day, trying to keep the column moving as fast as possible, trying to make the men believe that they had a chance.

They had to fight hard at one pass, a narrow notch in the hills, where the nearest clans had gathered in strength. If they had still had any scorpiones, the bolt shooters would have helped a lot. Instead, they had to carve their way through at sword point, for few men had pila or javelins left by this stage.

Ferox led them, letting his fears for his wife boil over into hate. They had to fight uphill and that was always hard, but these were grim, determined men, and after five attempts they broke through and slaughtered the fleeing enemy until their arms were weary and each man was covered in blood. Fifty warriors were hemmed in against a cliff face. None was spared.

The column had broken through, but the cost was heavy. They did what little best they could to sew up and bandage the wounded, and somehow found a way to carry them. For three days the Sun shone, lifting spirits, helping some of the sick to recover, but on the second day Clemens was badly wounded, struck in the face by a slingstone and with a javelin in his thigh. Ferox was the most senior officer left on his feet.

'Oh double shit,' Vindex commented cheerfully.

There were some desertions, especially cavalrymen who reckoned they could escape easier on their own, but Ferox was surprised how few there were. A prisoner assured him that the queen had ridden to the Novantae, and he wanted to believe it, but was kept so busy that he had only a little time to brood.

They came into more open country, and he was relieved when no one tried to stop them fording the big river. Yet the Damnonii had already gathered most of the harvest, and hidden it so well that they found little. The rain returned, making it hard to drag the few carts they possessed and their cargo of sick and wounded. Somehow they pushed on, the weak, half-starved and filthy soldiers heaving them out each time the wheels became stuck.

The miracle came when they reached the borderland with the Novantae, and he wished that he would dream of that moment, for even though he could close his eyes and picture it, it was not the same as reliving the emotion.

Claudia Enica rode out to meet them, and the most beautiful

woman he had ever known seemed even more beautiful than ever, reinforced because on either side of her there was a youthful image of herself.

'Girls, this is your father,' she said simply.

Beside them was Bran, half a dozen chieftains of the Novantae, the old king of the Selgovae, and even surly Vannus. They were escorted by warriors, and, though he was ashamed to admit it, the most beautiful sight of all were the hundreds of sheep and cattle and the dozen solid-wheeled carts piled high with sacks of grain.

The price to Rome for all this generosity would no doubt be great, but Ferox was sure that Hadrian would be willing to pay it to save the army. He was better than those old fools in the Senate centuries ago who had repudiated the treaty agreed by a proconsul with some Spanish town. He had saved the army, but the Senate would have none of it, and kept the army, but sent the general back to Spain, stripping him naked, putting him in chains, and dumping him outside the town. To their credit, the warriors inside would not take him, so eventually he went back to Rome. Ferox had heard the man even had a statue of himself made, showing him bound up and nude, and proudly displayed it in his porch.

Well, Hadrian was a better man than those fools, and certainly a practical man, so he would understand. Apart from that, Hadrian was not here, nor was anyone else, so the decision was Ferox's and his alone. Clemens mumbled assent through his smashed jaw, and the primus pilus was so fevered that he had not the slightest idea what was going on. The surgeons had taken the man's leg and were worried that this was not enough.

Three days later they met up with troops from the second, smaller army, and the legatus of Legio XX took over. He was eager to impress the newly arrived governor, Falco, who was said to be on his way north.

It all seemed an age ago, except when sleep dragged him back to that high valley and the wreck of an army.

'That is all very well,' Claudia Enica said suddenly, 'but will it be ready in time?' She shifted slightly, turning from her left side onto her right, so that she faced him, and said no more. In a moment the deep breathing returned, punctuated by grunting snores.

Ferox smiled, and reached out to touch her hair gently. She had always done this, and unlike other folk presumably she dreamed of negotiations and formal dinners, for she tended to blurt out bits of conversation without ever waking. It was better than nightmares, for she never seemed agitated and was always poised and calm. Like the snoring, this strange eccentricity made him love her all the more. He did not want to leave again, feeling that he must have earned more time with her after all these years, but Falco had summoned him and that was that.

He liked Falco, for he was one of those senators who actually had substance and talent under all the posturing and prosing. The man drove himself very hard and expected everyone else to do the same, so time and again in the last year or so Ferox had been summoned and given some task, whether temporary command of an auxiliary unit, some diplomatic mission or simply serving with the governor's cohort to advise. With more troops, the new legatus was aggressive, but thankfully understood that Rome's success depended as much on talking, bribing and forming alliances as it did on brute force.

So much had changed. Tincommius was dead, and some said illness and some said poison, and some even said that he had lost all will to live when he found out that one son had murdered another. Volisios was also dead, although not before he had claimed much of the credit for the slaughter of the Roman army and rallied many chiefs and warriors to his cause. Gannascus had caught up with him at the head of the pick of the royal army and a bitter battle had been fought in a high glen. The king's men won in the end, although at heavy cost. To his credit Volisios fought to the last, and dared to face Gannascus. Men said that there was not enough left to recognise of the prince's body when the fight was done, but no one doubted that he was dead.

The High King's empire fell apart. Some of his remaining sons claimed power and plenty of kings and chieftains did the same. They schemed, made alliances and promises, broke them, made fresh ones, and all the while fought. The far north was once again a mass of petty leaders and groups, their fortunes rising and falling with the seasons. The Wolf was doing well from this, becoming a great lord in his own right, his warriors preying on any neighbours who did not swear to follow him. Men said that he was guided by a child of Acco the druid, and Ferox feared that it was true.

Two summers ago, Falco led an army to the far north, and one of the things they did was go to the battlefield and bury in mass graves the remains of the fallen. Those were melancholy days, and one of the High King's sons was fool enough to muster an army and confront the Romans soon afterwards. He escaped, one of the first to flee, leaving most of his warriors to be slaughtered. The following month a king of the Venicones captured the lad and sent him to Falco, who duly forwarded the prisoner to Rome. It was something, but the north still rang to songs of the great victory, and there was plunder, captives and trophies as reminders of the glory. Somewhere among the tribes were dozens of signa standards and vexilla flags, as well as so much equipment. A lot of the heads were in the shrine of

Cocidius, in other sacred places, or fastened outside chieftains' houses.

For all his efforts, Falco had not managed to establish some sort of stability favourable to Roman interests in the far north – the sort that could so easily have been maintained through helping Tincommius and acknowledging Epaticcus as his heir in the first place. At the moment, this did not matter too much, as long as the leaders up there continued to tear each other apart.

Further south, Falco had made more progress, for it was easier to reach the tribal lands there and attack them if necessary. The leaders who had helped save the army were rewarded, which inevitably upset all their rivals and neighbours who had not contributed. Rivalries within and between the tribes intensified, raid following raid. It was said that some cattle were travelling hundreds of miles each year as they were stolen again and again. Even the Votadini, the usually so placid and industrious Votadini, were more inclined to fight than ever before. They chased marauders, then raided in reprisal. Most of the attacks and fighting were little affairs, waged between the tribes, but plenty of the leaders were Roman allies, which meant that they were involved, and as men got used to raiding it tended to spread. There were plenty of outcasts, masterless men who had lost out in feuds, and who banded together to make a living by the sword. If there was no repeat of the great coordinated raid into Brigantian territory, there were plenty of small attacks.

These days Falco's skin had a greyish tinge, for the governor was working himself into the grave. There were few operations involving a thousand men, almost none involving several thousand, for everything was local, but that made it so hard to control. The old king of the Selgovae choked on a chicken bone, and no one was well enough supported to replace him, so that the tribe became far less predictable, turning on each other, their neighbours and the Romans. Everywhere rivalries flared up, and the governor found himself dealing with dozens, even scores of leaders in every clan, let alone every tribe. Half the time, the middle-aged legatus Augusti went charging off at the head of a few hundred men, chasing raiders and bandits, riding to threaten or negotiate with some leader or other. Adding to all his worries was the frail health of his wife, back in Londinium. Men said that most aristocrats married for influence and money, but if that was true in this case, it did not prevent Falco and his wife from adoring each other. Yet he did his duty, staying on the frontier, driving himself harder than anyone else, and that meant Ferox could not refuse when he asked.

It was almost dawn, the light growing just a little in the room. Claudia Enica snored away beside him. He needed to go, for he had a long ride ahead of him to join Falco at Coria and then go north with him. His heart told him that his wife would not wake for a long time, for she had come to bed late and was never too fond of the early hours of the day. She would sleep on, attending dinner parties and dealing with friends and rivals in her dreams, and it was not fair to wake her.

There was a good chance that he would see Bran, for they were heading into the lands of the Selgovae and then the Novantae. The lad was doing well, becoming a great chief, while Vannus was much diminished in spite of the gifts he had received from the Romans. Vannus received gold and there was only so much a lord could buy with gold in the mountains. Bran was promised a bride from the royal house of the Brigantes to add to his gold. The idea had been the queen's and to Ferox's surprise Senuna was enthusiastic when her mother told her. His suggestion that perhaps one of the twins, a trained warrior, was a better match was met with the instant scorn reserved by the women of the family for his ideas.

'They're his sisters by oath,' the queen scoffed. Ferox knew that the Mother bound her pupils to be sister and brother and never to lie with each other, but had always assumed that such taboos lapsed once they had finished their training. 'And you know Bran better than anyone.'

'That's the point,' Ferox said, trying and failing to sound like Vindex.

'I love him, father,' Senuna assured him, as if explaining a simple fact to a slow child. His wife wanted it, his daughter was eager, and – most important of all – the governor approved, which meant that it would happen. Yet he still worried that she was so very young.

'Thank him, and say that we would like it all delivered by the end of the month,' Claudia Enica blurted out in the silence. As usual there was no more, presumably because that negotiation was satisfactorily concluded. The world of his wife's dreams sounded simple, far more efficient than the real thing.

She shifted to lie on her back, her breathing becoming softer. She did not stir.

Leaning over her, he kissed her lightly on the forehead, wondered whether his ancestors in the Otherworld were cringing and thinking that a true warrior should wake her and bid farewell by demonstrating his love.

He did not, even though she looked so very lovely. Instead he dressed and left.

XXVI

Three days before the Kalends of April,
the consulship of M' Acilius Aviola and
*L. Cornelius Neratius Pansa**, *at Vindolanda*

HADRIAN WAS COMING. Everyone had known that for the best part of a year, but now the imperial visit was imminent.

'A month or so,' Cerialis confirmed. 'He's bringing the new legatus Augusti and a whole new legion, VI Victrix from Germania.'

Ferox nodded, for he had heard the rumours, but Cerialis as the imperial procurator for Britannia was as likely as anyone to know the truth. It was an important job, a fine culmination for an already good career if that is what it proved to be. Ferox was never sure with Cerialis, and there were traces of the familiar restless ambition. Yet the man seemed old, his reddish blond hair now so pale that it was hard to say whether it was very fair or actually white.

'That's why this place is so splendid.' They were dining in the mansio, the way station for official travellers outside the garrison at Vindolanda. 'Fit for the first citizen no less, who would have thought it? They don't usually lavish this sort of thing on humble centenarii like me!'

---

* AD 122.

'I thought you tax collectors lived like kings wherever you were.'

'Ha. That's just the freedmen. We equestrians have to account for everything.' Cerialis scooped out an oyster. The sight still made Ferox feel nauseous after all these years, and he declined politely when his old friend gestured at the dish. The Silures believed that food from the sea weighed down and corrupted the soul, although Ferox sometimes wondered whether it was the sheer look of the things that turned his stomach. He drank some wine instead, making sure to dilute it well. There had been times when he had drunk too much. He still needed to be careful.

'Is it strange being back in this place?' he asked.

'Vindolanda? Hercules, I was so young when I came here. Those were happy times.'

'Apart from the attempts to abduct and murder you and your wife.'

'Well, yes, apart from those! But here we all are, still going strong. I can just remember the excitement of that first command. I miss my Batavians to this day. You knew where you were with them because they made it clear if they didn't like something... Odd being here and everything looking so different though. Perhaps it helps. Reckon I'd keep expecting to bump into old faces around every corner if the fort was the same.' He chuckled. 'Shame Flora has moved on though.'

Flora was an easterner who had run a highly efficient brothel on the edge of the *canabae* outside the old fort.

'She had gone before I came back from the east. No one seems to know where. I hope she is happy.'

Cerialis laughed. 'Yes, she was a decent old stick. Lepidina liked her, oddly enough, even went to get her advice about creating that bath we had in the praetorium. Do you fancy a bath, by the way? There is one here, the only bit of the building made wholly in stone.'

'That would be nice.'

Cerialis told one of the slaves to see to it, before returning to serious matters. 'Falco has leave to go,' Cerialis continued. 'Poor fellow is exhausted and his wife very sick. They're giving him Asia as proconsul in the hope that the warm climate will help her. Though from all Lepidina tells me, she'll be lucky to make it that far. Still Hadrian has said that he can leave now, instead of waiting for his successor. Falco's done such a splendid job that it is felt the situation is sufficiently stable, even up here.' Cerialis paused. 'I know that face of old. You don't agree?'

'Folk are saying that the tribes have broken the legate's spirit. That makes some of the chiefs feel strong and daring. Until this new legion arrives, the army is spread very thinly, and most it is labouring rather than ready to fight.'

'Do they say that the emperor is coming?'

'Yes.'

'Thought so. And no doubt that rumour started among the tribes before a word was breathed among senior officers. Yes.' Cerialis shook his head. 'I never will understand these lands and these people if I live to be a hundred. They just have a knack of knowing.'

'They listen, and they think. Sometimes they dream... And Romans never notice their slaves,' he gestured at a pair waiting quietly in the corner of this large and otherwise empty dining room. 'Slaves gossip and gossip spreads.'

'Well, I've seen enough not to doubt the result even if I don't understand how it works. Bit like the law, really.' He snorted at his own wit. 'Still, if they know Hadrian is coming, along with a new governor and lots of soldiers, won't that give them pause for thought?'

'Might make some think that it's well worthwhile striking now, before the Romans are stronger. The really ambitious or crazy, or both, might even think that Hadrian's arrival is a challenge. Imagine the glory of doing something under his nose, or to Hadrian himself?'

'Really?'

'Why not? They've killed a legionary legate after all.' Ferox regretted the words, but it was too late.

'And a tribune.' Cerialis reached over and patted him on the shoulder. 'It's all right, old fellow. I miss Titus, how could I not? And I feel sorry because I always drove the boy too hard. Lepidina often said so.' There was deep sorrow in his voice. Ferox and the queen had written to them, giving as much information as they could, and since his arrival in the province, every time they had met, they had covered it all again. Sometimes, when they were alone, Cerialis would listen to Ferox recall every detail he could of his time with Titus during those last months. Sometimes Cerialis would do all the talking, remembering older, better times and all the lost hopes. 'He was a good lad, always tried his best. I'm not sure that I was much of a father. You want the best for your sons, the things you did not have, and in this world many of those things come at a terrible cost.' His tone was very bleak.

'Why is that women understand these things so much better than us?' he went on. 'She told me, subtly at first, hinting, and then straight out because it had not got into my thick skull. Oh by the way, she writes to say that your wife is well, and your girls. Making quite the impression down there, so she tells me, just as she did, I suppose, back in the day.'

'She wants to turn them into proper young ladies,' Ferox said gloomily. It seemed an odd ambition after having them trained as warriors for several years, but then the queen's parents had done the same for her.

'I have missed your pessimism. Of course, she wants them to be fine ladies! They are after all. By the sound of it they and my Flavia are inseparable again, even though they haven't seen each other for years. And by the sound of it young Marcus is mooning over them like a lovesick schoolboy!' Cerialis roared with laughter. 'Oh don't worry, the lad knows how to behave. I tell him to take a dawn swim in the cold river every day and get plenty of exercise, the randy little devil.'

Ferox smiled dutifully. He could probably trust his wife and Lepidina to keep a close eye on everything, but the young were ingenious, and he did not know the twins well enough to gauge how sensible they were likely to be.

'Shouldn't he be with his legion?'

'Lepidina is trying to wangle a posting on the new governor's staff. You know what she is like. She has a cousin, whose uncle is married to the niece of someone else's cousin, who grew up next door to Platorius Nepos. That's the new governor, by the way, since you didn't bother to ask. I suppose some shepherd up a mountain told you his names months ago, before Hadrian had even chosen him probably – does that sound about right?'

Ferox grinned. 'About right.'

'Well, he is hanging around hoping that his winning smile will help convince Nepos when he arrives. Or Hadrian perhaps. The lad is ambitious.'

'Can't think where he gets that from!' Ferox smiled as the servants brought in new platters. Some seasoned lamb had the most enticing of scents. He noticed Cerialis eyeing one of the girls with more than casual interest. She was pretty enough, with that blank, I only see something if my masters want me to see something look you saw so often. Most Romans took it for granted, but it had always bothered him. Tended to make him wonder whether the owner had just spat in his soup.

'Thank you, my child,' Cerialis beamed at the girl. 'Regina isn't it, yes, what a pretty name. Thank you again.' He watched her leave with more interest than he showed the food.

'Well then, what's it like no longer being a soldier and instead becoming a book-keeper?' Ferox asked.

'Sorry,' Cerialis said as he snapped from his reverie. 'Oh that. A lot more travelling, and you develop a nasty suspicious mind that makes you mistrust anything anyone ever tells you. You'd be good at it!'

'And are you up in these parts to halve the subsidies to most of the chieftains, demand the rest pay debts they didn't know they had, or failing that hand over their nearest and dearest as slaves, before clearing off and letting the rest of us deal with the eruption?'

'Something like that, although changing the subsidies would mean changing the records and that costs ink and writing tablets, which is such a shocking waste that I probably won't bother… No, I'm mainly here to check on the princeps' great project. The amounts involved are staggering, truly staggering, so when numbers get that big even a little mistake can spiral into a vast waste very quickly. That's apart from checking that no one is stealing any more than is reasonable.'

'What, selling spades or pick axes to the natives at a vast profit!' Ferox suggested. 'Or thousands of stones from the quarries.'

'Who knows? Some people can find a way of making money out of anything. But if you do find a chieftain now living in a vast stone fort, then let me know – something might be up! … I don't know, the whole thing still staggers me. The numbers are enormous, simply enormous.'

Ferox felt the same. Two autumns ago Hadrian had written to Falco asking him to investigate an idea that was at once staggering and at the same time very Roman in its simplicity. He wanted a line of fortifications running from the east coast of Britannia across to the west.

'Lot of nonsense,' Falco said. 'So it's either divine brilliance or very mortal stupidity. Since it might be the latter, I thought of you,' he added, placing Ferox in charge of telling the surveyors where to look. 'If you send them into a swamp and they don't come back, that might solve everyone's problems.'

Ferox could not find any swamps in the right place, so instead brought them to the fringes of Brigantian territory, where the mouths of a river on each coast made the land as narrow as it could be, and left them to it. Most of them were serious men, happy in their task, and they worked their way in from either coast, taking sightings with the *groma*, sticking flags all over the place, and making cryptic notes.

Hadrian was delighted, and within two months of getting the report, he sent back detailed orders for a ditch and a free-standing wall, ten feet thick, running for eighty miles. That had been a year ago. Ferox could still remember Falco swearing for a long time as he went through the plans, ending in a morose, 'Wonder what he'll want us to build next month!'

Work began, with as many legionaries as the two legions could find, along with the handful from the vexillation who had somehow not been sent back with the rest several months ago. The legions had more craftsmen in their ranks and were simply better suited to big projects, so they did the work while the auxiliaries took on the chief burden of keeping the frontier in some sort of order.

'It's funny,' Cerialis said. 'I'd have thought that they would have started at one side and worked their way across, or even started at both sides and worked in, although I guess it would be more than a little embarrassing if they did that and missed each other. It's costing enough for one, never mind two.' All along the line marked out and chosen by the surveyors, there were more than a dozen work parties starting to build, and others quarrying stone. There were bits of wall, isolated towers, bare foundations nowhere near anything else. 'What do the locals say about it all?'

'Depends which ones you ask? There are plenty of farmers wondering about the flags spread out in a line across their fields. Reckon a lot of them don't want to believe it, it's all so strange, so unlike anything we have done before.'

'They've had forts built on their land though, haven't they?' Cerialis suggested.

'Some, but rarely on good farmland. We use so much turf that it makes sense to go where there is plenty of the stuff. That's usually not ploughed fields.'

'Huh! Never thought of that. Though at least I don't have to find too much in the way of funds for the bits they are planning in the west. That will be turf rather than stone.'

'Quicker, I suppose,' Ferox said.

'Possibly. The towers there are being made of stone though. No one has yet explained to me why. But to return to what the locals think about it all. What are the tribes saying, the Novantae, Selgovae and the rest? You know, the folk this wall is presumably supposed to inconvenience or intimidate.'

Ferox considered this, for there was not a simple answer. 'They're puzzled. If a farmer likely to see his land split in two and dug up into a ditch cannot really believe that this will happen, they've even less of a clue. Don't think any of them can really imagine it.'

'But they must see the towers going up, the gateways, the bits of wall. They must realise that something is going on.'

'Well, none of it joins up at the moment, and bits of wall start and stop for no reason, and are either foundations or low enough for anyone to jump across. I think we have them puzzled.'

Cerialis was amused. 'Well, that makes it all worthwhile I suppose. But they don't imagine it will end with that, do they?'

'Some probably do. But they all think we are mad in the first place, so they don't worry too much.'

'That's all right then.' Cerialis stretched his arms. 'Let's have that bath – one fit for an emperor, no less.'

Beltane, above the Vale of Wolf

He was alone, arms bleeding from his own knife, waiting to be guided.

'You will know what to do,' she had told him. 'The path is clear.'

It was cold, but what did that matter? The cold was nothing, even though the grass crunched beneath his feet with late frost.

'You will know.'

He missed her, for early in the winter she had gone down with a fever and her life had burned away. She had spoken a lot during those last days, often in languages he did not understand. Other times, the words were familiar but made no sense that he could comprehend. Yet near the end, she stared directly into his eyes and her voice and sense was as clear as it had ever been. No man could doubt the power of those words.

'It is soon. The great revenge.' Every word was clear, unslurred, and her eyes were bright even though he felt as if they saw straight through him to pierce the future itself.

'The path is clear. Your path. To bring death.'

She was old and the old died, for that was the way of things. Not even the most powerful druids lived forever in this world, for the Otherworld called to them all the time, its voice strong and seductive. That was the life of eternity, of uncovering all the greatest secrets.

'He will come.'

When she had fallen ill, he somehow knew that she would

die. He could sense that she knew it as well and accepted it as meant to be.

'He will come. Soon.'

Although she had guided every step he had taken for so many years, he was not frightened at the thought of losing her.

'Another will come before him.'

He knew that this was as much part of the plan as everything else. All was ready.

'You will know. The path is clear.'

Two of her women tended to her as she lay on her bower in the little hut that was all the shelter she would ever accept. They were both old, almost as old as she was, and he wondered whether she would choose one of them to guide him. She did not.

'Only you can walk it. Trust in your power. Listen for my voice.'

The only thing that surprised him was that he let his own woman tend to her. She was the only one allowed to feed her.

'She gives you strength. Use it.'

Within a day of the battle, he had discovered that his captive was not Enica of the Brigantes, called Claudia by the Romans. This Claudia was a former slave from the Trinovantes of the south, a whore turned courtesan and mistress of the commander, Priscus. She had her name because the master who had freed her was called Claudius and was a citizen, which made her a citizen as well.

He had learned this when some of his men brought in a prisoner, a Roman officer, and the man babbled and begged, telling him anything he wanted to know.

'In her you see Rome.'

He had been angry when he learned, and as they camped that night, he had taken her away from the others, dragging her inside the half-ruined walls of a sheep pen. She screamed and he hit her, and he was not gentle when he took her. He was a warrior and she was his prize in war. What she felt did not matter.

'And you see what is not Rome.'

She had fought him, and he had hurt her, for somehow she had saved a pride usually destroyed by slavery, and then, just at the moment of release she had called him by his name.

'Trust her.' The Silures gave children a name, their own real name, a name that was secret, known only to the child, the one who bestowed it and sometimes the parents. It was never again spoken aloud, for this was the name of the soul, the name they would carry when they walked the shadow lands of the Otherworld.

'Trust what she makes you feel.'

Claudia explained later that it was her brother's name as well, a brother she had lost when both were very young and sold as slaves. She did not know what had happened to him, or whether he still lived, but had called to him for help.

'There is no such thing as mere chance.' Those were almost the last words she said, repeating what she had told him when she had first seen his captive. Then he had wondered whether she intended Claudia as a sacrifice.

He no longer called her Claudia, her free name, or Hera, her slave name. She remembered being called Vinda by dim voices in her earliest memories. He liked that name.

She understood that she must never speak aloud her brother's and his name, not even to whisper in his ear as they made love.

'Like Rome.'

That was true in many ways. Vinda recovered quickly and became again very lovely. She was careful about her appearance, her cleanliness, her hair, for all combined to create her beauty.

She was also strong, recovering quickly from the injuries he had given her. Soon there was no sign of what had happened, nor did she do anything to suggest she remembered it.

'The face of Rome is a mask.'

He no longer took. She gave, and there was a pleasure that he had never before known. They did not marry, but she was his woman and the lady of his Hall. He gave her whatever she asked, and had even offered to send her back to the province with an escort and a great purse of gold.

'Rome is softness and Rome is strength.'

Vinda enjoyed power. She remained plump, if slimmer than when he had taken her. She had given him a son, the year before, and fretted until her figure recovered. The boy was strong, with the thick black hair of his people, and he was immensely proud.

'Rome is cunning.'

Vinda advised him. She would listen to whatever he chose to say, consider, and counsel him with subtlety.

'Rome is cruel.'

She advised him to raid, helping his power to grow in the months after the battle as the whole of the north was riven by rivalry and war. She suggested which men he should befriend and which he should kill. She saw past the bluster and reputation and spoke to him of great chieftains ruled by their wives and lovers.

'Rome is mighty.'

He could have taken the name of king if he wanted. He did not bother, but more and more families and clans pledged to support him. Instead of several hundred, he could now call on thousands to follow his standard of the wolf. Vinda had told him to make it, to be like the eagles of Rome, and to make it not of gold or silver, but of iron, for it was strength that mattered.

'Rome looks to the edge of the world and does not pay heed to the ground under its feet.'

He had about a hundred men trained in the ways of his people. Some of the others understood a little of this, but could not quickly learn all that there was to learn. They were his best. He had not asked them or even thought of it, but all had tattooed a wolf somewhere on their skin. They were hunters and killers and they were good. More than one chief who opposed him was ambushed and killed without need for battle.

'Rome rules through fear.'

He had made his neighbours fear him, and as month followed month, his reputation grew and the fear spread ever wider.

'Rome rules through guile.'

Men learn to fear what they cannot see. That was a saying of his people. Even accidental deaths were attributed to him, or to her magic. To his surprise, men spoke as if his new lady was also a descendent of Acco, with powers of her own.

'The fear, the guile, the softness and strength mean that Rome only seems strong from a distance.'

Whenever he could, he led or sent raids south, against the clans and chiefs allied to the Romans, and sometimes to the province itself. Two months ago, he had burned a villa of Ferox and his queen, the one all had spared in the great raid, so as to cast doubt on his loyalty.

'Rome is a giant and giants can be tripped and fall.'

Her words came back to him as he danced and chanted, and the visions were strong, of great statues tumbling to the ground, necks snapping, so that the carven heads rolled in the dust.

'It will be soon.'

She was dead, but she was with him. Vinda was beside him, somehow a part of her and something altogether different.

'Soon.'

His visions faded as the dawn rose behind a sullen sky. He walked back to the fort and did not hurry. The visitor was there, a Roman with cold enough eyes to be one of the Silures. It was the third time that he had come, and he warned that the next time he would most likely send someone else to carry the news.

That did not matter. The man was a traitor and was loyal, and it served both their purposes to work together.

'There is no such thing as mere chance.'

This man was here because of the captive they had taken at the battle, the coward who had begged and fawned. He was a greedy, ambitious man who had promised much in return for his life and freedom. Nothing about him was trustworthy except his ambition and his hatred of rivals. They were enough alongside the fear.

That man had gone free, taking an extra horse and money, promising to send word to someone with immense power.

He had done what he promised, and all that was asked of him since. Once he met the visitor for the first time, it became obvious why. If ever there was a man to fear, it was this one.

'No such thing as chance.'

They did not want what he wanted, but would give it to him nevertheless, and take their own mean prizes, for such things did not concern him.

The visitor brought much news and they talked and planned throughout the day, and for another day after that.

Soon. He knew what to do. The path was clear and he would walk it.

XXVII

The Ides of May, Londinium

THE FORUM WAS crowded, with people perched on walls and rooftops and anywhere else they could balance, however precariously. Guards, not the usual garrison troops, but immaculately turned out praetorians and singulares Augusti, stood at all the entrances of the basilica. The fortunate and favoured had been admitted early on and were permitted to stay throughout. Others waited, hoping that their turn would come before sunset and the session came to an end. Even when there was nothing to see, the crowd buzzed with conversation, wondering, questioning. No princeps had come to Britannia since Claudius almost eighty years ago, and he had stayed for little more than ten days.

Hadrian was here, and anyone who was anyone in the province had been desperate for an invitation to this ceremony, or failing that one of the smaller ones to be held in the following days and in a handful of other cities at a later date. Everyone else with a petition, some problem ignored or resolved the wrong way, and anyone who simply hoped that gaining the attention of the master of the empire would help them, had flocked to Londinium in the hope of getting to see him. There were no rooms left for hire, no inns with empty space, and even the outhouses or the flimsy shelters put up on any convenient wall in the yards and streets, were all full.

The prices were outrageous, because everyone could charge whatever they wanted, and plenty of folk were willing to offer more to find a place. The same was true for miles outside the walls, and there were tents dotted around, or folk simply sleeping on the ground. Inside, the streets were far filthier than usual, save for the paths carefully swept and cleaned for the use of the imperial party, a task that had to be repeated several times a day. Unseasonable heat helped magnify the stench of sweat and excrement. The public lavatories were overwhelmed, the public bath houses far too crowded to admit more than a few. Anyone who sold something did well, whether it was food or drink, fortunes or curses, or their bodies. So did the thieves, for it was so easy to slip away into the crowd. There were robberies and murder, and it was unwise for a stranger to wander away from his or her companions, especially if they were young and attractive, for people could vanish as easily as coins or jewellery, and they were never far from the port and ships that sailed far away.

Soldiers acted as sentries to keep the streets open, and sometimes they offered to help strangers who had lost friends or goods or had otherwise been abused. Sometimes they took the task seriously, especially when rewarded, and sometimes they did their job with great energy even without such incentives. The legatus Augusti was new, and men keen to stay on as part of his foot and horse bodyguard wanted to make a good impression. The praetorians and other guardsmen had seen all of this before in the Gauls, in Raetia, in Noricum and the two Germanies and took care to be appear efficient, disciplined and energetic. That was what Trajan had always demanded and the new princeps was every bit as much of a stickler. Armour and equipment gleamed as brightly as their faces, for the emperor noticed if he spotted anything, and informed the officers in charge, who passed the disapproval down, at each stage gaining in weight, like a boulder rolling down a hill.

Claudia Enica, her twin daughters, and immediate attendants were among the lucky ones with seats reserved inside the basilica itself. The day had started early, and they had gone together with Sulpicia Lepidina and her husband, who had returned only the night before. He had three soldiers from his staff, as well as a Batavian who served as his orderly, so Claudia took just two of her escort, both former soldiers and made to look as Roman as possible. She wore white today, dazzlingly bright, for she suspected that this and her red hair would make her stand out when most of the women present would favour colours. Lepidina was in pale blue, for she was fond of the shade and it suited her. The twins were in a deeper blue. All of them kept their hair simple, for Sabina, like the rest of her family, had rejected the elaborate confections common in the past. Claudia Enica had hers plaited and piled high on top of her head, which no doubt struck some Romans as an oddly foreign look. Lepidina had hers in a bun, while the girls each had a double bun. None of them were so crass as to copy the Augusta's style from her most common paintings and statues, but as they went through the streets and came to the Forum, they saw plenty who had done just that.

'It will be quite a wait, I'm afraid,' Cerialis told them as they were ushered into the basilica. The Sun had not yet risen, for Hadrian liked to start work early, which meant that everyone else had to be ready even earlier. The princeps had made it known from the start of his travels that he did not require the morning salutation from anyone other than his senior staff and officials. He had no wish to set the local worthies bickering over who should attend each day, let alone learn so many names. He made himself available in the daytime and that ought to be enough for them. Cerialis had attended on his own, as imperial procurator, the emperor's own man, able to send reports and receive instructions from the princeps wholly independently of the governor.

They were to the left of the podium at the far end of the great hall, already echoing to the flow of conversation. Some watched them enviously as they moved to so prominent a place. All but a few concealed it, and greeted Cerialis and his wife, for the procurator was one of the most important officials in any province, indeed the most important in all matters of finance and taxation, as well as the oversight of the substantial estates of imperial land. There were broad smiles and enthusiastic welcomes for him, and for his wife, since everyone assumed that she must have great influence over him, not least because she was clarissima femina, the daughter of a senator.

'I think I've been pinched raw,' Bellicia whispered to her sister while they were waiting for the king of the Atrebates to ask a favour of Cerialis.

'So have I,' Corotica added, reaching back to rub. In spite of the escort, the streets were so crowded that they had been jostled by the crowd.

'And neither of you killed anyone, so aren't you doing well?' their mother said sweetly. 'You will be proper young ladies in no time at all.' She was using the language of the tribes, and broadening the dialect to sound as Brigantian as possible, and hopefully incomprehensible to those close by. 'But a fine Roman lady does not rub her arse in public. What does a proper lady do?'

'Feign interest in everything a nobleman says, no matter how fatuous,' Corotica suggested.

'Listen carefully, waiting for the right moment to mock in a way that seems more like flirtation than contempt,' her sister added. 'Oh and don't let them know that you could slay them with ease.'

'Well done. You are learning.' They were, Claudia Enica allowed, remembering how she had had to learn the same lessons all those years ago. Memory made it seem easy, first living at Lugdunum in Gaul, then at Rome under Lepidina's guidance. Anything was easier when you had Lepidina as a friend.

Cerialis promised to do his best for the king of the Atrebates, and they set off again, the last few yards. Claudia Enica used the pretext of acknowledging friends and acquaintances to watch her daughters as they came behind. They did not walk like young Roman ladies, with demure little steps to keep dress and ornate coiffure in place, and eyes down amid strangers. They strode like panthers or some of the other big cats you saw in the arena. There was a confidence in them, a swagger that came from years of learning how to fight under the stern eye of the Mother. No one fought to the death up there, but they were given the belief that they could face and defeat anyone.

The twins were blossoming, their beauty still growing almost by the day. At the moment, they did not look feminine, at least as the Romans understood such things. What they needed to learn was to hide that side of them as she had done, unleashing the warrior only when necessary. It meant living as two people, always different from everyone else, and it was hard, but they were from the royal house of the tribe and must serve in that way as well as living in the world of Rome so that they could do the best for their tribe.

'They do so remind me of you at that age,' Lepidina kept saying.

Perhaps Claudia Enica had given off the same feral air in her day. She did not remember. For the moment it was still a shock for the girls to start living in Roman society, and the arrival of the princeps had thrown them into it rather more quickly than she had planned. It was probably for the best, and might even give her an advantage. If Hadrian noticed her daughters, and he was bound to do so, given that they were tall, redhaired, as near identical as it was possible to be, and would be just beside the podium, hopefully he would see them move. The emperor did not much care for women. Yet there was a good chance that the princeps would like two lithe young ones, slim and moving with the balance of athletes or warriors. They were close to the youths who fascinated him, a little fuller and plumper, which added to the attraction. Still, you would have to cut their hair short like the Spartan lasses of old, and bind their breasts as tightly as possible if the illusion were to be pushed any further.

That was not necessary with Hadrian. He had desires, very strong ones, but for more than a decade had controlled them, at least as far as Lepidina knew – and she would know as much as anyone in society. Whatever passions he had, the senator and now princeps had learned to keep them discreet, for the moment at least. As emperor no one would ever say no openly to any suggestion he made, which meant that it took an iron will not to indulge desires at least to some extent. For the moment, Hadrian would take no more pleasure than came from observing something or someone, and all in all, Claudia Enica reckoned that he would like to see her girls swaggering along.

They were certainly conspicuous. There were plenty of other kings and chiefs from the tribes gathered in the hall, the most important sitting fairly close to them. A handful of other Brigantes were present, some of them supporters and some not. All were at a distance. She was noticed because, age or not, she was striking – the dazzlingly bleached dress helped with that – and accompanied by the two younger versions of herself, and was with the procurator and his incomparable wife, sitting so close to the heart of everything. People whispered, pointing them out and explaining to friends who they were.

Hadrian arrived at long last with fanfares of trumpets, praetorians marching in, hobnailed boots stamping rhythmically as they marched and changed formation to each bellowed order. The princeps was not one for theatrics and ceremony, unlike some emperors, but had no choice on occasions like this, the first formal audience when he visited a province. There were prayers – and had already been sacrifices earlier that morning – and choirs, and speeches, lots of speeches. Hadrian needed to be welcomed and praised, even by Platorius Nepos, the new legatus Augusti, who had only just arrived on the same ship as the emperor.

After an hour, Claudia glanced behind her and noticed Corotica rolling her eyes.

'Feign interest,' her sister whispered and they both giggled. The queen glared at them.

It was another hour before the princeps gave his own speech thanking everyone for the welcome and telling them how important Britannia was in his heart. Claudia Enica had plenty of time to study the emperor and his party as the words flowed past her.

She had not seen Hadrian for seventeen years, when he had been about thirty. There was still the same restless energy, the quick brown eyes, with their intelligent gaze, giving off the sense that the owner was only with great difficulty refraining from telling you that you were wrong. He was thicker set now, face filled out, and if his limbs were still well muscled, he was no longer young. She was sure that there were a few flecks of grey in his beard. There were quite a few bearded faces in the audience. After the surprise, almost confusion, when statues, paintings and coins of the emperor arrived and showed a bearded face, plenty had adopted the fashion, something very rare apart from in the lower ranks of the army in the past.

Hadrian's comites, his distinguished friends and companions on this journey, were as clean shaven as ever, which suggested that they realised the emperor did not value such flattery. Aulus Platorius Nepos had a round face, thick hair and prominent ears, and could readily have passed for one of Augustus' family. He was just what most folk expected a Roman senator to look like. The other senators were older, most in their fifties and sixties, but all still vigorous. Septicius Clarus, one of the two prefects in charge of the Praetorian Guard – a precaution to prevent a single commander becoming too ambitious – was an odd contrast. He was short and very broad, and far from handsome, so that finding that beards were now fashionable was no doubt a great relief. The first thought was that someone had dressed up an ape from the arena as a soldier. He looked very strong, and rather fierce, neither of which were bad things for a senior guardsman. Yet Lepidina assured her that the looks were deceptive, and that this was far more of a cultured man of letters than a hard-bitten soldier.

Throughout the speeches, the Augusta scanned the audience constantly. Her eyes were a deep brown and large, and she would stare for some time at each person, with the hint of a smile on her face. Lepidina said that the emperor's wife had very poor vision at any distance, but that Sabina was convinced a regal expression and apparent interest in individuals would convey her concern for their welfare.

At long last, the welcomes and greetings came to an end, and business began. This meant more speeches, but ones with a clearer purpose. Hadrian had issued strict instructions that no one should speak for more than a quarter of an hour, measured on the official water clock used for public business. He had also made clear that brevity was more likely to win favour than grand orations.

The kings of the southern tribes were first, many of them the second or third generation of their family, descendants of men who had first pledged loyalty to Claudius and Rome. They wanted honours and rights, help with disputes involving communities in their lands and most of all to be considered important. Hadrian already knew the issues, for his staff had demanded that each petition be submitted in advance, and the decisions in each case had already been made. This was merely the way to honour all sides and make the ruling known in public, even in the case where the ruling was, 'and we shall consider the matter with all urgency'. Claudia Enica knew all about that one, for it was what she had been told for more than twenty years.

Once all these matters had been dealt with, almost three hours had passed. Soon there would be a break for refreshment, but before that there was one final matter.

'The res publica is the coming together of citizens and friends to make Rome stronger and greater. In renewing the friendships and alliances as we have done today, there is golden promise for the future.' He let the words sink in. They all liked that. 'Many tribes are present today, their leaders are Romans but also fathers for their own people, to extend the benefit of our peace and our justice to them.

'One great tribe has had no leader for many years, until today. I speak of the Brigantes, the folk of the north. Queen Cartimandua was a friend of the divine Claudius and always loyal, for among that people the leadership of women has never been feared or despised. That is not the Roman way.'

Claudia Enica could just see the Brigantian chieftains through the mass of bobbing heads. Several had perked up, and she could sense their expectation. It was hard not to smile.

'Yet today I name a Queen and a King for the Brigantes, and call them friends of the Roman people.'

There were murmurs of surprise. One of the chieftains frowned in confusion, and no doubt wondered whether the tribe was to be split into two.

'I speak of Flavius Ferox, the much decorated soldier Flavius Ferox, Prince of the Silures, and my friend, and of Claudia, descendant of Cartimandua, and an ally every bit as loyal to Rome. No one should ever forget her services just a few years ago during the troubles in the north.

'As we speak, her husband serves with our armies, so cannot be here today. Thus, I ask the queen to stand so that all may see her and know my faith in her. Come, Claudia, and take my hand and my blessing.'

She rose. The murmurs of surprise had grown louder, but someone was stamping his foot, and others joined, an old acclamation of the southern tribes. It spread through the great basilica until it echoed.

There were broad steps leading up to the podium, where Hadrian sat, Sabina beside him, the senators and commanders just behind. The noise grew, cheering joining the stamping of feet, and no doubt many had little idea of what this was all about, but wanted to show how impressed they were by the emperor's wisdom.

Claudia Enica inclined her head to the Augusta, who smiled broadly. She did the same to the princeps, who held out his hand for her to kiss.

'If you make a speech I might change my mind,' he said softly.

'A woman make a speech, my lord? Surely not.'

There was the slightest of smiles, but amusement in his eyes. 'That would be shocking, truly shocking. Is Ferox as gloomy as ever?'

'He is, my lord.'

'That is reassuring. Now what do you think of my wall?'

She thought for a moment. 'I have questions, my lord.'

'Good. I'll want you with me when I go north. Now turn and smile politely, but with restraint.'

'Hail the Queen of the Brigantes!' Hadrian called out. 'Friend of the Roman People!'

'Hail the Queen!' echoed through the hall. 'Long life to the princeps!' followed, and was repeated again and again until Hadrian raised his hand and a herald announced that business was suspended for an hour.

Plenty of people came over to congratulate her during the recess, some she knew, and many strangers using this to make an acquaintance. Claudia Enica enjoyed the moment less than she had expected. Part of that was the length of the wait, and a little the appointment of Ferox as king in his own right and not merely her consort. More was the sense that the long quest was over, so that there were far more important things to do now.

That evening there were two dinners, one hosted by Hadrian for the most distinguished men and the other by the Augusta for the ladies. The latter was a quiet, very proper affair, the food good, but taking great care not to be luxurious, the entertainment public readings of poetry. It was dull, but good practice for the twins. They seemed to have inherited her own fondness for clothes and jewellery, for they spent the few hours between the reception and the dinner fussing over each other and discussing different options with their slaves.

'Ladies, please congratulate your mother on my behalf.' The smooth voice was very familiar, and Claudia Enica forced herself to wait before she glanced back.

'I am sure she'll be delighted to know,' Corotica said and giggled in a way that was worrying.

The queen glanced back, saw the impudent fellow lean to kiss each girl on the cheek, give them a smouldering look, and then retreat into the crowd.

Marcus had gone off to his legion at long last, with a promise of future preferment if no immediate reward, and that had removed one worry. Now Pertacus, the same fellow who had done his best to seduce her only a few years ago, was obviously intent on bedding her daughters. That was offensive as well as concerning. He might be eager to ingratiate himself with her, given her formal recognition, but she doubted it. Pertacus had at long last received an appointment as tribune with a legion, one stationed in Dacia of all places, but had secured permission to serve on the new legatus' staff for the moment. Someone had won him this favour, which suggested that he did not need her patronage.

After the great disaster, Pertacus had briefly won some celebrity. He was the first man to reach an army garrison, or at least the first Roman and the first officer, since no one paid any heed to the irregulars who had made it back beforehand. By all accounts, Pertacus had played his part well, riding into Magna on a sweat-stained, exhausted horse, his head bandaged, clothes torn and bloodstained, his sword broken, and all in all coming off as the last man out of Troy.

Word had spread, for his was the first real news. Deliberately modest about his own deeds, letting his audience imagine his heroism, he had spoken of the defeat, and doubted the prospects of the survivors ever getting home. Priscus was dead with many more brave men. Titus Cerialis had shown his youth and inexperience by advancing too far from his defences, so that his men were overwhelmed. The stories spread, in a province desperate for news, and only when Claudia's own messages arrived, followed in due course by Ferox and his ragged army, did questions begin to be asked about Pertacus' version of events, and indeed his appearance on his own.

Yet his story was there, and it was what some wanted to hear and believe, especially the families of Ligustinus and Priscus. They needed someone or something to blame for the defeat, and an unwise young tribune, the first of his line to seek a senatorial career, was perfect. There had been a war of words, or of letters and even some pamphlets, ever since, for Sulpicia Lepidina was determined to defend her stepson. Claudia Enica and Ferox both played their part, as did plenty of others. The recovering Clemens also added his voice, though in an angry tone which did not always help.

Even at the dinner, Lepidina was careful to thank the Augusta for assisting her in the matter.

'Your boy was a great loss to Rome, my dear,' Sabina assured her. 'A great loss indeed. It is such a shame that the army only decorates those who live, for he was deserving of the highest awards.'

The empress talked very freely to those on the couches next to her. 'I was delighted to see you given your just reward,' she told Claudia Enica. 'Although I had wished, and argued too, that you be allowed to rule alone.'

'My husband is a good man,' Claudia assured her. 'And clever enough to understand his limitations.'

'You are fortunate. Is he kind? So many are not. Men can be beasts and...'

Sulpicia Lepidina tried to change the subject, asking Platorius Nepos' wife how she liked Londinium and what she had seen of Britannia.

'Men can be cruel,' the Augusta said, ignoring them. 'So very cruel.'

To break the uncomfortable silence, Claudia Enica asked whether as the wife and assistant of the greatest man in the world, the Augusta would favour her with some advice to help her rule well.

'That is hard. I do my best, you know, I really do.'

The steward, who had shown concern for some time, came over. 'My lady, I fear that you are not well.'

Sabina's eyes were glassy, she seemed almost frightened. 'Oh dear,' she said. 'Oh dear. I try so very hard.'

'You are tired, my lady. It has been a long day after a hard journey.'

'Yes,' the Augusta said. 'Yes, I am tired. I had better withdraw. Would you help me, dear Claudia?'

The empress shook off the arm of the steward, and let the queen help her up. She was not old, but there was a frailty about her. For a moment she leaned close.

'Trust no one,' she whispered.

XXVIII

Seven days before the Kalends of June, among the Novantae

'UP THERE,' VINDEX suggested. 'Either in the trees or in that dip in the ground. Two, I reckon.'

'Three,' Ferox said. 'And closer there are a couple more in the heather.' They were alone, in a high valley, having left the force of scouts and troopers several miles behind to follow this trail.

'That close! I must be getting old. So that's all five of them?'

'All five of the pony tracks we saw at least. Don't think the one on the sixth beast will be doing much.'

'And you're sure.'

'Fairly.' Ferox walked his horse forward, fingering the stone in his hand. It was smooth, probably from a river, and it was surely a sign. The tribes used stones and other things to leave messages and warnings, each tribe having its own system. This had been one he had not seen for a while. He went towards the heather and lobbed the pebble into its midst.

'Come out, you clumsy bastards!' Vindex shouted. 'We can see you!'

'Liar!' a voice said. 'It's that cunning bugger with you who's doing the seeing.' A man stood up among the heather, followed a moment later by another. 'Even then we had to make it easy for you.'

'Let's just kill 'em,' Vindex suggested.

Bran grinned. 'You could try, old man.' He called out and three warriors rode out of the trees. 'You hungry?' he asked Ferox and Vindex.

'Always,' Vindex replied.

'Then come with us.' Their camp was even higher up, in a sheltered dell. There were several farms dotted around the valleys below, and a few of the simpler huts used by the shepherds.

'They're good folk, but not rich,' Bran explained. 'No need to burden them by accepting hospitality. We have all we need.' He had four more men waiting here around a fire and roasting a stag. One of the men was big, towering over the rest.

'Ha, he said I was no good at hiding, so should wait,' Gannascus roared, slapping Bran on the back so hard that he almost knocked him over.

The German's hair and beard were pure white without a trace of dye, and there were heavy lines on his face, but his laugh was as strong as ever. 'I have news for you,' he said, as they sat down to eat.

The meat distracted him, giving Ferox a chance to talk to Bran.

'How is Senuna?'

'Rules with a rod of iron,' Bran assured him. 'The fort, the clan – me!'

'That's our lass,' Vindex said happily.

Bran grinned again. 'She wants you to come and visit when you can – even with this old fool of a Carvetian. There should be news for you before the year is out.'

'A young 'un?' Vindex asked before Ferox had a chance. 'Already? You don't mess about.'

Bran shrugged. 'Well, you know.'

'I'm her father, I'd rather not,' Ferox cut in. 'And I wish we could call on you. Might be the only way to calm the queen once she hears that she is going to be a grandmother. But you know it isn't so easy at the moment. Can you feel it in the air?'

'That's why I wanted to talk. The great ox over there,' he jerked his thumb at Gannascus, 'came to me not long ago because he wanted to talk to you. It's important.' His tone was suddenly very serious.

The German noticed, took another few bites of meat, licked his lips, and finally spoke. 'I've killed a Roman.'

'Well,' Vindex suggested, 'there's always more.' Ferox hushed him.

'He did not die straightaway,' Gannascus went on. 'He talked first.' He had never been a man whose talk flowed readily. 'He was on his way to see the Wolf.'

'You haven't caught up with him yet?' Vindex asked as the German paused again.

Gannascus worked a fragment of venison free from his teeth and spat it out. 'He has too many men and I have few left. His time will come.'

'Aye,' Bran took over. 'This Roman was a soldier, or had been, but was not dressed like a soldier, but like a trader, and even had a couple of slaves and donkeys with him.'

'They tried to steal a sheep and beat the shepherd when he complained,' Gannascus explained. 'We just happened to be nearby. I do not know why, but I just took a dislike to this man. He was not nice.'

'He was going to the Wolf, and carrying this,' Bran held out a wooden writing tablet in his hand. The seal was broken, and it was one of the ones where the wax could be melted and made smooth so that the page could be written on over and over again. 'I remembered the old trick they used to use, so scraped out the wax.' This particular sheet had only been used the once, before the wax was added, for underneath were four lines of neat letters.

'I cannot make them out,' Ferox said, after studying them and trying to see a pattern. 'But presumably my nephew could if it had arrived.'

'The man said he has been before, and others too,' Gannascus added. 'He said that he could not read it.'

'You believed him?' Ferox asked.

'In the end.'

'He told Gannascus that he was sent to tell the Wolf about Hadrian's visit,' Bran said. 'That he would be here soon, here in the north to watch his soldiers dig holes and build walls. The message had more detail, that was all he knew. Except for one thing. He knew about the man who sent him. Someone else whose time must come.'

'Sosius,' Ferox said as the realisation sank in.

'Oh shit,' Vindex added.

'He is a man I need to kill.' Bran's tone was flat. Years ago, Sosius had left a woman Bran cared about deeply, a sister through training, and let her be raped. It had shattered her, though she killed the attackers afterwards, but she had herself fallen only a little later.

'But isn't he Hadrian's man?' Vindex asked. 'What's that big bastard up to?'

'Maybe he used to be Hadrian's man?' Ferox wondered. 'I can't see the Wolf wanting to go back to the Romans.'

Bran rubbed his chin. 'Does he want revenge on you? Or to hurt you by hurting your family – the queen, your children.' His tone was becoming savage. 'Would Hadrian help with that?'

'Only if he benefitted from it.' Ferox thought for a while and shook his head. 'I cannot see how. So perhaps Sosius is doing this on his own. Maybe he wants to be free of Hadrian after all these years.'

'And do what, raise a family of sneaking little murderers?' Vindex was scornful.

'I do not know,' Ferox said.

'They need to die,' Bran said simply. 'Sosius and the Wolf.'

Ferox nodded, Vindex said, 'Aye', and Gannascus rumbled his approval. 'I don't know this Sosius, but I'll help kill him if we get the Wolf. I still have some men.'

'Any archers?' Ferox remembered the tall warriors with their powerful bows from years before, and felt an idea forming.

'Five good ones. As many more not bad.'

'Do you know when the raids are coming this summer?' Ferox asked Bran.

'Me, I'm a loyal ally of Rome, how would I know such a thing?'

'I heard late June or July,' Ferox said. 'Earlier than usual to take us by surprise.'

Bran smiled. 'Sounds about right. Not me though, I was wondering about heading north while everyone was away. See what they've left at home.'

'You won't have time,' Ferox told him. 'The Wolf will strike early, before everyone else goes in. He likes surprise and he likes to be talked about. I'll need you and your best warriors, your very best, men you can trust.'

'Hmm, that's thirty at most. No, better make it twenty if you want them really good.'

'Same for me,' Gannascus said.

'Fine.'

'So it's back to the old days, is it?' Bran asked. 'You in charge, the rest of us do what we are told. Guess it worked before and can work again – and we're all still here. Still, how do we do it this time?'

'I don't know.'

Vindex brayed with laughter. 'It really is like old times.'

They rode back to their men before sunset, and were pleased to see that they had kept a good watch. This was not hostile territory, not as such, but these were wild lands and you never really knew. They had come out this far, supposedly chasing a trail that they had lost, and since Ferox never lost a trail Vindex had to assume that he had planned to meet Bran from the very start, and not simply when he saw the other tracks.

On the next day they started south. They met some warriors, Novantae, and as the journey went on plenty more Selgovae and a few Votadini. None threatened more than a warrior always did, to show that he is strong, like the yellow bands on a bee warning of its sting. Most were friendly enough and willing to talk. They joked about the mad Romans and their low walls and stubby towers.

'Is it magic?' a few asked.

'Don't ask me,' Vindex replied. 'I am simply Carvetii. No one tells us anything.'

Some of the troopers were less amused. 'You wait, boys, one day there'll be a wall higher than a house. You can try raiding across that and see what happens?'

'The Romans are great liars,' the warriors said and rode on.

Before they reached the line of garrisons and the scattered work parties, word spread that bands of Selgovae had launched plundering attacks on the province much earlier than everyone had expected, while some of the Novantae had taken to boats and were ravaging the western coast. The Romans were not ready, not prepared, so there were alarms and panics, and hastily formed columns went on long chases and hardly caught anyone. Most of the successes came when the Brigantes formed their own bands and protected their farms or fought a band as it retired, recovering the booty and captives. There were not many such successes, for the losses of the great war meant that most chiefs had fewer men skilled with the sword to rally. Still, it was something.

At Magnis, Ferox found orders summoning him to await the arrival of the emperor. There was also a letter informing him that he was to be enrolled in the equestrian order. Another stated that he was now King of the Brigantes.

'So, we're really humped, aren't we,' Vindex concluded on behalf of the tribe and their kin.

XXIX

The day before the Kalends of June, the festival of the standards, Eboracum

THE DAY WAS always one of rest for the army, except for men engaged on vital duties. There were still guards to be mounted, lavatories to be cleaned, records to be updated and – for the truly unfortunate – sometimes skirmishes and battles to fight. As far as Hadrian knew the province of Britannia was quiet, not immediately threatened by violence great or small, so most of the army was able to parade, decorate the eagles, signa and other standards with wreaths and make sacrifice. He watched the ceremony at Eboracum, where two-thirds of Legio VI Victrix was settling down, with the remaining troops due in the next few days. The fortress had been neglected in recent years, since Legio VIIII Hispana went away, after which it had never been full and sometimes housed only small detachments. There would be a lot of work for the new legion to do, but that could wait for the days to come.

At dawn tomorrow, Hadrian and his escort would ride north. The praetorians and others could follow at their own pace. Sabina would stay here. She had been so eager to see more of these barbarous lands that it was easy to let her come this far, and the nature of the journey also made it easy enough to spend very little time in her company. The big praetorium of the legionary base was in good shape, a sign of someone thinking ahead or more probably a love of luxury in a succession of senior officers who happened to find themselves in command of the base in recent years.

The Augusta could stay there with her household and Nepos' wife, the legate of the legion's wife and Sulpicia Lepidina to give her appropriate companionship. He would also leave Clarus, the Praetorian prefect and Suetonius, so that they could sift through correspondence and only forward on to him anything that was truly important and urgent. They seemed to like Sabina, the gods alone knew why. Sabina would be safe enough here, safe from doing harm. Londinium was too busy, too close to Gaul and the Rhineland not to tempt the ambitious to come across and solicit the Augusta for favours. It mattered far less what she said and did, somewhere like Eboracum, where there were fewer people of note to pay attention and talk about it.

A close watch would be kept on his wife, and the freedman who was arranging it all did seem to know his business. The man was worried, though. A boy who helped check the lamps in the empress' bedroom and who was a reliable source had been found with a cut throat, floating in the river outside the fortress. Boys wandered off into dark streets and came to bad ends, so it may have been chance. No one had seen Sosius for a while, which might simply mean that the man was doing his job properly. It may also mean that he was suspicious.

When he rode through the main gate of the fortress the next morning, Hadrian felt an immense sense of relief, probably akin to many a man going through the same gates on a furlough. He was going to work, travelling hard and keeping very busy, but practical problems would be a relief after negotiation and endless speeches and fears about his wife. It was so much simpler, and easier to see when each task was completed and done well. After a few miles, he switched from horseback to coach, for that allowed him to dictate letters as he went.

They followed the roads, stopping at army bases, and he inspected guards at each gate and later parades of the unit stationed there. He liked talking to soldiers, and took care to find out something about a few men beforehand. There were even a handful who had served with him in the past, and he had a good memory for names and faces. On the way south, if there was time, he might inspect many of these units on manoeuvre. He wanted to make sure that every provincial army realised what was expected of them.

War was the most effective and cruellest of tutors. If an officer or soldier made mistakes against a real enemy, there were consequences. Trajan had fought longer, bigger wars than any emperor for a generation, which meant that those caught up in each campaign had to learn what really worked and what did not. There were always mistakes, training that was bad, habits that were dangerous. War punished such things savagely – at least most of the time, for luck was always there. Men died or they learned quickly how to do better.

Hadrian did not want such wars because the empire could not afford them. Apart from anything else, they had honed parts of the army while letting the rest rust away and weaken. The best men, the most ambitious officers in particular, had been drawn to the big campaigns. Some units who had had good wars, suffering a little, but not too much, and always winning in the end, so became superb fighting machines to rank alongside the divine Julius' veterans who seemed able to go anywhere, do anything and defeat anyone. Others, idling their time away in the quieter provinces, the refuge of the unambitious, the lazy, the stupid, and starved of good recruits, resources, activity and attention, went to seed. Rust like that tended to grow deep and last, whereas all the confidence and skill of the veteran war winners never lasted. Officers took other postings, men retired, and all grew complacent. Men who had fought for real too often became scornful about training, believing that they knew it all already.

'Training must be as real and as practical as possible.' Hadrian dictated the words as the carriage bumped along the roadway. Its repair would be another task for the army, as soon as there was time.

'Soldiers must learn the things that matter, repeating them until they become engrained habit. Officers must do the same, and also be ready to forget the old rules if the circumstances change.' He was not happy with the words. He wanted a set of official orders and a synthesis of all the best practice over the generations, condensed to make it as simple and easy to understand and remember as possible.

War was simple when you came down to it, its principles almost absurdly simple. Give yourself every advantage, inflict far greater damage on the enemy's spirit and resources than you suffer until he gives in. Different troops, different tactics had their inherent strengths and weaknesses. It really was not complicated in theory. The problem came in applying all these simple, sound ideas, when the weather was bad, your luck was out, and a clever and determined enemy was doing his best to kill you. No words could explain all of that, no set of rules be so exhaustive that they gave a man an easy, precise solution to each problem. It would be like a doctor feeling satisfied with his text because he had said that the object of the medical man is to keep the patient alive and healthy.

Hadrian wondered whether to include that thought, before deciding that humour would be a mistake. The smart officers would already understand that the rules could not be rigid and cover every circumstance, and the duller ones needed certainty to give them confidence. He wanted to keep it all as short and clear as possible, but it would also be good to inspect as many units as he could while they trained. That way, he could better convey what he expected, and encourage them to take the task seriously.

'Their drills are like bloodless battles, and their battles are blood-soaked drills.' That was something that Jewish fellow had said, and it was snappy even if it was not true. Still, a man who had rebelled, fought against Rome and eventually been hammered into the ground before changing sides, had an unusual perspective on the question.

No one could make training wholly real, because, whatever they pretended, everyone knew that it was not. Nor could a man, let alone a unit or an army, remain always perfectly prepared for a war even though no war was likely to happen. People did not work that way, and the world was about compromise and imperfection.

The thoughts stayed in his mind as he began his inspection at the River Tinea which flowed into the sea on the east of the island. The work parties were waiting, desperate to impress him. By the bank of the river itself, at their first stopping point, someone had erected a large wooden sign, declaring in bright red painted letters, that the first stone of the Vallum Aelium was laid here.

It was his idea, but he did not remember giving it a name, although admittedly he had toyed with the idea. He had drawn up instructions, a broad scheme, much like the set of army regulations he was trying to create. His design had gone to Falco, and he had meant it to act as a guideline rather than a rigid pattern. The governor had then had to turn it into orders for the legates of the two legions who would do the bulk of the preliminary work, and they in turn had to write and instruct even more subordinates.

Hadrian wanted them to think, to study the idea and then modify it according to the landscape, the resources of material and manpower, while always keeping its purpose in mind.

'I'm assuming that Falco did not think too much of the idea,' Hadrian said to Ferox, who had been waiting for him as ordered. 'And why aren't you wearing your ring?'

An eques wore a silver ring as a badge of his class, a symbol meant to be plainer than a senator's ring, although that rule was often breached. Ferox had one, because his wife had insisted, but hated wearing anything on his fingers so had the thing on a string around his neck.

'Kept slipping off, my lord. It's being altered.'

Hadrian did not believe a word of it. 'And you have not thanked me for making you a king.'

'I am a soldier, my lord. I go where I'm sent and do what I'm told.' Ferox's face was rigid, the wooden expression of a soldier tolerating a senior officer, but he let it soften for a moment. 'My wife is delighted though, so thank you.'

Hadrian grunted in amusement. 'And Falco.'

'Obeyed orders, my lord. A good man, that, if you do not mind a mere equestrian saying so.'

The emperor sighed. Ferox was almost as irritating as he was useful. 'But?'

'The former legatus Augusti was very busy, my lord. There was so much to do – chasing raiders, fighting sometimes when there was an enemy we could strike, and talking a lot more. He never spared himself, not once, and he was tired... I think he did not have the energy left to embrace the project. But he obeyed, my lord, and did his duty. None better.'

Falco had delegated the task to his juniors, and Hadrian could not blame him, even though he wished that there had been one mind overseeing the project, rather than many. His instructions had been copied, embellished and then interpreted in ways that were surprising.

Some of what they had done was good, very good indeed. The bridge over the Tinea was coming along very well, but then the army built a fair few bridges so usually had men with experience of doing the job in the past. His knack for faces came in useful when he remembered a centurion who had worked on Trajan's great bridge over the Danube.

'Good to see you again, Sabinus,' he called and then asked in detail about the construction and all those little peculiarities that marked any project. Hadrian did not mind getting dirty, climbing over the building site and getting down into the mud by the river.

In the days that followed they worked gradually eastwards. The land climbed, which meant so did the planned line of the wall, up and down the gently sloping sides of the hills.

'You tell me that this is nothing compared to the country further east?' Hadrian asked.

'It's pretty low for a good way after this bit, then proper hills for a stretch, and then easier and flatter all the way to the far shore,' Ferox confirmed.

Each day Hadrian chose to ride for a short while with Ferox, trailed by a pair of singulares Augusti from his Horse Guards, and then the rest of the imperial cavalcade at a distance.

'Talking to you tends to make me suspicious of everyone,'

the emperor claimed. 'I learn, I mistrust, and it is all the more refreshing to return to polite conversation with my officers and *comites*.'

Ferox had arrived with the reports of the raids from the Selgovae and the rest. He had added his suspicions that more were to come, and admitted his surprise that these had happened so soon.

'Then you are fallible after all, thank Jupiter for that!' Hadrian had already responded by issuing a new order to Nepos. The western third of the wall was being made in turf rather than stone. The army knew how to build in turf and timber better even than it knew how to make bridges, for all marching camps, and plenty of others used the material. They understood it, could do it quickly, so he had ordered the legatus to concentrate on getting that section complete by the end of the summer in broad terms, and by the end of the year for the more complicated features, like the guarded gateways built roughly every mile. The west was clearly the most immediately vulnerable sector, so they would get everything in place there as quickly as possible.

'I had not appreciated how much land around here was farmed,' Hadrian said. 'Thought it would be too cold and too wet except in the best patches.' They were riding past a family farm, watched with fascination by two very young and muddy children. In this stretch the path of the wall was no more than a line of flags and pegs driven into the earth, with squares where the towers would be and larger rectangles for the defended gateways. Hadrian winked at the children, who ran away screaming. 'Oh well, I suppose they do not see too many emperors in these parts.'

'Or beards, my lord.' Two pairs of eyes peeped out warily from behind the shelter of a fence.

'So do they use ploughs, or just scrape the earth and shovel it into rows to plant the seeds?' Hadrian's curiosity extended to many things, and often he thought aloud, not wanting an answer because he liked to work puzzles out. 'I really had expected more woods.'

Trees were a problem, or rather the lack of them, as the centurion working on a stretch of foundations some way ahead explained when they arrived, the whole staff now clustered around him.

'Not stone?' Hadrian asked.

'No, my lord. There's plenty of stone to be had, just about everywhere. I don't reckon we'll have to carry it far from the quarries anywhere along this stretch, or anywhere else I've been for that matter. Reckon half a mile at the most, and often it will be less. It's rough, not the prettiest stuff I've seen, but it'll do the job. We'll save the best stuff for the facing on either side, and the middle will be anything. Clay will probably pack it down well enough and sometimes we can leave it loose. So that means we should have plenty of mortar to go around.'

'But not wood?' the emperor was still puzzled.

'No, my lord, begging your pardon. You see we can only build a wall free so high.' The centurion held his hand level with his chest, palm flat and facing down. 'You can't go higher, not unless you have something to stand on.'

'Scaffolding,' Hadrian said and at last it was so obvious.

'Yes, my lord, spot on. We need timber to build frames and platforms to stand on. Then we can take it up another level,' again the hand was held out to show, 'and then another and another and so on. At the moment, we've got more men that we can use, because there isn't enough decent timber left to spare for the work. Once we finish at one stretch, we have pull the scaffolds apart and take them on to do another stretch.'

That all made sense, and was another reason to send more of the soldiers to the west where they could use their standard equipment to finish the turf sector. Still, it irked him a little that he had not understood the problem much quicker, for it really was so obvious.

'Should be easier when we get over to the west,' the centurion went on, for he sensed Hadrian's interest and rare understanding, so began to talk as engineer to engineer. 'It's new to us, you see, a free-standing stone wall like this. No one had done it before.'

That was true, and Hadrian took pride in the original idea. Fort walls were backed with earth banks, even when they were made in stone, which meant that the man was right, no one in the army ever practised building a stone wall on its own, especially one this size. Last year in Germania, he had inspected a wall of sorts, but that was really just a big fence, a simple stockade made from a single row of poles, easily found in that land of forests. It was simple because it did not need to be anything else, merely a barrier to help the army prevent anyone getting into or out of the province without permission.

He had something different in mind for Britannia, and not simply because even he realised that the place lacked the endless ranks of towering trees of Germania. There was no river of the right size and running the right way to serve after the manner of the Rhine and Danube, no mountains or other sort of barrier. Thus the simplest solution was to build one. Yet as with war, achieving the simple was rarely easy.

'Why are they so wide?' Hadrian asked.

The centurion stared down at the two hundred paces of foundations he had his men had almost completed, almost as if he saw them for the first time. He frowned, scratched his chin, felt a little stubble, which was embarrassing, and then remembered that he was in the presence of the princeps and stiffened to attention.

'Orders, sir.' There was silence, so after a while, he added, 'It's what they said they wanted. Ten feet. No more, no less.'

Hadrian managed to stop himself from sighing. It was not the man's fault, but illustrated the difference between instructions meant as guidelines and the way they were implemented. Thinking back, he remembered worrying about having a free-standing wall. He did not want to use the finest cut stone and ample mortar to fix it firmly. This needed to be something easy, using only local materials, and as quick and cheap as possible. It also needed to stay up in spite of all that wind, rain and frost could throw at it. That meant a simple construction, and that it needed to be solid, and therefore wide. He dimly remembered a phrase along the lines of 'well made to resist the rigours of the climate and not need frequent repair, so perhaps as much as ten foot wide, where necessary'.

Somewhere along the line, as orders were copied, embellished and passed on, that had turned into 'build me a wall ten foot wide.' He was sure that must have provoked plenty of sucking in of teeth and shaking of heads. These men were soldiers, but the ones in charge were engineers as well by inclination and experience, and engineers were all alike.

The tour continued, stopping at every spot where even the slightest work had taken place. Hadrian had announced that he wanted to see everything, so that is precisely what senior officers were doing. For long stretches there was nothing, only flags, but it was fascinating to be free to ride and to wrestle with this problem. He was already drafting one change of order in his head, reducing the wall from ten to somewhere between seven and eight feet, as appropriate. The saving in stone and hours of work would be immense.

On the first few nights they stayed in some of the temporary camps made for the work parties, or at a more permanent base if one was close. Although the escort immediately with the emperor and his staff rarely numbered more than fifty men, there were several hundred singulares Augusti in the wider area, supported by similar numbers of auxiliary cavalry and many more legionaries and auxiliaries on foot, stationed as pickets or out patrolling in the wider area. Any tower already completed, whether on its own or above a protected gate, was manned night and day. Ferox still worried, for only a fool did not in country like this.

'Worry comes with power,' Claudia Enica told him one night, 'you'll have to get used to it.'

'I was hoping to leave all that to you.'

'Huh, typical man. Now remember, whenever you get a chance, see if you can nudge the princeps to make it simpler for folk to claim compensation when their land is cut through by his wall. It is too complicated at the moment... and stop doing that, this is important... now where was I? Yes, at the moment they need written proof, which no one has, and then... I said stop and I meant it. Stop or I'll have you executed. The chiefs know who owns what, and I can keep an eye on the chiefs... uh, uh... stop. We're in a tent, you know. Act your age. That's better. They should need no more than a respectable witness. And they don't want money. They want something useful. Understand?'

'Yes, and what do I get.'

'Nothing unless you behave. You need to do this, husband, for my people – your people as well now. And you need to do it before you leave us. When is that?'

'The day after tomorrow. The emperor does not need me for a while and I need to... see to some things.'

'Will it work?'

'I do not know. But be very careful. Very careful.'

'Yes, my king,' she said meekly, mocking him. Later, much later she slept and he stared at the tent roof and listened as every now and then she uttered clear, coherent sentences.

'Good, we will proceed with this,' was one of them. The Romans liked their omens and saw them in all the wrong places and understood them in the wrong way. If he was really a citizen and an eques as they told him, he would probably have been cheered by this, thinking a god inspired her to speak and predict success.

Instead he lay awake and tried to think of all the different possibilities, all the attacks and how to match them. Mostly he worried about losing the woman lying beside him, wrapped in most of their blankets, and snoring softly away.

A few days before the festival of Lugh, in the mountains

HE SPENT THREE *days on the mountain top alone, listening and not hearing. That did not bother him. The path was as clear as ever, and he would walk it. There was nothing more for her spirit to tell him until it was over. He went not to learn, but to grow, to nurture his power inside him, and be calm for the trials to come. He felt that she was there, watching, and simply had nothing important to say.*

He had made love to his woman before he left and would not take her again until he returned. This was not a time for love, for flesh freely given, for that risked his strength. He would succeed if his power was at its greatest and his purpose clear.

Yet he bade Vinda farewell when he went back to the fort to gather his men. She said that there was another child in her belly from that last night together and perhaps she was right. The thought pleased him, in a way, but his soul was no longer with the hearth, not for the moment.

Revenge was near. The bald-headed freedman, this Sosius, was here. He had information, fresh information, from someone very senior, who knew where Hadrian would be and when.

At sunset, his chosen warriors would start slipping south, travelling in twos and threes and fives. That was the way among the Silures and what he had taught them. A raiding band dispersed, all knowing where to meet when they were close to what they wanted. They would go mostly by night, and some would go disguised as traders and travellers. One group, special men, would ride openly as escorts to Sosius and some other Romans, protecting the hides on the packs of their mules. Some of his men would walk in chains as slaves to be sold.

There were other packs with the mules, carrying things that they would need and must be hidden until the last moment. More than twenty of his men were former soldiers, or had been taught to look and act close enough to the real thing. By now there was full equipment to outfit them properly and they would be able to do more than pass at a distance. Even the emperor would be proud of their turnout, until it was too late. Sosius had helped, and grunted in satisfaction as he watched them go through their final paces

There was no need to rush. They had plenty of time, so could go carefully, making everything seem natural. No one could trust the Novantae or Selgovae, but there was no reason that they should notice a few isolated travellers.

He rode alone, apart from a boy, going ahead of all the others, travelling only by night. Sosius had given him a lot of information about a place that seemed ideal. He knew it, remembering it from the great raid when they had passed nearby. The Silures taught their sons to understand the land, and to look always for places to evade their foes and places to kill them. Last summer, he had gone there again, curious at what the Romans were doing.

For three days he walked, leaving his horse to graze in the care of the boy. He wondered briefly whether there would come a day when he would have his own son to perform this task, then dismissed the thought. She had not promised him long life, but she had promised him revenge. Hopefully his son – or sons, perhaps – would grow to be strong and healthy, to be warriors who preyed on their enemies and lived free.

The Romans had done a lot of work since his last visit, and there were a few things that Sosius and his spies had not seen, or perhaps did not understand. The freedman was a killer, but he was not a warrior, still less a child of the Silures.

He watched them for a long time, saw the patrols and work details coming and going, and marvelled at the arrogance of men who thought that they could tame the landscape as they might train a dog. Men who kept dogs rarely understood wolves.

The next day he hid in another place, one of many patches of woodland in the river's winding valley, and again he studied the soldiers and their routine. It would be different when the emperor came, but even so men tended to follow the familiar paths out of habit.

Satisfied that he had seen all that he needed to see, and that he would remember it, that night he went back to the horse. On the way, he had a sense, no more than that, of someone watching. He went still, sheltered by a bush, and below him a slope running down to the chuckling river. There was nothing in that direction, so he lay flat and waited.

The sense faded and a wolf howled, lonely and sad. Wolves were rare in this country, driven out by the farmers and the herdsmen. They lived in the hills and mountains, especially at this time of year when men brought their flocks to the high pastures.

It howled again, a little further away, and faintly he heard the answer of the pack.

The path is clear, she had said, and so it was.

XXX

Eight days before the Ides of June, between Banna and Magnis

THE IMPERIAL PARTY had settled at Vindolanda, with the emperor in the mansio built for that very purpose, a few other favoured individuals sharing with him, and the rest distributed around the praetorium and the more respectable buildings in the canabae. Much to his delight, Cerialis discovered that someone had hired Flora's old house, given it a thorough clean and found some furniture to make it suitable. Apparently there had been no shortage of beds.

'Pity they haven't kept on the staff as well,' he said.

Claudia Enica liked the procurator, and, as the most intimate friend of his wife, knew that the man had almost always taken his pleasures outside the marriage bed. The arrangement was satisfactory for both parties most of the time, and was common enough among well-to-do Romans.

'You should be careful, Lepidina told me to keep my eye on you,' she told him, grinning. For some reason she thought of that other Claudia, the mistress of Priscus, and wondered what had happened to her. Hadrian was not the sort to encourage that sort of indulgence among his staff.

The procurator was almost as pleased when he realised that quite a few of the singulares Augusti were his countrymen. The unit was nicknamed the Batavians, but such names often meant little in the army, especially as time passed. It was recruited from the pick of men forwarded to Rome from the auxiliary alae and, every so often, the cavalry of the cohorts if a man displayed truly exceptional courage or talent. There were Gauls, Syrians, Mauretanians, Thracians, a fair few Spanish and Germans, but still a few Batavians, led by a grey-bearded veteran called Soranus, who hailed Cerialis as his king.

'Where did you learn to use a bow?' Cerialis asked him, for his people had no real tradition of archery.

'The army,' the man said. His Rhineland accent was still strong, and surely deliberate for he spoke Latin and Greek clearly. The singulares had always let some turmae and some individuals use different weapons, something that Hadrian wanted to encourage in the rest of the army. Soranus was a horse archer, his bow one of the carefully made composite types, invented in the east and copied by the army.

'They say he is very good,' Claudia Enica told the procurator.

'You've been listening to soldiers' gossip.'

'Yes, I have. One told me that the whole regiment swam their horses across the Danube so that Hadrian could impress a delegation of tribal leaders. Your Soranus shot an arrow high, then hit it with a second shaft before it landed.'

'He is to stay by you, along with another trooper – and yes, another of my folk. It's a favour to Ferox, so please let them. The princeps knows and approves.' Cerialis was to return to Eboracum the next morning, for there was a problem with the returns supplied by the men in charge of a large imperial estate.

Claudia knew that she would miss him. There were a few slave girls at the mansio, and obviously in the garrison commander's household, but the queen was the only respectable woman with the imperial party, although some of the older, more traditional might question that description. As time passed, the sight of Claudia Enica wearing breeches, boots and riding astride grew more familiar, and gradually less shocking. However, the princeps valued her opinion, and often sought it on questions of her own people, and their neighbours, whether kin or enemies. There was knowledge and intelligence in all the answers, as well as a good deal of wit. Slowly, she managed to charm most of the senior men, as well as almost all the juniors, so that even those unmoved by her looks, whether because they preferred darker complexions and different shapes or age, or had limited interest in women at all, started to be won over.

There was some hard riding in the rugged country near the middle of the land, and sometimes even the emperor preferred to go on foot. Pertacus seemed to be everywhere, helping to marshal the outlying screen, but somehow always managing to appear and offer his help. One morning the eager tribune followed the princeps' instructions and had men stationed on all the sites where towers were planned, but not yet built. Pertacus himself came up with the idea of each one have a pole, some twenty feet high and ending in a bright red streamer to simulate something of the height of the tower.

Hadrian was impressed, as he and the staff rode along the road, down in the valley behind the crests which the wall would follow.

'Good.' Whoever had laid this section out had understood his intent.

'They cannot always see each other, my lord,' another centurion explained. 'But they can be seen from the road and from the bases.' The emperor seemed to be spending a lot of time talking to centurions from the legions, and felt all the better for it.

'What about there?' Hadrian pointed back towards Vindolanda. 'Is that tower the one on the hill above the fort?'

'Yes, my lord. The men up there can see any signal or send one. The fort won't be able to see the wall itself, but it can see the tower and the tower can see the wall. We've done this a few times, if there wasn't a direct line in the first place. A couple of other spots just meant felling a tree or two that was blocking the way. That's more common over towards Banna. Lots of woodland there, but we're clearing it for use and to open everything up.'

'Don't they need to see each other as well?' Nepos asked, trying to understand the principle. 'The towers, I mean. They're what, never more than a third of a mile from one of the gateways. That would be the quickest source of help. Along most of the line at least.'

'But not much help if there are a lot of enemies,' Hadrian told him. 'These men are there to watch, not fight. They give warning, like a dog barking when it smells a burglar. The warning might be enough to frighten the burglars away. If not, it means we can start thinking of how to deal with them. Remember, they not only have to get over the wall, they also have to get back across it on their way home.'

'And we hold all the gateways,' the centurion said enthusiastically, before realising that he might just have interrupted the emperor. His face went pale.

'Quite,' Hadrian said. 'We hold the gates, and they won't be able to take one unless they come in big numbers and are willing to take losses and waste time doing it. It's all about time – time for the alarm to go up, time for us to find out what is happening and where, and then the time to put together enough troops to catch them.' His eager tone now matched his centurion's. 'That's what all this is for. To make everything harder and slower for them at every stage. To make it easier and faster for us to realise that there is an attack. Then respond and crush. That's the final stage, but without it nothing else matters. We have to catch them before they get home and crush them. Thetatus as the lads say! They don't get home to boast and show off their spoils. They don't get home at all.'

The emperor stared at the faces around him, especially Nepos and the senior officers, and wondered whether they fully understood. Like the free-standing wall, no one had ever done anything quite like this, but then no province offered such a narrow point to defend – if you could call eighty miles narrow! In essence other provinces bordering on more or less hostile country worked on the same principle, but the solutions had to be different in more extensive lands.

'What if they don't come, my lord?' The question came from the Queen of the Brigantes while the others had nothing to say. He saw a sparkle in her green eyes that suggested she felt in on the joke, and understood that what she was asking helped him to explain.

Hadrian spread his arms wide and smiled. 'That's actually the aim. If this wall and the troops on it make it so difficult to raid the settled lands then eventually no one will try. They'll see the wall running across the hilltops and see in it the overwhelming might of Rome. Like a warning about guard dogs. Try to cross this and you will suffer immense pain. You probably won't come back. It may take time, but in the end they will learn. Once they have, then we will probably be able to reduce the number of soldiers permanently stationed here. They simply will not be needed because of the wall. That's the whole point, let stone and turf and sharpened stakes do the hard work instead of men.'

Nepos nodded several times. Hadrian could not tell whether

he really understood or was simply showing open support to please the princeps. One of the minor joys of supreme power was that everyone was inclined to agree with you. What was it he had been told one learned senator had said about him – you don't argue with a man who has thirty legions! The price of that was the difficulty in knowing what everyone really thought and believed. Did they understand well enough to make this work?

'We will need a lot of cavalry,' Nepos said after a while. That was good, suggesting that he had some real appreciation. 'To catch them before they get away.'

'Yes, we will,' Hadrian agreed. 'But then we always do. Speed is such an asset. Though remember that unless they take a gateway, then they'll probably be on foot. Hard to get a horse over a fifteen-foot wall after all!'

There was the usual laughter, for how could there not be when the princeps was witty.

'You could use a big ballista,' Nepos suggested, and his seniority, and Hadrian's ready laugh, ensured that this was also hugely enjoyed.

Yet Hadrian was starting to worry, a thought nagging at the back of his mind. It was not about whether or not his governor and the other officers really understood everything, but a doubt about his own conclusions. He kept thinking of the wall as if it were finished. The need to rush the turf sector was sign of that. Wanting something to happen did not make it appear instantly and work as well as it had in your mind. There was a real danger of trouble before it was all in place, especially if the tribes realised what its completion would mean. A few defeats and everyone would be talking about the emperor's grandiose and useless folly.

There was also a deeper worry. It was all about catching

the enemy before they escaped and killing or capturing them. Who was going to do this? Again, he had planned for the final version, a perfect, complete work that would rarely if ever actually have to deal with a raid because its simple existence had rendered such a raid virtually impossible. Something else, or perhaps several other things, would be needed to make it all function in the short term.

'Remember that there will also be honest folk needing to cross,' Claudia Enica said once the laughter had subsided. 'Not everyone is a bandit. Some of my own people will live north of the wall. They will still be Brigantes, my subjects and loyal allies of Rome.'

'Yes gentlemen – and lady or course – that is something we must always remember. Rome does not stop here. This is a barrier to those who mean us harm, not to us.' Hadrian stretched his arms high, the closest an emperor could come to yawning in public, even somewhere like this. 'Come on, enough work for today. Let's give these horses a run back to Vindolanda!'

The next day they went west, setting out before dawn and riding a fair distance. The prefect at Magnis had tried to convince the emperor to stay at the fort, offering to give up the praetorium altogether, presumably by evicting one of his centurions and slumming it in his rooms for a night or two. Hadrian thanked him for his kindness, but refused. They had built this mansio at Vindolanda far grander than it needed to be, and the least he could do was stay there as long as possible. Apart from that, he liked the place, in spite of the midges that swarmed in the air outside every evening. Another advantage was that riding out each day to inspect another position gave him more time to understand the land, and on the following day they headed west again, using the road.

A good architect worked with the ground, only changing

it when he had no other choice, because in a contest between landscape and man, the landscape started out with a big advantage that was hard to beat. Better to seduce the land than try to rape it. The thought amused him, and since it was about the right time and the horses were warmed up, he gave the signal to trot and then canter. He was feeling well, accustomed to riding often and far as he had not been for quite a few years. He also thought that he had the solution to making the wall work properly from the start. It meant more building, a lot more building, and that was a concern, for even rough calculations in his head hinted at the cost in material and labour, much of it requiring high levels of skill. His other idea was simpler, a lot simpler, but could not work on its own.

The emperor was almost certain, and felt that today would make his mind up one way or the other, for today the army of Britannia would show him the most fully complete section of the wall. Armies were always like this, toiling to present a few things honed to perfection, whether a particular drill, a building, an engine, or simply a guard of soldiers, each one prepared with more care, sweat and attention to detail than the vainest and most fashionable matron in Rome. Everyone knew how it worked, and whoever was performing the inspection, whether commander, governor or the emperor himself knew the score and understood that he had a role to play, and part of that was to be suitably impressed and pretend not to notice that this was artificial, what the unit could do rather than what it normally did. The trick as far as Hadrian was concerned, was to be impressed by the displays, commenting and criticising as appropriate to prove that you were really looking, but at the same time to sniff out all the things that they did not want you to see and decide how far these mattered.

Before the end of the first hour, they came to a burgus on a rise just beside the road, and although this was not part of the formal inspection, it would be rude for a princeps to pay no attention to some of his soldiers. There were plenty of these little forts around the empire, enough to house a detachment and keep an eye on traffic along the road and enforce the laws over a wider area. Its commander was an eager centurion, the local regionarius, and reported that he had seventy-four men under his command, sixty-two of whom were present and fit for duty, including the sentries at the watchtower. Hadrian had noticed the tower up on the ridge to the north west. It was bigger than the ones planned for the wall, but was so conveniently placed that the planners had sensibly decided to include it, even if it would look a little different to the rest.

Hadrian was struggling to remember every name in time when he was meeting so many officers, but in this case the sight of the tower prompted a memory of a report from Ferox and the regionarius himself.

'Felicio, isn't it? Yes, of course it is. You're an old hand up here and doing a splendid job. Well done, well done. One day I am sure that I will need you for greater things, but for the moment keep up the good work – and that goes for all of you!' he added, raising his voice.

As they rode away, past a camp filled with rows of tents for legionary work parties, he acknowledged the salute of a picket standing in front of the main gate, with armour so highly polished that they almost sparkled. There were more of them than regulation required, so someone else was putting on a show.

They stopped at a quarry, and he dismounted and was shown around by a plump optio who sweated profusely in the presence of so many senior officers. The place seemed well enough run, with plenty of building stone already cut out and piled neatly waiting for use. Hadrian felt it best to ignore the slogans carved on the remaining cliff face, the insults, boasts and pictures of penises.

The road was fairly straight, on the southern slope of the valley, because a stream ran through its bottom. To the north the crags were like the crest of a high wave. There were a few more towers, some of them no more than stubs, and plenty of flags to mark the line of the wall. Hadrian wondered how often the wind had blown them over, and how often someone had to go and hammer them down again. The emperor was visiting, so everything must be perfect, if only for a few hours.

A promising morning turned grey and cloudy, and before long the air was damp, almost raining, if not in droplets you could feel. Hadrian did not mind, for it would prevent the day getting too hot and they had a lot to do. He patted the neck of his stallion, one of his favourites, and decided that it was time for another canter, slowing only when the slope started to edge down into a shallow valley just beyond Magnis. He had already inspected the fort and its garrison, which meant that there was no need to do it again. The prefect was there, with a guard of honour, even though the imperial party did no more than walk their horses past.

Also, there was the tribune Pertacus, who was a good-looking man and must have been a delightful youth. He was supervising the outposts of troopers and soldiers to cover the land on both sides against any barbarian fool enough to attack when the army was at its most vigilant. Hadrian could tell that the tribune was galloping around, giving orders, then sitting high in the saddle and staring out towards the horizon with a look of stern resolve. The fellow obviously liked an audience. That was not necessarily a bad thing, and promoting local aristocrats was how the empire worked and how it had always worked. He sensed that the queen did not like Pertacus, and remembered the war of words over assigning blame for the defeat in the north, and the 'concerns' pointedly expressed over his escape. So, the tribune looked the part, but might not have real talent or courage. That should not matter too much as long as he was never in a position where everything depended on him alone.

They pressed on, the road climbing gently again and coming closer to the line of the wall.

'Ah,' Hadrian could not help stopping and staring for a moment at the view. His staff were slow to react, so Nepos and a few others clattered past, bumping against each other as they made sure that they did not nudge the emperor's horse. Hadrian had thought about this for many hours, drawn sketches, written down his thoughts and calculations, yet nothing quite prepared him for seeing all those ideas brought to life.

Ahead of them was a miniature version of the burgus, a rectangular enclosure somewhere between a quarter and a third its size. It was well built, the walls thick, presumably ten feet thick, and fifteen feet high to the crenulations on the parapet. There was a gate on the north and south sides, and over the northern gate a rectangular tower some thirty feet high. It had an open platform on top, and an auxiliary stood straight, bronze helmet glinting dully, shield uncovered to show its green field and bright decoration, spear held erect. He was not quite at attention, but close enough, gazing north over the winding, wooded valley to his front. Smoke rose from the shingle-roofed buildings just visible behind the walls.

Hadrian knew that he was smiling like an excited schoolboy. To the east there was simply a short stub of curtain wall extending from the front wall of the little fort. To the west was the wall itself, thick and wide, with so many sentries pacing earnestly along its walkway that they must have been given a signal to tell them that the emperor was about to arrive. The wall was the same height and width as the walls of the little fort, and all in the same dark, almost drab grey stone, not pretty in itself, but impressive because of the sheer scale. A tower rose up around a third of a mile away.

In front of the wall was a neatly cut ditch, deep, essentially V-shaped, and making use of the natural slope whenever it helped. Between ditch and wall were rows of sharpened stakes, thrusting up at an angle, some of them supporting beams from which more wickedly sharp sticks extended to make a thick hedge.

It was beautiful. Hadrian imagined this wall, snaking along over the heights, running straighter on the plains, stretching from coast to coast, and he knew his eyes were moist. It was lovely not in the natural beauty of a dome or row of columns or of polished marble, but because it was so vast, so functional. No one had ever done anything like this before.

'I wonder whether we might ride for a while in front of it,' he said eventually. There was surprise, murmuring, for this had not been the plan. Still, no one argues with a man who has thirty legions, and the mild wish of a princeps was naturally a command. He let them adjust before explaining. 'I should like to see how it will appear to a tribesman.'

'Shall I paint myself blue and stage an attack?' Claudia Enica suggested brightly.

The emperor chuckled, as did everyone else, if an instant later. 'Perhaps next time, dear lady.'

They rode in front of the ditch. Pertacus and other officers were galloping around and shouting, moving some of the outposts to give the imperial party more space. Hadrian studied the wall itself and also the lands in front of it, for they had come down a little from the higher ground to the east. It was still hilly, open in patches, but there were dips and ravines as well as a lot of woodland offering concealment from the eyes of sentries, even ones walking along the wall or on top of a tower. As Hadrian and his entourage rode west, the land started to slope down into the deep valley of a river, which came from the north before meandering westwards. This was perfect ground for raiders or anyone wishing to slip by without being seen, which was the main reason it had been chosen as the site for this showpiece stretch of wall. If the idea could work properly here, then it could work anywhere. He was pleased to see signs of initiative. In front of each of the towers, the ditch angled back so that it was almost right up against the wall, which meant that no one could hide in it and not be seen – or struck with a missile. He had not suggested that in his plan, so it was good to see. He wondered whether they had mounted a scorpio in each tower. That would make them very dangerous to approach.

They went down into a ravine, some of the slopes almost cliffs, with a brook rushing down to join the main river, and his stallion stumbled more than once as they climbed again. Ahead was another little fort, what in his plans he had called a fortified gateway, because he could not think of a better name, other than something vague like *praesidium*. It was not really large enough to be a burgus and was built into the wall, so really part of that.

This one matched the first one, a mile back, with a front wall some sixty foot in length. On the slope, the tower over its arched gateway loomed high above them. The sentry on top could equally have been the twin of the man at the other one, standing intensely alert in a way that would have done Pertacus proud.

Hadrian sniffed. 'Let's join them for something to eat. That smells good.'

'Open the gates!' Pertacus shouted the order, the man seeming to pop up everywhere, even though Hadrian had not seen him pass. One of the gates squeaked as it was drawn back, and Hadrian imagined the garrison commander wincing because he had forgotten to check that the hinges were oiled. There was a causeway of solid earth, the sides strengthened with timber to take them over the ditch.

With a crash, two files of infantrymen stamped to attention, lined up on each side of the road. Hadrian's stallion flicked its ears and wanted to run, not because of the noise, but because the road climbed sharply as it ran to the gate on the rear wall. A little pressure with his legs, a tug on the bridle and the beast calmed, but its rider was almost as surprised. Hadrian had to stifle a smile, because the base of the far gate was at eye level, so steep was the slope.

'At ease,' he told the soldiers. 'Is that bread I smell, centurion?'

'Yes, my lord. In the oven over there.' He pointed to Hadrian's right, where a clay oven stood next to the corner where the side wall met the front wall.

'Splendid. I love a proper army loaf when it's so fresh that it's still warm. Nothing quite like it. May I share some of your meal?' Hadrian had the momentary thought of what he would do if the man refused.

'Of course, my lord. Would you care to eat in my quarters?' The tone was doubtful, a mixture of wild hope that he might entertain the emperor and fear that he could only do this meanly, for the pair of rooms allocated to him were scarcely lavish.

'No, let's eat out here.' Hadrian turned, seeing the leading members of his staff were clustered in the archway behind him. 'Nepos, get someone to take the horses through and tend to them. Let's take a look at this place.' The emperor jumped down and held out his reins to a soldier who was so nervous that he almost dropped his spear as he fumbled to lean it against the wall. There were two long buildings either side of the track, each with a low veranda. They had stone foundations and lower courses, and rendered, half-timbered walls above. There were several doors on each, as well as windows – windows with glass panes no less. Yet still they were on this formidable slope, which must make placing the cots for sleeping quite a challenge. It was a well provided little base, carefully built, although he could not help noticing that the stone was rough. Presumably it was the best that the nearest quarries had to offer.

'Thank you,' Hadrian told the nervous soldier, and strode off to his left where stone stairs led up onto the wall. Plenty of permanent forts still used ladders or had earth steps cut into the bank behind the wall, so it was quite a surprise to see them and he bounded up, cloak flying. The centurion rushed to catch up, noticed that the legatus Augusti was also now on foot, realised that he should not push in front, was uncertain whether he should beckon to his commander, and then was relieved when Nepos followed the emperor without prompting. A woman appeared, a handsome woman, unmistakably so in spite of her manly attire, and he realised this must be the queen of the Brigantes. She smiled at him, which was nice, and went on up the steps after the governor. He had to presume that this was also all right.

Hadrian climbed to the tower, the last stage by a humble ladder through a trapdoor in the ceiling. 'At ease, man,' he said as his head came through, not wanting the sentry to become any more disciplined and stand more firmly at attention in case something snapped under the strain. 'No need to stand on ceremony.'

The view to the front was impressive, the valley stretching out ahead of them, although again there was so much cover. The wall ran out to his left, heading downhill, although since it was no more than three courses of stone it was little more than a dark line running through the countryside. It turned to follow the river until the water swung sharply south. That was a spot he wanted to see, once they had finished here. Beyond there was another steep climb to a hill that was a mass of trees.

'Is that the place the locals call Banna?' he asked the sentry.

'Yes, sir.'

Hadrian glanced back to his right, realised he was smiling again as he saw the wall in its proper height and glory, gave himself a moment to recover and then walked to the parapet at the back of the tower. With the slope, he could only just see over the far wall to the fields beyond, which rolled away to the horizon, large swathes of them covered in high ripening barley. Half a mile away, perhaps less, was the road, although he could not see it. He could just make out the top of one of the towers of a burgus, much like the one they had seen at the beginning of the day. The sight brought home to him just how peculiar this place was, not simply because of the slope.

'How many men do you have here?' Hadrian asked the centurion who had just joined them.

'Thirty soldiers, a duplicarius and myself, sir.'

That looked about right, in little barrack blocks just like a proper camp, snug rooms with proper windows, ovens for baking, and his own little world for a centurion to command. Hadrian sniffed. There were eighty-one of these places in the plan, which meant eighty-one centurions and two and a half thousand or so other soldiers to man them. If they provided guards for the towers, that left hardly anyone to respond to a problem, which was fine if there were not any problems. In the meantime men were away from their units for what – months, even years. This was a comfortable little billet if you did not mind leaning over to stand straight, and soldiers liked to settle down somewhere and keep out of harm's way. That was fine for them, but meant discipline and training were likely to fall away.

'Too big and at the same time too small,' Hadrian said softly.

'My lord?' The centurion was wondering what he had done wrong.

The wall was a grand measure, and not to be spoiled because it lacked the resources to work.

'Nepos, we need forts. May as well be on the line of the wall itself, because that is never too far from the road.'

'Yes, my lord,' Nepos said. What else could he say?

In the valley

'PITY YOU DON'T *have any archers. Good ones, I mean,' the Roman said. The man was bold now, full of swagger, so that it was an effort to recall the same man gibbering in fear when they had taken him after the great victory. 'There will be plenty of chances for a good shot. The emperor likes climbing to the tops of towers and usually rides at the head of his staff.'*

'An arrow rarely kills cleanly,' he said in response. 'It might miss because the wind blows at just that moment or the emperor moves.'

'You're right,' Pertacus conceded. 'We need to be sure. The empress is counting on us.'

He said nothing to that, for he did not care one heartbeat about Hadrian's wife.

'The queen,' the tribune went on. 'It would be well if she dies.'

He was not about to argue, or tell the man that if the emperor died, then no doubt his wife could persuade the new emperor to dispose of any petty king or queen. The Brigantes always talked far too much, but Pertacus was nervous for all his bluster.

'Hadrian first. The others if we can,' he said levelly. 'Now we should go.'

The tribune had a bodyguard with him. The man was a gladiator or wrestler, with the over-trained muscles that made his arms and legs appear taut and bloated, and the battered face of the trade. He was dressed as a soldier, a legionary no less, but no one would mistake him for anything but a professional hard man and it was common enough for the rich to be accompanied by such men, even in the army. Proper soldiers tended not to like them and contented themselves with being wary. Any officer who felt the need for such protection was obviously nervous and suspicious, so better not to cross without good reason.

The tribune, the gladiator riding just behind him, led him and twenty men dressed as auxiliary troopers as they rode out from the south towards the burgus. They had spent two days and two nights hiding in a secluded wood waiting for the moment. He had chosen the insignia of his old cohort for their shields, even though the unit was far away in Pannonia. With the emperor visiting, there would be plenty of unfamiliar faces and symbols around, and no one was likely to raise questions, especially when they saw the familiar sight of the tribune and his bodyguard. They looked just like any other turma of cavalry going about its duties. He had a high yellow crest on his helmet to act as their decurion.

They went straight to the burgus, half of them riding under the arch without difficulty because the gates were open. The rest stayed outside.

'Is the centurion here?' Pertacus asked the sentry standing on the tower.

'No, sir. He and his men are on picket duty. Decius is in charge, sir.'

Decius appeared, fiddling with the chin tie of his helmet. 'Sir!' He saluted with great formality. His nervousness and curiosity were obvious, although he did not ask what was happening.

'I need men for an extra covering party. The emperor wishes to see more of the work than we expected. How men do you have left?'

'Twenty-six, sir, including myself. The rest are out with the centurion.'

'Parade them all! Now!' Pertacus turned around. 'Rufus, rest your men and fill the water skins.'

'Sir,' he said. Rufus had commanded his turma. He had been a small man, one of those officers who had risen as far as they were ever going to reach and resented it, so took it out with small acts of viciousness. Eventually one of the men had snapped, killing him before deserting.

It seemed a suitable name to assume.

The garrison turned out quickly, Pertacus shouting at them to hurry. 'You,' he pointed at one of the disguised warriors. 'Get up that tower and tell me whether you can see the imperial party. Go on, get a move on!'

He noticed one of the garrison roll his eyes at the fussing officer. The man was an old sweat and had seen it all before.

Decius slammed his foot down as he came to attention and saluted again. 'All present, sir!'

'Right, take twenty men and come with me. At the double!' Pertacus turned his horse and trotted back through the gateway. 'Come on!'

There were muffled curses, a distinct omnes ad stercus *and the detachment stumbled into a run, equipment noisy because they had not had time to strap everything on properly and fasten it well.*

Four men were left in line in front of the house.

'Who said you could dismiss!' he snarled at them.

Habit took over, and with rigid expressions they stiffened back to attention.

'Hercules' balls,' he told them. 'There's a good chance that the emperor himself will take a look at you and this is how you turn out?' He remembered some of the many harangues he had

faced from the moment he had sworn his oath to Trajan and Rome and kept going. 'Soldiers? I've seen eunuchs with bigger balls…'

They listened, still at attention, for that was what soldiers did. Just stand there, let it all flow past and don't pay any attention because it was just words and he had the power and you did not. Never give him an excuse, never show any emotion, and when you get back at him, make sure that you don't get caught. All his hatred for Rome and its army flooded back, all the resentment at the way they took warriors and treated them like dogs, and he realised that he was spitting as he yelled at them.

'Lucky for you, you get this warning. Now in a moment, I am going to dismiss you and you will go and you will clean your kit until it would please Mars himself.' He smiled, the way some officers felt that they could simply become your friend. 'Now, do you have any barley for my men's horses?'

The four men on parade died a moment later, for this was the signal and during the tirade one of his own men had come to stand behind each one. The soldiers had known they were there, but could not turn, and had not paid attention as they lapsed into that half-asleep state of men listening to abuse from a senior. One hand grasped each mouth, while the other drove a pugio into the neck, between helmet and armour. They struggled, one even managing to bite hard into the fingers of his attacker, but the surprise was so sudden, his men so good, that there was no real noise. There was a lot of blood, as it pumped from the men's necks, but that could not be helped. The sentry on the tower died as quickly, with no more than a gasp of pain that would not carry to anyone who mattered. Dragging the corpse to the side, the warrior took the sentry's place.

He drew his sword as a man appeared in the doorway of one

of the buildings, a knife in his hand. It was Sosius, his shaven head and round, placid face easy to recognise.

'Anyone else?' he asked.

'Three slaves,' Sosius replied. That had been a problem, for while you could order a parade of soldiers, there was no way of weeding out all the others likely to be in any base. The freedman leaned down and used the hem of a corpse's tunic to wipe the blade of his dagger clean.

There was no need to ask whether or not Sosius had dealt with them. 'The storeroom is over there,' the freedman pointed at a building. 'You'll see the oil and the sacks. There's a fire burning in that one.' He nodded at another building. 'It's all ready.'

'Good.'

'Is there anything else?' Sosius asked.

He shook his head.

'Then I need to go. So that we can be sure.'

The corpses were being dragged into a barrack block as the freedman left. Another warrior ripped open a grain sack and spread it across the blood.

Pertacus had assured him that no one would come looking before they were ready, but you never really knew with the army. Two men, as well as the one on the tower, were to stay behind to do what needed to be done. The warrior pretending to be a sentry would tell them when, waiting until the Wolf and the others had vanished over the horizon, then counting to five hundred.

He was walking the path and knew where he was going.

XXXI

By the river

'I CONFESS I am tempted to try, my lord,' Claudia Enica said, 'if I did not remember the fate of Remus.'

Hadrian laughed, for he was in a good mood and had always enjoyed the company of women who enjoyed wit and best of all those who possessed it.

'Well, I did not bring a spade,' he told her. 'And I will admit that even I am tempted to jump this fellow over the great wall.' He patted the neck of his stallion.

The great wall was barely eighteen inches high, for all its broad width. They were behind it now, for with the ditch so close to the steep banks sloping down to the river, there was little space in front. Trees thick with summer leaves meant that they could rarely see the water, but they could hear its flow. The trees were small, trunks twisted as they clung to the slope, so that they were unlikely to be much use as precious scaffolding. Still, they would have to be cleared away when the wall was raised properly.

'That will have to go,' Nepos said, waving an arm towards them. Hadrian felt that the legatus was understanding more and more of how this was all going to work.

'Yes, when there is time. No sense letting the enemy creep up on us.'

'And how close together do you want these forts, my lord?' Nepos asked. There had been little time to discuss as Hadrian ate some food and asked the soldiers questions, but now that they were riding again, it was easier. This stretch of wall undulated with the land, so that they could not see far in any direction.

'We'll work out the details later. My guess would be ten miles at the most, and probably less than that. It will mean plenty of troops near every sector. No one will get to spend too long at any tower or gateway. We don't want them getting slack. At most it should never be more than a few hours' walk from any spot on the wall to reach a big garrison. And if there are plenty of horses, news – and help – can go much faster. They might not need to be there for ever, but it will make the wall so formidable that the locals will learn to fear it. As we said before, you may get across, but—'

Hadrian's head snapped around to look back. He held up his hand. 'Did you hear that?'

Nepos frowned.

'It was a scream,' Claudia Enica said.

'A bird, probably, dear lady, at a distance they can sound uncommonly like—' Nepos stopped because a horn brayed harshly from somewhere behind them.

'My lord!' One of the fifteen singulares Augusti in the close escort was shouting and pointing back towards the high ground. A plume of black smoke rose above the ridgeline, getting thicker by the moment.

'Is that the burgus?' Nepos asked, sounding more puzzled than anything else. 'What is going on?'

'You!' Hadrian called to the guardsman who had shouted the warning. 'Ride up there, take a look, and report back as soon as you can.'

'Sir!' The soldier cantered away, horse racing up the hillside. A horn sounded again, closer, and there were faint shouts and screams.

Nepos rallied. 'Must be an attack. Do we make a dash for the gateway? It has solid walls and plenty of men. Shall I take a few men and see what is going on? There must be pickets and patrols nearby, surely.'

Hadrian hesitated. He remembered the plot to kill him at that hunt in Dacia. Not all his enemies were barbarians. Still, Nepos was right, there should be soldiers fairly close by on every side and they could not all be traitors.

'Go!'

The legatus Augusti of Britannia beckoned to some of the singulares and headed off, a couple of the other senior men following as well. When they vanished over the edge of the dell, the emperor was left with fourteen singulares Augusti, a couple of tribunes, a body slave, and the queen. There must be hundreds, even thousands, of soldiers within a mile.

Claudia Enica nudged her horse alongside the emperor, Soranus and the other Batavian just a few yards behind. For an instant Hadrian's eyes flashed with suspicion.

'This is a bad spot, my lord. We cannot be seen, but we cannot see anything either.'

Riders spilled over the crest to their left, the hoofs of their horses flicking up clods of mud. An officer was in the lead, a tall man, a tribune, and Hadrian quickly recognised Pertacus the Brigantian. Behind him came a dozen troopers, all angling down the slope to follow the line of the wall. Someone's horse started to ride ahead, and soon the imperial party jerked into a trot, the wall beside them.

'Beware, my lord! Ambush! You must get to safety!' Pertacus was pointing westwards, along the line of the wall. 'There is a camp by the bridge, my lord!' he called. 'You will be safe there. Follow me!'

The horses sensed the nervousness of their riders and they were bunched together, so that as one began to canter they all did. Soon, Hadrian and the rest were galloping, over another rise into a meadow. There was a tower ahead, complete by the look of it, with a sentry on top and two more standing in front, shields propped against their legs. They gaped as the cavalcade came charging at them, and stood to attention.

'Not far now, my lord,' Pertacus shouted. His men were stretched out behind him, almost in a file, the wall running parallel with Hadrian and his escort, and barely higher as they got closer. On the other side, beyond the low wall, the ditch had not yet been dug, and after ten or so paces the land sloped sharply down to the river.

Claudia Enica's horse was barged by one of the praetorian tribunes riding with the staff, and the mare stumbled and almost fell. Clinging onto a saddle horn, she straightened herself up, and realised that Pertacus was watching her, as was his bodyguard. The moment she looked back, the tribune bared his teeth in a satisfied smile, before waving his arm ahead. In the distance, a long bowshot past the tower, the ground rose slightly, and more auxiliary troopers were coming into view. There was a decurion at their head and they were heading straight for them.

Hadrian raised his hand. 'Halt!'

The order was not neatly obeyed, for no one had expected it, and this crowd of experienced soldiers and a collection of officers had been riding because everyone else was. It was not quite a panic, but nor had anyone been thinking too much. Horses reared as riders sawed at their reins. The praetorian tribune's horse slipped, its front legs going down, throwing him forward onto the grass.

The auxiliaries riding beside them were caught by surprise, but they were almost in a file and not too bunched together. No one fell, and in a moment their horses were turning.

'Now!' Pertacus shouted. 'Murder!'

Troopers hefted spears and threw them. One hit the emperor's stallion in the chest, driving deep, and the animal screamed as it fell. Hadrian jumped free, landing hard with his shoulder on the rough core of the low wall. Two of the singulares Augusti were down, and a tribune screamed as his horse fell and rolled over him in its dying throes.

Claudia Enica glanced across the wall, ready to jump her mare over, and then all at once the bushes and stunted trees on the river bank were alive with men, warriors with little shields and long spears. Mouths opened in screams as they boiled up over the edge and charged towards them. There was no prospect of escaping that way and swimming their horses over the river.

The singulares were trying to form a rough line, stabbing with their lanceae to keep the attackers back. Officers fumbled with swords as they drew them, but men were fighting back and a trooper reeled away, clutching at his throat as it fountained blood. Riders were mingling with each other, stabbing with spears or hacking with swords.

Hadrian pushed himself up, then ducked to let a javelin whisk past his shoulder. 'The tower!' he yelled. It was close, barely thirty paces away and as long as the men there were just soldiers, it offered the best sanctuary.

The singulares Augusti were good. They had originally been recruited from Batavians and other Germans because the Romans knew that such warriors saw an oath to a chieftain as sacred and would not think before sacrificing their lives to save his, for otherwise they would be disgraced. These days many races served in the Horse Guards, but all accepted the same faith as a tradition. They were the emperor's men, and if it came to it, their bodies were there to shield him, for that was the price of the pay, the prestige and the pride of serving with the finest cavalry in the empire.

Four of the guardsmen were on the ground, dead or badly wounded, as many more fought on, in spite of gaping holes in their armour. One bareheaded man, helmet gone, thigh cut open, threw himself at one of the Wolf's riders, grabbing the man by the throat and bearing him to the ground. Another thrust his spear through the belly of a trooper, punching right through the iron rings of his mail, and while he reached for his sword he knocked another enemy out of the saddle by slamming his shield boss into the man's face. Soranus put an arrow into the mouth of one enemy, then swung round and dropped a warrior charging up from the river.

'Come on!' Claudia Enica wished that she had a sword, but while the emperor had permitted her to ride with his staff, doing so armed would have stretched even his indulgence too far. She had a slim-bladed knife tucked into her right boot, but that would be no use at all at the moment. Unable to think of fighting, she pushed her horse forward to be level with Hadrian. She called the Batavians after her.

The emperor had his own gladius in hand as a bare-chested man came screaming towards him, spear levelled. Hadrian surprised the warrior by going forwards, grabbed the shaft just behind the head, slid his blade beneath the square shield and thrust into the man's stomach, twisting the blade to free it. Another warrior bounded up from the side. Soranus saw the danger, aimed and loosed, but as he did so another horse barged into his and the shaft went low, driving through the warrior's thigh. The man yelped and stumbled.

Hadrian ran, diving between Claudia Enica's mare and the

other Batavian's horse and heading for the tower. The two soldiers on guard were running forward and Pertacus was shouting at them.

'Kill him! Kill the tribune!' the queen screamed. One man raised his spear, but did not throw, until a trooper peeled off towards them. The javelin hissed in the air, plucking the rider from the saddle and the two auxiliaries came forward, the second man throwing and grazing the side of Pertacus' horse, which wheeled away. The other horsemen, the ones led by the decurion, were closer now, spurring into a gallop. Hadrian noticed that they had the same shield device as the ones with Pertacus. It was familiar, but it was not a unit here.

'Into the tower!' he yelled.

A tribune, a fresh and rather timid young man, pushed into a career by his family, surged past them, waving a sword already slick with blood and headed straight at the decurion and his men. He was screaming at the top of his voice, a strange mixture of fear and rage, and he slashed hard at the decurion, shattering the man's oval shield and making him slam back against the horns at the rear of his saddle. A stone, lobbed by the sentry on top of the tower, hit the rider behind, and the tribune was in the midst of them, slashing wildly. Swords flashed, and Claudia Enica could not see the man die as he was struck from all sides, but it gave them precious moments. The open door to the tower was just a few paces away and clear. Hadrian sprinted, the Batavian following. Soranus was shooting behind him as he came, and then both riders jumped down as the emperor went through the doorway.

'Lady!' Soranus called, just as Claudia's mare fell, neck arched and teeth bared in agony, and there was a blow on her back, a hard blow, so that she was thrown through the air and slammed into the ground, winded and bruised. Soranus stepped back towards her, heard a rider bearing down on him, put an arrow to his string and loosed in one smooth motion, the result of years of training.

'Go!' Claudia gasped, trying to push up, when something hit her head and she felt the vomit in her throat. The world went black.

XXXII

Across the river

FEROX HEARD THE horn sounding and knew that he was wrong, utterly wrong. Men's heads turned towards him, not needing to ask the question.

'Wait,' he said.

The old warrior, the leader of the queen's escort, nodded, while Ferox tried to think. He had expected a diversion, but not up there, so close to the tiny fort at the end of the mile of solid wall. It had to be a diversion, because even the best warriors in the world could not hope to reach the emperor through so many soldiers and with the protection of his new fortifications. Treachery or not, that made no sense, unless the betrayal was on such a vast scale that there was little chance of stopping it. That did not seem likely, for you did not sense that folk resented Hadrian. For most of the empire, one princeps was much like another, as all powerful and as distant as Jupiter.

Ferox stared across the river at the little camp next to where a work party was to build a bridge on the line of the wall to carry patrols across. Hadrian liked bridges, and there were not too many in his grand plan, so it was obvious that the emperor would come there and take a look. It was likely to be as far as he went today, before turning for home. There were patrols on the hill rising behind him, on this side of the river, and he could see others on the far side, high in the hills. Those men were stirring, catching the distant sound and wondering what to do.

This was where he would have killed Hadrian, putting men in the woods that came within fifty paces of the camp, and more in the bushes and trees of the river bank on either side. They could have waited until the imperial party was staring at the foundations of the bridge, then burst out, trapping the emperor against the river. They would have taken losses, heavy losses, but anyone trying to kill the master of Rome must accept that. The only escape route was across the river, and he had wondered whether there might be men waiting here as well. There were not, as he had learned in the early hours of the night when he scouted the position in this fir wood, before going back to fetch his men. He was here to react if he was wrong, and if he was not to shut off the enemy escape, and ideally help the emperor swim across to safety. The singulares were supposed to be good at that, after all.

Bran and three others were somewhere on the river banks. Ferox was not sure what side and where, but trusted his friend to have found as good a place as possible. There was too much risk in sending more men forward, partly because that would make staying concealed so much harder. Even worse, they might be mistaken for enemies by the Roman covering forces.

Gannascus was too big to hide and not made for stealth, so he and Vindex had taken the bulk of the men and were further back, horses at the ready, staying beyond the perimeter set up by the Romans. They were in a couple of groups – again he had trusted them to make the right choices – so that they could catch the Wolf and his men as they tried to escape. Whatever happened, his nephew could not survive to boast of his deeds.

Ideally, they would get Sosius as well, if the freedman was truly involved, but that was less likely and less urgent. The Wolf could rouse the tribes by telling of how he had almost killed – or even slaughtered – the high king of the Romans, and there would be red war for years before Rome restored its reputation.

Ferox had planned to meet the ambush he would have set if he were his nephew and had guessed wrong. Now he had to work out was happening and do his best to counter it. The diversion was raging, and now there was smoke rising from somewhere on the far side of the hills. It was thick and black, growing in spite of the drizzle, which meant that if was quite a blaze. Was it another distraction or the main attack?

'Get the boats,' Ferox told the old warrior. 'I'll take three men. Keep the rest here in case they still come this way.'

The 'boats' were coracles, the little bowl-shaped frames covered in hides that poorer folk used to catch fish. Ferox and one warrior went in one, and two more Brigantes in the other, paddling furiously against the strong tide. It seemed a better bet than wading and swimming across, which would mean ditching their armour. Ferox wanted to keep his helmet and look as much like a Roman centurion as possible. Hopefully that would stop any soldiers from shooting at them.

'Faster! Faster!' he called, as he and his companion drove the stubby paddles through the water. The river was not that wide here, but it rushed because of the slope and they had to steer hard left as they tried to go straight.

Soldiers outside the camp saw them, shouting a warning.

'Stand fast!' Ferox bellowed in his best parade ground voice, ruined a little because he stopped rowing and the round coracle lurched sharply down stream. 'I am Ferox of II Augusta!'

A pilum spun through the air and splashed into the river where they would have been if they were going straight.

'You stupid mongrel! Put that man on a charge! I'm a centurion!' He glanced back at the warrior behind him. 'Paddle before those damned fools try again!'

Hadrian pulled the ladder up behind them. He did not feel good about it, but if he died there would likely be civil war, so it was his duty to prevent that. There was an inner chamber halfway up the tower, a door either side level with the walkway of a wall not yet built. Thankfully someone had taken the job seriously and there were doors already in place, so he checked that they were bolted. He had done the same with the door on the ground floor, but it was not sturdy enough to hold out for long against a determined enemy.

'Get up top!' he ordered Soranus. The other Batavian had gone back when the queen's horse went down. Hadrian had seen the man punch with his shield at a warrior on foot, but another had chopped down from behind, cleaving through the shoulder doubling of his mail shirt.

He must survive, which meant being selfish and not indulging in misguided heroics. The man might survive, and hopefully Claudia would do so, but that was not up to him. He had this horse archer from his singulares, and the sentry on top of the tower, which made three of them, but only two to take all save the most essential risks. Hadrian heard pounding on the door downstairs, and the splintering of wood as the timber began to break.

'Take this,' he called, struggling to hold the ladder he had drawn up and pass it through the trapdoor onto the roof.

Soranus appeared, reaching down to grab it.

'No, Hadrian ordered. You shoot, get the other fellow to do this.'

'Dead, sir.'

With much cursing – and apologies on the part of Soranus each time he swore in front of his emperor – the ladder was drawn up onto the open platform at the top of the tower. Hadrian scrambled up the other ladder, the one from this floor. It was chained in place, so there was no way to haul that up as well. He would just have to hope for the best. Hadrian walked over to the parapet to see what was happening, Surely help must be coming soon, with all this noise.

'Stay back, you stupid bastard!' Soranus barked as he would to a raw recruit. He paid no more heed to his lord and master and turned back, drawing an arrow and loosing it.

Hadrian heard a scream and did what he was told. No sense in getting this far and taking a stone or javelin in the face while looking down. He realised that there was a gash on his right thigh and his breeches were torn, and he could not remember taking that wound. It did not seem too bad, but he drew his gladius again and clumsily cut some material from his cloak to bind it.

Trumpets, Roman tubicines this time, sounded, and two groups of a dozen or so cavalry appeared on the ridge to the south. Given the recent ambush, that did not mean that they were friends, but they were coming on quickly.

'You beauties!' Soranus yelled in delight, and in spite of the risk Hadrian went closer to the parapet and his heart leapt as he saw two turmae of his own singulares coming up from the east along the line of the wall. They were galloping, rushing to beat the other troopers in the race to join the fight and whether that was in case of any suspicion of their loyalty or from sheer pride in their own unit did not matter.

The noise had dropped, and Hadrian had the sense that the fighting was over, or almost over, in the way you sensed a storm was passing. He went to stand so that most of him was sheltered by a crenulation. There were dead men and horses strewn all around, a lot of them. Quite a few of the men disguised as troopers had long-shafted arrows sticking from their corpses, which suggested that his Batavian had done remarkable work. Hadrian searched for his officers and saw several corpses. There was no sign of Claudia, although she might be buried by other dead.

Soranus shoved him hard as a javelin whipped towards them. The Batavian's face was close, and he saw him flinch as the spearhead flashed past, just inches from his face. Somehow it went between them without hitting either except when the last part of the shaft grazed the guardsman's cheek.

Hadrian staggered, making himself go back into the middle of the platform. It took a moment to gather his wits and breath. 'I know, *commilito*,' he said. 'I'm a stupid bastard!'

Soranus nodded. 'Not for me to say, sir, begging your pardon. But you're a live bastard, and that's what matters.' There were tears in the man's eyes and on his cheeks. 'But the lady, sir, the lady.'

Bran had spent a cold and wet night in a hollow set into the south bank of the river. He knew that there were warriors hiding little more than a hundred paces to the east. They were good, but not quite good enough, for he had heard the soft noises of movements, and one man whose bowels seemed more than usually active. The rush of the water covered a lot, as did the showers of rain, but the signs were there for those able to notice them. Once he had crept close enough to watch and see a little movement. He guessed that there were twenty or more men waiting and had no doubts about who they were.

After that Bran went back to the hollow and his men. They huddled together, covered in their cloaks, sheltered by the sides of the bank and a bush hanging low over it. He doubted anyone slept, but these were good men, all older than him and yet willing to accept his orders. Two were Germans, followers of Gannascus from the old days, and they carried bows as tall as themselves, each one carefully wrapped, with the strings kept separate, to keep out the damp.

Four against twenty, probably far more, apart from anyone else the Wolf would bring to this ambush. The odds were not good, but nor were they so simple. Hadrian would have his escort, presumably good men. They would be taken by surprise, but then so would the ambushers when his little band took them from the side or rear.

Dawn came, a cold grey dawn, scarcely less damp than the night, and still they waited, hour after hour. The third man was one of the queen's escort, a former auxiliary, with them to help Bran convince any Romans that they were on the same side. The fellow kept rubbing his legs to keep some sort of life in them.

They must all have fallen asleep, drugged by fatigue, the cold, and the endless waiting, for Bran's eyes jerked open when he heard the sound of an ox horn trumpet. He nudged the others gently, and was relieved when none of them moaned or said anything in that short time when a man is still too sleepy to think straight. They were all stiff, aching and chilled, and they started to move slowly, as quietly as possible, to get ready. The Germans unwrapped their bows.

Bran put his fingers to his lips, pointed to himself, then gestured for them to stay. He crouched to get on the bank, then crawled forward. There were plenty of bushes and bent trees to his left, but even so he was careful. He came to the lip of the bank, saw a tower not far ahead, and on either side a wall that did not seem to be much more than foundations. Hadrian and his escort were coming along behind it, shadowed by a file of troopers led by a fancily dressed tribune or the like. Bran whistled, giving the signal they had arranged, and no one seemed to notice, for there was silence and he was about to repeat the call, when the troopers swooped in to attack and a rush of yelling warriors burst out of the treeline. There were more troopers to the right, coming in fast. He glimpsed Claudia Enica's red hair in the chaos, as men and horses were going down, saw the emperor fall, and then his men jogged up beside him, knowing that stealth no longer mattered.

Bran led them along, nearer to the tower and the combat. The second group of troopers swept in, until a lone rider appeared among them and they foundered as they clustered to cut him down.

Bran pointed at the milling auxiliaries. 'Start killing them,' he told the Germans. He and the Brigantian went round, to take the men coming up from the river in the flank. Each had a sword and shield and wore mail. Helmets and spears had seemed too cumbersome to take when they needed to creep and hide for so long.

A horse fell like a stone as an arrow went into the side of its head, its rider falling. The trooper beside him shook in the saddle as an arrow burst through the boards of his shield and only just stopped as it touched his mail. The next went past the rim of the shield and punched through the armour. The rider gasped, staring down in horror, the breath knocked out of him.

'Hey, mate!' Bran called to a warrior clad in a dark tunic and trousers. The man turned, puzzled, his shieldless right to them, and Bran stabbed once, ignored the man's scream, yanked the blade free and went on. The next one was ready, jabbing with a thick-hafted spear. It banged against Bran's own shield, slashing a rent in the calfskin cover so that it hung open. He thrust at eye level, making his opponent flinch and duck, and then swung his weight left and punched with the boss of his shield, forcing the warrior back. Another man was coming at him, but the Brigantian was there, covering his side. Bran punched again, the man's boots slipped on the grass, giving him an opening, and he sliced his blade across the warrior's belly, punched once more and went on.

The densest fighting was near the tower. He saw Claudia Enica riding with another man, sheltering someone, realised that it was Hadrian as a purple-cloaked figure bounded towards the entrance to the tower, then the queen's horse was falling, but a shrieking warrior, face painted black with red stripes on the cheeks slashed at him with a gladius. Bran dodged, gaining room, pretended to slip, saw the man grin and raise his sword high to slash, for although he had the weapon of a soldier he was not trained to use it. Bran thrust above the shield, the man was slow trying to meet it and managed only to push the blade high. Instead of spearing into his throat, the point of Bran's sword went through one painted cheek. The warrior dropped his sword and Bran used his weight to thrust harder, and he saw the eyes roll back and heard the ghastly choking sounds as the man died.

'We're with you, you fools!' The Brigantian shouted as an auxiliary trooper came at him on foot. The man ignored him, stabbing with a broken hafted spear, and Bran saw the same shield device carried by the ones following the tribune, the ones who had attacked the emperor.

'Kill him!' he shouted, jabbing at the man, who blocked the blow with his shield. The Brigantian was bleeding near the wrist, where the spear point had brushed past him, but still had plenty of strength and slashed, striking against the trooper's shoulder. The mail held, but the man crouched and grunted with pain. Bran sliced low, carving into the man's leg and he went down on the other knee, but the Brigantian hacked even harder, notching the blade of his sword as the rings snapped. Blood flowed, and he struck again, and again, but the warrior was already dropping.

Horsemen were cantering through the fight, heading for the river. There was an auxiliary, perhaps an officer, hands clutching a face that was bloody and one of the troopers leading his horse. Bran saw the officer, thought he looked familiar, and saw the man slice at a wounded guardsman and miss as he passed. Another man, thick limbed and squat, was with him, and he had something draped over the neck of his horse. Bran saw red hair, shaken loose, waving, and realised that it was not something but someone.

'You stay. Make sure they know the Germans are on our side!' he told the Brigantian, as he looked for a horse to follow. He saw one, its reins hanging loose, happily cropping the grass amid all the chaos. Bran ran, dodged a spear, went left to pass a warrior covered in wounds, but still brandishing his sword. The warrior came at him, so he slammed his shield into the man's face and let go, then leapt up. The horse quivered, but did not stir. He patted it and his hand came away wet from its neck, but it was too late now to seek another. He gathered the reins, nudged the horse around, saw a cavalryman, one of the singulares Augusti no less, heading for him, so screamed, 'Go hump yourself, you mongrel! I'm on your side!' The man grinned, whether he believed him or not, but was still some way away and Bran kicked the horse to make it run, drove it straight at the low wall, felt the muscles tense and then the leap, and felt and heard a back hoof clip the edge of the wall. The beast stumbled, the front left pommel of the saddle drove painfully into Bran's stomach, but he was still there and the animal started to run, pushing between some bushes, and it almost fell again as the bank dropped suddenly a good five feet. Bran clung on. He could not see the tribune, or the soldier carrying the queen, but another trooper was forcing his horse up the far bank. He reached the top and vanished into the woods above the river. Bran followed.

Claudia Enica hit the ground hard. Her eyes opened, but she could see nothing and her mouth was full of the grass that was everywhere.

'Are you hurt?' a voice asked softly. 'Let me help you.' A hand grasped one of her arms, another rolled her onto her back. There were branches above her, a thick canopy of woodland, and a handsome face smiling.

'Thank Taranis,' Pertacus said. 'I was worried. But I cannot see anything more than a few cuts.' He ran his hands over her hips and legs to check. She was too breathless, too sore and too confused to protest. Just about everywhere seemed to hurt, but nothing hurt more than anything else.

'The princeps is safe, I think, but there was still fighting and I wanted to get you to safety. I am a Brigantian after all, as well as a Roman! And of course, I am a man, and you are... well, let's just say that we all had a narrow escape and leave it at that.'

Another face appeared, round, battered and scarred, with tiny eyes. Nothing about that face looked thankful or safe.

'I was worried that my warning came too late,' the tribune said. 'I was late realising that those men were not soldiers, but traitors or something. Who knows what madness has taken them?'

'You shouted "murder!"' she croaked. Her throat was thick with bile.

Pertacus shrugged, his face embarrassed. 'Not very original. All I could think of on the spur of the moment. Now can you get up? We probably ought to find a patrol – a large one we can be sure are true servants of the emperor. I am so glad that you are not hurt.'

'Take my arm,' she said, holding out her left and trying to work out where the bodyguard had gone. She did not believe a word she was hearing, even with her mind sluggish. There would probably only be one chance. Pertacus held her arm, lifting her. She moved slowly, deliberately awkward, and her right hand went to her boot and slipped the knife free. She thrust up, and there was agony as her arms were pinned and pulled back.

Pertacus gasped in surprise, straightened up, and then sighed. 'Ah well, I suppose it was too much to hope that you were fooled.' He reached for her hand and prised out the knife. 'Dear me, not very ladylike is it?' His other hand swung and slapped her hard so that her cheek stung. 'Bitch.'

'Hadrian will know,' she said, gasping because the gladiator's grip was like a vice. 'Your only chance is to beg for pardon and accept exile. If you harm me not even that will save you. My husband will find you wherever you go. You know that don't you?'

Pertacus hit her again, using the back of his hand this time. Her lip started to bleed.

He sighed. 'We have so little time, my dear, and if only you had been nice in the past this would not have mattered. But you aren't nice, are you, you're ambitious and cruel, with beauty like the Morrigan's and with her lust for blood.' He dropped the knife and grabbed the top of her tunic with both hands. He yanked hard and it stretched, but did not tear, so he kept on tugging until it did and then he ripped it open, pulling it off her completely. She could not break free. He hit her again, then grabbed her breast strap and tore it away.

'My father was killed serving your brother, did you know that?' Pertacus asked. He was panting, face flushed with rage.

'I knew he died when you were young. I was never sure how?'

'Bitch.' He hit her again, then began to fumble at her belt. She kicked out, but he was too fast and dodged. 'Why should you care? So you did not know that Ferox, your precious husband, our king,' he spat the word, 'killed him like a dog as he stayed loyal to your brother, the true king.' The buckle came free and he pushed her breeches down, even as she kept trying to kick out. He hit her twice more.

'I so wish that there was more time, but then I wished that you had burned all those years ago at the villa, because that meant that I have had to wait, and now we are in a hurry. It was not easy arranging that attack, making it happen at the same time as the big raids, and after all of that no one who really mattered died.

'I want you to suffer, and I want that bastard husband of yours to suffer because I want him to come for me so that I can kill him.' He reached out, brushing fingers across her bruised cheek almost tenderly. 'I really wanted to enjoy every moment of this. Be nice as well, if you were your usual stylish self. I do have standards, after all, and fine clothes and make-up help to disguise the fact that you are so very old.'

He took her chin in both hands and kissed her. 'Cold as the Morrigan herself.' He started to lift his own tunic and armour and unfasten his snug riding breeches. 'Well, woman who is not a goddess, you should know that you have not won. Hadrian will die, for this was not the whole plan, and before the end of the month we will have a new emperor. Do I see surprise in your eyes? You have lost in every way, and you will die when I am done with you.'

'That won't take long!' she said and spat in his face.

He hit her again, although less hard than before. 'The new emperor and the old empress will reward those like me who supported them. So, my sweet queen, exile is not my fate. I have won.'

'Are you well, sister?' a familiar voice asked.

Claudia Enica was spun around as the gladiator turned, still holding her too tight to break free. Bran was there, his clothes and armour spattered with mud. He paid no attention to her nakedness, and his eyes were on the two men. Like her, he had been taught by the Mother, which made them kin by oath, apart from anything else such as being married to her daughter or his long friendship with Ferox.

'My apologies for taking so long, but my dog of a horse broke its leg and died on me.' He smiled. 'So, my friends, you have a choice. You can let the lady go and be on your way. I doubt you will get far as there are a lot of embarrassed and angry soldiers swarming everywhere and desperate to redeem themselves after letting the emperor nearly get killed. Probably best to give yourselves up and plead for mercy.'

'Or?' Pertacus asked, fastening his trousers. 'You said there was a choice.'

'Oh yes.' The grin became even broader. 'I kill you and we get it over with.'

'Felix,' Pertacus commanded, and Claudia Enica was pushed down hard onto the ground. The tribune and his bodyguard drew their swords, spreading apart to take Bran from either side.

'It's nice when things are simple,' Bran said, and drew his spatha. Claudia Enica struggled for breath. Her trousers were bunched beneath her knees, pinning her legs together.

The gladiator came forward, well balanced for all his bulk, and quick on his feet. He lunged, Bran dodged, cut back and the blades met and clanged. Pertacus came in from the other side, swinging wildly. Bran leaped back and the gladiator took another step and was about to thrust again when the queen grabbed his ankle with both hands and pulled as hard as she could. It was like tugging at the column of a temple, but the man grunted and looked down, giving Bran the chance to slash into the gladiator's side. It was a hard blow, but his armour was good and although the edge carried between two of the hooped plates and through the jerkin underneath it was not a crippling wound. Pertacus slashed at him again, hitting almost the same spot, and Bran's mail split apart before he could jump back.

The gladiator grunted softly, turned and tried to stamp on the queen with his other boot. She let go, rolling away, cursing that her legs were still pinned, but the trousers were too well fitting to kick off easily over her boots. She rolled again, pushed up on her hands, thinking that if she could stand then maybe she could haul the wretched things up. Then she saw the knife and lunged for it, falling again, but she had the blade and that was something. At last, she was back on her knees, and using one hand pressed on the ground, she managed to stand.

Bran had nicked the tribune on the arm, and added a fresh scar across the mangled nose of the gladiator. The price was another rent in his armour. Both wounds pulsed blood, and he would start to weaken if nothing was done. The gladiator was also slowing, his tunic and leg beneath the cut in his armour darkly wet.

The queen of the Brigantes tugged with all her might at the top of her trousers and managed to haul them up most of the way, so that she could walk.

'I remember your father now, Pertacus!' she called, voice harsh, but strong. 'He was a...'

The expression was one that none of them expected a queen to know and for just a moment the fight paused. Bran roared with laughter. Pertacus turned, so saw a dirty, mud-stained and nearly naked woman holding a little knife.

'And what do you expect to do with that, lady?' He came towards her, his gladius held out. 'Oh well, I would have preferred to use another sword on you, but this will do.'

The gladiator found a burst of energy and charged. Bran went back, seemed to slip, but the veteran of the arena knew a trick when he saw it and slowed before he got close. He saw the hand move, scooping mud, so started to pull away, turning his face before it could be thrown to blind him.

Claudia Enica took a pace back. The knife was sharp and light, but no match for the reach of a sword. She remembered Vindex telling her a story, and an idea came.

Bran did not throw any mud, but used his crouch to spring forward. His left hand grabbed the gladiator's right arm at the wrist, trying to hold back the thrust. The man was as strong as an ox, and the point of his gladius kept coming, pressing into Bran's mail shirt. He was stabbing forward at the same time, and the bodyguard was a fraction late taking hold of his arm. Bran grunted with effort and pain as the gladius broke through the rings and drove into his flesh, but strong though his opponent was, all his own weight was behind his attack and his spatha had a much longer blade. The gladiator's eyes were pale like a child's, and he saw them blink, although that was all the emotion there was, and then the sharpened tip of the spatha drove into the man's right eye. Bran felt the force slacken on the sword in his own body, and pushed harder until his enemy went limp. The gladiator's great weight helped to pull the spatha free, but also tore the man's sword out, widening the wound.

Bran knew the wound was bad, but he was alive, on his feet, and Claudia Enica was in danger.

'You got the balls to fight me, or only women?'

Pertacus' head snapped around, registering shock to see his man stretched on the ground. Claudia threw the knife, as she had heard Ferox had done in the first of his duels, and her aim was good and the distance short. The slim blade buried itself deep in the side of the tribune's neck. He gasped, stared at her, then back at Bran and the blood spurted out so fast that it pushed out the knife. The tribune sagged, like an old building collapsing.

Claudia Enica wiped her bleeding lip. 'That's a pity, I could have done with talking to him.'

XXXIII

That evening

FEROX REACHED THE fight when it was all over, to find the emperor safe, the queen gone and Bran gone after her. To his surprise, one of the first people he saw was Marcus Cerialis at the head of half a dozen cavalrymen from Legio II Augusta. Ferox was by far his senior in the legion, could see that plenty of troops had arrived or were on their way, so ordered Marcus to follow Bran. 'That way!' he said, pointing towards the river. 'Try not to get lost or your parents will never forgive me!' The lad gave him a cheerful grin, as Ferox began his search through the dead. His nephew was not among them.

'You!' He chose one of the singulares who seemed to be well mounted. 'Give me your horse!'

'Sir!'

'Do as he says!' Hadrian was leaning over the parapet of the tower.

Ferox nodded his thanks, and rode to find a trail and then find Vindex and Gannascus. It took time, but he found all three, largely because he did not do what the regulars were doing, and kept mainly to the valleys of the little streams and the rest of the close country. Five horsemen were heading north, already past the cordon established to protect the emperor. That did not surprise him, because in the panic after the ambush, everyone was rushing around and very few were thinking.

There were fifteen of them altogether as they followed the fugitives along a winding path, keeping to cover as much as possible. When they had climbed to the far side of the valley, Ferox sent four men off on either side, to take the open paths and hurry in the hope of getting ahead of the enemy. Gannascus and Vindex stayed with him, refusing to leave.

'You draw trouble,' the German told him. 'So we will find them and I will kill him.'

They pressed on, and after an hour found the corpse of a man, stretched flat on his back, legs and arms neatly arranged and bare sword laid beside him. He had the stump of an arrow sticking from his chest.

'My men are good,' Gannascus said with great pride.

That meant four fugitives, and a spare horse, but they were still gaining, and Ferox suspected from the tracks that one or more of the remaining men were also wounded and slowing everyone down. It did not sound like the Wolf to coddle men like this, unless these men were bound by a solemn oath of the sort the Silures sometimes swore before they tried to do something especially risky.

Two hours later, he judged that they were barely a mile behind, for the dung from the fugitives' horses was still soft and very moist as the flies swarmed over it in delight.

'Let's take it nice and slow,' Ferox said. Gannascus growled, but obeyed.

Ferox led, fifty paces ahead, and he went warily. His nephew ought to guess that they would be followed, and if he had let them come so close, perhaps that was because he wanted them near. He could be expecting to meet up with more of his warriors.

They were in a winding valley again, the brook at the bottom less than a foot deep and barely wider. Ahead the ground climbed to a gap between woods. Ferox stopped and stared at it. He beckoned to Gannascus and Vindex, who came up on either side, then gestured for the other men to watch both sides of the gully.

'I see two,' he said softly. 'Only two, one on either side of the track. But there could be more.'

'Do we wait?' Vindex said.

'Might be what they want,' Gannascus suggested.

Ferox drew his gladius. 'Let's just walk at them, and see what they do.'

Vindex drew out his wheel of Taranis and touched it to his lips. 'You know, one day, I'll stop listening to you.'

'Not today,' Gannascus growled. They both drew their swords, and unlike Ferox had their shields.

They walked forward in a line.

'Lads, you don't have to die here!' Ferox called.

A man came from the left first, screaming as he ran at them, sword ready and oval shield held up.

'Watch out!' Ferox yelled at Vindex, who was on his right, because a moment later another man came from that side, charging in silence, spear raised ready to throw.

Vindex spun his horse around in time to take the spear on his own shield. Gannascus was cantering at the other man, cutting down with a dull clang as his blade drove the man to the ground, a dent in his helmet. Vindex killed the other easily, for there did not seem to be any real heart in the attack.

They discovered the reason as they rode on. Ahead of them,

two horsemen stood their mounts in the path. Both were in Roman uniform, and both were badly hurt.

'Are you Ferox?' one asked. His right arm hung limp, broken and useless.

'I am.'

'That is him,' the other man said, and began to unwind the bandage that covered his face.

Ferox knew the voice at once, for this was his nephew, the one they called the Wolf.

'An arrow,' the other man explained. 'It struck from the side.'

The Wolf's left eye was gone altogether, leaving an empty socket, his nose was smashed and his right eye a ruin, all done as he chased the emperor, and Soranus shot that one last arrow before fleeing into the tower.

'The last thing I saw was Hadrian!' he said bitterly. 'It would be a bastard Roman, and worse, he was getting away. I'm guessing he is still alive?'

'He is.'

'Then you had better kill me and end it,' the Wolf told them.

A blind chief was no chief, especially when he was a man who had no kin in these parts and had power only because he was a warrior. Ferox turned to Gannascus. 'Your choice?'

'You killed my son,' the German growled.

'I killed many,' the Wolf said.

'There must be a price,' the German said, but Ferox could sense his reluctance. Whatever else his nephew was, he was brave and warriors could not help admiring bravery. They also understood vengeance.

'Sister's son, do you remember the tales of our people?' Ferox asked.

'I do.'

'The story of Camulorix?'

The Wolf hesitated and licked his lips. 'You're a bastard,' he said at last.

'You will be remembered, whether you live or die, always remembered.'

The blind man smiled. 'I agree.'

They all dismounted as Ferox recounted the story, and after the Wolf had taken a long drink of wine, he lay down on the ground.

'This is sharp,' Ferox said, offering Gannascus his sword.

'This is heavy,' the German replied, holding up his own blade, but he did not smile.

They held the Wolf down, and the big man took careful aim and severed the man's right wrist. Then he cut off the left foot.

The warrior with the broken arm could not do it, so they tied off each limb and bandaged the stumps.

'Take him to Fanum Cocidius,' Ferox told the warrior. 'The priests will help, and if he does not live it is a good place to pass.'

'We're not going with them?' Vindex asked.

'Why should we?' Ferox said, but as they began to walk their horses away, he stopped for a moment.

'Farewell, Rues,' he called. 'We will meet in the other world.'

'Well, he shouldn't be hard to recognise,' Vindex said.

XXXIV

Seventeen days before the Kalends of July, Vindolanda

FEROX STARED AT the ceiling. It was an honour, so they assured him, to be among the handful of guests allowed to stay in the mansio with the emperor, even if it meant occupying this tiny cubicle of a room and this hard-framed box of a bed, less than four foot across. At least it was summer and the nights were mild, because he had long since lost the battle of the bedclothes to his wife. The queen had done this and somehow occupied the centre of the lumpy, badly filled sack mattress. Ferox was on his back, and if he kept his legs straight and arms at his side then he just fitted onto what was left of the bed, albeit at the cost of the side of the frame digging into him.

He could not sleep, so he listened to Claudia Enica's bouts of snoring. She had not talked much so far during the night, but he suspected that that would come, most likely if he ever did manage to drift off.

She was recovering, for although nothing seemed to be broken, she had ached in her back, side and limbs for days after the ambush. She had not been able to sleep well at the start, which meant nights of her lying awake and talking, consciously this time, while he tried not to touch her even accidentally because she hurt so much at every movement.

Bran seemed to be improving. His wound was bad and

the journey in a waggon to get him to the fort's hospital can only have been nightmare of pain. Yet he had received the full attention of the emperor's own physician and the lad was still alive, so all in all it was encouraging. Soon, Ferox, Vindex and Gannascus would take him back to Senuna.

Apart from his wife's familiar noises, the mansio was never quiet. There were sentries outside the emperor's room and at every entrance, for no one wanted to take any risks after the attack earlier in the month. The queen had reported Pertacus' words, and his confidence that the plot was still underway, and although Hadrian was inclined to dismiss such concerns, he agreed that some precautions were prudent, at the very least to make his senior officers and guards feel better. During the night the sentries paced, and were relieved every second hour, and inspected half way through, which meant booted footsteps, the clank of armour and equipment and low-voiced conversations. Some went on for a long time, the sort where he could pick out a few words, but not enough to satisfy his mind's urge to make sense of what they were saying.

Ferox heard it all, just as he heard the other sounds, as the slaves went about their duties. The staff were quiet, but lamps needed checking, the fire to heat the bath needed tending, and at regular intervals someone went to clean the latrine's floor and seats, to take away any dirty sponges and bring clean ones, and to open the sluice and wash out the channels underneath the seats.

Ferox had lived all these years by relying on his senses, watching and listening, and unless he fell asleep quickly, he was finding it more and more difficult to drop off, especially when he was somewhere unfamiliar, like this.

There was a soft grating sound and then a low swish of water coming from the tank on the roof of the building, as a slave flushed the latrines through. The toilet was next to his room, which was another reason he questioned just how much this was an honour. He heard the grating again as the sluice was lowered back into place, then footsteps as the slave finished and went off to perform another task.

Ferox waited, but the sounds had brought a fresh dilemma. His body was telling him that he needed to urinate, which seemed unfair, because he had gone several times during the night and did not remember drinking much of anything the evening night before. If he got up again, he would probably wake himself up even more, apart from the risk that during his absence the queen would annex the rest of the bed, for she had a knack of sprawling diagonally to fill all the available space. He did not really fancy the floor, but holding on and defending this strip of bed to the last did not make the sense of urgency go away.

The queen turned onto her back. 'We need the marble to be bright,' she said.

Fair enough, thought Ferox, making up his mind. He rose, hand reaching for the pugio lying beside the bed as it always did. He reached out for it and stopped, remembering where he was. Even so, it was an effort to leave the weapon behind and simply put a cloak around his shoulders, but a man wandering about with a dagger near the emperor's bed chamber might have a lot of explaining to do.

Then he heard something, a hiss that could have been his wife's breathing, except that she had rolled again onto her front and he did not think the sound came from so close by. His instincts were warning him, and he decided that if he had to explain, then so be it. Ferox slid the pugio from its scabbard. He put it in his left hand, fastening the cloak properly with a brooch so that the folds would conceal it.

He lifted the catch on the door gently, baffled because his bladder was no longer demanding his attention with the same relentless fervour, and eased the door open. The corridor was dark, which it had not been before, since lamps were mounted in sockets and kept burning at all hours. There was light from the open door at the far end, the emperor's room, and a hunched shadow on the floor in front of it.

Ferox searched in each direction, wondered whether to shout an alarm, for the shadow in front of the door was not moving, and was surely the praetorian guardsmen who should have been on watch. Instead, he ran towards the door, keeping his dagger low in his left hand, for a warning would be heard by everyone, including an assassin if one was already in the emperor's room.

His bare feet slapped against the polished floorboards, the noise echoing. A man appeared in the open door, silhouetted against the light. His hood was thrown back and the skin of his shaven head glinted. There was a gladius in his hand, held low, and the blade was dark.

'You,' he gasped.

Ferox ripped his cloak off, snapping the pin of the brooch, and flung it at Sosius, for he knew the face and the voice.

The freedman struggled, head buried under the garment and Ferox dashed forward and punched the dagger into the man's belly. He ripped the blade free and stabbed again and again, his right hand trying to grab the freedman's throat. Sosius grunted, and there was blood everywhere, and the freedman yelled in pain and then slumped down, the cloak falling away.

He stared up at Ferox, eyes blinking, his life draining away. 'Why?' he said softly and went still.

Ferox went into the chamber, fearing the worst, for there was a slave lying dead in the corner, head unnaturally back and throat gashed open, so that his white tunic was bright against the dark pool around him.

The figure on the bed was hunched, and the shade from a canopy over the bed meant that it was hard to make out the details. Ferox's heart was pounding, his left hand sticky with blood, and he lowered it and the dagger and went closer.

There was another sound, a sound of soft breathing.

'My lord!' Ferox called.

The emperor stirred.

'My lord Hadrian!'

Hadrian sat up, stretching his arms and yawning so wide that it was almost theatrical. Well, people slept and woke in different ways, something that being married to Claudia Enica constantly reminded him.

'Ferox?'

'Are you hurt, my lord?'

'Bit stiff, but well enough.' The emperor noticed the dagger. 'Hercules' balls, what are you doing?'

'Saving your life, you ungrateful sod,' Ferox said before he could stop himself.

'What!' Hadrian leapt out of bed. He was naked, which was scarcely dignified, but there was no trace of any wound.

'Sosius,' Ferox explained. 'He was here. He's killed two, maybe more.'

Hadrian glanced at the murdered slave. 'Where is he?'

'Thetatus.'

Hadrian sighed. 'Then hadn't we better give the alarm, centurion?'

'Yes, sir, sorry, sir,' Ferox said and then shouted for the guards.

Epilogue

The day before the Kalends of July, Vindolanda

'So, if I understand correctly, the fate of the empire was decided by your bladder?' Cerialis was grinning broadly. 'That will be an interesting despatch to be read out in the Senate. Not that it will, of course.'

'Of course,' Claudia Enica agreed. 'The attempts to assassinate the emperor never happened, officially that is.'

'Quite. There was a border skirmish near where the emperor was – and wasn't our princeps terribly brave, just as you would expect – before the whole frontier burst into flames.'

That at least was true, for the raids had come in quickly and they were heavy and frequent, as the news that the emperor had almost been killed spread, and fed the pride of many warriors, their doubts about Roman strength, and their contempt for Hadrian's odd little walls and towers. Nepos had a war on his hands, which meant rounding up nearly all the work parties and turning them back into soldiers for the rest of the season. The Romans would win, eventually, for the new legion and the auxiliaries who came with them meant that the army was far stronger than it had been for a generation.

It also meant that the great wall, the Vallum Aelium, would take much longer to complete, especially since Hadrian had ordered a raft of changes to the design, adding forts to the mix so that the garrison immediately manning the wall would be much larger.

'I hear he is considering something quick to finish to form a barrier behind it all, something that can be ready in a year or two at most,' Cerialis commented. 'I am hoping for a ditch of some sort. As procurator I feel that would be good. Ditches are cheap.'

'What about Sosius?' Ferox asked.

'And my husband's heroic bladder,' Claudia Enica added. 'Yes, how soon will its story be set to song!'

'Sosius?' Cerialis asked. 'Now who could that be? No, I don't think anyone of that name has ever existed.'

Claudia Enica sighed softly. 'As I thought. So it is done, then?'

They were walking together on the parade ground, the area quiet apart from a handful of recruits practising with wooden swords and wicker shields against the posts set up at the far end. There was no one nearby, but even so Cerialis glanced around to check. Ferox was aware of a duplicarius with the recruits and was sure the man was silently fuming at the sight of strangers strolling about on his drill ground as if they had a right. Still, no one so junior was likely to yell at a procurator or a stylish lady.

'Lepidina tells me that the princeps already knew a good deal,' Cerialis explained, 'and had men in place with orders to act instantly. He had realised Sosius was more loyal to the Augusta than to him – a family connection apparently. She has been foolish rather than clever or capable, which sadly sums up her character. Angry at her husband for years, it simmered away until she started to think dangerous thoughts, and win over some of the imperial household. It's not clear how much they really knew or how far they took her seriously. As I see it, the plan was that once Hadrian was dead, the Augusta would use her authority to proclaim a new emperor. Nepos was the obvious choice, for he is on the spot and in command of three legions. She would declare that her husband had thought so highly of his legatus that he had marked him down as a likely successor, maybe even a candidate for adoption.'

'Would that have worked?' Claudia asked. Ferox just listened, for the more he heard the more he doubted that this was the real truth.

Cerialis considered for a moment. 'Lepidina thinks that it might have done. There could still have been a civil war, who knows? It seems fair to think that the Augusta thought that it could work, and Sosius – who of course was never there – was a shrewd political operator. They might have made it work.'

'So what happens now?' she wondered. 'A divorce still seems unlikely. Has any princeps ever divorced his wife?'

Cerialis had the habit of staring into the sky when he was thinking. 'Only the mad ones, I think,' he said after a moment. 'Can't remember whether Claudius divorced Messalina before she was executed, but then she was scarcely a typical wife!... But no, he will not do that. Officially there was no plot at all, hence no threat to the continued rule of the Lord Hadrian.

'There has been a scandal, a minor one, vague in nature, and people will discuss it without getting too worked up. The Lady Sabina Augusta, wife of our emperor, has been indiscreet, or has allowed members of the household and staff to be indiscreet around her – the details will never be announced, so that will allow plenty of salacious gossip. Those involved, chiefly the Praetorian prefect and poor Suetonius, the *ab epistulis*, will bear the blame, although again since nothing will be stated in any detail, no one will know blame for what. Both are dismissed to private life, along with a few others. No one will die, at least no one anyone has heard of. It is clear that Nepos himself knew nothing whatsoever of the plot. The Augusta was confident that with the emperor dead and an army at his back, and with her support, he would readily have done what was asked.

'So Nepos remains governor, and Hadrian frightens his wife, shows her up to the public as injudicious and even sillier than everyone thought, but appears as the loyal husband in the best traditions of the res publica by standing by her.'

Claudia Enica's tone was scornful. 'How very Roman.'

'It's what created the empire, so I'm told,' Cerialis allowed. 'That is politics, I suppose, and better than the alternative of chaos and war... Well, on that note of profound reflection, I had best bid you both 'Good Day.' Remember that you are to visit us in Londinium over the winter. Queen and king or not, my wife commands it, so it must be so!' He strode off towards the carriage waiting for him on the road next to the training area. Hadrian had gone to Uxelodunum in the west the day before, inspecting the turf wall and helping to organise the response to the raids. After that, he was due to return to the south of the province, so that he could sail back to Gaul before the autumn.

Cerialis turned and waved before climbing into the carriage. It was a small raeda, and Ferox wondered whether it was the same one the procurator and his family had used all those years ago, when he was the prefect in command of Vindolanda.

'Let's take in the view before we go and see Bran,' the queen suggested, so they strolled over to the far side, where the valley rolled away to the west. They did not speak, but her hand found his and they stood for a long time. It was bright and clear, and the Sun might get oppressive later, but for the moment it was most pleasant. The shouts of the duplicarius carried to them as he berated his recruits, and a little later the cornu sounded to mark the start of the second watch.

Ferox smiled, for the sounds of the army were so familiar after all these years that they were comforting. Hadrian had announced that he was retiring him as centurion, which allowed his legion to fill the slot he had held for so long. He was named as prefect, a more fitting rank after his admission to the equestrian order, and told that he would be expected to serve with Nepos' staff and with every legatus who succeeded them. While it was a wrench to think that he would have to spend a lot of time away from his wife, it was probably for the best. He did not thrive on inactivity.

'So what do you think, husband?' the queen asked eventually.

He stared down fondly into her green eyes for a while before answering. 'That you are very beautiful, and that I am the most fortunate of men.'

Her bruises, even the harsh blackness around one eye, had largely faded, so that she needed only a little make-up to conceal them. She had not told him all of what had happened, of what Pertacus had been about to do before Bran arrived. Ferox was angry enough at the best of times, and as her fellow ruler of the tribe, he needed to be more judicious in his conduct.

'Hmm, when the Silures turn to flattery a wise man reaches for his sword and watches his back, or so the old saying goes.'

Ferox leaned back, studying his wife's rear with obvious appreciation. 'I have never heard that one before,' he said.

'That's because I just made it up. I did not say how old after all, but something is bothering you and I would prefer to know what it is. Surprising as it may seem, you are occasionally right.'

He thought for a while longer and she let him take his time. 'Sosius,' he said, struggling to find the right words. 'What he did, did not make sense.'

'The plot? But the man was an intriguer. The gods know we

have been caught up in his schemes often enough, you most of all. As Hadrian's man, he murdered, plotted and discredited a lot of important people – probably far more than we know. I should have thought murdering an emperor would be easy enough after all that.'

'But why? He was Hadrian's man as you said. So we're supposed to believe that after all this time he wanted his master dead.'

'Slaves and former slaves have little cause to love their owners, no matter how benevolent the owners consider themselves to be... And will you stop staring at my arse.'

Ferox straightened up and put his arm around her waist. 'Fine, let's say he was really loyal to the empress all along, or that he came to loathe Hadrian, or that he came to believe that for all his past service, the new princeps had come to feel that it was better not to have him around in case he revealed some of the things Hadrian has had him do. He knows a lot, far too much to make him safe.'

She leaned towards him, and if proper Romans were not supposed to show such affection in public, she did not care. 'You know, you have a mind as suspicious and crooked as any senator. You might even make a good king, were I not a better queen.'

Ferox kissed her on the forehead, before going on. 'What we are supposed to believe is that he decided to kill the emperor. He helped arrange an ambush that did not work.'

'It nearly worked.'

'Did it? Still, maybe that was chance and they struck before they were quite ready, so Hadrian got lucky. But that fails, and Hadrian is alive and heavily guarded everywhere, including here at the mansio. Problem one, if the emperor is so well protected, how does Sosius get in?'

Claudia Enica felt her certainty slipping away, but wanted to follow the logic through. 'He was good at what he did, we all know that, very good indeed. And he knew the emperor's habits and household as well as anyone.'

'Fine, then there's problem two. This cunning spy and assassin sneaks past all the guards, although he murders one of them, and does it with the man barely making a noise. Then he cuts the throat of a slave, again without any noise.'

'He was good, as we said.' Her tone was dubious for it did not add up.

'And our third problem is that after doing all this, the sleeping emperor remains unharmed and Sosius comes out through the door and meets me.'

'Well, that's a shock for anyone.'

Ferox pinched her bottom and she gave an exaggerated squeal, drawing attention from a squad of recruits jogging along behind them. One man tripped and fell and a senior soldier leaned over, screaming at the tiro to get up and pay attention.

'Behave!' she told him, 'you're a king after all... But perhaps he changed his mind at the last moment, had second thoughts and realised that he did not want Hadrian dead.'

'Really?'

'No,' she conceded. 'That does not seem likely.'

'Now if I was a suspicious man...'

'Perish the thought!'

He pinched her again, prompting merely a mild complaint this time. 'As I was saying, if I was suspicious, then I would think that Hadrian was not asleep at all. You could smell the fresh blood in there, the place reeked of it, and surely anyone, most of all an emperor who knows that people are after his hide, would be woken by that. It didn't seem quite real at the time, the way he woke up and pretended to be bleary eyed and groggy. Too much like an act. I heard talking before I got up, could have been from there. Perhaps Sosius wasn't a surprise at all, even if he had to sneak in. Maybe he was still Hadrian's man, working in the shadows as he had always done.'

Her eyes widened. 'And Hadrian is worried and annoyed by his wife's loose tongue and interference in public life. So, he gets someone to convince her to plot, so that when it fails, he can use it against her. She's embarrassed and not likely to try anything again and a mild scandal makes everyone take her even less seriously.' She sighed at the coldness of it all. 'Sosius could arrange something like that, couldn't he? There would be the dead guard and slave to show an attempt at assassination. All that could be thrown in the Augusta's face to make her compliant. And Sosius was waiting until he heard a sound, then could rush out of the chamber and escape, as if surprised before he could deal the fatal blow! Sweet Minerva, it's brilliant in a cruel way, that is.'

'That's what I wonder,' Ferox said. 'And then I wonder whether it was no coincidence that Hadrian insisted we stay in the room so close by. He did not seem that bothered to find Sosius dead.'

'Well, he could not do anything else, could he? That way his plan still worked and... Oh, no surely not... that way he could dispose of Sosius and make sure that no one ever knew the truth – about this and all the other things over the years.' The queen frowned. 'But that meant knowing you would be prowling about seeking the lavatory at the right time.'

'As I say, I am not sure. That might have been chance... I might even be wrong, but this is what I wonder. About the same time, double the usual number of guards had come on duty all around the outside of the building. Legionaries as well as praetorians. Marcus was in charge of arranging it, so it was someone outside the household, someone Sosius did not know. I'm not sure he would have got out as easily as he got in.'

'That does not mean that he would be killed?'

'Then or later, it would not really matter, would it? He could not talk to anyone who mattered – mattered politically that is.'

'Sosius would not be easy to fool,' Ferox went on, 'but with the praetorian dead, Hadrian could claim that the slave killed the soldier, then tried to stab him, but the Immortal Gods woke him in the nick of time and he was able to slay his assassin. Sosius might have believed that that was the plan, if he still trusted Hadrian.'

They lapsed into silence for a long while, and the Sun did not seem quite so warm.

'What should we do?' Claudia Enica asked eventually.

'Nothing. I might be wrong,' Ferox said, 'and anyway what could we do? Show the world that Hadrian is a clever, treacherous bastard. He calls himself that, you know? If he fell, then what would we get? Civil war and eventually a new emperor. Who can say whether he would be a good man. The odds are against him being smarter. You don't have to like Hadrian to accept that he does a good job. Just don't get on his wrong side.'

'And that's it?'

'What else should there be? He'll govern well, you are Queen of the Brigantes as you have always deserved, our youngest daughter is married to a wounded brigand and the twins will soon be off to terrorise fashionable society in Lugdunum. The world is as it should be.'

She laughed, long and deep. 'Let's go and see Bran,' she said once she had recovered, 'and you can apologise again for killing Sosius before he could.'

'That's family for you,' Ferox said, and together they walked towards the main gate of the fort.

Historical Note

The Wall is a novel, just like its predecessors *The Fort* and *The City*, and also the *Vindolanda Trilogy* which first introduced Ferox, and it is only fair to let readers know how much of the story is grounded in fact and how much is pure invention. Ferox himself, along with Vindex, Claudia Enica, and all the other characters from the tribes are fictional. Flavius Cerialis, Sulpicia Lepidina and their family are known from the Vindolanda writing tablets, but only through this source, which provide us with glimpses of their life. Although I have tried to ensure that nothing in any of the stories ever conflicts with the information from the tablets, their characters are largely inventions. This is also true of what happened to them after they left Vindolanda, about which nothing is known. I have given Cerialis a splendid career for an equestrian officer, culminating in his appointment as procurator in Britannia at the time of *The Wall*. In fact we do not know who the procurator was at this time, so unless new evidence turns up in the years to come, this conjecture is possible at least.

No detailed narrative history has survived for the Roman empire in the second century AD, which means that even many major events are not well understood. This was the heyday of the empire, a time of prosperity and optimism, but chance of survival has meant that there are many gaps in our knowledge. When it comes to a province like Britannia, even less is known about what was going on at any time. This is frustrating for the historian, but offers opportunity for the novelist to create a story.

Hadrian is remembered as one of the 'good emperors', a man who ruled well, but the most detailed account of his life is in the Historia Augusta, a collection of sensational biographies written in the fourth century, by which time the empire and society had changed a great deal. To give an idea of its reliability, the author pretends to be several authors, some writing in earlier periods. Overall, the earlier lives appear a little more sober and reliable than many of the later ones, but even so this is not a source that anyone would choose to rely upon; it is simply that there is nothing better and it supplies information, some of which seems plausible, that is not preserved anywhere else. Originally there were plenty of other accounts, for instance the History of Dio Cassius, a senator who wrote in the early third century, but this survives only as very brief epitomes.

We can be confident about the bare bones of the major events, and the novel follows these. Trajan appointed Hadrian as governor – legatus Augusti – of Syria in the closing stages of his eastern campaigns. By 117, the emperor's health was failing badly, and on the journey back to Rome Trajan fell ill in Cilicia and died. It was announced, largely on the authority of his widow, Plotina, that in his final hours he had adopted Hadrian, thus marking him as successor – something he had singularly failed to do up until this point. By chance, we have a memorial to Phaedimus (fully Marcus Ulpius Phaedimus, since like all freedmen he took his master's name), Trajan's chamberlain/ butler. He died on 12 August, just a few days after Trajan, although his ashes were not carried back to Rome from Cilicia for another twelve years. The Epitome of Dio says that Trajan believed that he was being poisoned. We do not know the cause of Phaedimus' death, but he was only twenty-eight and it seems more than a coincidence.

Whatever happened, Hadrian acted quickly, helped by allies in Rome and elsewhere, and was soon acknowledged universally. There were some arrests and executions, followed by the alleged conspiracy of Nigrinus the following year. This seems to have occurred during a hunt, although few details are known, and it led to the deaths of Nigrinus, Lusius Quietus and perhaps some others. Killing a number of senators in this way forever soured relations between Hadrian and the aristocracy, and ensured that the tradition about him was generally hostile. Attempts to pass the blame onto subordinates failed.

If the main events of Hadrian's reign are understood in little more than a broad outline, there is very little information about what was happening in most provinces, including Britain. The sources do say that there was serious military trouble in Britain late in Trajan's reign that continued under Hadrian. During the course of this and subsequent fighting, there were significant Roman losses, severe enough to be remembered in later years and cited as an example of heavy fighting. This was the context for a significant reinforcement of the garrison of Britannia, and an emphasis on a heavier deployment in the north, seen most of all in the construction of Hadrian's Wall. However, none of this is understood, least of all the chronology, scale and nature of the fighting or the Roman decision making in response.

Vindolanda was written to suggest what the northern frontier might have been like before the building of the Wall, and in part to lead towards an explanation of why it was created. Acts I and II of this story are set in the same pre-Wall era, the evidence for which comes primarily from archaeology, aided by inscriptions, the writing tablets and such things as slogans on coins. In the eighties AD the Romans under Agricola had penetrated well into the north of what would become Scotland, but plans for long-term occupation were soon cancelled, the permanent bases constructed in the area abandoned. This retreat occurred in several phases, all of which may – or may not – have been ordered because troops were needed elsewhere, notably on the Danube.

By the beginning of *The Wall*, there were no Roman bases significantly north of the east-west road running from the Tyne to the Solway. This is normally called the Stanegate, but like the names of other Roman roads in Britain, such as the Fosse Way and Watling Street, this is a later Saxon name. We do not know what the Romans called it, nor can we be certain when a well demarcated track was turned into a properly paved road, although there is a good chance that this occurred under Trajan.

Several forts are known along the line of this road, including Corbridge (Coria), Vindolanda, Carvoran (Magnis) and Carlisle (Luguvalium). Opinion is divided over whether or not to call this a frontier system. Some of the action at the start of our story occurs near the fortlet (burgus) at Haltwhistle Burn, not far from the famous and often photographed Cawfields Milecastle subsequently built on Hadrian's Wall. Haltwhistle Burn has been excavated, which revealed that it was one of the first military installations in Britannia to have stone walls, and finding a number of internal buildings. Today, the outlines of these can be seen on the ground, giving an idea of the outpost's size and its position above the burn. The tower is what would later become Turret 45a on the Wall, which was originally built as a free-standing structure. This is one of several towers apparently built well before Hadrian's Wall, and most likely serving as signal stations to the forts and fortlets along the road.* Apart from Haltwhistle Burn, a similar installation is known at Throp to the west and there may have been others.

Compared to later periods, and indeed earlier ones, the Roman military presence in northern Britain was smaller in these years. Overall, the province had gone from having four legions at the time of conquest, to three and then to two. At least, this is our best guess, but as with so many things certainty is impossible. While most assume that Legio VIIII Hispana left Britain sometime early in the second century AD and disappeared from the army list through disaster or ignominy later in the century, no one really knows what happened or when. Recently, one scholar argued that the evidence could still be interpreted to have the legion in Britain *c.*117 and that it could just possibly have been involved in a defeat contributing to the memory of heavy losses in the province around this time. He does not claim that this is the only, or even the best way, to interpret our evidence, simply that it is possible.

I have opted to send the legion away – and readers of *The City* will know that it plays a central role in that story, set far to the east. However, I also have the scratched-together cohort of veterani and other men left behind to play a role in *The Wall.* There is no doubt about the army's abandonment of all its bases substantially north of the Stanegate in the late first and early second century, and an overall running down of the garrison makes sense, even if we cannot be precise. It is even harder to know where many auxiliary units were at any one time than it is with the much larger legions. Trajan's priorities

* However, a tower identified by Sir Ian Richmond near what would later become Birdoswald (Banna) fort has been shown by the current excavating team to be neither a tower nor so early in date. On-going work on Hadrian's Wall continues to throw up surprises and challenge existing views.

were his wars against the Dacians and later his expeditions in the east and invasion of Parthia. In each case, perhaps a quarter of the army's entire manpower, and perhaps even more, was involved in some way or other in the theatre of operations. It seems unlikely that at such times, Britannia was given much priority when it came to resources and manpower.

Within this background, the narrative in our story is pure invention, but seems logical. The ailing Spurius Ligustinus is an invention, as is Priscus. We do not know who was governor of Britannia before Falco, or who commanded II Augusta at this time. Tincommius is another invention, as is my version of the politics within and between tribes. One of the greatest problems of understanding the frontiers of the empire is that we rarely know anything at all about the desires, ambitions and capacity of the peoples living beyond them, so that all discussion tends to be about Roman aims and priorities, giving the false impression that the Romans were free agents.

Heavy raids into Roman and allied territory seem a very likely opening to any conflict, for raiding was common in so much of the ancient world. Such attacks were likely to prompt reprisals by the Romans – in essence counter raids of their own – which in turn would lead to more violence as the communities to the north defended themselves. The history of most frontiers in many periods of history suggest that vengeance and reprisals by all sides had a tendency to fall on people who had little or nothing to do with the original grievance, encouraging conflict to spread. Much of the cost for all this fell on the more or less civilian populations on each side.

The Brigantes were one of the largest, if not the largest tribe or tribal confederation in Britain. As always, our evidence for their identity comes primarily from Roman sources or evidence produced by those among them adopting aspects of Roman life, which surely does not represent the whole picture. Thus much of the depiction of them, let alone the stories of Claudia Enica and her family, is invention. We do not know what happened to the royal line of the tribe in this period or how long it lasted. Excavations at Aldborough or Isurium Brigantum, the tribal capital built to conform to Roman ways of doing things, show at least some in the tribe trying to fit in to and benefit from the imperial system. There is much we simply do not know, but I have done my best to fit the episodes set there with the evidence from this research.*

Act II of our story focuses on Priscus and his expedition to the north. This is all invented, although as usual I have tried to represent the Roman army in the field as accurately as possible. There is no specific evidence for the raising of numeri/irregular units of Britons for use in the province at this time, although some did serve elsewhere. However, it is a plausible enough thing for the Romans to have done when short of regular troops. I have been vaguer than usual about the identity of most of the auxiliary units with the army, because we are not always sure which ones were present at this time, and which arrived later as the Wall was developed.

Roman battlefield defeats were relatively rare in the first and second centuries AD, and detailed descriptions of them are even rarer. Most of the time, discipline, command and control, equipment, training and tactics gave the Romans a huge advantage in any encounters in the open field. Thus there was a need to create a convincing explanation for a serious defeat. The build-up to the battle in our story is very, very loosely based on the overwhelming Zulu victory over a British army

---

* See Rose Ferraby & Martin Millett, *Isurium Brigantum. An archaeological survey of Roman Aldborough* (2020).

at Isandlwana on 22 January 1879, as I suspect some readers have noticed. In *The Wall*, the Romans suffer several thousand casualties in this defeat, as a reminder that in this era a disaster did not have to be on a vast scale to be important – compared for instance to the losses against the Cimbri and Teutones, who wiped out a succession of Roman armies in the late second century BC. The cenotaph at Adamklissi in Romania, which may commemorate the fallen from a defeat in the conflicts against the Dacians and their allies, has space for some 3,800 names.

Early in his reign Hadrian sent Falco to Britannia, most likely to deal with the crisis there. At some point, perhaps then, perhaps later, a tribune named Titus Pontius Sabinus was sent with 3,000 legionaries from the units in the Germanies and Spain to reinforce the garrison of Britannia. In the story I have placed this in the aftermath of Priscus' defeat. There may have been other reinforcements, but no one is quite sure when they occurred. Hadrian appears to have brought Platorius Nepos and Legio VI Victrix with him when he came to the island in 122. Falco may have left the province before they arrived, for a diploma – the bronze copy of a document granting discharge and citizenship to a time-expired auxiliary – has this man and others discharged by Falco, but this was formally confirmed by Nepos. Falco was sent to Asia, a non-military province, but his wife appears to have died on Samos during his term of office or before they arrived.

Hadrian's visit to Britannia was one of many provincial tours he made during the course of his reign, travelling more widely and more often than any emperor since Augustus. Before looking at Hadrian's Wall, it makes sense to consider the story told by the *Historia Augusta*, of the dismissal of senior staff, including the Praetorian Prefect Septicius and the senior civil servant Suetonius – more famous to us as the author of biographies of the first twelve Caesars as well as other works. The offence was some over familiarity with the emperor's wife, Sabina Augusta. This is placed immediately after the description of Hadrian's visit to Britain and before his return to Gaul, which allows some scholars to place the incident during the visit – and certainly gives sufficient justification to include it in our story.

Hadrian and Sabina clearly did not get on well and grew to loathe each other. A later source includes the claim that she often boasted of making sure that she never became pregnant by him. They never divorced, since that was not something a good emperor did, and the details of the relationship are impossible to know. Whatever the nature of the scandal, and whether the empress was more victim than cause, a political aspect made sense for our story, even though all the details, and Sosius himself, are invented. In later years, Hadrian is said to have grown suspicious of Platorius Nepos, so having the conspirators plan to name him as emperor offered a reason for this distrust to grow in later years.

The most famous thing Hadrian ever did with regard to Britain was order the construction of Hadrian's Wall. A souvenir cup bearing the name Vallum Aelium – Aelius being Hadrian's family name – suggests that the Wall was actually named after him, at least in the early days. The Historia Augusta says that the Wall was eighty miles long and its purpose was *barbaros Romanosque divideret* – 'To separate/divide the barbarians and the Romans' – which is not particularly helpful, apart from all our concerns about this source's reliability in the first place. Hadrian's Wall is barely mentioned in other surviving ancient literature, which means that its story is known from archaeology, backed by inscriptions. (As yet, no writing tablets at Vindolanda or elsewhere in the region that are legible can be dated definitely to the period of the Wall itself in its final form.) At Vindolanda, excavators uncovered a substantial building outside the wall of the contemporary fort, which they interpreted as a mansio or official way station and conjectured that this was built to house Hadrian on his visit, hence the inclusion of this in our story. One tablet has been interpreted to suggest that someone was hoping to petition the emperor on his visit.

On the whole, scholars have tended to assume that Hadrian ordered construction of the Wall during his visit in 122, although this assumption has never been universal. In recent years, timber used to construct the frontier palisade in Germany inspected by Hadrian in 121 has been dated and shown to have been felled several years earlier. This greatly strengthens the case that work had already begun and that some parts of the Wall were already visible, and a few even complete, so that the emperor could come and see what had been done, as in our story.

It is certain that a succession of modifications to the original design were ordered within a relatively short period. At the start, the plan was for a wall some eighty Roman miles long, made in turf for the western third and stone for the rest. The stone wall was to be ten Roman feet wide, which scholars refer to as the Broad Wall. Every mile or so there was a small fortlet or fortified gateway allowing travel through the wall and in addition to the two main gates in line with existing roads. We call these small fortlets milecastles, but do not know what the Romans called them. Between each set of milecastles were two towers which we call turrets to distinguish them from free-standing structures.

Probably the first change was to reduce the width of the stone wall to something like seven and a half feet, which scholars call Narrow Wall. Debate rages over how much was ever built to full height at the original Broad Wall width, but at best it was a very small proportion of the total. However, Broad Wall foundations can clearly be seen in a number of places today, while several turrets and milecastles had stubby wing walls to the Broad Wall gauge built when they were constructed. These had later to be joined to Narrow Wall. Apart from anything else, this confirmed that the wall and its installations were not built in a simple sequence, but sections done or partially completed in different stretches at different times.

The second major decision was to add auxiliary forts to the Wall itself, rather than relying solely on the smaller number of bases on the Stanegate for immediate support. This meant that in several cases forts were built on top of existing milecastles or turrets – something easiest to see today in the north wall at Housesteads. This added a lot of troops, and also more gateways to the line of the Wall. Then, at some point, perhaps quite quickly after this decision, work began on a feature known by scholars as the Vallum, a wide entrenchment running south of the Wall. (The name comes from a mistake made long ago, since vallum means wall and the feature is essentially a ditch.) This is not well understood, and in its initial phase it had very few crossing places, so that anyone coming through the gate of a milecastle would then have to travel some distance if they wanted to proceed further south.

Why the western section of the Wall was made in turf is unknown. It cannot have been a shortage of suitable stone quarries, because it was subsequently rebuilt in stone later in the second century (and in some cases the stone wall followed a different line, which means that we can still see traces of the earlier turf wall). A plausible suggestion is that the western sector was the most threatened, and therefore work here was done using the quicker and far more familiar method of working in turf, earth and timber. Milecastles in this sector were made from turf and timber, but turrets were stone from the start, which is harder to explain other than to suggest a plan for an all stone construction abandoned early on because of the need for haste. In addition, the line of milecastles and turrets without the wall itself was continued around the Cumbrian coast, suggesting that there were problems with raiders coming by sea.

Elsewhere, a case has been made for priority in building going to areas that were perceived to be especially vulnerable, such as the river valleys of the Tyne and the Irthing, and more generally to the turrets and milecastles – or perhaps only the latter's front wall with a tower over the gateway – to create a line of observation points as soon as possible. For all the apparent rigidity of the initial design, the men doing the work showed a good deal of flexibility on the ground. Thus the distance between milecastles varies a fair bit, but each is carefully positioned to be visible to a fort on or behind the line, whether directly or via another tower as a relay. In contrast, several have gateways opening onto what are effectively precipices, and at least one never had a front gate at all. This suggests that observation from the tower was more important than the ability for a body of men to travel through at that point. However, no one is really sure who crossed the Wall via the milecastles, and how often, whether as military or civilian traffic – even before the addition of forts and the Vallum complicated matters.

The picture that is emerging is of work parties active in lots of different places at once, determined by available manpower, local and wider priorities, and such things as the access to timber for scaffolding. Our story draws on the suggestion that some of the Wall, most notably a mile or so between milecastles 47 and 48 (the numbering running east to west from a notional zero at Wallsend) was prepared as a sample for Hadrian to inspect as he does in our story. The milecastle where he stops to climb the tower and eat and chat with the soldiers is milecastle 48 at Poltross Burn, which is well worth a visit. These two milecastles were larger than all other known stone milecastles and all but one of the turf milecastles. They are still significantly smaller than other Roman fortlets, for instance Haltwhistle Burn and Throp – the latter just a short distance away from Poltross Burn. They are also built to Broad Wall standards, and the internal buildings are larger and more lavish than those in other milecastles, with ovens, glass in the windows, and the stone steps – the only steps surviving anywhere on Hadrian's Wall and thus the only physical indication of its height. Another notable feature of Poltross Burn – and other spots along the Wall – is that it is built on a very steep gradient.

If you walk to the west along the line of the Wall – and on my last visit this meant a detour because the path under the railway embankment was blocked – you will see a long section of Broad Wall later finished as Narrow Wall. That is why there are only a few courses of stone in place in our story. The turret where Hadrian seeks refuge is 48a at Willowford East, where you can see wings of Broad Wall joined onto Narrow Wall, suggesting that the tower was built to its full height before the curtain was joined to it. The reconstruction picture on the information board for this turret shows it open, whereas at 48b it depicts the turret with a roof. This is one of many mysteries surrounding the Wall, since we simply do not know whether turrets had open tops or were roofed (and, if so, what shape the roof was). Similarly, there is not universal acceptance that there was a wall walk running on top all along the curtain wall. Personally, I believe that there was and that this makes best sense of the evidence, but it is impossible to prove the point.

One persistent myth about Hadrian's Wall which has a tendency to recur in some general studies of Roman history (in which of course, the author does not have space to discuss the question in any detail, so the failing is understandable) is that the Wall was weak from a military point of view. This is nonsense, based on a misunderstanding of the threat it was likely to face. There was never an expectation of massed assaults on long stretches of the Wall in the manner of the chapters in Kipling's wonderful *Puck of Pook's Hill*. In the case of large-scale attacks, Roman army doctrine was to fight in the open, advancing to confront a threat – just as Titus Cerialis does in our story. The more immediate problem was raiding by small or moderately large bands of warriors. The Wall was not impenetrable to such attacks, but it made it far more difficult to get across without being seen. Once the Romans were alerted, they could begin to respond, gathering a force to hunt down and defeat the raiders, who still had to cross the Wall to get back home.

Hadrian's Wall was never meant to be a barrier to the Romans, as its lavish, even excessive provision of gates makes clear. The Roman army was designed as a mobile force, and its strategy and tactics were aggressive. It is worth noting that a high proportion of the troops stationed on the Wall, somewhere between a fifth and a quarter, were cavalrymen, adding to the immediate mobility of the army there. This made it easier to locate and catch raiders, and made patrolling in advance of the Wall far easier. In addition, as well as adding forts to the Wall itself, Hadrian also placed several new forts as outposts to the north. One of these was at Bewcastle, Fanum Cocidius. Although only partially excavated, the unusual shape of its ramparts and outer ditches are still visible on the ground today. It seems to have been built around and enclosing an existing shrine, which may suggest that the Romans wished to supervise and observe the cult and perhaps wider meetings were held there. My depiction of the shrine is invention, exploring this possibility.

We do our best to understand the traces of the Wall, even though only a tiny fraction of the original structure has ever been excavated or is still visible today. That means that figuring out what the Romans intended and how well or not it worked out is extraordinarily difficult. Even worse, as mentioned earlier, we have nothing from 'the other side of the hill', from the viewpoint of the locals, whether the more or less hostile tribes to the north or the folk who found a wall being built through their fields. I have tried to suggest ambitions and rivalries within the tribes and their leaders as central to what happened, with a few being fixedly pro- or anti-Roman and most more concerned with their own advantage. There was certainly something happening, which justified the construction of the Wall, the more rapid completion of the western section, and later, after Hadrian was dead, prompted its abandonment and decommissioning when the army went north and built the Antonine Wall. We have no real idea why all this happened, and what had changed, although it raises the possibility that senior officers, perhaps even Hadrian, did not envisage the Wall as something to operate and man indefinitely, even though in fact it was soon reoccupied and this continued until the end of Roman Britain.

Even this brief discussion should show how many puzzles remain concerning Hadrian's Wall. As an introduction to some of these, I would suggest my own *Hadrian's Wall* (2018), as well as Nick Hodgson, *Hadrian's Wall. Archaeology and History at the limit of Rome's Empire* (2017), and Matthew Symonds, *Hadrian's Wall. Creating Division* (2021), both of which came out too late to be mentioned in my book and each of which considers the planning and construction of the Wall in some detail. Also well worth a look is David Breeze and Brian Dobson, *Hadrian's Wall* (fourth edition, 2000), while no serious visitor to the Wall should go without a copy of David Breeze, *J. Collingwood Bruce's Handbook to the Roman Wall* (fourteenth edition, 2006) in his or her pocket.

The last few decades saw something of a revolution in thinking about the design and construction of the Wall, and Peter Hill, *The construction of Hadrian's Wall* (2006) and John Poulter, *The planning of Roman roads and walls in Northern Britain* (2010) are both well worth a look. The late Peter Hill, a stone mason turned scholar, brought an especially practical eye to the question, for instance raising the issue of scaffolding as a major factor in the speed of construction. Another fresh approach was offered by David Wooliscroft, *Roman Military Signalling* (2001), which considered the question of visibility to and from installations with particular attention to the siting of turrets and milecastles. The scene where Pertacus has men holding tall flags to mark the position of turrets is a homage to experiments by David and his team using poles and lights.

The Wall drew inspiration from the many scholars who have and continue to work on Hadrian's Wall in all its aspects, and indeed the many who study the Romans, especially the army, and the Iron Age communities. All of them have my thanks.

GLOSSARY

ad stercus: literally 'to the shit', the expression was used in military duty rosters for men assigned to clean the latrines.

agmen quadratum: literally a square battle line, this was a formation shaped like a large box and used by a Roman army threatened by attack from any side. Units were deployed to form a rectangle, sheltering baggage and other vulnerable personnel and equipment inside.

ala: a regiment of auxiliary cavalry, roughly the same size as a cohort of infantry. There were two types (a) *ala quingenaria* consisting of 512 men divided into sixteen *turmae* and (b) *ala milliaria* consisting of 768 men divided into twenty-four *turmae*.

auxilia/auxiliaries: over half of the Roman army was recruited from non-citizens from all over (and even outside) the empire. These served as both infantry and cavalry and gained citizenship at the end of their twenty-five years of service.

Batavians: an offshoot of the Germanic Chatti, who fled after a period of civil war, the Batavians settled on what the Romans called the Rhine island in modern Holland. Famous as warriors, their only obligation to the empire was to provide soldiers to serve in Batavian units of the auxilia. Writing around the time of our story, the historian Tacitus described them as 'like armour and weapons – only used in war.'

***Beneficiarii*:** experienced soldiers selected for special duties by the provincial governor. Each carried a staff with an ornate spearhead.

Brigantes: a large tribe or group of tribes occupying much of what would become northern England. Several sub-groups are known, including the Textoverdii and Carvetii (whose name may mean 'stag people').

***burgus*:** a small outpost manned by detached troops rather than a formal unit.

centurion: a grade of officer rather than a specific rank, each legion had some sixty centurions, while each auxiliary cohort had between six and ten. They were highly educated men and were often given posts of great responsibility. While a minority were commissioned after service in the ranks, most were directly commissioned or served only as junior officers before reaching the centurionate.

***centurio regionarius*:** a post attested in the Vindolanda tablets, as well as elsewhere in Britain and other provinces. They appear to have been officers on detached service placed in control of an area. A large body of evidence from Egypt shows them dealing with criminal investigations as well as military and administrative tasks.

***clarissima femina*:** 'most distinguished woman' was a title given to women of a senatorial family.

cohort: the principal tactical unit of the legions. The first cohort consisted of 800 men in five double-strength centuries, while cohorts two to ten were composed of 480 men in six centuries of eighty. Auxiliaries were either formed in milliary cohorts of 800 or more often quingeniary cohorts of 480. *Cohortes equitatae* or mixed cohorts added 240 and 120 horsemen respectively. These troopers were paid less and given less expensive mounts than the cavalry of the *alae*.

commilito/ commilitones: 'comrade/s' or 'fellow soldier/s'.

consilium: the council/meeting held by a Roman magistrate (including a general) to discuss any important matter and issue his decision.

curator: (i) title given to a soldier placed in charge of an outpost such as a *burgus* who may or may not have held formal rank. (ii) The second in command to a decurion in a cavalry *turma*.

decurion: the cavalry equivalent to a centurion, but considered to be junior to them. He commanded a *turma*.

duplicarius: an auxiliary soldier who received double pay and had more authority than an ordinary soldier.

equestrian: the social class just below the Senate. There were many thousand equestrians (*eques*, pl. *equites*) in the Roman empire, compared to 600 senators, and a good proportion of equestrians were descendants of aristocracies within the provinces. Those serving in the army followed a different career path to senators.

frumentarii: soldiers detached from their units with responsibility for supervising the purchase and supply of grain and other foodstuffs to the army.

***galearius* (pl. *galearii*):** slaves owned by the army, who wore a helmet and basic uniform and performed service functions, such as caring for transport animals and vehicles.

gladius: Latin word for sword, which by modern convention specifically refers to the short sword used by all legionaries and most auxiliary infantry. By the end of the first century most blades were less than 2 feet long.

hastile: a spear topped by a disc or knob which served as a badge of rank for the *optio*, the second in command in a century of soldiers.

legate (provincial): the governor of a military province like

Britain was a *legatus Augusti*, the representative of the emperor. He was a distinguished senator and usually at least in his forties.

legate (legionary): the commander of a legion was a *legatus legionis* and was a senator at an earlier stage in his career than the provincial governor. He would usually be in his early thirties.

legion: originally the levy of the entire Roman people summoned to war, legion or *legio* became the name for the most important unit in the army. In the last decades of the first century BC, legions became permanent with their own numbers and usually names and titles. In AD 98 there were twenty-eight legions, but the total was soon raised to thirty.

***lemur (lemures)*:** ghosts or unquiet spirits of the dead.

***lixae*:** a generic term for the camp followers of a Roman army.

***omnes ad stercus*:** a duty roster from the first century AD from a century of a legion stationed in Egypt has some soldiers assigned *ad stercus*, literally to the dung or shit. This probably meant a fatigue party cleaning the latrines – or just possibly mucking out the stables. From this I have invented *omnes ad stercus* as 'everyone to the latrines' or 'we're all in the shit'.

***optio*:** the second in command of a century of eighty men and deputy to a centurion.

***pilum*:** the heavy javelin carried by Roman legionaries. It was about 6–7 feet long. The shaft was wooden, topped by a slim iron shank ending in a pyramid-shaped point (much like the bodkin arrow used by longbowmen). The shank was not meant to bend. Instead the aim was to concentrate all of the weapon's considerable weight behind the head so that it would punch through armour or shield. If it hit a shield, the head would go through, and the long iron shank gave it the reach to continue and strike the man behind. Its effective range was probably some 15–16 yards.

***praesidium*:** the term meant garrison, and could be employed for a small outpost or a full-sized fort.

prefect: the commander of most auxiliary units was called a prefect (although a few unit COs held the title tribune). These were equestrians, who first commanded a cohort of auxiliary infantry, then served as equestrian tribune in a legion, before going on to command a cavalry *ala*.

procurator: an imperial official who oversaw the tax and financial administration of a province. Although junior to a legate, a procurator reported directly to the emperor.

pugio: Latin name for the army-issue dagger.

***res publica*:** literally 'public thing' or state/commonwealth, it was the way the Romans referred to their state and is the origin of our word republic.

scorpion *(scorpio)*: a light torsion catapult or *ballista* with a superficial resemblance to a large crossbow. They flung a heavy bolt with considerable accuracy and tremendous force to a range beyond bowshot. Julius Caesar describes a bolt from one of these engines going through the leg of an enemy cavalryman and pinning him to the saddle.

***signifer*:** a standard bearer, specifically one carrying a century's standard or *signum*.

Silures: a tribe or people occupying what is now South Wales. They fought a long campaign before being overrun by the Romans. Tacitus described them as having curly hair and darker hair or complexions than other Britons, and suggested that they looked more like Spaniards (although since he misunderstood the geography of Britain he also believed that their homeland was closer to Spain than Gaul).

***spatha*:** another Latin term for sword, which it is now

conventional to employ for the longer blades used mainly by horsemen in this period.

***tesserarius*:** the third in command of a century after the *optio* and *signifer*, the title originally came from their responsibility for overseeing sentries. The watchword for each night was written on a *tessera* or tablet.

***thetatus*:** the Greek letter theta was used in some military documents to mark the name of a man who had died. This developed into army slang as thetatus meaning dead/killed.

tribune: each legion had six tribunes. The most senior was the broad-stripe tribune (*tribunus laticlavius*) who was a young aristocrat at an early stage of a senatorial career. Such men were usually in their late teens or very early twenties. There were also five narrow-stripe tribunes (*tribuni angusticlavii*).

***triclinia*:** the three-sided couches employed at Roman meals.

Tungrians: a tribe from the Rhineland, many Tungrians were recruited into the army. By AD 98 a unit with the title of Tungrians was likely to include many men from other ethnic backgrounds, including Britons. In most cases, the Roman army drew recruits from the closest and most convenient source. The Batavians at this period may have been an exception to this.

***turma*:** a troop of Roman cavalry, usually with a theoretical strength of thirty or thirty-two.

About the Author

Adrian Goldsworthy studied at Oxford, where his doctoral thesis examined the Roman army. He went on to become an acclaimed historian of Ancient Rome. He is the author of numerous works of non-fiction, including *Caesar*, *Pax Romana*, *Hadrian's Wall* and *Philip and Alexander*. He is also the author of the Vindolanda series, set in Roman Britain, which first introduced readers to centurion Flavius Ferox.